Hayner PLD/Large Print
Overdues .10/day. Max fine cost of
item. Lost or damaged item: additional
$5 service charge.

TOGETHER FOREVER

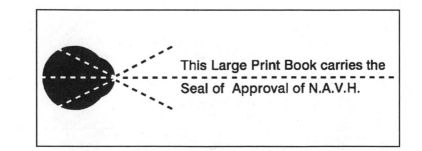

ORPHAN TRAIN, BOOK 2

TOGETHER FOREVER

JODY HEDLUND

THORNDIKE PRESS

A part of Gale, a Cengage Company

Farmington Hills, Mich • San Francisco • New York • Waterville, Maine
Meriden, Conn • Mason, Ohio • Chicago

LIBRARY OF CONGRESS CIP DATA ON FILE.
CATALOGUING IN PUBLICATION FOR THIS BOOK
IS AVAILABLE FROM THE LIBRARY OF CONGRESS.

ISBN-13: 978-1-4328-5144-6 (hardcover)

Published in 2018 by arrangement with Bethany House Publishing, a division of Baker Publishing Group

Printed in the United States of America
1 2 3 4 5 6 7 22 21 20 19 18

And he said unto me, My grace is sufficient for thee: for my strength is made perfect in weakness. Most gladly therefore will I rather glory in my infirmities, that the power of Christ may rest upon me.

2 Corinthians 12:9

CHAPTER 1

New York City
June 1858

Marianne Neumann's fingers were shaking so hard she could barely pry open the first record book. There were half a dozen more in the drawer. How could she possibly search through all of them?

At a scuffing in the hallway, she glanced at the closed office door and froze. She held her breath and prayed the footsteps would pass by. After only two weeks on the job, she couldn't afford to be caught snooping in the director's desk.

For an eternal moment she remained motionless, listening to the steps as they faded down the hall. Releasing a breath, she returned her attention to the record book bound with a plain brown leather cover.

She opened it gingerly to the front page. The date at the top read *April 1855*. With trembling fingers, she paged through the ledger, noting that the entries were varied in length. The handwriting changed frequently. Several pages were wrinkled and the ink unreadable where perhaps coffee or some other liquid had spilled on the page. The final entry was dated late in 1855, nearly three years ago.

She snapped the book shut and stuffed it back into the drawer where she'd found it.

Her hand slid over the spines. She had to find the records from last autumn. But which ledger contained the information she needed? She attempted to pull out another volume, but it stuck to the others on either side. The June evening had begun to cool, though not enough to lessen the humidity and heat that permeated the second story of the Children's Aid Society building.

"Come on, come on," she whispered. This would likely be her one and only chance to investigate. Which meant she had no choice but to find the information she needed about her lost sister.

Even as her shaking fingers pried another record book loose, she tried to grasp at the last vestiges of hope. Tomorrow she was leaving on her first placing-out trip and would be gone for weeks. She had to have some clue, some small hint to guide her search while she was traveling. She couldn't go without anything.

She flipped open the book to the back entry. *March 1856.* She was getting closer. She returned it and reached for the next one. Would it have records from the autumn of 1857 when Sophie disappeared? Surely the book was here somewhere.

She hadn't resorted to sneaking into the director's office just to come away empty-handed. Not only was she displeasing God once again with her sinful scheming, but she was putting her job in jeopardy. If the Children's Aid Society didn't fire her, at the very least they wouldn't allow her to accompany the children on the trip west.

At another hollow echo of footsteps in the hallway, Marianne paused. When the slapping halted outside the office door, her pulse sputtered faster. She pressed the drawer to close it.

When the doorknob rattled, panic overtook her and she dropped to her knees behind the desk. She hardly had time to duck her head before the door squeaked open. She held her breath and tried to make herself invisible. Thankfully the desk was massive.

If she'd had a moment's more notice, she might have been able to move the chair out of the way and wedge herself farther under.

As it was, she'd have to pray whoever had opened the door would only peek into the office and not come inside.

The click of the door closing, however, sent a tremor through her. As someone began to cross the room, she pinched her eyes closed and shrank lower. *Go away!* Her mind shouted the silent command.

But the steps drew nearer.

Don't come around the desk. Please . . .

When the footsteps stopped at the front of the desk, she didn't dare breathe. Her heart was racing so fast it tripped and thudded against her rib cage.

The person fidgeted with something on the cluttered desktop, scattering papers and shifting books around. The whole workspace was rather messy, shelves overflowing with books and papers, crates filled with letters and stacks of newspapers. Even though it was the largest office in the building, it was still cramped and had only one window, which was half open.

Finally, all rustling on the desktop ceased. Marianne opened her eyes and glanced at the shoes showing underneath the desk. A black pair of leather oxfords that had been polished to a shine.

Oh no. She squeezed her eyes shut again, yet knowing it would do no good. Blocking out the surrounding images wouldn't make her disappear from this predicament, even though she desperately wished it would. And closing her eyes wouldn't make the man on the other side of the desk vanish either.

What if Reverend Brace had returned? He'd left the building over an hour ago. She thought she'd waited long enough before sneaking into his office, but had she been wrong about his schedule?

The man on the other side of the desk cleared his throat.

She cringed.

Silence settled over the room, which magnified the chatter of the children downstairs, along with the busy evening noises arising from nearby Broadway Street — the clomp and clatter of horses and carriages and the calls of vendors closing up their shops.

The stillness in the office stretched on. She would have almost believed the man had left, except when she peeked, his shoes hadn't budged from the spot in front of the desk.

"So . . ." came a hesitant voice.

She jumped. She shouldn't have been startled to hear him speak, but she was. She'd sincerely hoped to avoid detection.

11

But apparently her hiding spot hadn't been secretive enough. She wished the floor would swallow her up whole and she could disappear without a trace. But since that wasn't about to happen, she scrambled to find some excuse — anything — to explain her presence on the floor behind the desk.

"Can I be of any assistance?" The voice was younger than that of Reverend Brace and was unfamiliar.

Perhaps she should remain frozen and pretend she hadn't heard him. Maybe he'd get the hint she didn't wish to be discovered and would leave. However, as much as she wanted to pretend the entire situation wasn't happening, she also knew she had to salvage what she could of her reputation and job. This man might not be Charles Loring Brace, the founder of the Children's Aid Society, but he very well could tell Reverend Brace she'd been in his office.

Marianne attempted to school her face into a mask of pure innocence while she patted the floor around her. "I was just searching for my pen." She quietly whispered a prayer of apology for her further deception. She felt awful enough for sneaking into the office. Now she was making matters worse with her lie.

"Any luck?" the man asked.

"None." She started to push herself off the floor, but before she could grab on to the desk to hoist herself up, the man was at her side, taking her arm and assisting her.

Part of her was afraid his grip would tighten like a chain and that he'd drag her from the room, march her downstairs, and expose her misdeed to the other workers who were still present. So she was surprised, when she was finally standing, that he gently steadied and then released her.

"Thank you," she managed past her constricted airways.

"You're welcome." His voice had a slow Southern drawl to it.

Even though she wanted to duck her head and slink from the room, she couldn't keep from glancing at him. And when she did, her attention jerked back and stayed on his face — his incredibly handsome face. His features were chiseled with equal measures of strength and suaveness. A dimple in his chin added an aura of irresistibleness to his appeal.

His tanned skin made his sandy hair appear lighter — not blond, but much lighter than her own dark brown waves. The layer of whiskers on his jaw and chin was a shade darker than his hair. His brows rose, revealing wide eyes that weren't green, but neither were they blue. Although not distinct in color, they were filled with humor.

Humor was better than anger, wasn't it? She attempted a small smile, which felt more like a grimace. "I'm Miss Neumann."

His smile broke free with the abandon of summer sunshine coming out from behind the clouds. He flashed perfect teeth in a devastating smile that had the power to knock a girl off her feet — if she was the kind of girl who was easily turned by a handsome smile, which she wasn't. "I'm Andrew Brady."

"Mr. Brady —"

"Drew."

"Ah. Well. Pleased to meet you." She wasn't really pleased to meet him. She was actually chagrined to be caught in Reverend Brace's office by someone like him. What must he think of finding her hiding on the floor? And then crawling around feigning looking for an imaginary pen?

She inwardly sighed but outwardly attempted to keep herself composed. She smoothed a hand down her skirt, relieved she was wearing one of her new cotton print dresses for summer. It had repeating yellow-and-white vertical stripes with purple and red flowers dotted throughout. The full bell-shaped skirt had so much material it could have been cut apart and made into dresses for an entire tenement of young girls. Well, perhaps not quite. But it was a much fancier dress than any she'd owned while growing up.

In fact, all of her clothes in recent months had been beautiful and dreamy. Her older sister, Elise, had insisted on giving her the clothes. Marianne hadn't protested too heartily, if at all. She could admit she'd appreciated shedding her filthy threadbare rags for the luxurious garments.

"Miss Neumann." Mr. Brady spoke her name as though trying a foreign word.

"Yes, Miss Neu-mann." She enunciated it carefully. It was a typical German name. She supposed she still spoke it with a trace of her German accent, which, try as she might, she couldn't completely shed, even after almost eight years of living in America. "I've been working at the Children's Aid Society for two weeks, and I leave tomorrow for my first trip taking children west."

"And I suppose you're sneaking around Mr. Brace's office attempting to get information on a long-lost child you hope to find while on the trip?"

"Exactly."

His smile widened, and his eyes turned a shade lighter, almost blue.

"No, of course not," she said quickly, wanting to pound her palm against her forehead. "What I meant to say is, I was hoping to find my pen so I wouldn't have to leave on the trip without it."

He cocked his head toward the drawer of ledgers she hadn't been able to close all the way. "Maybe you should check for your pen in the drawer."

She stepped away from the incriminating evidence. "Thank you, Mr. Brady, but I should be going. I still have a good deal of packing yet to do this evening."

"You certainly wouldn't want to leave the *pen* behind, now, would you?" he asked. "Especially not after daring to come into Mr. Brace's private office to find it."

Was he baiting her into telling the truth about why she was in the office? She paused to study him, hoping to read his expression. His grin only inched higher, and the spark in his eyes told her he was enjoying teasing her.

Her ire flamed to life. She didn't appreciate anyone making merry at her expense. "I don't see that my presence here is any of your business. In fact, perhaps you're the one who should explain what you're doing in Reverend Brace's private office, not me." There, she'd switched the focus onto him.

After all, he was as guilty as she was for trespassing. "Who are you anyway? And why are you here?"

She hadn't seen him in the offices since she'd started working. She crossed her arms in a show of accusation, but the effect was lost in the drooping material of the wide pagoda sleeves. "Maybe you're an intruder. Maybe I should alert the authorities."

"Don't worry about me, darlin'," he said in a particularly heavy drawl and a wink. "I promise I won't tell anyone you've been in here."

For a brief moment, she was speechless. This man had clearly seen her ruse. Even so, she couldn't let him know he was correct. The best course of action was to leave while she still had a sliver of her dignity remaining.

She started for the door. "Since I have nothing to hide, you can rest assured I won't worry about you, Mr. Brady." She tried to infuse confidence in each step and forced herself to exit the room without glancing over her shoulder at him. She only made it a step into the hallway when screams erupted from the first floor. Frightened screams.

What was going on? Was one of the bigger boys bullying a younger child?

She raced toward the stairway. She'd already been hard at work all day helping the orphans to bathe, distributing their two new outfits, and cutting and delousing hair. Nevertheless, she was supposed to be supervising the children this evening and throughout the night.

At this late hour, most of them were eating in the dining room under the watchful eye of the woman employed to cook meals, along with two other agents who were helping prepare for the expedition. Even so, Marianne choked against the guilt that was tightening an invisible hand around her throat and squeezing.

Hadn't she learned her lesson when she'd resorted to deception last fall when the Seventh Street Mission had closed and she'd found herself jobless and homeless? When her lies had cost her Sophie? Sinning never accomplished anything worthwhile. She'd only end up disappointing God again and earning more censure.

At the heavy tread of footsteps behind her, she suspected Mr. Brady had heard the commotion and was rushing to investigate the situation too. When she reached the bottom that led into the front room, she stopped short at the sight that met her.

In the dining room doorway stood a

18

stoop-shouldered man wielding a pistol. He wore baggy trousers with a stained and tattered coat. His head was hatless, revealing strands of stringy hair. He swung the gun at the long plank table, where at least a dozen children were still seated on trestle benches on either side.

"Tell me where Ned is," the man yelled in a slurred voice, "or I'll start blowing off heads!"

The two agents crouched near the table, shielding several of the children who were crying in terror.

The man took a wavering step into the room and pointed the gun unsteadily at the nearest child, a boy who didn't appear to be a day older than five. The orphan's eyes widened in his pale face, but he didn't move or speak. He simply stared up at the man almost resignedly, as though he'd faced such violent overtures before and would accept his fate whatever that might be.

"Tell me where my boy is, you child-robbers," the man called again, swinging the gun toward the nearest agent, grandmotherly Mrs. Trott. "I ain't letting you take him away."

"Who's your boy?" Mrs. Trott asked in a wobbly voice.

Marianne didn't consider herself a brave

person. But she couldn't stand by and allow a drunken brute to harm any of these poor, innocent children. Her gaze swept around the front sitting room, taking in the clusters of children already finished eating who were attempting to make themselves invisible behind the sparse scattering of chairs and tables.

Her sights landed upon a poker near the fireplace. Before she could start toward the makeshift weapon, Mr. Brady shouldered past her, brushing her aside in his haste. He barreled toward the intruder, his jaw set with determination.

Marianne wanted to reach out and stop him from doing anything foolhardy. Certainly he wasn't planning to confront an inebriated man who was waving a gun around. It was much too dangerous.

Yet much to her horror, Mr. Brady reached for the drunk, swung him around, and punched him in the stomach. Even as the man stumbled and started to double over, he let loose a slew of vile curses, raised his gun, and pointed it at Mr. Brady.

Aghast, Marianne watched as the drunk's finger closed around the trigger. She screamed a warning, but it was too late. The bang of the gun drowned out her voice. More screams and cries filled the air along with smoke from the discharge. Marianne expected to see Mr. Brady lose his grip on the man, stagger backward, and fall to the floor. Instead, he slammed the man's hand against the doorframe, knocking the gun loose so that it clattered to the floor.

Within moments, Mr. Brady had yanked both of the man's arms behind his back and had subdued him into a sniveling, whimpering mass. A black hole in the ceiling showed that somehow Mr. Brady had managed to knock the barrel of the gun upward, thus saving himself from a nasty gunshot wound. A mixture of surprise and relief weakened Marianne's knees, forcing her to grab on to the stair railing to keep from buckling.

"Wally." Mr. Brady cocked his head in the direction of one of the boys standing near the front door. "Go fetch the police officer on the corner of Broadway. Tell him Drew Brady asked for him."

The thin lad nodded solemnly and then slipped out the door and was gone before Marianne could instruct him to bring back *two* police officers just to be safe.

The drunk started cursing again. Mr. Brady yanked on the man's arm. "None of that now," he said. "This here's a God-fearing place full of women and young children. You better watch your language or you'll force me to make sure you do."

"Give me back my boy," the man spat. "That's all I want."

Mr. Brady made holding the intruder look effortless. But from the way his muscles bulged against his shirtsleeves, he was expending a great deal of strength to keep his grip on his prisoner. "You said your boy's named Ned?"

The man nodded. "Heard tell he's heading west — to Illinois — with a trainload of other kids."

The children were mute, still cowering as they watched the interaction, the remainder of their meals growing cold on the table before them.

Mr. Brady kicked the gun so that it slid across the wood floor, stopping only inches from Marianne's feet. He didn't need to say anything for her to realize he meant for her to pick it up and make sure the drunk didn't get his hands on it again. She bent and grabbed the weapon, the metal colder and heavier than she'd expected.

"If I asked Ned why he ran off from his home," Mr. Brady asked, "what would he tell me?"

"It ain't any of your business —" The man's curse was cut off as Mr. Brady yanked his arm.

"He's probably got plenty of good reasons for leaving, doesn't he?"

"The law says I got a right to keep whatever he earns."

"He's a human being created in the image of God Almighty. And he has a right to be treated with dignity."

"I can raise my boy however I see fit."

"If you treat him worse than a dog, don't expect him to show you any loyalty."

Marianne didn't know who Ned was or if he was in the building. But she'd certainly never turn him over to this man. Marianne knew exactly what kind of person Ned's father was. It hadn't been all that long ago that she'd been in a situation much too similar to Ned's.

"You can't keep him from me," the man shouted. "And if you won't tell me where he's at, you can be sure I'll find him. I always do."

"You don't want him to end up like you, do you? A violent drunk?"

The man started to speak but couldn't seem to find the words.

"Don't you want him to have a better life?" Mr. Brady persisted.

Marianne willed the man to answer with a resounding yes, but she wasn't surprised when he cursed Mr. Brady and at the same moment lashed out, flailing with his legs and twisting to free himself.

Mr. Brady wrestled with the intruder for several moments before renewing his grip. This time he thrust the man forward toward the building entrance. One of the boys opened the door and held it wide. Only when Mr. Brady was in the doorframe did Marianne notice the blood seeping through his sleeve. The bright crimson covered the back of his upper arm so that the sleeve stuck to his skin.

Marianne sucked in a breath. "Mr. Brady?"

He shot her a hard glance over his shoulder, one taut with warning.

She bit back her words. But once the door closed behind him, she sprang into action. "We need to send someone for the doctor. Mr. Brady's been shot."

CHAPTER 2

Drew Brady winced at the pressure on his wound. Thankfully, the bullet had only grazed his skin. Even so, the abrasion stung and was still bleeding.

"You could have gotten yourself killed." Miss Neumann's pert lips pressed together into a disapproving frown, which somehow managed to be entirely too alluring. From the moment she'd crawled out from underneath the desk in Brace's office, he'd been struck by her delicate and yet elegant features, especially her dark brown eyes that were framed with long lush lashes.

He wasn't normally drawn to brunettes, but maybe he'd just never met one as attractive as Miss Neumann. Or maybe he'd never met a woman who'd shown her attraction so clearly the second she'd laid eyes on him. What man wouldn't be flattered by such wide-eyed admiration? Even if Miss Neumann tried to hide behind a façade of sassiness, he'd seen past it.

And he'd also seen right past her excuse for why she was sneaking around Mr. Brace's office. Her expression had given her away. Even if it hadn't, he didn't need to be a genius to figure out she'd been searching through the books in Mr. Brace's desk.

She released the rag from his arm and dipped it into the basin of warm water on the edge of the desk. As she swirled the cloth around and then wrung it out, the liquid in the bowl turned red.

He was bleeding more than he'd suspected and had already ruined his shirt — not only from the excessive blood but also because he'd ripped it open to expose the wound.

"You shouldn't have approached the man without having a way to defend yourself," she said, laying the cloth back against his wound.

He sucked in a breath at the pain but attempted to mask it with a grin. "I'm flattered you care so deeply about me already."

Her expressive eyes flashed with chagrin before her beautiful lashes lowered to veil them. Nevertheless, her face was all too readable. She liked him.

Truthfully, most women did. His looks had always been his biggest asset, especially because, as a second son, he'd never had much else going for him. He'd used his handsomeness and charm to the best of his ability instead.

"I hardly know you, Mr. Brady," she said, clearly attempting to infuse dignity into her tone. "Any care I'm showing you is out of sisterly concern."

In the first-floor office where she'd led him after he returned, the quarters were tight. The large desk took up much of the room, along with the two chairs on the other side. Unlike Brace's office upstairs, this one was used by all the agents for meeting with parents, other relatives, or even friends of the children brought to the Society's attention. It was spartan in its furnishings and had no files or anything else that might be confidential.

In the close confines of the room, she stood near enough that he caught the faint scent of lavender, either from her soap or from a satchel she placed with her clothes. She was also close enough for him to notice her lovely figure, perfectly rounded in all the right places and pronounced by the slimness of her waist.

"It's okay to admit how you really feel." He couldn't keep from flirting with her. It was his normal way of relating to ladies, and it had worked in the past to put women more at ease around him.

"I'm engaged to be married, Mr. Brady," she responded stiffly. "My affection and my adoration belong to my fiancé and to him alone."

"Engaged?" He studied her features and again saw the uncertainty, even guilt write itself in bold letters. She was too readable and didn't realize it.

"Reinhold, my fiancé," she said hurriedly, "is already in Illinois working and saving up money so we can be together."

"I take it you're hoping to see him at one of the stops?"

"Perhaps."

"So he doesn't know you're coming?"

"Something like that."

"Then it will be a delightful surprise," he said, pouring on his best charm. "I can't imagine anyone not being happy to see a beautiful woman like you."

At his praise, her lashes fell again but not before he caught sight of the pleasure his compliment brought. He relaxed against the hard spindles of his chair, mentally patting himself on the back for working his magic.

She removed the rag and examined his injury.

"Will I need stitches?"

She cocked her head and lifted tentative

fingers to the wound. As she made contact, he tried not to flinch at the burning pain that shot up and down his arm. "One area is slightly deeper. We'll see what the physician says once he arrives." She glanced toward the open door as if expecting the man to walk in at that moment.

Usually on the day before a trip, the building was noisy with all the children who would be staying there for the night. Some had been collected from the Nursery Department of the House of Refuge on Randall's Island. Others had been plucked directly from the alleyways, empty buildings, and cellar doorways of the worst parts of the city. Two had been delivered to the New York Children's Aid Society by a father who'd lost his job and couldn't afford to feed and clothe his children.

In all, he counted twenty-eight orphans for this placing out. On his previous trip, he'd had forty. Hopefully they'd have better luck placing everyone than they did the last time.

He followed Miss Neumann's gaze to the empty hallway outside the office. Gone was the thrum of excitement that had permeated the atmosphere when the children learned they would get to ride on a train tomorrow. The incident with Ned Colson's dad had changed the mood. Drew wished it hadn't occurred here. On the other hand, if Mr. Colson had gone to the Lodging House, there was no telling what might have happened, especially because Drew wouldn't have been there to intervene.

"So, Miss Neumann, tell me more about yourself since I clearly have much to learn."

She moved to the basin and rinsed the blood from his rag again. "And exactly what would you like to know, Mr. Brady?"

"I don't know anything about you other than that you're searching for a missing child . . . er, pen. And that you're engaged to a very lucky man somewhere in Illinois, who may or may not be expecting your visit."

She frowned at his attempt at humor. "I'd say that's more than enough for you to know about me, wouldn't you?"

"Not at all, since we're to work together for at least the next six weeks."

In the middle of wringing out the bloody rag, she froze. Her eyes widened, revealing both surprise and worry. Why would she be worried about riding with him? Hadn't he proven he was decent and charming?

"Why am I working with you?" she asked with a note of despair in her voice.

He sat forward. "Because you're privileged

to get my expertise and the joy of my presence."

"But I've never seen you before —"

"I work at the Newsboys Lodging House when I'm not on a placing-out trip."

"Oh." She stood back and studied him more carefully.

"Do I pass your inspection?"

"I don't know."

"What else would you like to know about me? Ask me anything."

"How long have you worked with the Children's Aid Society?"

"Two years."

"And how many placing-out trips have you made?"

"I've gone on four. This new one will be my fifth."

Her nose wrinkled at the bridge. "You're much younger than the other men working here."

"True. I'm twenty-four."

"And why the Emigration Office? What makes you want to work with orphans?"

He ignored the pricking deep in his chest, the one that still occasionally reminded him of all he'd left behind, a dark past he didn't want to think about, the mistakes he'd made that had altered the course of his life forever.

"My spiritual mentor, Reverend Lyman

31

Giles, introduced me to Mr. Brace four years ago, right about the time he founded the Children's Aid Society. Giles thought I'd be a good fit for Brace's new ministry. And as it turns out, he was right. I think the mission of the Society is a noble one and I'm glad of the small part I can play in giving children a wholesome life away from the vices of the city."

"So you're a personal friend of Reverend Brace?" Worry shifted over her face like the shadows lengthening in the room at the approaching dusk.

"I already promised I won't say anything about you being in his office earlier looking for your *pen.*"

She pursed her pretty lips together and moved to place the rag back against his arm. Whatever she'd been doing was something she didn't want to confide to him. He could respect that. After all, he harbored enough heartache of his own that he didn't want to discuss with anyone.

He expected her to press harder this time, to punish him for his teasing — which she obviously didn't like. So when she dabbed him gently, he relaxed against the spindles. "My turn," he said.

"Your turn for what?"

"To ask you questions."

"Maybe I don't want to answer any questions."

"How long have you lived in America?" Her slight trace of an accent told him she was German.

"Almost eight years."

"What's your given name?"

"Marianne."

He grinned. "See. This isn't too hard, is it?"

She tentatively smiled in return, and the smile only made her prettier.

"You're young, not like any of the other women Reverend Brace has hired as agents." Even if he was mimicking the same age issue she'd just said to him, the fact was she was far too young for the job. Some of the older boys from the Lodging House weren't much younger. And as pretty as she was, they'd certainly notice. He'd have to question Brace on the wisdom of hiring Miss Neumann and in particular sending her on one of the trips. Surely Brace would have had the same concerns.

"I'm nineteen. I'm old enough." She straightened her shoulders as though that helped to make her appear taller and older. Instead it only served to highlight her womanly appeal. Not that all the other women agents were old spinsters. But they'd likely been hired for their experience and wisdom in dealing with children. What kind of experience would a nineteen-year-old have?

"How many arms did you twist to get the job?" he teased.

Embarrassment flickered across her face. He really liked this ability to tell exactly how she felt. Most of the Southern belles he'd grown up with had perfected the art of turning on and off their emotions like a water spigot.

"I may as well tell you the truth about my employment here." Her shoulders sagged. "I'm sure you'll find out from the other workers eventually anyway."

"Your father is friends with Mr. Brace?"

"My brother-in-law."

"Ah. And who is this illustrious brother-in-law that has the power to sway Charles Loring Brace to go against sound reason and hire a nineteen-year-old girl as one of his placing agents?"

"Thornton Quincy."

He whistled. The Quincys were one of the wealthiest families in the country. Wellington Quincy, who'd recently died, had left his fortune and company in the hands of his son, Thornton. And it was no secret that Thornton Quincy was one of the top financial supporters of the Children's Aid Society. In fact, without Thornton's generosity, the Society would be in trouble.

"Say no more," Drew said.

She didn't need to. Her expression spoke loud enough of her guilt and shame. But she continued nevertheless. "I feel terrible for using Thornton to get the job."

He wanted to tell her that was obvious, but he nodded with what he hoped was understanding. "You must have really needed the position."

"I did. It was the only option I had left."

"Option for what?"

She shook her head. "What I meant to say is that I need work. I couldn't live off my sister and Thornton's charity any longer. This job seemed like something I could do to help make a difference in the lives of orphans."

Like earlier when he'd caught her in the office, he could sense she wasn't telling him everything. And if there was one thing he'd learned from his own past, it was to not push people to share more than they wanted or were ready to. "So Thornton Quincy is married to your sister?"

She nodded. "Last September, my older sister, Elise, went to Illinois on one of the Children's Aid Society trains that were helping place unemployed women in jobs in the West."

The Panic of '57. That was what some were calling the recession that had occurred last year. Banks and businesses all along the East Coast had collapsed, leaving thousands of people jobless, hungry, and homeless. In New York City alone, he'd heard reports that unemployment had reached as high as forty percent. One hundred thousand people without work in Manhattan and Brooklyn. The joblessness led to homelessness and hunger. Thousands were left destitute, having to take shelter in police stations, particularly in the wintertime.

Worst of all, the number of homeless children on the streets had risen. With the continuing flux of immigrants into New York City, poverty, illness, and crime had become rampant. Under such conditions, children were abandoned or left orphans by parents who died of disease, drank themselves to death, or simply couldn't take care of them anymore. Once the recession hit, the number of orphans had escalated to new alarming levels. Although there was no way to count the number of homeless children, some believed there were as many as thirty thousand.

"Elise happened to meet Thornton on the

train ride to Illinois," Miss Neumann continued. "They became friends. Thornton arranged for her to have work in a new town in Illinois that he was developing at that time."

"And while they were there, they fell in love, got married, and lived happily ever after?"

"Well, it wasn't quite that simple. But, yes, eventually they overcame a lot of obstacles and got married."

"So you live with them here in New York City?" Although her gown was pretty and stylish, it wasn't anything fancy, not something he'd expect of a young lady residing under Thornton Quincy's roof.

"They're splitting their time between Illinois and New York. So I live in a boardinghouse nearby. Besides, I didn't want to intrude on them since they're newlyweds." At her mention of the word *newlyweds,* she shifted away from him and ducked her head. If she'd been a blushing girl, he guessed her cheeks would have been bright pink.

"From what I've heard about the Quincy mansion, I doubt you would see them enough to intrude on their privacy."

She gave a soft laugh. "True."

"So what's the real reason you aren't living there?"

She met his gaze directly. The brown of her eyes was mesmerizing as it flickered with the raw honesty of her emotions. "I can't deny I appreciate the help my sister and Thornton have given me." She caressed the folds of her skirt, and suddenly Drew understood that she owed everything to them — not just the job but her clothing, the funds for the boardinghouse, and perhaps all she had. "I've relied upon my sister my entire life, even before she married Thornton. And now part of me needs to go out and prove I can be strong enough on my own."

He knew what it felt like to live in an older sibling's shadow. He'd hated it. And he knew that driving need to prove oneself to be strong and different. He'd had to do that too — was still doing it.

For a long moment, she busied herself with soaking the rag, rinsing and then squeezing and repeating. Her motions were brusque, and he could see she was chagrined at revealing so much about her personal life so hastily to a stranger.

But he didn't mind at all. He felt connected with her, as though she was a kindred spirit. When she lifted her hand to replace the warm compress on his arm, he stopped her by capturing her wrist.

"I'm glad you're coming on the trip, Miss Neumann. I think we'll make a good team." Maybe she was a little young to be an agent, but now he understood why.

Before she could respond, Wally rushed into the room, followed by the physician. "What's this I hear about you being shot by an angry parent?" Dr. Morrow asked as he brushed past Marianne. The doctor was one of the supporters of the Society and gave of his time and medical attention freely as a gift to the ministry.

Marianne stepped aside, relinquishing her position to the doctor. Drew wanted to tell her not to go just yet, but the doctor probed his wound, making him forget about everything but the pain in his arm. Well, almost everything. He caught sight of Marianne's slight smile as she turned away. And he decided it was one smile he'd never get tired of seeing.

CHAPTER 3

Reinhold Weiss jabbed at the dark soil, then dropped the potato cutting into the hollow. He made sure the piece landed with its eye facing upward before raking dirt over the spot and patting it firmly with the flat end of the hoe.

The leather strap of the potato pouch cut into his shoulder and rubbed against the blisters that had formed there hours ago. At least the bag was almost empty. And at least the sun was low in the sky. Even though the burning heat from midday lingered in the warm soil, it wasn't pounding on his head and back and shoulders anymore.

He paused and leaned against his hoe. Surveying the rows upon rows he'd walked that day, a surge of satisfaction coursed through him like the cool evening breeze that was just beginning to tantalize his sweat-drenched shirt. He slipped off his hat and let the rush of air comb through his sticky hair.

He'd made good progress. If the weather held, he'd be able to finish the potato planting on the morrow. Of course, he wouldn't get a full night's sleep if he hoped to cut the rest of the seed potatoes into pieces in readiness for the remainder of the planting. But in the end, all the hard work would be worth it because Mr. Turner had promised him a percentage of the profits.

Profit enough, hopefully, to go toward the purchase of the adjacent acreage. His very own farm.

The thought spurred him to pick up the hoe and shuffle forward a foot to dig the next shallow hole. Dig. Drop. Cover. Pat. The motions came effortlessly and with little thought since he'd been doing them since sunup with only a break at noon to rest in the shade of a lone elm at the edge of the field. He'd eaten corn bread and a thick slice of dried ham Mrs. Turner had sent with him. Then he'd lain back in the tall grass, heedless of the flies that had come out to feast on his flesh.

Early June was late for the potato planting in central Illinois. From what he'd heard, the seedlings should have been in the ground in April or the early part of May. But he'd been too busy helping Mr. Turner harrowing the fields, turning up the moist earth with the implement's sharp teeth so that the soil would be mellow and smooth. Once the land had been prepared, they'd sown the grains — first a field of wheat, then one of rye, and finally a field of oats they would use to feed the cows and horses next winter. The biggest job had been the corn planting. They'd worked for weeks from sunup to sunset to get the seeds in the ground.

Mr. Turner had said they'd be plenty busy once the weeds started growing. They'd spend their days fighting off the thistles and choking sprouts that had no place in the fields. In the interim, Mr. Turner was breaking his calves. When Reinhold had approached him about planting the potatoes, the man had grudgingly agreed to the plan, allowing him to use two acres.

The clang of a distant bell stirred the hunger pangs that had been gnawing Reinhold's stomach for the past hour. The hunger was nothing like it had been the last few weeks in New York City when he'd been out of work and trying so desperately to provide for his mother and siblings. Thankfully now, he was earning enough that he could not only send them money but also save a little each month.

He marked the spot where he'd planted his last potato cutting and then started the trek back to the farm. The shadows of the gray fence posts had grown long, and the few wisps of clouds in the sky were tinted with a glow of pink and orange.

As he walked the winding dirt path, the two-story white clapboard house came into view, along with the barn, henhouse, and the smoke shed. The outbuildings were arranged in a U-shape with a large fenced-in vegetable garden growing in neat rows behind the house, and a pigpen behind the barn. He breathed deeply of the scent of damp earth and clover, relishing the freshness of the prairie wilderness.

Weariness settled through every bone of his body, but the soreness was strangely satisfying. He'd done a good day's work, and eventually he'd have something to show for it, unlike all the construction work he'd done while living in New York City. Of course, he'd been grateful for the employment, which had freed him from having to sew like most of the other people in his tenement. And yet he'd never felt fulfilled the way he did here on the farm.

"Nice of you to show up now that the chores are mostly done," Higgins remarked as Reinhold strode into the barn. The comforting waft of hay and horseflesh greeted him and reminded him the other hired laborer was only a temporary part of his life — like a sliver under his thumbnail that he had to endure for a little while, but not forever.

Higgins stepped out of the shadows of one of the cow stalls and wiped his hands on his trousers. Chewing on a piece of hay, the young man's thin face was masked with freckles from spending hours in the sun. Although Higgins claimed to be a year older than Reinhold's twenty years, he was scrawny compared to Reinhold's stocky frame.

Soon the barn would be shrouded in darkness, and Reinhold would have to finish the chores by the light of a lantern. A quick glance around told him that most of the chores hadn't been done yet, in spite of Higgins's claim to the contrary. The stall floors still needed to be mucked out and the mangers filled with fresh hay. The water troughs were empty, and the young calves were bleating for attention.

"I'm going to supper," Higgins said, brushing his fingers through his short-cropped hair before putting on his hat. "But old man Turner won't take kindly to you showing your face at the table until you do your part with the chores."

Reinhold let the strap from the potato bag slide from his shoulder and fall to the floor. He reached for a rake and then crossed toward Higgins with strong menacing steps. Higgins shifted uncomfortably, fear flashing in his eyes. Reinhold knew he shouldn't feel satisfaction, but he did anyway. Every once in a while Higgins deserved to be put in his place. And this was one of those times.

Rake in hand, Reinhold walked straight up to Higgins and glared at him. Higgins glanced at the door as though gauging how long it would take him to reach it and bolt from the barn.

Reinhold adjusted the rake to his other hand, which caused Higgins to flinch. But just as swiftly defiance flared in the man's eyes. "You're the one who wanted to plant potatoes."

"He offered it to you too."

"I already work hard enough."

Reinhold had to hold back a laugh. "You didn't do your fair share of chores tonight and you know it." The man never did his fair share with anything, but that was beside the point.

A smirk curled Higgins's lips. "How could you know everything I've been doing if you haven't been here to see it?"

Reinhold had learned it wouldn't do any good to argue with Higgins. He was slippery, much like one of the trout they fished for in the nearby creek. He'd wiggle and squirm his way out of any situation and glide off downstream smoothly and effortlessly.

"Don't provoke me, Higgins."

"Or what?" Higgins's annoying grin widened. "We both know you're too nice to do anything to me."

Reinhold stared at the man a moment longer before he made a point of bumping Higgins's bony shoulder with his brawny one so that the farmhand was forced to move aside. Then he lowered the rake into the soiled hay and began to toss it aside, ignoring Higgins.

Over the past several months of laboring alongside Higgins, Reinhold had learned the only thing he could do was put up with the man and, at best, ignore him.

After a minute of working, Reinhold sensed he was alone, that Higgins had made his escape and gone to supper. Reinhold paused and rolled his aching shoulders. By next spring he'd have his own place, he'd be plowing and harrowing his own fields, and he wouldn't have to put up with Higgins or rely on anyone else ever again.

Not that Mr. Turner was a bad man to work for. Even if he was rough at times, the farmer paid decent wages, fed him, and let him bed down in the barn. After getting used to the smells and noises, the barn wasn't a bad place to live. It was more spacious and cleaner than the two-room tenement apartment where he'd subsisted with his family in Kleindeutschland.

In fact, the more he worked and lived on the farm, the more he was convinced he wanted a farm of his own. Even though he'd only been a hired hand since February, he'd fallen in love with every aspect of living off the land. He loved the livestock, the soil, the fresh air, the openness of the prairie, the solitude, and even the hours of toil.

The first time Mr. Turner had mentioned there was still plenty of land left in central Illinois for sale, Reinhold had realized maybe it was possible for him to make a better life for himself, that maybe America actually did hold opportunities for men like him. The overcrowded streets of New York City had never held much promise, and he'd all but given up hope that his existence would ever amount to more than drudgery.

But here . . .

Reinhold took a deep breath, and as he exhaled, his stomach rumbled with a fierceness that spurred him to pick up his rake again. If he worked hard and fast, he might be able to finish in time to get a plateful before Mrs. Turner and her daughter started to clean up the evening meal.

When he'd completed the chores, he hoisted himself up the ladder to the loft. He debated heading to the farmhouse without changing his shirt first. But if he showed up wearing the sourness of a day's worth of sweat, Mrs. Turner would only shoo him out of the house with the enormous wooden spoon she carried in her apron pocket.

The rafters forced Reinhold to duck low as he crossed to the spot where he bedded down and kept his possessions. The hay still bore his impression from the previous night, and the letter he'd started writing to his mother lay abandoned in the scattering of straw. He reached for his haversack, which contained everything he owned: a small bundle of clothes, an extra pair of shoes, letters, blank paper, pen and ink, and his father's pocket watch. The glass case was cracked in a dozen places, making the numbered face underneath nearly impossible to read. Although it had stopped ticking long ago, it would always work to remind him of the kind of man he never wanted to become.

As he pulled out a clean shirt, he stopped short. The hay behind his bag had been pushed aside and scattered as though an animal had been clawing it. A cat? Or mouse? Or . . .

His gaze shot across the loft to where Higgins slept, to the thin blanket strewn in the straw, the scattering of dirty clothes, and the empty haversack.

With his pulse pounding an ominous rhythm, Reinhold dropped to his knees and started digging in the hay, his fingers groping for the leather pouch he'd buried there. At the brush of the smooth purse, Reinhold allowed himself to breathe again. It was still here. Higgins hadn't taken it.

Reinhold had tried to be careful not to remove it when his fellow farmhand was present. He didn't think Higgins knew of his hiding spot. Even so, he needed to find a new, safer place to keep his earnings.

He sat back on his heels and lifted the flap of the pouch to reassure himself that the coins Mr. Turner gave him at the end of every month were still there. But as he widened the pouch, his stomach dropped with a sickening thud. All that met his touch was the dry leather interior. The money was gone. Every last dollar.

With a groan, he tossed the purse onto his

bed of hay. Four months of hard labor. Four months of going without any luxury for himself. Four months of saving for his own place. In an instant, all of it had been ripped away from him.

The weight of his loss crushed him, bending his head and shoulders, pinning him with the dejection that had been his companion in recent years. He should have known his new employment was too good to be true. He was only a poor immigrant with no skills. What made him think he could rise above his station? Do something more with his life and find fulfillment?

He was still just an ignorant, uneducated, simple man of peasant roots. Maybe that would always be his lot in life. Maybe he was destined to be disappointed if he dared to dream of life beyond what he'd always known.

"No." He straightened his shoulders and lifted his head. The effort was like trying to toss off a load of stones, and he almost buckled under the depressing weight once again. "No. I won't give up." He spoke louder, and the sound seemed to lend him the strength he needed to stand. He crossed to Higgins's side of the loft and rummaged through the man's meager belongings. He didn't expect to find anything, but his gut told him Higgins had taken the money today while he'd been planting potatoes.

Perhaps that was why Higgins had decided to stay back. Maybe he'd been planning all along to get his hands on Reinhold's savings and had been waiting for the right opportunity. Why work hard from sunup to sundown when he could earn the same amount by thieving?

With a cry that was half aggravation and half anger, Reinhold jumped up. His head bumped against the rafter, and this time he roared with all the emotion pumping through him.

Without another moment's hesitation, he climbed down the ladder and stalked out of the barn. He took long strides across the barnyard and didn't stop to wash his face and hands at the big iron kettle that sat next to the well. He made his way directly to the back kitchen door where Mrs. Turner had instructed them to enter for meals.

Stomping inside, he let the door slam behind him. He didn't stop until he'd passed through the kitchen into the dining room where everyone was gathered at the table. At his appearance, silence descended over the room.

Mr. Turner sat on one end of the long table. His gaze flickered to Reinhold for only an instant before returning to the last few bites of his honey-glazed dried apples. He was the tallest man Reinhold had ever met, easily grazing doorframes with the top of his head. Even sitting, he reached as high as Reinhold's chest.

The oil lamp at the center of the table was lit, casting a golden light over the leftover radishes, onions, and lettuce picked from the vegetable garden the women tended. A few dried, tough-looking pieces of roast beef sat on one platter, and a dark end piece of bread remained on another. Otherwise the meal had been picked clean, with Mr. Turner's daughter already clearing off the table. At his appearance she'd frozen, a collection of empty bowls and plates in her hands.

"Reinhold," Mrs. Turner said, her sharp eyes scouring him, "you get on back outside and wash up before coming in here. You won't get a crumb from this table until you do." The woman was almost as tall as her husband but much more portly. She ran the house with the precision of an army commander, neat, organized, and efficient. Lucinda, their only child, resembled the couple in her height, but was as quiet and timid as Mrs. Turner was loud and forceful.

For once, Reinhold ignored Mrs. Turner. Instead, he stalked over to where Higgins sat, grabbed a fistful of the man's shirt, and pulled him up from his chair. "Give me back my money."

Higgins had a mouth half full of dessert. "Hey!" he mumbled past the dried apple. "Get your hands off me."

"Reinhold Weiss!" Mrs. Turner barked his name. "Stop the fighting this instant or I'll boot you right out the door without a drop of supper."

"I want my money." Reinhold tightened his hold on Higgins's shirt, twisting it into a bunch and yanking Higgins so their faces were only inches apart.

"I don't know what you're talking about." Higgins spoke the words so innocently that for a fraction of a second Reinhold was tempted to believe him.

"The money I've been saving for the land on the other side of the creek."

"You know that's my land." A gleam sparked in Higgins's eyes. "I claimed it first."

Higgins had shown no interest in the farmland across the creek until after Reinhold had brought it up a couple of months ago at dinner. Even though Higgins claimed he wanted to purchase the land too, Reinhold always suspected Higgins was only saying so to aggravate him.

What if he'd been wrong? What if Higgins was serious about buying the farm? Serious enough to steal from him?

"Reinhold and Higgins!" Mrs. Turner had risen to her feet and taken her wooden spoon from her apron. Her large face, framed by a puffy mound of brown hair, made her even more menacing.

She'd have no qualms about slapping him with the spoon, but he couldn't make himself let go of Higgins's shirt. "I see what you're doing. You're stealing from me so you can try to get the land first."

Higgins jerked away, trying to free himself. Although the young laborer was strong, Reinhold knew in a battle of fists, he'd win. Not that he'd ever hit the man. Even so, Reinhold had earned his muscles from years of construction work and was the bigger man, which was apparently why Higgins had found another, more passive way to fight him.

"Go ahead, look through my stuff," Higgins said. "I ain't got nothin' to hide."

"Where did you put it?" Reinhold yelled. If he didn't find the money, he'd have to start over again saving up. What if he didn't have enough for a down payment by autumn? And what if Higgins beat him to buying the land?

"Boys!" Mrs. Turner towered over them, the spoon raised.

Higgins's expression was unrelenting in its taunting. His lips quirked in the beginning of a grin, and his eyes were alight with satisfaction.

Reinhold started to shake Higgins, but Mrs. Turner swung the wooden spoon between them. The large end cracked against Reinhold's hands. Pain radiated through his skin down to his bones, forcing him to release Higgins.

Mrs. Turner lifted the spoon and brought it down again, this time grazing Reinhold's shoulder. As new pain sliced through him. A clatter and then crash of porcelain against the floor startled them all to stillness.

On the other side of the table, Lucinda's eyes were fixed on her mother's wooden spoon and round with terror. She was so focused on the spoon she didn't seem to notice she'd dropped the plates, platters, and bowls and that now they were shattered into dozens of pieces at her feet.

"Lucinda May Turner!" Mrs. Turner gaped at her daughter, her eyes bugging out.

Reinhold didn't waste the moment of distraction. He backed toward the kitchen, his shoulder and hand throbbing with each step.

"What has gotten into you, girl?" Mrs. Turner said.

Lucinda's eyes darted from the spoon to Reinhold. And then her gaze dropped to the table, and her cheeks flamed a bright red. "I'm sorry, Mother." The young woman's voice was a breathy whisper, hardly audible.

For a moment, the scrape of Mr. Turner's spoon against his bowl was the only sound. He was apparently intent on eating every last drop of honey without any concern for the tumult circling around him.

Higgins had also used the opportunity to dart from the table in the opposite direction into the front sitting room. The click of the front door meant that Higgins had gotten away. Again.

Frustration coursed through Reinhold. Unless he had solid proof Higgins had been the one to dig through his belongings and take the money from his leather pouch, what could he do? Higgins would only continue to deny having a role in the thievery.

The shock on Mrs. Turner's face over her daughter's accident was turning into hard lines of anger. "I ought to turn this spoon on you and teach you not to be so clumsy.

But we all know that won't do any good, will it?"

Lucinda's chin dropped a notch so that it almost touched her chest. Her black hair was pulled back into a tight bun and parted down the middle in a perfectly straight line showing her white scalp.

"No matter how hard I've tried and no matter how much I've disciplined you over the years, you're destined to be the clumsiest girl I've ever met."

Except for the dinner hour, Reinhold rarely saw Lucinda. Even though she hardly ever spoke, he'd learned plenty about her from Mrs. Turner, who had a lot to say about her daughter, particularly about her failings. Not only did Mrs. Turner criticize Lucinda for being clumsy but also for being inept, lazy, ungrateful, too shy, and the list went on.

He'd learned she was of marriageable age, perhaps a year or two older than him, but that somehow she'd failed to win the heart of one of the local neighbors, a young man Mr. and Mrs. Turner had hoped would come live on their farm and perhaps take it over someday since they didn't have any sons of their own.

Reinhold wasn't sure what had happened to deter the match, except the young man had ended up marrying another woman, and now Mrs. Turner lamented the lost beau at least once every meal, along with making a point of telling Lucinda she would end up a spinster.

At times, Reinhold felt sorry for the young woman. While he'd never spoken more than a dozen words directly to her, he tried to show her a modicum of kindness whenever he could. It couldn't make up for Mrs. Turner's harshness, but it was a small token. After all, he knew what it was like to be the despised, scoffed, and rejected one. He'd experienced that enough to never wish it upon anyone.

Ignoring the ache and sting in his body from where he'd been lashed, Reinhold retraced his steps to the table and crossed to where Lucinda stood accepting the tongue-lashing from her mother without a word of protest.

"I'll help you clean up," he said quietly.

She stood at least two inches taller than him and didn't look at him. But she nodded, and her cheeks flushed a deep red again.

He knelt and began to gather the broken pieces of pottery.

"This is all your fault, Reinhold," Mrs. Turner said, stuffing her spoon back into her apron. "I think we should charge you for the cost of replacing everything that was broken."

"No, Mother," Lucinda said in her whispery voice. "I'll buy it." She knelt next to him, and as she reached for the first shard of porcelain, her fingers trembled so much that Reinhold was afraid she'd cut herself.

Mrs. Turner snorted loudly. "And just how are you planning to buy me new dishes?"

Lucinda's chin dropped again, and her hands fell idle to her lap.

Mr. Turner's chair scraped across the floor as he pushed away from the table.

Reinhold willed the man to rise to his daughter's defense and ease her embarrassment, but he only stood, scratched his belly, released a loud belch, and then lumbered toward the front room.

"Take the cost of the broken dishes out of Reinhold's next earnings," Mrs. Turner called after her husband.

He grunted a reply.

Reinhold reached for another jagged piece of plate, and his spirit deflated. He wanted to protest, but the honorable thing to do was to take responsibility. Lucinda wouldn't have dropped everything if he hadn't stormed into the room and picked the fight with Higgins.

He swallowed the words that burned in his throat, the words about how unfair life was sometimes. Instead, he finished picking up the pieces. At least he had plenty of experience at it since his life had been a series of broken mishaps.

If only, for once, something would go right.

CHAPTER 4

Marianne checked her list again — for the twentieth time. Three jars of raspberry jam, six loaves of bread, two heads of cheese, and five bundles of newly picked carrots she'd managed to purchase yesterday from a farmer selling his produce out of the back of his wagon. There were the raisins and figs, and she'd even snuck in a package of peppermints.

The food was stored in several boxes they would have with them in their passenger car. She'd also been responsible for packing the rest of the supplies that would see them through the next week of travel. The two other boxes that needed to fit into their train car contained knives and spoons, bibs, towels, washcloths, soap, a small sewing kit, blankets, knitted shawls for the little ones, and an assortment of medicine and remedies for ailments the children might suffer.

The younger children each would have a

bundle of clothing on the train — the second of the two new outfits provided for them by the Children's Aid Society. But the older children's extra clothing was stowed in the Society trunk. She'd packed a trunk of her own personal items as well. Although she hadn't been given a set return date, other agents had remarked that the trip could last anywhere from weeks to months.

Not only would she be helping to situate the orphans in new homes at stops along the way, but once the children were placed, she would have the responsibility of revisiting each of them and making sure the placement was suitable. At least that was what she'd been told.

Marianne closed her notepad and stuffed it into the valise she planned to carry with her on the train. She counted the boxes on the platform again and prayed she'd remembered everything. She'd hardly slept the previous night because her mind had raced with all the details for the trip. Not only that, but she could admit she was nervous about traveling with close to thirty children, all of whom were strangers to her.

Yes, she'd met many of them yesterday when they started arriving at the office. But she'd been so overwhelmed with the many aspects of getting them ready that she'd scarcely been able to remember their names.

Two other agents had come to the train station to help oversee the departure. They stood with the children near the train car, herding them together much like shepherds with their sheep. With the busyness of the depot, the people milling about, the various train workers shouting instructions and calling to one another, it would be easy for one of the children to wander off and get lost in the crowd. Some of the younger boys seemed particularly fond of wrestling with each other, and in a place near trains that had such speed and power, Marianne dreaded to think would could happen if they weren't careful.

That dread only escalated every time she thought about the fact that within the hour, the other two agents would leave and she'd have to handle all these children by herself, especially if Andrew Brady didn't show up. She chewed on the inside of her cheek and glanced around again for at least the tenth time, hoping to catch sight of Drew. His handsome face wouldn't be hard to miss, even in a busy train station. But she hadn't seen him anywhere.

Last night, after the physician had sewn six neat stitches into Drew's arm, he'd left with the doctor, claiming he needed to return to the Newsboys Lodging House. She, on the other hand, had spent the night at the Children's Aid Society building, along with the other two ladies in order to supervise the children.

She'd expected Drew to do the same, but maybe sleeping on the floor was beneath him. For her, bedding down wherever she could find a spot was nothing new. She'd done it for many years while living in her uncle's tenement in Kleindeutschland. Of course, she wouldn't complain about her bed at the boardinghouse. She had to admit she rather liked having a bed again after so many years without.

Whatever the case, she'd been restless and had held her breath at every strange noise throughout the long night. She hadn't been able to stop thinking about the drunken father who'd shot Drew or wondering if there were any other irate parents who might show up.

Everyone knew and accepted that the orphanages and Children's Aid Society program weren't just for true orphans — those who'd lost both of their parents. Rather, some only had one parent who'd given them up. Many of those parents did so with no intention of ever reclaiming them.

Other mothers and fathers placed their children in orphanages or asylums during times of crisis. If parents lost jobs or became ill and couldn't feed or clothe their children, they would take their children to orphanages or to the Children's Aid Society for placing out. The separation was usually only temporary, and the children were brought back home as soon as the parents could provide again.

In such situations where a parent or relative was still alive, the Children's Aid Society was supposed to make sure the caretakers were in agreement with the plans before sending the children westward on trains.

But sometimes the agents didn't know the whole background behind why a child was being dropped off at the Society. Most of the time the children weren't consulted about what they wanted, at least from what she'd seen. Even if they were, Marianne suspected many children were too young to comprehend what was happening.

"Miss Neumann," called Mrs. Trott, the elderly matron who reminded Marianne of her grandmother, who passed away shortly before her family had moved to America. "It's time for the children to board."

Marianne examined the boxes and supplies one last time. It was too late now to add anything she'd forgotten. She may as well allow the porters to finish loading.

She went to the children, and as she did so, their wide eyes watched her with expectation and trust. Some of the older girls were holding hands with the younger ones, having been paired by the agents with strict instructions to help guide them.

The initial enthusiasm the group had shown at the sight of the trains had abated. Now silence shrouded them. Even though their faces were scrubbed until they shone and their hair cropped and combed neatly with bows for the girls and smart hats for the boys, there was no grooming away the wariness that lined each of their faces, a wariness that perhaps reflected her own.

She wanted to believe she was doing the right thing for these children by escorting them to new homes. She wanted to reassure them everything would be all right and they would be happy wherever they were going. But would they? She prayed so.

However, a niggling of doubt haunted her. What if some of them had been ripped away from people who loved them? Family who would miss them and mourn for them each day they were gone? Family who wouldn't know where they were or what had become of them and would search for them until the day they died?

Oh, Sophie, where are you? Why won't you let us find you?

Marianne's gaze flitted to each of the sweet upturned faces following her every move. She had to control her misgivings and fear. She couldn't let the children see anything but confidence, so she forced a smile. "You all look so nice in your new clothing."

For a moment, her comment distracted the children, reminded them of the fancy garments they'd been given — likely the first time most of them had ever worn something clean, much less new. The little girls stroked the smooth calico, the ruffled edges, the lacy ribbons. Even the boys proudly straightened their bow ties, swelled their chests against the vests and coats, and tapped their shiny black shoes. For some, the shoes were the first pair they'd ever owned.

Mrs. Trott patted Marianne's arm. "You'll do fine, dear. Always remember, our responsibility is to God for these children. They have the same capabilities, the same need of benevolent and good influences, and the same immortality as the little ones in our homes. We bear in mind One died for them even as for the children of the rich and happy."

"Thank you," Marianne responded, allowing the woman to fold her into an embrace, glad for the chance to hide her face, which would surely give away her insecurities. The other agents thought of her only as Thornton Quincy's sister-in-law. None of them knew the more sordid details of her dismal past, of the fact that a year ago she was as desperately poor as these children, that for a time she'd been homeless on the streets and had to live off the good will and charities of others in order to survive. Even if her situation had improved — for which she was grateful — she still didn't consider herself to be a part of the rich and happy echelon of society.

With a final pat, Mrs. Trott released Marianne. "Don't forget when your burdens grow heavy, that God is walking alongside you, waiting for you to cast your cares upon Him."

Marianne tried to brighten her smile. Was her fear that easy to read? "I'm sorry. It's just that I'm worried about Mr. Brady's whereabouts. He should have been here by now."

"Mr. Brady might be impulsive and irregular at times, but he has a kind heart and he's good with the children." The shake of the grandmotherly head spoke louder than her words. The woman was relieved she didn't have to make the journey with Drew Brady. That thought did nothing to ease Marianne's worries.

The whirlpool of uneasiness in Marianne's abdomen began to swirl faster. The storm only brewed as she helped situate the children in the passenger car that had been reserved for their group. Thankfully, they had the whole car to themselves and wouldn't have to worry about disturbing other passengers. The children had grown loud again, standing on benches, crawling under them, peering out the windows, and opening and closing the closet door at the back of the car.

Marianne stowed the food and supply boxes at the front of the car and already had to chastise two young brothers who'd glimpsed food and attempted to pilfer a snack. From all the hauling and shoving and situating, she'd become overheated and was in the process of attempting to open some of the windows when silence fell over the car.

Her spine prickled, and she craned her neck toward the entrance in time to see that several teenage boys had come aboard. She wasn't good at guessing ages, but they looked to be young men in the range of fifteen or sixteen years. They weren't particularly big or tall, yet there was something overly mature in their expressions, a hardness from having to fend for themselves for so long, and an anger at life that simmered beneath the surface.

One of the boys, the lankiest with smallpox blister scars on his face, fixed his attention upon Marianne. He elbowed the other two and cocked his head toward Marianne. "Well, well, what do we have here, boys?" His lips curled into a surly smile, one that told Marianne he enjoyed intimidating others. "And you thought we'd be bored."

Marianne abandoned her effort at opening the window and turned to face the newcomers. She straightened her shoulders and attempted to lift herself to her full height, which at five-foot-five wasn't enough to intimidate anyone in return. "Who are you boys and what are you doing here?" She tried to make her tone strict.

"Who are we?" The lanky one lifted an eyebrow at his companions and then sauntered down the aisle. "Everyone knows who we are, don't they?" He glared at the orphans as though daring them to defy him. From the fear on their faces, it was clear the children were familiar with the boy.

Marianne guessed he was from one of the many local street gangs that lived in the alleys, who made terrorizing, stealing, and fighting a way of life. She wouldn't be a match for these boys if they decided to harass her, and the thought made her muscles turn to jelly. But she forced her feet to carry her to the aisle toward the newcomers and not away as she was tempted to do.

"Apparently your fame isn't as widespread as you believe, because I have no idea who you are." If only she was braver like her sister. Elise would have known what to do to scare them off the train before they hurt someone. Instead, Marianne floundered, praying the boy couldn't see her ineptness.

When his grin inched higher, Marianne knew her prayers were for naught. The boy realized she was afraid and was planning to use that to his advantage.

"You better do what we were told," one of the other older boys said, his voice hinting at worry, "or you'll git us kicked off." He was the shortest and thinnest of the three boys with a swarthy complexion that highlighted a long white scar across one eyebrow. A purple half-moon colored the skin under one of his eyes, likely the result of a fist-fight.

71

Did these boys believe they were coming along on this trip?

She took in their clean trousers and pristine shirts along with their shiny shoes. Alley boys, especially those belonging to gangs, didn't dress like this. In fact, none of the children in Manhattan wore such fine clothes . . . unless they were part of the Emigration Plan. The Children's Aid Society believed the orphans must look as well groomed as the children in the community where they were going in order to offer them the best chance possible of attracting a family to take them in.

Who had given leave to these boys to join their group? She frowned her displeasure. "I don't know what you think you're doing barging into our group like this, but you're not welcome."

"Come on, Liverpool," the boy near the door said again.

Liverpool? What kind of name was that? Marianne knew she shouldn't be surprised. Nicknames abounded among the street urchins — Smack, Yankee, Picket, Smalley. Left to their own vices, the children became expert thieves, liars, profane swearers, and beggars, taking names to suit their lifestyles and often to avoid detection and repeat offenses with the police.

Liverpool didn't listen to his companion but continued toward Marianne until he was standing only a foot away. The pockmarks on his face were more pronounced up close. Even though his face had been scrubbed, a line of scum still rimmed his hairline.

"How about if I make myself welcome?" Liverpool took off his hat, licked his hand, and smoothed his rusty brown hair back. "I've been told I'm a good kisser."

Some of the children around her tittered.

Marianne didn't know whether to laugh or to slap the boy on the cheek for his forwardness. Before she could decide, a man's voice carried through the passenger car, making everyone jump.

"Liverpool, I told you to stay away from Miss Neumann." Drew Brady ducked into the car. His tone was deadly, his expression severe.

The sight of him relieved her so much she sagged back a step. "Since you seem to know these young men, Mr. Brady, I'd appreciate it if you'd escort them off the train."

Drew's scowl was trained on Liverpool's face as he shouldered his way past the other two and made his way down the aisle. "You didn't touch Miss Neumann, did you?"

Liverpool lifted his bony shoulders and

shrugged. "How was I supposed to know this was Miss Neumann?" Even though his expression was full of innocence, something glittered in his eyes that said he'd known well enough.

Drew stomped toward Liverpool. "I warned you."

The boy spread his feet and lifted his chin. "You told me to stay away from the pretty young lady. You didn't say anything about the girls."

Pretty young lady? Drew Brady thought she was pretty? A flush of warmth spread through her at the realization.

Before the boy could react, Drew grabbed Liverpool by the shoulders, spun him, and locked his head into a tight hold. "I'm not an idiot," Drew growled, "so don't treat me like one."

Liverpool's lips pressed together, and his fists clenched. Although he clearly wanted to lash out at Drew, he didn't move.

Drew twisted Liverpool back around and looked the boy in the eye. "I want you to go on this trip. I really do." Drew's voice lost its edge. "But if you come, you have to do what I tell you to."

Liverpool's eyes flashed with defiance.

"Can you follow my orders?" Drew asked. "Because if you can't, you'll have to get off right now."

For a long moment, their compartment was absolutely quiet, which magnified the noises of the other locomotives coming and going around them. A steam whistle wailed with a long burst followed by a short one. Wheels clattered and scraped against railroad tracks. Train cars rattled in passing.

Marianne had taken her first train ride earlier in the year when she'd gone to Illinois to visit Elise in Quincy. She'd hoped to see Reinhold on her trip. Her longtime friend had moved to Quincy shortly after Elise had gone there. He'd done construction work in the new town, sending money back to his destitute family in Kleindeutschland. When he'd left Quincy, he hadn't told anyone where he was going. Even now, six months later, Marianne still didn't know where Reinhold was.

Guilt nagged at Marianne for having told Drew yesterday that Reinhold was her fiancé. Although she wished it were true and had always fancied Reinhold, he'd technically never made any mention of marrying her. She just hoped that this journey would help her not only locate Sophie's whereabouts but also find some link to Reinhold.

Whatever the case, she was thankful for already having the experience of riding a locomotive so that amidst all the other anxieties, at least the sounds and sensations of the train wouldn't be new.

"I believe what I told you last night," Drew said, his sights sweeping over all three of the older boys. "This trip could give you a better life, better than anything you could dream or imagine."

The stiffness began to ease out of Liverpool's shoulders until finally he nodded. "Fine. I'll do what you tell me."

"Good." Drew released his grip on the boy and propelled him toward his friends at the front of the car. "You fellows sit in the front rows."

Liverpool rolled his shoulders as though shaking off a disease. He walked lazily back to his friends, a grin playing on his lips. He slid across the first bench and swung his legs up, taking up the whole space. His friends glanced between Liverpool and Drew, the uncertainty on their faces almost comical. It was clear they feared both man and boy. They both sat on the opposite bench that faced Liverpool's.

As the children resumed their conversations, Drew turned to her, concern creasing his forehead. "He didn't touch you, did he?"

She shook her head. "No. I wouldn't have let him."

"He's a strong kid."

"Well, I'm stronger than I look." At least she wished she were stronger.

"If he bothers you again, I'll send him back to the city."

"I didn't realize we had any more children coming."

He shrugged. "I was hoping more of the boys from the Lodging House would want to come this time. But I only convinced the three."

She wanted to ask Drew why he was bothering to bring such a hardened, troubled boy in the first place, but now was neither the time nor the place. She returned to the window she'd previously been trying to open, and she yanked on it. "I hope we have enough food for everyone."

"I'm not worried. If we need more, I'll buy it along the way."

"Very well." She tugged on the window, but again it didn't budge. "I'll add them to the list of children and will get their information from you later."

He reached an arm around her, released a leather strap, and slid the window down effortlessly. The breeze rushed into the stuffy compartment, bringing cooler air but also the fumes of burning coal.

When she turned around, she found

herself practically in his arms. Flustered at the impropriety of the situation, she attempted to put proper distance between them and flattened against the window.

Apparently noticing their close confines, Drew took a rapid step away and cleared his throat. "Are we all set to leave?"

"I believe so." She was keenly aware of the children around them watching every move they made. Although there were certainly no romantic inclinations between herself and Drew Brady, she would have to be careful to conduct herself with the utmost integrity to be above reproach in all things.

The agent who'd trained her had warned that she was not allowed to fraternize with the other agent during the journey. Their attention was to remain focused on the children. Her instructor had implied that any reports of misconduct between agents could be the cause of dismissal.

As though remembering the same, Drew retreated another step, bumping into the bench directly across the aisle.

"Mr. Brady," called one of the younger boys several seats back. "Will you sit with us?"

Drew made his way to the cluster of boys, speaking to each by name, ruffling hair, joking with them, and drawing grins from even the most timid. He did the same with a pair of siblings sitting across the aisle.

Marianne's heart warmed at the smiles and giggles and renewed excitement that were quickly replacing the fear that had been present only moments before. With a sense of relief, Marianne lowered herself to the bench in the middle of the passenger car where she'd decided to sit for the journey. She'd hoped being at the center of the activity would allow her the best position for overseeing the orphans.

But as Drew settled himself into the group of boys, she wondered if she should have sat with the children too. She'd wanted to keep appropriate boundaries. The youngsters needed to know she was in charge, that she wasn't their friend, didn't they? The agent who'd instructed her on her duties had said she shouldn't form attachments; otherwise the orphans might have a difficult time leaving her when the time came for them to part ways.

No attachments to the other workers. No attachments to the children. It was bound to be a lonely trip. She released a brief sigh. Good thing she was used to loneliness.

Retrieving her notepad from her valise, she opened it and added three more digits to the end of the list, bringing the total number of children from twenty-eight to thirty-one. She was tempted to march right up to the three newcomers and get their names and information herself. But after glancing at Liverpool and the hardness of his contours, she decided she'd better wait for Drew. She'd been around enough boys like Liverpool to know they were unpredictable and easily provoked.

When the train lurched and the steam whistle blew, the children's voices rose in a clamoring of anticipation. The younger ones pressed their faces against the windows in their eagerness to experience the train's increasing speed. Even the older children vied for spots at the windows where they could watch the shifting scenery.

Marianne couldn't keep from staring out the window as the buildings began to whiz past at an almost dizzying speed. Although the train would eventually gain speeds of thirty miles per hour, the current pace was faster than any carriage could travel, faster than most of them had ever gone. She felt the children's exhilaration in her own blood.

When the busy and crowded thoroughfares of New York City gave way to a more rural landscape of farm fields and woodlands, she expected the children to settle into their seats. But they continued to crowd against the windows, making exclamations about everything they saw.

"What's that, mister?" The questions flew at Drew, who reclined with both arms spread across the back of his seat, his legs stretched in front of him. He answered every question with saintly patience.

"Look at them cows!" squealed one girl, her eyes round in wonder. "My mother used to milk cows."

"What's a-growin' in that field, mister?"

"Ah, fellers, see all the sheep!"

On and on the exclamations rose at each new sight. Many of the children had never seen anything but the crowded tenements and streets of the city. Marianne could completely empathize with their excitement. She'd felt the same way on her first trip out of the city, like she'd traveled to a whole new world, one she'd never realized existed except in fairy tales — a world that was clean and fresh and beautiful. So unlike the filthy, crowded, stale streets and alleys that were home to far too many people.

Some of the children extended their arms out the few windows that had been opened, and she was tempted to insist they draw back inside. But Drew sprawled in his seat, his posture relaxed as if he were on a pleasure trip instead of supervising thirty-one orphans. He didn't seem to be worried about the possibility of a younger child falling out. So Marianne bit her tongue and swallowed her apprehension.

After almost an hour of high-pitched enthusiasm, many of the children returned to their seats. Some were already quiet, contemplative as if realizing how different their lives would be, how much was changing, and how far from home they were going.

"Everyone's attention, please!" Drew's voice boomed through the passenger car. The orphans swiveled to face him, and their clamor dimmed.

He was standing in the aisle, one hand holding the bench to keep himself steady against the lurching movement of the train. With the other hand, he held his hat. "As we start our trip together, I don't want to neglect the most important part of the voyage."

Marianne nodded and opened her notebook wider, pressing on the spine and smoothing her hand down the pages. After the long walk to the station, as well as the busyness of the depot, they surely needed to make sure each child was accounted for.

She should have thought of taking roll call herself.

"Let's bow our heads and ask God to be present with us on our trip," Drew said.

Was he praying? Did he think that was the most important part of the trip? Marianne's pencil slipped from her fingers, and she fumbled to grasp it only to knock her notepad off her lap. It fell onto the plank floor with a slap.

Over the heads of the children, Drew's gaze met hers. The sincerity in his green-blue eyes and the earnestness of his expression told her he was serious about his statement. He believed prayer was the most important aspect of their journey. And something in his eyes beckoned her to join him in his effort.

His words from last night came back to her. He'd told her he was glad she was coming and that they would make a great team. At the time, she'd appreciated his confidence in her and was relieved that, in spite of her poor background, he still wanted to be her partner.

But if he expected her to pray with him, he was in for a big disappointment. God wasn't about to listen to her prayers, much less answer them. She'd sinned too often, displeased Him too many times. And now she deserved whatever ill will might come her way.

Yet she didn't want Andrew Brady knowing she felt unworthy of God. She wanted him to see her as the person he did last night — the one he wanted as a partner and not the failure she really was.

Dropping her sights to the notepad on the floor, she broke the connection with Drew. She bent and fumbled for it, fidgeting with the pages, opening and closing them at least three times before sitting up and shutting her eyes as though waiting for him to begin his prayer.

He was silent a moment, and then his voice carried through the compartment above the clacking of the wheels. "Father, we need you to guide us each step of the way. We ask you to go before us, that you prepare even now a home for each of these children, that you bring them to a place of love and joy like they've never experienced."

Drew's prayer was so personal and sincere that Marianne at once sensed God's presence in a way she hadn't in a long time. From the peace that emanated from Drew, she knew God was listening to him and that he was a righteous man. Part of her liked him even more for it. But another part shrank at what Drew would think if he ever saw deep inside her.

As handsome and sweet and godly as he may be, she'd have to keep her distance from him during the voyage. She simply didn't know how she could live with herself if she let one more person down.

CHAPTER 5

They'd been traveling for twelve hours, yet it felt like twelve days.

Marianne combed the sweaty strands off Dorothea's forehead. The little girl was asleep with her head on Marianne's lap and her legs curled on the bench. The stench of the girl's vomit still lingered in the air around them, having splattered not only on Dorothea's new outfit but also onto Marianne's.

The three-year-old had been heartbroken at the sight of the red jelly stains on her pretty dress. And Marianne had to question the wisdom of the agent who'd decided they should have jam sandwiches for their meal. Why not cheese or even just bread and butter?

Marianne let the cool night air from the open window brush the hair from her overheated face and tried to make herself more comfortable on the hard bench.

On the other side of her, seven-year-old Jethro had laid his head against her arm and finally dozed. He'd been sick from the motion too but thankfully hadn't vomited like poor Dorothea. His coarse, prickly hair stood on end like a rooster's crest and was nearly as bright red. His impish face was sprinkled with freckles, and he'd lost his top front teeth so that he spoke with an adorable lisp.

He'd told her bits and pieces of his life, particularly about his time doing odd jobs on the docks, how he'd dressed in sailor's ragged castoffs, which had been much too large for him. With his father in prison and his mother deceased, he'd resorted to gathering up the twigs and chips left behind on the docks after piles of firewood were loaded onto steamers. He'd sold the wood shavings until he saved up twenty-five cents.

After that, Jethro went to the match factory and worked as a match boy for a while, buying his wares at wholesale. With his quarter, he'd been able to afford ninety-seven bunches to sell for a penny apiece. He said he had to walk street after street all day long, knocking at every door he passed, usually having them slammed in his face. Still, by the end of the day, he'd sell all the matches.

Marianne hadn't been surprised by Jethro's tale. She'd seen too many children in his same position. But it made her sad, nonetheless, to think that a boy of no more than seven had already experienced such a difficult life. Even more, it pained her that he hadn't known the love and safety of a family.

Marianne hugged him to her side a little tighter, knowing she shouldn't care so much about the children already, but she couldn't seem to stop herself. After spending all day in such close confinement, how could she keep them at arm's length? How could she stay aloof and impartial as Mrs. Trott had instructed?

The steady clacking of the wheels against the track and the constant creaking of the train car drowned out the snores and heavy breathing of the children who'd managed to fall into an exhausted slumber. Some lay on benches. Others were curled up on the floor under benches or in the aisles. They were experts at sleeping wherever they found a spare spot.

A gentle brush against her shoulder was followed by a large form sliding onto the bench opposite her. Andrew. He lifted the legs of the boy who already occupied the spot and made room for himself by draping the boy's legs across his lap.

"How are you faring?" Drew asked.

The darkness of the car was broken only by the soft glow of moonlight filtering in through the windows. It was enough light to see the outline of Drew's features, including that irresistible dimple on his chin.

"I'm tired," she admitted.

"You did well for your first day."

"So did you." She'd actually been quite impressed with his interactions with the children. After Mrs. Trott's rather ominous warning about him, she wasn't sure what to expect. Certainly not the bottomless kindness and the tender, sweet way of interacting he'd shown thus far. He wasn't afraid to discipline when needed, was in fact strict at times. His methods seemed to be a winning combination of both soft and hard, and the children adored him.

"How is your wound?" she asked. He'd gone all day without a single complaint about his arm and the stitches, but she was sure it had to hurt.

"It's sore, but nothing I can't handle." He nodded at Jethro and Dorothea. "Looks like you made a couple of friends."

She brushed her fingers across Dorothea's forehead and into her loose hair. In the dark, the silky texture could have been

Sophie's. How often had Marianne slept next to her little sister and done this very thing to her hair, smoothing it off her forehead, telling her stories to ease her fears, trying to distract her from the cold and hunger and loss that had been their companions all too often?

Sophie. Her sister would have turned sixteen recently. A deep, familiar ache welled up within, an ache that had been growing over the past months until at times it radiated through Marianne's whole body and she hurt all over. She still had no clue, no information about where Sophie may have ended up. After weeks of scouring the alleys and crowded tenements of the city, Marianne had resigned herself to the fact that Sophie was no longer there. Her brother-in-law, Thornton Quincy, had even hired a detective to search for Sophie. Thornton had been kind enough to spare no expense, and yet he was unable to locate the young girl either.

Marianne had begged Elise and Thornton to help her get this job with the Children's Aid Society for one main reason — so she could continue her search for Sophie. Yes, she wanted to have the work to prove she could live independently from her sister. And yes, she'd wanted the job because she genuinely wanted to help orphans who had no way of helping themselves. But mostly it was because she suspected Sophie had left the city on a train with a group of orphans. At first, Marianne hadn't believed Sophie would resort to the placing out, but the more Marianne thought about it, the more she suspected her sister had done so in an effort to track down Olivia and Nicholas.

The two abandoned children had been Sophie's charges. At only one and two years of age, the pair had seen Sophie as their adopted mother. And Sophie had grown close to them as well. Too close.

When Olivia and Nicholas had been sent west through the Children's Aid Society without Sophie's knowledge or permission, she'd been devastated. Without a job or money to pay for a ticket, perhaps Sophie decided she had no other option than to join a placing-out group. Whatever the case, Marianne had decided that visiting the various towns the Children's Aid Society traveled to for placing orphans might bring her one step closer to finding her sister or maybe even Olivia and Nicholas.

If only she'd been able to find solid evidence in Reverend Brace's filing cabinet. The name of a town would have been a start. Even a sentence to confirm names would have been helpful. But after Drew's interruption, Marianne hadn't had the courage to sneak back into the reverend's office and search again.

She couldn't even be sure Sophie had gone anywhere at all. In fact, she wasn't certain Sophie still lived. What if she'd been murdered and tossed into the Hudson or east Rivers? Although the image of her sister's body decaying in the muck of a riverbed was too awful to contemplate, that wasn't Marianne's worst fear. The worst strangled her with nightmarish images, causing her to sob into her pillow at night. It was the picture of her beautiful sister trapped in a basement cellar somewhere, never seeing daylight, forced to give her body over to prostitution night after night.

"You seem sad," Drew said softly. "What are you thinking about?"

Marianne couldn't tell Drew she was thinking about her lost sister. If she did, he'd figure out whose records she'd been searching for, along with her ulterior motive for being an agent on the trip. Instead, she tried to lighten her demeanor so he wouldn't grow too suspicious. "Have you ever put yourself in the children's shoes?" she asked, avoiding his question.

Drew lifted the small shoe of the boy

whose leg rested on his lap. "Would this fit?"

"Not literally," she chastised, though his quick grin told her he'd merely been teasing. "How strange all this must seem to them — leaving their homes, starting out for the unknown, not knowing their fate."

"It's the beginning of a much better life for them." He spoke with such assurance, Marianne could almost believe him. For just a few seconds. But then all the doubts came rushing back again about Sophie, Olivia, and Nicholas.

Even when she, Elise, and Sophie left uncle's tenement and had been homeless and hungry, they'd cared for Olivia and Nicholas as though the infants were of their own flesh and blood. When they'd gone to live at the Seventh Street Mission with Miss Pendleton, Olivia and Nicholas came along. And when Marianne moved in with Reinhold's mother and aunt, she brought Olivia and Nicholas.

She'd never intended to part ways with them. Never intended for Reinhold's aunt to take them to the depot and put them aboard a train with a group of children leaving with the Children's Aid Society. What must the two children have thought when they were riding the train, having been ripped away from the people who loved them? Marianne's heart broke every time she imagined their fear and confusion and homesickness. They'd likely huddled on the hard benches, silent and withdrawn, tears in their eyes, praying someone would take them back to the sisters who'd become their family.

"What if some of these young ones didn't want to leave the city?" Marianne whispered, brushing Dorothea's cheek and imagining it was Olivia's. "What if they were torn away from a family who loves them?"

No matter how much Elise had tried to placate her and assure her that Sophie running away and losing Olivia and Nicholas weren't her fault, Marianne would blame herself until the day she died. And she wouldn't stop searching until she found them. Even if she had to look for her entire life.

Drew was silent a moment and seemed to study her.

"Hypothetically, of course," Marianne added, suspecting he could see much deeper into her thoughts than she wanted him to.

"If they were *hypothetically* taken away from a loving family," he said slowly, as if choosing his words carefully, "then that family can rest assured the children are being well cared for in another loving home with two parents — a mom and a dad, in a wholesome environment away from the vices of the city. A place where they'll flourish and grow and have plenty of food. A place where they'll have godly influences, be taken to church, and also be given an education. A place where they'll have fresh air every day and room to play and have the kind of work that will strengthen their character."

She soaked in his words like parched soil did with a gentle rain. She wanted so much to believe him. If Olivia and Nicholas had found a home like that, then maybe they were better off. Maybe they'd been confused, maybe even terrified, at first. But hopefully over time, they would forget about their life in New York City. Perhaps it would become a distant dream, replaced by new and beautiful memories with a family who truly loved them.

Sophie, on the other hand . . . Before Marianne could stop herself from asking Drew another question, it was out. "And what about an older child, someone in her teenage years? What kind of life could she expect in the West?"

Again, Drew took his time answering, and she found herself waiting breathlessly for his response, desperate for the reassurance

Sophie might have found happiness too.

"Hypothetically again," he finally said, "such a young woman would likely find herself hired to work on a farm or perhaps as a domestic for a family in town. She'd find herself in a wholesome environment as well, away from the temptations and evils of the city. No doubt she'd be required to work hard, but such work would be good for her, help build her character, and train her to run her own house someday. And of course she'd be taken to church and given an education."

Marianne felt her body relaxing at Drew's description, the tension and anxiety easing from her muscles. "You make the new lives and new families sound a bit like heaven."

"For most of them, the difference is like moving out of hell into paradise." His slight drawl made his words all the more soothing. "And our job is to ensure that, to put them with the best possible families."

Oh, how she prayed he was right, that Nicholas and Olivia were indeed in a better place and that Sophie was happy. If only Marianne could know for sure, then she might rest easier at night. She wouldn't give up her search for them, but at least she'd be able to let some of the heavy load of guilt slip away.

Next to her, Jethro whimpered, as though crying in his dreams. She rubbed a hand over his arm, then bent and placed a kiss into his coarse hair.

"You're good with the children," Drew remarked.

"It's easy to love them," she said. "But I'm worried I'll grow too attached and they to me if I'm not careful."

"Most of them have already had too little love. In fact, for some of them, our love might be the first they've ever experienced. Besides, I always say it's better to give them more love than not enough."

She nodded, and it was her turn to study him. He leaned back, looking completely relaxed, as though he hadn't a care in the world. What kind of life had this man come from where he could so easily dismiss his concerns? In some ways, his confident manner reminded her of Thornton. Was Drew a man born into wealth and privilege? He certainly was nothing like Reinhold, who took life as seriously as it had been given to him.

"Since we're to be partners on this trip, I really should know more about you," she said.

He didn't say anything but instead turned his head toward the window, staring out at the moonlit landscape passing by — lush forestland, thick and black, the pointed tops of spruce and pine illuminated faintly in an ethereal glow.

"I'll tell you more about me," he finally said, "but only if you promise to do the same."

"Of course." Surely, she could find some things to share with him. She wouldn't have to tell him every sordid detail.

In hushed voices they talked for miles upon miles of train track. She was fascinated to learn — but not surprised — that he was from Georgia, his father a prosperous plantation owner. His family had more slaves than he could count and grew not only cotton but also invested in tobacco, wheat, oats, and sweet potatoes. Although Drew sided with the growing abolitionist movement regarding slavery, he saw no way to end the institution without severely crippling the South's economy.

Drew didn't go into much detail about his family but mentioned he was the second of two sons and that because his older brother had made it his life's ambition to take over the plantation, Drew had decided to go to seminary to study theology. He hadn't finished his training but instead pursued becoming a teacher. He'd taught for a few years in Georgia before moving to New York City.

When it was Marianne's turn to share, she told him about her family's history, how her Vater had been a baker in Hamburg, Germany, but how he lost his business when a wealthy count slandered him. Her family then moved to New York City, where Vater started a new bakery. But the competition proved too difficult, and Vater's debts had grown until finally he was forced to sell everything. Marianne believed the loss was too much for him to bear. His heart failed soon after and he died.

Marianne skipped the years when she and her two sisters and Mutti lived with Uncle and his family in his tiny apartment in Kleindeutschland, the years she and Elise and Mutti worked in a tenement sweatshop sewing men's vests. They'd worked twelve hours a day for six days a week and still never made enough money to do more than buy food and pay Uncle what they owed for rent.

Instead, she told Drew about Mutti dying last spring and how hard that had been. "You know the rest," she finished. "After Mutti died, Elise went to Illinois as part of the Emigration Plan for women who needed work. She met Thornton, got married, and now here we are."

Surely, Drew didn't need to know about all that happened after Mutti's death, how they'd run away from Uncle and were homeless and hungry, slept in dirty alleys and ate out of garbage cans. Olivia and Nicholas were with them, and Nicholas became sick. But God worked a miracle and brought the wealthy Miss Pendleton into their lives. For a short while they lived together happily and worked at Miss Pendleton's Seventh Street Mission, which was a safe house for destitute women.

Unfortunately, the mission experienced financial trouble and had to close its doors. That was when Elise applied at the Children's Aid Society and the Emigration Plan — their program to help seamstresses and domestics find work in the West.

During those awful months when Elise was in Illinois and Marianne was in charge of everyone, Marianne made the decision to pretend to be pregnant with Reinhold's baby, so that his mother would take her in and support her. At the time, Marianne thought the lie was only a tiny one. She justified telling it because she needed a place for her and Sophie and Nicholas and Olivia to live. She wanted to keep them together and avoid subjecting them to the hardships of being homeless again.

But the lie backfired. Now here she was six months later trying to make atonement for her mistakes.

"And your fiancé?" Drew asked. "How does he fit into your story?"

She squirmed and wished she hadn't told him about Reinhold last night. She'd been too quick-tongued. For a few moments, she fingered a loose strand of Dorothea's hair and tried to figure out how she could refrain from answering him. Expelling a long breath, she decided she might as well tell him the truth now before the lie grew too big to handle — like it had when she'd told Reinhold's family she was pregnant.

"Reinhold lived in the same tenement as my uncle. That's where I first met him."

"It was love at first sight?"

She pictured meeting the strong, handsome young man when she first moved in with Uncle. "Yes, I guess I have always loved him. But . . ."

Drew waited.

She swallowed hard. "Well, we're not engaged yet."

"I see."

"But we will be very soon. Just as soon as we're reunited."

"Where does he live?"

She hesitated, considered making something up, but then forced herself to be honest again. "I'm not exactly sure. I was hoping Elise would know by now, that perhaps she would have gotten a letter from him telling us where he's settled."

"And why wouldn't he send such a letter to you?"

Her cheeks began to grow hot, and she was glad for the darkness that hid her flush. "He probably has written to me. But I've been in transition, moving so often that the letters have likely missed me altogether." At least that was what she wanted to believe, what she'd clung to all these months since he left the city and took her heart with him. He'd probably written to her numerous times and thought about her daily, if not hourly, as she did him. Well, maybe she'd stopped thinking about him hourly, yet he was never far from her mind.

She shook her head. "Enough about that. Now that I've opened my heart and given you a peek inside, you must do the same for me."

He gave a low chuckle. "Darlin', all you'll see are skeletons in my heart."

"You don't have a sweetheart somewhere waiting for you?"

His smile faded, and once again his attention turned to the window and the darkness of the night. The hill they traveled through had been blasted away to make room for the tracks so that now slabs of stone rose sharply outside the window.

Even though their compartment's interior became darker as they passed through the imposing rocky landscape, she could see the battle warring across Drew's face. Was he having the same problem as her? Deciding which parts of his past to divulge and which to keep buried?

"I was engaged once," he said so softly she almost didn't hear him.

She waited for him to elaborate. But he only stared out the window as though he'd disappeared into another time and place.

"You loved her very much?" she finally dared to ask, more curious about Drew's past love than she wanted to admit.

Again Drew was silent. But the silence said it all. He'd once loved a woman, and that love had cost him his heart.

"I'm sorry," she whispered.

His attention flickered back to her. "It's in the past. And that's where I prefer to leave it."

"Then I won't bring it up again," she said earnestly.

"Thank you."

Silence settled in around them. The rocking of the car with the steady clack of the wheels began to lull her until her eyelids felt heavy.

"You should get some sleep." His voice drifted to her but sounded a dozen miles away.

She nodded and let her eyes close all the way. Her last thoughts before falling asleep were that she wished somehow she could heal Drew's heartache and make him happy.

CHAPTER 6

"Don't go too far from the depot," Drew instructed the three older boys, who'd already hunkered down in their new coats and pulled their hats low as they strode away from the train platform.

The only one to acknowledge his command was Ned, who glanced over his shoulder and squinted in the bright morning sunlight. "Sure thing, Mr. Brady." The bruise under the boy's eye was healing, but the scar across his brow would never go away. Neither would the inner scars, the ones inflicted by a father who thought nothing of taking a leather belt to his son's face. From the way Ned explained the incident, he'd merely been in the wrong place at the wrong time — sleeping on the floor in a spot that had caused his father to trip and fall over him.

Drew had seen Ned's face after that particular beating, a gruesome portrait of cuts and bruises, the worst where the belt buckle had cut deeply, requiring two layers of stitches to heal properly.

Drew pressed a hand against his upper arm and winced. The gunshot wound still stung. But better him with the bullet wound than Ned. Hopefully now, Ned would never have to face his father's drunken abuse again. Drew prayed Ned would finally be free to make a good life for himself.

Some opponents of the Emigration Plan, like the directors of the Juvenile Asylum and the House of Refuge, believed the trouble-some juveniles — the most morally de-graded types along with beggars, vagrants, and petty thieves — should remain in the asylums so they could be reformed first through a period of institutional incarcera-tion before being placed into families in the West.

Brace had been accused of scattering poison over the country because he per-sisted in placing children who had not been officially corrected. His opponents had a pessimistic view of human nature and saw the poor as having intrinsic evil character. They believed children of the poor were strongly disposed to be criminals by birth, and they thought the best way to fight against such a tainted nature was by rigid discipline and punishment.

Brace had privately confided in Drew that he thought the controversy stemmed in part from financial considerations. The Juvenile Asylum and House of Refuge were afraid the Emigration Plan would take away their inmates and thus their funding would decrease. After all, the Emigration Plan was much cheaper than institutional care. The statistics from the previous year proved it. It cost the Children's Aid Society a onetime payment of ten dollars per child to place them with a good Christian family. In contrast, it cost the House of Refuge eighty-five dollars to care for a child in a crowded building rife with disease and unrest.

Drew watched the three boys head down the unpaved street past shops just opening for the day. Brace's words from a recent article pushed to the forefront of Drew's mind: *"If there is a good family in the West that is willing to take in a poor boy from the city to give him social and Christian instruction, why in God's name should they not do it? What if the boy is bad? If enough families can be found to serve as reformatory institutions, is it not the best and most practical and economical method of reforming these children?"*

"Amen," Drew breathed. Brace's declaration had become Drew's litany of hope whenever he faced a boy as hardened as Liverpool, or as scared as Ned. They deserved a second chance every bit as much as the infants.

Behind him, the shouts and squeals of the younger children filled the air. Marianne had led them to a grassy field to the left of the train depot, where several silos and granaries had been placed in a strategic location close to the tracks. The children were running in the field, which glistened with dew. Several were chasing a white butterfly, while others raced around in circles, their energy finding release after the past day and night spent cooped up inside their train car.

Marianne knelt with some of the girls to examine a patch of purple wildflowers. She smiled at their gasps of delight. When one of the girls slipped her hand into Marianne's, she pulled the girl into a tender embrace.

Drew couldn't stop himself from watching her for just a moment longer, appreciating the way she interacted with the children. Although at first yesterday she'd attempted to remain aloof, likely instructed to do so by some of the older agents who were kind but impersonal with the children, he'd noticed her gradually succumbing to her desire to lavish the children with the attention they craved.

By the time he'd had the chance to speak with her last night after the children were asleep, she'd been surrounded by the children. They adored her because she couldn't hide the fact that she adored them. That love was in her eyes and written on her expressive face.

As she straightened, she glanced in his direction and caught him staring. He supposed the polite thing would have been to look away, to pretend he hadn't been staring, to save her the discomfort. But he'd never been particularly conventional when it came to women. He'd always liked flirting and had been rather good at it.

He let his lips curve up into a practiced half smile that always worked its magic. Her velvety brown eyes widened and filled with telltale admiration before her impossibly long lashes descended and she angled herself away. Strangely his pulse sped, and he felt flustered in a way he hadn't experienced in a long time.

Was he reacting to her beauty? Amidst the lush green of the long grass, her light cotton print dress made her look like a delicate flower. Even after sleeping in her clothes all night, she was somehow fresh and especially pretty with her wide hat accentuating her wavy brown hair that was styled in a pretty twist.

Or was he reacting to the closeness he felt after talking with her last night? While he'd sensed she hadn't shared everything, he empathized with her losses. Maybe he hadn't lost his family to death, but he'd lost them nonetheless.

Or maybe he was reacting to her because of how she'd looked after she'd fallen asleep. He'd been too tired to return to his original spot — at least that was what he'd told himself. He'd been content to watch the moonlight coming in from the open window highlight her elegant features, which were so peaceful in slumber. He'd relished — perhaps more than he should have — observing her without her being aware.

Or was he reacting to the knowledge she wasn't engaged? He'd never made a habit of flirting with married or engaged women. He hadn't appreciated when other men flirted with his fiancée and had gotten into some bloody fights because of it. But now that Marianne had revealed the truth about her status, he could have a little fun now and then, couldn't he? She wasn't taken yet.

In fact, he had the suspicion this Reinhold of hers didn't deserve her, not if he hadn't attempted to write and let her know his whereabouts. He sounded like the type of man who led a woman on, promised her what she wanted to hear, but then eventually moved on regardless of the pain he left in his wake.

Marianne bent to pick a flower, and as she straightened she peeked at him again. At seeing him still staring directly at her, she brought the flower to her nose as though she could hide her reaction. Even so, he saw her smile.

So she liked when he stared at her?

He swaggered forward, unable to keep his grin from inching higher. If she liked him staring, he would oblige her. That would be no trouble at all.

"Time for a few races," he called to the children. The boys bounded over to him first, shouting their enthusiasm and full of questions as always, but the girls hung back. "Come on, ladies. You too."

Some of the youngest girls giggled and skipped toward him. But Marianne and the older ones didn't move, watching him with interest but obviously not planning to take part. He inwardly chuckled, intending to rope Marianne into the fun.

For the first couple of races, he lined up the children and had them compete with one another in a simple footrace. They ran with abandon, letting the cool morning air rush against their faces, their shoes and hems dampening with the dew.

Then he shot a sideways glance at Marianne and the older girls. "Time for the ladies to race." Marianne shook her head, but he continued, "With another long day on the train, don't you think the ladies should exercise before we board?"

"Yes, I suppose that's a good idea." She started to steer the girls in his direction.

"You too, Miss Neumann."

Her expression turned indignant. "Surely you jest."

"Do I look like I'm jesting?" He attempted to make his face serious, except his lips wouldn't cooperate and twitched into a smile.

She balled her hands on her hips and stared at him as though she were attempting to decipher ancient hieroglyphics.

"Maybe you're scared because you can't run." He waited for her to take the bait.

"I can run just fine," she said. "Maybe you're the one who can't run."

He grinned. She was responding the way he'd hoped. "Is that a challenge, Miss

Neumann? Are you daring me to race you?"

Around him, the excited murmurs and giggles told him he had the orphans on his side.

"Who would like to see me race Miss Neumann?" he called out.

His question was met with a chorus of cheers from the children, who were ecstatic at the possibility of seeing their two adult leaders compete.

Marianne looked from him to the children and back before narrowing her eyes as though she'd figured out his ruse.

He shrugged. "We can't let the children down, now, can we?"

"True." She bent and fidgeted underneath her petticoat. It took him a moment to realize she was removing her shoes.

"Are you running barefoot, Miss Neumann?" He wasn't easily surprised, but this was something entirely new. He'd never met a Southern lady who would bare her feet in the presence of a man. Come to think of it, he'd never met any lady who'd do such a thing.

She dangled a pointy high-heeled shoe from her finger. "I can hardly walk in these without tripping. You don't expect me to run in them, do you?"

"Very well," he responded, bending and

tugging on the lace of his shoe. "If you must run barefoot, then I will too."

His news brought another round of cheers from the children. Before he knew it, his shoes were off and damp grass tickled his toes. He stood on an imaginary start line next to Marianne and waited for the oldest boy present to give the shout that would start the race.

"What prize do I get for winning?" He lengthened his leg and stretched his hamstring, making a show of loosening his muscles.

"I don't think you should wonder what you'll receive, Mr. Brady," she said in that sassy tone she sometimes used. "Rather, you should ponder what you'll be giving me once I beat you fair and square."

"I suppose you'd like me to allow you a head start?"

She huffed and kicked aside her discarded stockings and shoes.

He chuckled and pretended to finish stretching his other leg. He shook out his arms, then circled his head first one way and then the other while jogging in place. Finally he nodded at the boy. "I'm ready. But I can't speak for Miss Neumann."

"I'm as ready as I'll ever be." Her eyes glinted with something he could only classify as excitement.

He loved that she was being such a good sport about his impromptu challenge. Plump Mrs. Trott wouldn't have played along with him, not even if someone bribed her with a hundred dollars. Most of the other agents would have frowned on him for his silliness.

But Marianne Neumann . . . she was proving to be unlike most women.

"Ready?" the boy shouted.

Marianne nodded and trained her sights down the field to the finish line, a large oak tree. She chewed at the inside of her cheek nervously. The motion tugged at his gut, and he couldn't stop himself from admiring her full lips. The dip in the middle of her upper lip was particularly flattering — in a kissable kind of way.

"Go!"

For a moment, he was too busy admiring her to realize the race had begun. Before he realized what was happening, she'd darted forward and left him standing at the start like a big oaf.

Some of the children jumped and screamed at him to run while others whistled and cheered for Marianne. With a surge of energy, he forced his feet forward. So what if she had a slight head start. She'd need it. He was doing the gentlemanly thing by going easy on her. After all, he didn't want to embarrass her. He simply wanted to claim a prize from her when he won.

At first he ran with a lazy stride. But as Marianne rapidly put distance between them, he watched her in surprise. Her lithe body was light and her legs long beneath her skirts. Her bare feet skimmed the grass, scarcely seeming to touch the ground at all.

As he watched, he realized his mouth was wide open. He snapped it shut and willed his legs to pump faster. Maybe this wouldn't be such an easy win. His feet pounded the earth, his tender soles unaccustomed to the hardness. He swung his arms and lowered his head in an effort to make up the distance between them. But when he next glanced at her, she was even farther ahead.

The children ran alongside him, calling him to go faster. Their laughter and the glee on their faces warmed his heart. "I'm trying my hardest," he said. "You have to believe me, I really am." But even at his best, Marianne reached the oak tree well ahead of him.

As she touched the bark, she turned to gauge where he was. Her face broke into a delighted smile at the sight of him so far behind and now struggling to finish through heaving breaths. A moment later, he reached the oak and had to bend to gasp for air.

The children swarmed around him, patting him on the back and shoulders, but their real admiration was directed toward Marianne. They reached for her, tugged on her skirt, and clamored for her attention.

She made a point of hugging the littlest ones and accepting handshakes from all the others. When the din diminished and Drew's breathing returned to normal, she held out a hand to him. "My condolences, Mr. Brady. Next time perhaps I'll need to give you that head start."

Laughter bubbled up inside him and rolled out.

She smiled innocently, yet the gleam in her eye gave her away. She was enjoying the thrill of her victory.

"It looks like I underestimated you, Miss Neumann," he said, combing strands of hair back from his forehead.

"Looks like you most certainly did, Mr. Brady."

"You win the prize."

"And what prize is that?"

"Anything you want."

Her brow quirked. "Anything?"

"Absolutely anything." With the bright sunshine bathing them in its glory, and the coolness of the morning lingering in the air, anything seemed possible. Strangely, he found himself wishing he could do something special for her.

"Why don't you surprise me?" Her voice held the hint of a challenge.

Pure pleasure surged through him. He not only loved surprises, but he also loved challenges. To be able to combine the two was something he'd anticipate. "Very well, Miss Neumann. You'll have your surprise before the day's end."

The morning passed quickly, especially because Drew was an endless source of entertainment for the children, as well as for Marianne. He kept the children busy, solving riddles and playing various games, one of which required them to spot certain things either on the train or in passing that began with certain letters of the alphabet.

When they stopped at midday, he carried their box of food off the train and to the shade of a nearby grove of trees, where Marianne knelt and began to slather bread with red jelly just as she'd done for every meal.

Although she was already tired of the simple fare, the children accepted the food she gave them without complaint. During their meal, Drew disappeared. When he returned a short while later, he snuck up behind her and covered her eyes with his hands.

The pressure of his warm touch made her forget about everything else for a moment. She could sense his presence, the strength of his arms, the solidness of his chest.

"I have your prize." His voice was threaded with excitement.

"So soon?"

"Keep your eyes closed," he instructed as he assisted her to her feet.

Marianne closed her eyes beneath the blindfold that Drew's hands formed. "What is it?" she asked as the children giggled.

"If I told you, it wouldn't be a surprise." Drew propelled her forward, the pressure of his hands gentle and firm at the same time. Shivers of delight ran up her backbone — from the anticipation of the surprise and not from his touch, she told herself.

Not far away, she could hear the boiler man on the water tower shouting orders to the train crew. He would be positioning the spigot from the water tower over the boiler that carried water necessary for the steam engine to function. In addition to the water, the coal tender would also need refilling.

The frequent stops to refuel and take on

new passengers made the trip longer, yet the breaks were a blessing in disguise, allowing the children to get out of the cramped and stifling train car to stretch their legs and release energy.

Drew spun her and moved her back the way they'd already come.

"I think you're purposefully marching me around in circles," she said and followed his lead regardless of his antics.

"Maybe I am, maybe I'm not." His voice rumbled near her ear, the sound sending another shiver up her spine.

Her smile couldn't get any wider and probably made her look like a painted puppet wearing an extra broad grin. After a moment he stopped.

"Promise to keep your eyes closed until I say so?"

"I promise."

His hands fell away, and she lifted her chin to let the warm afternoon sunshine caress her skin. Around her came the ringing voices and scuffling of the children who'd followed her and Drew to wherever he was taking her.

"Don't worry, Miss Neumann," Jethro said next to her. "If Mr. Brady tries somethin' funny, I'll protect you." His steady chatter had kept her company all day.

Thankfully he was getting used to the train's motion and hadn't been as sick today.

"Thank you, Jethro," she replied. "I'm counting on you."

His hand, sticky with jam, slid into hers. She squeezed it tight.

"All right," Drew said, "you can open your eyes now."

She lifted her lids and blinked against the sunlight. They were standing near the train platform. On the ground before her was a rectangular box covered with Drew's coat.

He lifted the box, careful not to disturb the makeshift covering that hid what was inside. "Are you ready?" he asked as he positioned the box in front of her.

"Yes!" came a chorus from the children.

He lifted the coat away. Oohs and aahs and gasps of delight rang out around them and echoed her own surprise. The box was filled with several dozen, perfectly ripe strawberries.

"Where did you get them?" she asked, clapping her hands together.

"They're grown locally." He beamed as though he'd created them himself out of nothing.

She couldn't remember the last time she'd eaten a fresh strawberry. Probably not since she was a little girl helping in her father's bakery in Germany. Even then, the straw-berries hadn't been nearly as large and red as these.

The children began jostling each other, eager to try the fruit. Several reached into the box to take a strawberry. But with a laugh, Drew lifted it out of their reach. "Don't worry. You'll all get to taste them. But since Miss Neumann won the race, she gets the first pick."

Just as eager as the children, Marianne stood on her tiptoes and peered into the box that Drew still held high. She found the biggest strawberry and, with a flourish, lifted it to her mouth. As she bit into the fruit, sweetness filled her senses. It was tender and lush against her tongue. She savored it for an endless moment.

She could feel the eyes of every child upon her. They were waiting for her reaction with hushed anticipation. She smacked her lips together, pretending to taste the strawberry. "Mmmm . . . I suppose I better try one more just to make sure they're good enough for the children."

Drew's brows rose. Before he could say anything, she picked out another strawberry and bit into it. As she finished chewing, she once again pretended to test it.

"What do you think, Miss Neumann?"

one of the older girls asked. "Are they all right for us?"

Several younger children mimicked the question.

"I think I need to test a few more." She reached to take the box from Drew. "I might even need the whole box."

Drew's laughter rang out. The sound was contagious, and the children joined in, even though the youngest of them likely had no idea what was so funny.

As she lowered the box and offered the strawberries to everyone, her gaze connected with Drew's above their heads, and they shared a smile. The blue-green of his eyes was clear and warm and beautiful. And filled with an appreciation that made her breath stick in her chest.

When his eyes focused on her lips still covered in sticky strawberry juice, she quickly used her tongue to wipe away the residue. As she did so, something flared in his expression, something that caused sparks in her belly.

For a second, she wondered if he was thinking about what it might be like to kiss her. But as the children's questions surrounded her, she forced her attention back on them, all the while conscious of Drew's presence.

"What're they called?"

"How do they grow? From trees?"

"What about the black dots on the outside? Them ain't bugs, are they?"

Some ate the whole berry, tops and all, while others nibbled more carefully, savoring each morsel of the strange new fruit. When the three older boys arrived back to the train platform, the strawberries were almost gone.

"Would you like to try a strawberry?" she asked, holding the box out to them.

Liverpool ignored her and swaggered past. Since Drew had reprimanded him on the train, he'd made a concerted effort to snub her, as if to prove he didn't need a supervisor, especially one as young as her.

At the sight of the box and the few remaining strawberries, the thin boy with the scarred face veered toward her. She'd learned his name was Ned, the boy whose father had stormed into the Children's Aid Society the previous night. When she realized he'd made his escape from New York City and his abusive father, she'd been relieved. Even if Ned didn't like her any better than Liverpool, at least he seemed to trust Drew.

Although Ned tried to hide his eagerness by forcing his brows into a scowl, he couldn't conceal the interest that glowed in his eyes. He picked up one of the remaining berries, but before he could raise it to his mouth, something hit him in the back of his head, causing him to cry out in surprise and pain.

He spun around in time to see Liverpool reach for another stone near the tracks.

"Hey, now!" Drew said sternly, starting toward Liverpool. "Put the rock down."

Liverpool tossed the rock into the air and caught it in his palm, his pockmarked face a mask of defiance. All around, the other children had turned silent. Fear and intimidation could be one tactic for bending the will of children, and apparently it was Liverpool's primary method of leadership.

"You goin' soft on me?" Liverpool sneered at Ned. The other older boy, Timmy, stood next to Liverpool and was the quietest of the three. In fact, if Timmy did talk, Marianne had never heard it. Even now he stared at Drew bearing down on Liverpool, his eyes widening in fear. He elbowed his companion in warning.

"You can't tell me if I can have a strawberry or not," Ned replied, though his voice lacked the same conviction as Liverpool's.

"You eat it, I kill you," Liverpool said. He

raised the stone, his eyes daring Ned to defy him.

"Over a strawberry?" Ned asked with a shake of his head. "You're crazy." With that, he stuffed the berry into his mouth.

Liverpool's fingers closed around the stone.

"Mr. Brady, watch out!" Marianne called, afraid he'd get caught in the cross fire. Yet as soon as the words left her mouth, Liverpool dropped the stone and smirked at her.

If he'd hoped to make her look like an overanxious ninny, he'd succeeded. Drew was glaring at the boy as he reached him. "You can't bully people into doing what you want."

"Just following the example of my leader." Liverpool didn't back down from Drew's stare.

"You think I'm bullying you?" Drew asked.

"You wouldn't bring it up if it weren't true."

"You know it's not true."

"All I know is, you don't mind roughing me up when it suits you."

Drew fisted his hand enough that Marianne could see the veins in his wrist. He continued to stare at Liverpool, his eyes radiating frustration as the muscles in his jaw flexed. Liverpool's gaze was raw with disrespect.

The anxiety in Marianne's stomach twisted again. She was afraid for Drew, although she didn't know why she should be. He wasn't in any danger from a boy half his size.

Ned grabbed two more strawberries before darting away without so much as a thank-you. As he scampered back over to Liverpool and Timmy, Liverpool finally broke eye contact with Drew and started to walk away.

"You need to respect and obey authority, Liverpool," Drew said after him. "Otherwise the farmer who takes you in will send you right back to us."

Liverpool shrugged and hopped onto the stairs leading up to the train car. The other two followed.

Watching the older boys disappear inside, Drew exhaled and shook his head slightly. Marianne wished she could have Drew's optimism regarding the boys, but she couldn't help but think that bringing them along on this trip had been a big mistake.

CHAPTER 7

"I wanna go ho-me." Dorothea's heartbroken sobs tore at Marianne. She hugged the little girl in the crook of her arm and attempted to rock her back and forth to the rhythmic swaying of the train.

"I wanna go ho-me." Dorothea had been saying the same thing over and over for the past hour, and nothing Marianne said or did consoled her. Yesterday Dorothea had apparently been too sick and miserable from the motion of the train to cry. But ever since their midday stop for strawberries, Dorothea hadn't been dry-eyed.

Marianne noticed that several other younger children had been weepy throughout the day too. At first, Marianne assumed they were just tired and restless after being cooped up in such tight quarters. But once Dorothea started talking about wanting to go home, Marianne wondered if the others were homesick too. After the excitement of the train ride and the thrill of seeing so many new sights had worn off, perhaps they were realizing the permanence of the trip, that they were going far away from all they'd ever known and would likely never return.

Even if what they'd known had been difficult, even if they'd been deprived and hungry and neglected, at least New York City was familiar. Maybe some of them still had friends and family who cared about them and would miss them, whom they would miss in return.

Just like Marianne desperately missed Sophie. She'd discreetly asked about Sophie at every train depot they'd stopped at along the way. But with so many passengers and children who rode the trains, the stationmasters couldn't recollect one girl among the many who passed through every day. If only Marianne had a photo of her sister. But her family had been too poor after Vater died to do anything but try to survive.

Marianne pressed a kiss against Dorothea's silky blond hair. She wanted to ask Dorothea about her home, about all she was leaving, yet she was afraid such probing would only disturb the girl all the more. Instead, Marianne held her and tried to console her with promises of how wonderful her new life would be, praying the promises didn't sound as empty to Dorothea as they did to her.

Drew had been doing his best to soothe the other children, as well as pair them with some of the older girls who could keep watch over them. He also continued to engage the children in riddles and games, which Marianne now realized were not just a fun way to pass the time. The activities provided a distraction. He was especially talented at telling stories and seemed to reserve his tales for when the children were at their worst. He'd launch into tales of bygone days, usually involving historical figures like Joan of Arc, King Arthur and his knights, or Julius Caesar. Somehow he managed to bring the characters to life by dropping them in the midst of a dangerous adventure.

During such storytelling, the train car would grow silent except for the rickety sounds of the train itself. Marianne noticed even Liverpool listened to the stories, although usually with his hat pulled low over his eyes as he feigned disinterest.

Directly ahead of the engine with its plumes of billowing black smoke, the sun was nearing the horizon, leaving an amazing display of colors across the sky, swirls of pink and lavender and orange. She'd tried to direct Dorothea's attention to the beauty of the sunset, something they couldn't see among the crowded narrow streets of the city where brick buildings and laundry lines strung from open windows blocked the sky. But Dorothea had apparently had her fill of the new landscape and couldn't take in anything more.

Across the bench from her, Jethro and another boy named Sammy were peering out the window, attempting to follow the burning orb as it disappeared from sight. The two boys had been somber most of the afternoon too, occasionally voicing questions about what was coming in their new lives. She'd tried her best to keep her answers positive. But the truth was, she didn't know what to expect either.

Drew had informed her that by tomorrow they would reach Chicago and would switch trains. They'd then start their southern trek on the Illinois Central into the rural towns of Illinois. By tomorrow afternoon or evening they might reach the first destination where they would begin the process of placing out the children. She supposed the closer they got to the destination, the more worried the children would become and the harder her job would get.

She couldn't imagine it getting worse

when already Dorothea's deep sobs wrenched her heart and made her want to weep right along with the little girl. "You'll be just fine, sweetheart," Marianne whispered again. "Your new momma and papa will love you so much."

Dorothea pulled back to reveal puffy eyes and cheeks streaked with tears. "I wanna go home." This time she spoke the words firmly, ending with a half sob, half hiccup.

Marianne used a handkerchief to wipe the girl's damp cheeks, then brushed away a few strands of hair from her eyes. What else could she tell Dorothea? A three-year-old couldn't understand what was happening, where she was going, or the new life that awaited her.

Dorothea's brown eyes looked up at her, wide and trusting but brimming with fresh tears. What could she say that hadn't already been said? Perhaps she ought to try Drew's method of using distraction.

Bending down, she tugged her valise out from under the seat and unlatched it. She dug around until her fingers connected with the item. She hesitated, unsure whether she should expose her most treasured possession, the only connection she had left to the memories of a beautiful and sacred past, to those years when everything felt normal, when she'd had a father and mother's love, when she'd had security, when she'd been utterly blissful and free of any worries.

She closed her eyes briefly to ward off the deep stab that came whenever she thought of all she'd lost, of how she'd never be able to regain that security and love. Perhaps this was how these orphans felt. Maybe they weren't able to put into words their feelings, but they too were losing so much and would never regain it.

Pushing aside her own pain, Marianne lifted the music box. It consisted of a pale oak pedestal with the wooden figurine of a young girl tending her four geese underneath the protective shade of a tree. The miniature carvings were hand-painted in bright greens, reds, and white.

Dorothea's sob cut off abruptly at the sight of the box, and her eyes widened.

"This was my Mutti's," Marianne said. "She gave it to me just before she passed away."

Even though Marianne never parted from the music box and brought it with her everywhere she went, she hadn't turned the crank once since Mutti died. Mutti had instructed her to keep the music box as a reminder to always sing and never lose sight of the music and joy that was found in living, no matter how difficult her situation.

And although she'd promised Mutti she would, she never realized how difficult life would get and how all too often she made things worse for others instead of better. If Mutti had known the mistakes Marianne would make and the trouble those mistakes would cause, she wouldn't have given her the treasure.

I'm sorry, Mutti, Marianne silently apologized. *I'm so sorry . . .*

She hesitated and considered slipping the music box back into her valise. But as her fingers brushed against the figurine of the girl tasked with watching the geese, Marianne swallowed the ache in her throat. Maybe she'd lost Sophie and Olivia and Nicholas, but she could do better now with these children, couldn't she?

With trembling fingers, she rotated the wooden hand crank. The geese and tiny tree began to turn to the German folksong *"Alle Meine Entchen,"* which meant "All My Ducklings." At the familiar melody, she pressed a hand against the sharp pain in her chest.

The sweet chiming song wasn't loud, yet it drew the attention of Jethro and Sammy away from the window. Soon they were on their knees in front of the music box on her lap. Like Dorothea, they were mesmerized by the movement of the figurine and the melody coming from within the pedestal.

When the spinning slowed, Marianne rotated the crank again, the children watching her with growing fascination. For some time she allowed the three to take turns carefully cranking the handle whenever the geese came to a standstill. Before long the others in the surrounding seats pressed in to see the music box as well until it became the train car's main attraction.

Finally, when darkness forced the children to return to their seats, Marianne placed the music box in Dorothea's lap. "Would you like to hold it for the night?"

The little girl nodded, her worries having dissipated along with her tears. She caressed the pedestal with her delicate fingers and leaned her head against Marianne's arm. Her lashes fluttered down, and within a minute her heavy breathing told Marianne she'd fallen into an exhausted slumber.

Maybe sharing this treasure with Dorothea and the others was the right thing to do. She hadn't been able to speak any words to ease their hurts, but music seemed to have a way of soothing and healing and bringing hope.

Fingers brushed against her shoulder —

Drew's strong, capable hand. In such a short time of knowing him, she'd recognize his touch anywhere. She glanced up at him. In the darkness, his face was unreadable, but when he spoke, she heard the warmth and admiration in his voice. "You were great today. The kids loved the music box."

Drew's praise was a balm to her spirit. "You were great too," she said.

His hand on her shoulder lingered a moment longer before he moved on, making his way down the aisle to check on the children. Marianne hoped he'd come back and sit on the bench across from her so they could talk again as they had last night. When he passed her by and returned to his spot farther back, she tried to quell her disappointment.

The next morning, they reached Chicago and left the passenger car that had been their home for the last two days. Walking through the train station with thirty children along with their belongings was harrowing. They were jostled by passengers coming and going, and Marianne was afraid that even though the children were holding hands, one or more of the littlest would end up separated and lost in the vast depot.

By the time they reached the Illinois

Central train and boarded, Marianne was hot and perspiring and as exhausted as though she'd worked a full day in a sweat-shop. All the while, Dorothea clung to her, never once leaving her side. The sobs hadn't returned, however, even after she'd relinquished the music box back into Marianne's bag.

Drew instructed her to wait aboard the train with the children until departure. Of course, the older boys left just as soon as Drew did, ignoring her calls for them to remain on board.

As the minutes passed, Marianne only stewed in her worry. She couldn't stop from fearing that somehow Drew would miss getting back to the train on time and she'd be all alone with the children. The more distraught she became, the rowdier and louder the children grew.

When a fight erupted between several boys, Marianne expelled a deep breath and tried to release her own tension. She suspected they would follow her suit — if she remained calm and positive, they would be too. At least that was how it appeared to work when Drew was with them. He had a way of making everything seem as if it would turn out just right.

After she settled the dispute between the

boys, she persuaded everyone to return to their benches with the promise of a story. Once the car was silent and all eyes were upon her, a small wave of panic rippled through her. She hadn't told any stories since Sophie ran away. Like her music, she'd wanted to cut that part of her away, hadn't wanted to think about all the memories she'd lost.

Thin fingers wound through Marianne's, and she glanced down to find Dorothea peering up at her with her big brown eyes. The sadness and fear that had been there yesterday had been pushed aside somehow. And now in their place her eyes radiated trust.

Marianne kissed the girl's forehead. Then she made herself tell one of the fairy tales Sophie had loved hearing, one about a young woman whose father died, leaving her an orphan in the care of a callous and wicked stepmother who had two very spoiled daughters.

She hadn't paid attention to the passing of time until she neared the end of the story and noticed Drew leaning casually against the train car door, watching her with rapt attention. She hadn't seen him come in, and at the realization that he was staring at her and listening to her story, she fumbled over the last couple of sentences, completely self-conscious. Quickly she closed her tale with "The End."

Drew clapped with exaggerated slowness, a smile creeping up the corners of his mouth. And when the children noticed his clapping, they joined in, until soon their applause filled the car. When the noise faded, Drew said, "It would seem Miss Neumann is not only the faster runner, but she's also the better storyteller." At the genuine admiration shining in his eyes, Marianne could only nod and duck her head, not sure if she was embarrassed by his praise or pleased.

"Perhaps Miss Neumann and I will have a storytelling competition this afternoon," he continued, "and you'll be the judges — clapping loudest for the story you like the best."

Marianne shook her head in protest. She'd already gone above and beyond for the children by sharing her music box and then a story, neither of which she felt comfortable doing. But seeing Drew's grin and wink, she stopped herself. There was something in his eyes that pleaded with her to understand. This would be the most difficult afternoon of the trip yet. The closer they got to their first placing-out stop, the harder it would be for the children as the reality of what was to come later today began to sink in.

She nodded and tried to muster a smile. Drew Brady, among his many other admirable characteristics, was turning out to be a persuasive man. She was embarrassed to admit he had the power to get her to do his bidding and with little effort on his part. And the longer she was with him, the less resisting she was inclined to do.

CHAPTER 8

The sound of the children's laughter echoed in the air and made Drew smile. All around on the grassy embankment along the canal, the orphans ran in wild abandonment in a game of tag.

Earlier, when they received news their train would be delayed in leaving Chicago for several more hours due to a problem with the engine, the stationmaster allowed them to step outside until further notice. Although Marianne was concerned something might happen to one of the children amidst the busyness of the town, Drew made the best of their delay by occupying everyone with games. Thankfully he had an endless supply of them at the ready from his days of being a schoolteacher.

The summer day was hot and cloudless, and the humidity had rolled in, making everything damp and sticky. His sights kept returning to the canal, to the cool water that would refresh them all. But as much as he wanted to take a dip, he wouldn't do it. It would only incite the children to follow his example, and before he knew it they'd all be swimming.

He'd learned his lesson that fateful day when his old life had ended, when he left his home and family behind. And he wasn't about to make the same mistake again. In fact, he'd told the children to stay away from the canal, that if he caught anyone even putting a hand into the water, he'd march them back to their train car.

At the canal's edge, Marianne sat in the shade of a willow with several girls around her, along with a few infants. A breeze tousled the tangled willow branches, which provided a little relief from the heat. She was using the opportunity to teach the older girls how to braid hair and wrap it into stylish coils.

"She sure is purty, ain't she?" Redheaded Jethro spoke beside him, peering up at him with his freckled face, his smile revealing the gap of his missing front teeth.

Drew considered pretending he didn't know who Jethro was referring to. But after living on the streets, sometimes Jethro was too smart for his own good and he'd see right past Drew's charade.

"She is mighty pretty," Drew admitted, admiring Marianne's bright eyes, flushed cheeks, and animated features as she rose to help one of the girls twist a braid. Her head bumped against a branch, which knocked off her fashionable hat. Before she could bend to capture it, the hat rolled down the embankment and fell into the canal.

The current was lazy today. Even so, the straw hat with its colorful ribbons began to drift away from the shore.

Marianne and the other girls started forward, getting much too close to the edge for Drew's comfort.

"Stay away from the canal!" he shouted, bolting toward the group.

At his terse command, the girls all backed up and watched his approach — all except Marianne. Instead, she got down on her knees and started to reach for the hat.

"Miss Neumann!" he called, sprinting toward her. "Don't try to get the hat!"

At the sharpness in his tone, she sat back on her knees and glanced at him, a frown creasing her brow. When she returned her attention to the hat, she gave a cry of dismay. "Now look. It's completely out of reach."

Drew dropped to the grass next to her. He stretched out over the canal and tried to grasp the hat, but it drifted farther away.

Marianne began to unbuckle her shoes.

"You *can't* go in," he said more forcefully than he intended.

"I'm not losing my best hat." She had one shoe off and was unrolling her stocking.

"I'll buy you another."

"The river is shallow here. I'll wade out for it."

He put a hand on her arm to stop her and then softened his voice. "Please."

She halted and searched his face as though attempting to understand his hesitation. "Are you offering to make the rescue for me?"

He'd longed to take a dip, but with all the children crowding around them, he didn't want to risk any of them getting in the water with him.

"Since you don't think I'm capable of rescuing my hat," she added with a grin.

"Do you know how to swim?"

"No. Do you?"

"I'm an excellent swimmer."

"Then I dare you to get it."

A dare? He loved a good dare. How could he refuse?

"Unless you're not as excellent as you say you are," she said, her eyes glimmering with the challenge, making him all the more eager to prove himself.

"I can do it," one of the younger boys piped up.

"No," Drew said quickly. "If everyone agrees to stay out of the water, I'll go in to rescue Miss Neumann's hat."

The children clamored their agreement and clapped in their excitement, which only spurred Drew on as he shed his shoes and socks, shrugged out of his coat and vest, and emptied his pockets. With Marianne's eyes still brimming with her challenge, he jumped in. The water came up to his thighs, and even though it was cold, it felt good.

He waded out farther until he was up to his chest, letting the water soothe his over-heated skin. Within easy reach of the hat, he grabbed it and started back to the shore.

"I could have done that," Marianne said, crossing her arms, clearly unimpressed.

He tossed her hat onto the shore so that it landed at her feet. Then he dove under the water, submerging himself. He swam to the middle of the canal, flipped on his back, and floated downriver for a few seconds. Then he paddled around and waved at his audience on the riverbank.

This time she was smiling as widely as the children. With a showy flip, he went back under and returned to the shore with a few effortless strokes.

As he climbed out, the children chorused their praise. He was dripping wet and wouldn't dry easily in the humidity. But the cooling off was worth it, and so was the sight of Marianne's delighted smile at his accomplishment. Her brown eyes sparkled with an admiration that warmed his blood.

"Did I prove myself, Miss Neumann?" he asked, standing before her and letting rivulets of water trail down his shirt and trousers to form a puddle at his bare feet.

"Yes, very much so." Her gaze dropped to his wet shirt plastered to his chest. Her eyes widened, and she glanced away, but not before he caught sight of the curiosity and interest in her eyes.

She fiddled with the brim of her hat, still dripping with river water, and looked everywhere but at him.

He reached for the hat, which she relinquished without a word. "Since I rescued it, then I beg you to allow me the honor of returning it to your head." He spoke gallantly and waved the hat with as much drama as he could.

The children giggled at his antics.

"You may do the honor, sir," she said, playing along with him. She bowed her head before him, the sunlight warming her hair to a glossy sheen.

His heart swelled with fondness for this young woman before him, at her ability not only to put up with his playfulness but to go along with it, even seeming to enjoy herself. He couldn't remember a time when any other person, much less a woman, had accepted him so readily for who he was and not who they expected him to be.

As he gently lowered the hat onto her head, water dripped into her hair and down her face. But instead of making a fuss or being irritated, she lifted her face and beamed up at him as if he were her knight in shining armor.

Drew stretched his arms high above his head and let the chilled night air wake him up. He hadn't planned to arrive in Benton at three o'clock in the morning. But the delay in Chicago had lasted much longer than he'd anticipated. Even after they returned to the train from their time along the canal, they'd still had to wait.

He'd telegrammed Reverend Smith, the minister of the Presbyterian church in Benton, and informed him they would arrive late and would need to postpone the placing-out meeting until the next day. Reverend Smith was in charge of the committee Drew initiated several weeks ahead of their arrival. While Drew could admit he wasn't the most organized agent working for the Children's Aid Society, he still attempted to form committees in the towns they would visit over the next few days. Such committees usually consisted of clergymen, merchants, newspaper editors, doctors, and lawyers.

Drew counted on the committee to publicize the arrival of the orphans by posting advertisements around town. The committee also located lodgings for their party at a local hotel or tavern, arranged a site where the children could be distributed among willing families, and helped specify the merits of the people applying to take in the children.

After his previous trips, Drew realized the committees were invaluable to his job. He needed them to make the placing out run smoothly. His group of orphans wouldn't stop at every small town along the Illinois Central. Brace had encouraged the agents to choose well-established towns situated in prosperous farm country, those boasting a population of three to four thousand and having good schools and churches.

Benton, Mayfield, and Dresden had qualified. They were also clustered fairly close together, so that on the return trip the work of following up on placements would be easier to accomplish and take less time.

"Is this it?" came Marianne's sleepy whisper behind him.

He turned to see she'd awoken and had followed him out of the train car. She stifled a yawn behind her hand.

"Yes. We're finally here."

Above, the sky was sprinkled with stars and a bright full moon, which lit the deserted train platform as well as the town beyond. The businesses were closed, the storefronts black, and even the tavern was quiet. The only sounds were the hiss of the engine and the train workers busy refueling.

"What will we do with the children?" Marianne asked, coming alongside him. "Will the train wait until dawn to leave?"

Drew shook his head and searched Main Street for the church and the parsonage. Did he dare attempt to wake Reverend Smith at three in the morning? Or was it better for the children to make themselves comfortable on the station's platform? After all, it was a warm night, not a cloud in the sky. The children actually might enjoy sleeping under the stars.

"No, we can't delay the train. It's already running behind schedule. We'll have to sleep out here on the platform until morning."

He expected her to protest, but instead she nodded. "At least they'll have more room to spread out here."

They worked together to rouse the children, carrying the youngest in an attempt not to disturb them. It took some time before all the orphans and their belongings were off the train. By then the children were wide awake. He agreed with Marianne when she told the children they must all lie down and try to sleep until daybreak. The littlest ones resumed their slumber, while the older ones, who were too excited to sleep, rested quietly.

Drew positioned himself in the middle of the boys, staring up into the sky and trying not to think about Marianne with the girls only a dozen feet away. His thoughts returned to the way she'd looked earlier in the day when he'd put her hat back on and helped her to her feet, how pretty she was. Or when he'd observed her telling a story to the children. Her delicate features were animated and more beautiful than ever, even more beautiful than when she'd tasted the strawberries.

Heat coiled in his gut at the thought of her lips covered in strawberry juice. Kissable. That's what her lips were. Pert, pretty, sassy, and kissable. He almost smiled at the thought but then gave himself a mental shake.

What was he doing letting his thoughts drift in that direction? As much as he enjoyed flirting, that was all he wanted. He had no desire to get into a relationship. Not ever again.

For a brief moment, his mind flashed to another time and another place, the week before his wedding, the last kiss he'd shared with Charlotte, when she still loved and wanted him. But the final week of school had changed all that. One tragic instant had changed everything.

His body stiffened, and he sat up in protest of the memories he never wanted to ponder again. He blew out a pent-up breath and in the process felt a pair of eyes upon him.

He shifted, and across the slumbering children, he saw Marianne. She was lying on her back and had tilted her head to watch him. When his gaze connected with hers, something in her expression said she was thinking about the strawberries too, that she was remembering his reaction and was wondering what it would be like to kiss him.

What would it be like to go to her at this very moment and pull her into his arms?

151

He'd never do it. He cared too much about his job and the example he set to the children to ever do something so rash around them. Nevertheless, the image of bending in and gently exploring her mouth with his set him on fire.

Her eyes widened as though sensing his wayward thoughts. And she did that chewing thing with her inner cheek that only made him want to kiss her even more.

He made himself break the connection and lie back down. As tempting as it was to glance at her and think about kissing her, he stared straight up into the sky, to the fading stars. He was surprised at the strength of his reaction to her. He couldn't remember having such a strong physical reaction even to Charlotte.

What was wrong with him?

He'd admonished himself to treat Marianne like a friend and nothing more, yet his body was betraying him. Was he growing attracted to her because he'd spent so much time with her during the last three days of travel?

Was it because he genuinely admired her kindness to the children? He could tell she cared about them with a depth that rivaled his.

Was it because she was always surprising

him? Like when he'd walked in on her telling the children a story?

Or was it because she was so open with her emotions and thoughts? He never had to guess how she was feeling or what she was thinking. There was no pretense in her nature, which was a welcome relief from the way most women he'd known acted.

Whatever the case, he liked Marianne Neumann. Probably a great deal more than he should. Although he knew he should be more careful in the future to make sure he guarded both of their hearts from attachment, he inwardly shoved away the concerns.

He didn't want to worry about it. In fact, he made it a policy not to worry whenever possible. Not about the future, and most definitely not about the past. He liked to live in the moment, taking one day at a time.

There was no sense in worrying about what might or might not happen with his feelings toward Marianne. After all, even if she showed interest in him, once she found Reinhold, she'd run back to him and forget Drew ever existed.

CHAPTER 9

Dawn came too soon. The sun had barely begun to lighten the sky when the children woke up. Soon their excited chattering rang in the air. Before Marianne could stop them, they were running off the train platform in all directions to explore the town. She attempted to corral them, especially the youngest, but Drew shrugged off her concern with one of his easy grins and "Everything will be just fine" responses.

"Don't worry, they won't wander far," he said. "Their rumbling stomachs will bring them back soon enough."

At the very least, she tried to make sure the youngest were paired with the older children. She ambled hand in hand down Main Street with Dorothea and another little girl, hushing groups of children whenever they became too rambunctious.

"Remember, we want to make a good first impression on your new mommies and daddies," she said. "We don't want them thinking you're obnoxious street ruffians, do we?"

Mrs. Trott had instructed her on the importance of making sure the children were clean and in their best clothing before the meeting. If the orphans looked proper like all the other children, then families would take greater interest. Marianne understood, but still didn't like the idea, that people couldn't accept the children in their ragged state, that they must be cleaned and polished to be made acceptable.

Mrs. Trott had also told Marianne the children must be on their best behavior, that she would need to teach some of them to say *please* and *thank you* because they'd never learned any manners.

As Marianne walked around town and tried to keep a semblance of order among the children, Drew headed for a spacious two-story parsonage that sat next to the church. He'd informed her that Reverend Smith was in charge of the Emigration Committee for Benton and that he needed to speak to the reverend to discover the arrangements for their food and lodging.

Marianne kept peering in the direction of the home where Drew had gone, willing him back outside to help her keep track of the children. The sun was fully visible by the time he exited the parsonage. At the sight of Drew, the children came running back. Marianne realized Drew had been right, that their hunger had spurred them to return.

He led them across the street to a tavern and hotel called the American House. There weren't enough tables and benches to seat all the children, so they had to take turns eating breakfast comprised of eggs, bacon, and thick slices of warm bread. Marianne ate standing up, trying to hide how much she was enjoying the hot meal after the endless jelly sandwiches. The twinkle in Drew's eyes told her he'd noticed and was amused.

When they finished eating, the hotel proprietor showed them to the rooms where they could wash up and change into their spare outfits, the second set of new clothing they'd been given by the Children's Aid Society. Marianne supervised the washing of hands and faces and the combing of hair, doing her best to make sure the children looked their best.

"Try to keep yourself absolutely clean," she admonished as they walked down the street toward the church. The children were mostly silent now, their faces reflecting the uncertainty and fear over what was about to happen.

"When are the new mommies and daddies coming to get us?" Jethro asked, falling into step next to Marianne and Dorothea. Strands of his red hair stood on end, unwilling to submit in spite of her vigorous combing.

"I think they'll all arrive sometime this morning," she replied, noting the town had come alive during their reprieve inside the hotel. The clomp and clatter of horses and wagons and the greetings of tradesmen opening their shops echoed in the crisp morning. The yeasty scent of baking bread wafted from a nearby bakery, reminding her of Vater, of family, and that she had neither anymore. In some ways she was every bit as much an orphan as the children she was helping. And so was Sophie.

Her inquiries around Benton about Sophie had been met with the same responses she'd had so far all along the way. Among the many immigrants who'd passed through over recent months, no one remembered seeing a blond-haired young girl of about sixteen.

Though disheartened, Marianne told herself she'd only just begun. If she didn't find any clues regarding Sophie's whereabouts on this placing-out trip along the

Central Illinois Railroad, perhaps she would on the next journey along a different railroad with other towns. She'd ride all the railroads if she had to until she found Sophie.

Their large group drew the curious stares of everyone they passed. People clustered around windows of businesses to watch them walk by while others stood in their doorways. Marianne didn't see any hostile expressions, but neither did she see any that were particularly enthusiastic.

What were the people thinking? Were they happy to have the orphans? Or did they resent having the homeless children brought to their town? Marianne knew people had mixed opinions about the Emigration Program. Some were willing to participate and believed it their God-given duty to show charity. Others thought Reverend Brace was dumping New York City's trouble onto their doorsteps. Marianne prayed the citizens of Benton were the charitable kind.

"Will they take me home in one of their wagons?" Jethro watched a wagon rolling into town, a man and his wife on the bench with several small children in the back.

"Yes." At the thought of parting ways with Jethro, she had to speak past a constricting throat. "I suppose they will." Even though she'd only known the boy for three days, she couldn't bear the thought of handing him over to complete strangers. Apparently this was why the other agents had cautioned her against getting too close to the children, because they'd known how hard it would be to watch them ride away.

"Will I get to go out and work in the farm fields today?" Jethro asked with his adorable lisp.

"Your new family will want to get to know you first." At least she prayed they wouldn't be inclined to send a seven-year-old into the fields like a slave boy. But who would stop them if they did?

At the thought, a shudder skimmed up Marianne's backbone. Dorothea looked up at her with frightened eyes as if sensing Marianne's growing trepidation.

Stop worrying, Marianne. Try to be positive like Drew. He was walking at the rear of the group, and his voice was cheerful and encouraging.

She smiled down at Dorothea and squeezed the little girl's hand. But Dorothea didn't smile in return. She rarely did. With an enormous bow tied in blond hair and silky natural ringlets hanging to her shoulders, Dorothea had an angelic aura. She was a pretty girl, and any family would be lucky to have her.

But would the new family be sensitive to the girl's homesickness? Would they be tender and sweet to her while she adjusted? Maybe Marianne would have to give Dorothea's new parents a few instructions about how to comfort her if she cried again.

Marianne could only imagine the little girl in a strange new place, alone, frightened, and crying. What if her new parents were too busy to comfort her? Or didn't care? Or worse yet, grew frustrated by it? Marianne sensed any amount of frustration would only send Dorothea further into despair.

Once again, Marianne's throat tightened as tears burned the back of her eyes. This was awful. If just the thought of parting ways with these precious children was hard, how would she handle giving them up when it really happened?

"Maybe my new home will have cows and pigs and sheep." Jethro's steady stream of chatter continued. "I might like a dog, especially if he was a puppy. I might like a few cats too. Do you think my new home will have chickens?"

Several other boys joined in the litany of what farm life might be like, which was a welcome distraction. But as soon as they stepped through the doors of the church into the stillness of the empty sanctuary, the children became silent and somber. Even the three older boys secmed subdued, as if they finally realized the gravity of what was about to happen.

They filed to the front pews to sit until the townspeople arrived. After Reverend Smith gave his opening address, Drew announced a few brief instructions about what they were to do. When people began to arrive, Drew squeezed into the spot next to Marianne. His arm pressed against hers, as did his thigh. She tried to make more room for him, but the children on the other side of her were already packed tightly together.

Drew didn't seem to notice he was practically sitting on her lap, so she decided to pretend she hadn't noticed either, although it was hard for her to ignore the delectable pooling of warmth in her stomach that seemed to come all too quickly whenever she was near him.

He held out a black book that was about an inch thick, similar to the ones that had been in Reverend Brace's desk drawer. "I think you'd be better suited to keeping the record book than me. You're more organized."

"True." The plain cover was worn and tattered in one corner, the pages appearing well used and nearly full.

"Since I'm more experienced, Brace thought I should handle the book on this trip," he explained in a low whisper. "But if you're willing to do the job, I'd be more than happy to hand it over to you."

She took the book hesitantly. While she could read and write, she wasn't proficient at it since she'd had to quit school and work in the sweatshop after Vater had died. "What do I need to record?"

"You don't need to write much." He dug in his coat and as he did so, his body pressed against hers even more. He withdrew a pen and offered it to her. She took it, careful not to let her fingers brush against his, but his grazed hers nonetheless.

She could feel herself flush at the intimacy of it, and she quickly opened the book to divert her thoughts away from Drew, though that was becoming harder to do with every passing day.

The book fell open to the last page that had been written upon near the end. The handwriting was in scrawled cursive, hardly legible. It read, *John Dublin, American, Protestant, thirteen years, orphan, parents died in Maine, a snoozer for four years, most of the time in New York, intelligent, brown eyes, hopeful. Placed in Iowa City.*

"What's a snoozer?"

"Street name for a thief that robs someone while thcy're sleeping."

She studied the entry and thcn paged through older entries. The handwriting varied, some neat and clear, others too difficult to read. Overall, however, none of the information about each child was very long. "The details are so sparse."

"Not much is needed."

"Don't you think we should record as much as we can? What about families searching for their children . . ." Her pulse came to a crashing halt, and hcr hands froze on thc book.

What if these pages contained the information about Sophie or Olivia and Nicholas that she'd been looking for that day she'd snuck into Reverend Brace's office? She didn't know how many record books the Children's Aid Society had, yet if this particular book had the names and descriptions of children placed over the past year, then there was a good chance Sophie's name could be there.

Marianne's fingers trembled at the thought. She clutched the book tighter to keep Drew from sensing her sudden excitement. She certainly didn't want him taking the book away from her until she'd had the chance to read through it more carefully.

"The most important thing in charity is the personal relationships we establish," Drew was saying in answer to her question. "Besides, there really is no way to keep track of everything. Last year we placed out over seven hundred children. Since the founding of the Children's Aid Society four years ago, we've placed nearly three thousand. If we decided to record more details, we'd have to hire someone full time to do so."

"Even so, surely we can do better," she whispered, attempting to keep their conversation private, although she was sure the children around them were hearing every word. She bit back the need to argue with Drew, especially because some of the residents were filing into the church in anticipation of the meeting.

Drew rose and began to make his way around the church, introducing himself and making his acquaintance with families. She wondered if she ought to do the same. But with the thick record book in her hands, she couldn't make herself get up. She could only sit and stare at it, and tremble at the realization that her months of searching might end today.

"Miss Neumann," called one of the boys in the pew in front of her. It was Peter, a young boy of about ten who had been one of the quieter children on the trip. He hadn't yet spoken to her directly, although his younger brother, George, was more outgoing and had told her that since their mother had lost her job, they'd been living on the streets. They'd found refuge for a while in a grocer's coal box and then for some time on a ferry, where a kind deckhand had let them sleep in the engine room.

Peter and George's story of survival was like many other children in the group, so sad and desperate. Surely any new life here in the West was better than what they'd been accustomed to. She had to remember that. She had to keep telling herself the children would be better now.

"What do you need, Peter?" she asked.

"I c-c-can't," Peter stuttered, and his face flamed with embarrassment.

She tried to pretend she hadn't noticed his stuttering, and she waited patiently for him to continue.

He opened his mouth and attempted to formulate a word, but nothing came out.

"It's all right," she said in what she hoped was a soothing voice. Inwardly, however, her heart ached for the boy. No wonder he hadn't spoken much during the trip and had let George do most of the talking for him.

The boy on the other side of Peter finally turned with an exasperated frown. "What Pete's trying to say is that he can't find George."

"Can't find George?" Marianne scanned the pews of orphans, looking for the brown-headed boy who resembled Peter. "Where could he be?"

"Pete ain't seen him since before breakfast," the boy offered before turning back around.

The words sank into Marianne and filled her with dread. When she met Pete's gaze this time, she could sense the dread and worry in his eyes too. "You're sure he's gone?"

Peter nodded vigorously.

Marianne stood, her heartbeat tapping at double speed. She surveyed the sanctuary and found Drew at the back speaking with an older couple. She wound her way around the pews toward him. As she approached, his gaze swerved to her as though he'd sensed her urgency — or perhaps read it on her face.

"What's wrong?" he whispered, turning away from the couple.

"It appears we've lost a child," she whispered in return.

"Lost?"

She pressed her lips together and nodded. "Yes, George. Peter's little brother."

"Are you sure he's not just hiding for the fun of it?" Drew ducked to look under the pews.

"Peter said George didn't come back for breakfast this morning."

Drew straightened, his expression grave. She'd learned Drew was rarely without a smile. So she knew the situation was serious.

His body had gone from relaxed to tense and alert in an instant. He bolted into action, gathering the group of boys Peter and George normally played with. He drilled them with questions before he finally sought the reverend.

"We're forming search parties," Drew said as he returned to where she stood near the pews trying to control the children who were fidgeting and growing anxious.

Drew's eyes were the most serious she'd ever seen. Any hint of humor was gone, replaced by a gravity that made her insides quaver.

"The boys said the last place they saw George was at daybreak when he was heading out of town across a bridge."

Marianne's blood ran cold. It only grew colder — in spite of the warm June sunshine

— as the day progressed. One man after another swam into the deep and murky part of the creek under the bridge and attempted to locate the boy's body. Other search parties scoured the surrounding woods, and still others walked rural roads, hoping to find the young boy and praying he'd merely strayed too far from town and lost his way.

By nightfall, the search was called off, most believing George had drowned in the creek and had been swept far downstream. Dripping wet and exhausted, Drew only shook his head when Marianne begged him to stop for the evening. She was afraid he'd grow so faint that he'd drown too, but he dove under the water again regardless of her pleas.

Marianne finally led the rest of the children back to the American House for dinner. Their faces were sunburned and sad as they sat silently around the tavern tables and ate. Peter was inconsolable and had gone up to the boys' room, curled in a tight ball in a corner and wouldn't speak to anyone.

After the long day and with the heavy weight of the loss upon them, the orphans were soon all asleep, some of the youngest sharing beds, the rest asleep on the floor. As much as Marianne longed to fall into bed herself, her worry over Drew kept her awake.

Deep into the night, when she heard the front door of the hotel creak open, she tiptoed downstairs. The tavern was shrouded in shadows.

It took a moment for her eyes to adjust to the darkness, and when they did, she found Drew sitting at the table closest to the door, his body slumped in a chair, his head resting on his arms on the table. The dejection oozed from his body as surely as the water dripping from his clothes into puddles on the floor.

She crept up behind him and hesitated only a moment before laying the blanket she'd brought with her across his back and shoulders. He didn't move, and for a moment she wondered if he was so exhausted that he'd fallen asleep. At a deep ragged intake of his breath, she realized he wasn't asleep. She couldn't be sure, but she thought maybe the sound had been a sob.

At the thought of this strong and kind man diving under the water and searching for a lost orphan all day, a sob welled up in her own chest. She'd watched Drew hour after hour over the past days. She'd seen his tenderness and his compassion for each of the children shine through in every moment he spent with them. He was tireless in his efforts to love them and endless in his drive to give them a better life.

Andrew Brady was a good man. A man she was proud to know.

She wrapped the blanket more securely around his shoulders, careful of the tender spot on his arm where he'd been wounded by Ned's father. When he released another shuddering breath, she pushed aside reason and held the warm blanket tighter until she'd wound her arms across his chest and was hugging him from the back.

She tried to keep her embrace somewhat proper and impersonal, but at the chill emanating from his body, she couldn't resist leaning into him, pressing her body against his back, and laying her face in his damp hair.

The ache in her throat tightened, and several hot tears slipped on to her cheeks. She felt his coldness, his pain, his frustration, and his disappointment in the tightness of his muscles and in the rigidness of his spine. She wished there was something more she could do to ease his pain, but she knew of nothing but being here for him, holding him, and somehow trying to reassure him she cared about how he was feeling.

Squeezing him tighter, she pressed a kiss against his head and then moved her hands to his upper arms. Above the blanket, she rubbed his biceps, wanting to warm him up. But when he stiffened beneath her touch, she wondered if perhaps she'd overstepped what was proper. She started to pull away, but his hands reached out and captured hers. He tugged her hands to his chest, forcing her to lean her body against him once more. "Don't go." His whisper was hoarse.

She laid her head into his hair again. She told herself she'd comfort any of the children this way, that Drew was only a friend, her partner, a hurting man who needed someone to care.

But when his arms folded over hers, she closed her eyes and relished the solid feel of his body much more than she should. She held him that way for an endless moment. She didn't want to let go, but she was sure he'd think she was being improper if she held on too much longer. So she kissed his head again and untangled her arms from around him.

This time he released her. But as she started to straighten, he pivoted in his chair, snaked an arm around her waist, and dragged her down onto his lap. Before she could resist, he wrapped his arms around her and buried his face into her hair. Although she was still wearing the dress she'd changed into that morning, she'd already uncoiled and brushed her hair so that it hung down her shoulders in long thick waves.

"Please, Marianne," he said, his voice close to her ear, "I need you. Stay."

She nodded, keenly aware of their proximity, of the fact that she was on his lap with his wet arms around her. They would be setting a poor example if any of the children happened upon them. And yet he was clearly hurting.

I need you. The words tumbled around inside her mind. When had anyone ever needed her? Even after Elise had left for Illinois and had put her in charge, Sophie hadn't looked to her for leadership or help or even comfort the same way she had Elise.

Olivia and Nicholas hadn't needed her either. They'd always wanted Sophie. Truthfully, Reinhold had needed her even less. He was so strong and independent. She'd been the one who'd needed him.

But here, now, in this moment, Drew needed her. She put aside her reservations, melted into his embrace, and rested her head against his, drawing in a shaky breath at the pleasure of knowing she was important to someone else. For a while he just held her, and she was content to listen to his heartbeat gradually slow its pace.

"I'm to blame for losing George," he finally said.

"If anyone's to blame, it's me," she replied, pulling back so she could see his face. In the dark, his features were shadowed but still as handsome and winsome as always. "I was the one in charge of watching the children when he ran off."

"But I shouldn't have left you to watch them all by yourself," he whispered. "At the very least I should have listened to your concerns about keeping them from running off in all directions."

Even though she'd been chastising herself all day for not doing a better job of keeping track of the children, she also realized the impossibility of the task. "Even if we both do our best, the job of supervising thirty-one children is challenging — especially children who are used to doing what they want whenever they want."

"I don't know." His voice was laced with self-doubt.

She lifted her hands to either side of his face, trapping him, and forcing him to look at her. "Andrew Brady, you are the best leader these children could ask for. You're a special, special man, and their lives will be blessed for having known you."

She couldn't see his reaction, but she could feel him tremble slightly at her words. When he cupped her cheeks in return, she almost smiled. But before she could move, his mouth descended to hers. The heat and pressure of his lips against hers was so unexpected she lost her breath. When he moved, he gave her no choice but to move against him in return.

She quickly grew heady and breathless. She'd never kissed a man before, not even Reinhold, although she'd dreamed about it plenty of times. Never had she imagined a kiss would be like this.

When his hand slid up into her hair and tangled there, a warning in her heart told her to be careful. His lips broke from hers and found her neck. At the first touch, she closed her eyes, feeling as though she might swoon with the pleasure of his lips grazing her skin.

But the depth of the moment frightened her. What did this mean? This emotional draw to him — where would it lead? Was she only heading for trouble once again? She'd already brought enough upon herself with her past sins. She needed to be cautious. "Drew?" she whispered.

His lips stilled. For a moment he didn't move. Then he pulled back with a moan. "I'm sorry, Marianne. I shouldn't have kissed you."

"It's all right," she said as she extricated herself from his lap. She hated that he was apologizing, didn't want him to be sorry for kissing her. She wanted him to like it and relish it as much as she had.

"You were just trying to be nice," he rushed, "and I took advantage of the situation —"

"No, we were both caught up in the moment. That's all." He'd been grieving and had been emotional. He'd needed someone to comfort him, and she'd been there. He probably would have done the same to any other woman who'd come to him in the middle of the night, wrapped him in a blanket, and then thrown her arms around him. Maybe she'd led him on. After all, she'd kissed his head when she was hugging him. If that wasn't an invitation, she didn't know what was.

He shook his head and ran both hands through his damp hair, clearly frustrated with himself.

"Come on," she said, reaching for one of his hands. She had to salvage the situation for them both. "We're tired. Let's each go to bed and we'll forget this . . . this moment between us ever happened."

He allowed her to help him to his feet. "Then you're not mad at me?"

"It's hard to be mad at you for anything."

He was silent as he trailed her to the stairs. At the top, his fingers connected with hers, and her heart flipped at the soft touch. "Thank you," he whispered.

The contact was as brief as his words. When he entered the boys' room, she realized she'd never be able to forget about their moment together, nor did she want to.

CHAPTER 10

Reinhold's chest churned with the ferocity of a summer storm. From the way the dark clouds towered on the horizon, he guessed the weather was about to match his mood.

He halted the horses and wagon in front of the general store but didn't move, not wanting to go in. He'd probably have a letter from his mother or aunt begging him to send home more money. And this time he wouldn't have any. Not even a penny. Not after Higgins had stolen his savings. Not after he'd agreed to pay Mrs. Turner to replace the broken dishes.

After finishing the potato planting, he'd attempted to figure out another way he could earn extra income. He'd gone over every possibility including doing construction work in the evenings after completing his farm work. But the Turner farm was several miles out of town, and he didn't think Mr. Turner would let him ride one of the horses to another job. Walking to town and back wouldn't be feasible. Besides, Mr. Turner would find more work for him around the farm if he mentioned he wanted an additional job.

Even now the back of the wagon was filled with the new fence posts Mr. Turner had ordered. When Reinhold returned to the farm, he'd have the task of fixing the fence around the pigpen. The spring piglets still kept getting loose, and no amount of repairing the old posts had worked to keep them contained. Of course, Higgins had weaseled out of the job, citing his inability to do any building compared to Reinhold's expertise.

Reinhold exhaled his exasperation with Higgins and prayed somehow God would bring about justice. He had the suspicion it wouldn't happen without divine intervention.

He jumped down from the wagon and rubbed a hand along the horse's flank, patting her and letting her know he appreciated her faithful help before brushing a hand over the muzzle of the other horse. He'd never had the chance to care for horses in New York City, though he'd always admired them from a distance. It wasn't until Mr. Turner hired him that he'd had the opportunity to learn more about the magnificent creatures. It was just one more thing he'd come to love about working on the farm.

He hitched the team to the post in front of the store and then lumbered up the plank steps. At the door, he hesitated. The tempest inside warned him not to go in and certainly not to check for mail. But at the sight of Lucinda at the counter, he knew he had no choice but to help her carry out the few bundles she'd purchased.

A bell on the door tinkled as he entered, and the waft of coffee beans, coal oil, and pickled eggs welcomed him. Wilson's General Store contained just about any amenity the small farming community of Mayfield needed, and the shelves lining the walls were filled to overflowing with everything from ribbons and thread to gardening tools. Barrels, crates, and piles of goods filled every nook and cranny, making walking through the store difficult for all but the thinnest of people, like Lucinda.

"There he is, even as we speak," said Mr. Wilson, who finished tying string around Lucinda's last package.

"Good morning," Reinhold said to the proprietor.

"Miss Turner was just finishing her shopping, and I can tell she's anxious to get home and start on her newest sewing project." Mr. Wilson snipped the string with his scissors and pushed the package toward Lucinda.

The young woman towered above the proprietor, who was as short and round as Lucinda was tall and thin. She glanced sideways at Reinhold, giving him a glimpse of the embarrassment creeping into her face before she ducked her head.

"She has enough material here to sew shirts for an entire army of men." Mr. Wilson chuckled, and his protruding belly bounced up and down, wiggling like a bowl of custard.

Lucinda's face melded into a deep crimson, and she scooped up her packages. In her haste, several toppled to the floor. She bent to retrieve them but only managed to drop everything.

Reinhold rushed to the counter to rescue her from her clumsiness. He supposed that was why Mrs. Turner always insisted he accompany Lucinda into town. The girl was liable to run herself over if left to her own devices.

Before he could assist her, Mr. Wilson shoved a paper in front of his face. "Told Miss Turner to tell her pa we've got another trainload of orphans coming through here tomorrow."

Reinhold had no choice but to take a look at the sheet Mr. Wilson was holding. It was an announcement concerning the arrival of children from New York City, who all needed homes with good families here in Illinois.

"Supposed to come in this morning," Mr. Wilson said. He rubbed a hand over his bald head, polishing the already-shiny skin there. "But I got a telegram last night saying they've been delayed a day."

Reinhold scanned the newsprint: *"All children received under the care of the Association are of special promise in intelligence and health, and are in age from two years to fifteen years, and are free to those receiving them, on ninety days trial, unless a special contract is otherwise made."*

Special promise in intelligence and health? Reinhold almost laughed at the exaggeration. The orphans gathered from the alleys and doorways of New York City were scrawny, disease- and lice-ridden, and most probably hadn't attended school.

"I know Cal Turner talked about getting himself a couple of orphans." Mr. Wilson laid the advertisement on the countertop. "He's got you and that other fellow now, but you can let him know anyway in case he wants more help."

"He said he can't afford any more help right now."

"Well, these here boys are for free." Mr. Wilson then spread another piece of paper out on the counter. At the top it read, *Terms on Which Boys Are Placed in Homes.*

Reinhold read the first paragraph: *"Boys fifteen years old are expected to work until they are eighteen for their board and clothes. At the end of that time, they are at liberty to make their own arrangements. Boys between twelve and fifteen are expected to work for their board and clothes until they are eighteen, but they must be sent to school a part of each year, and after that it is expected that they receive wages."*

Such an arrangement didn't seem fair. If the boys were working long days, wouldn't they deserve to have paid wages every bit as much as he did?

" 'Course, now I don't know how many of the big boys will be left by the time the train reaches us tomorrow," Mr. Wilson said. "I heard the older ones are usually the first to be taken since they can be the most useful and productive."

"I thought the orphans would become part of families and be treated like sons and daughters."

"Oh, they do become part of families," Mr. Wilson said. "But they've got to work just like the rest of us. None of us can survive out here without lots of hard work."

The muscles in Reinhold's back and shoulders still burned from his days of planting potatoes. He knew about hard work. But at least he was getting paid.

Lucinda had picked up all her packages and now stood trying to balance them with one under each arm, one under her chin, and several more stacked in her hands. Reinhold reached to relieve her of her burdens. She relinquished several with a shy smile.

"Anyhow, let Cal know we're meeting tomorrow morning at eleven o'clock sharp to distribute the orphans to anyone who wants one."

"The children are given to anyone?"

"Absolutely. I'm one of the men on the placing-out committee in Mayfield, and we're looking for people who might be willing. Seems like we have more children needing homes than families willing to take them in. 'Course, lots of families around here are struggling to feed the mouths they already have and can't afford to take on one more."

Reinhold nodded, although there was an unsettled ache inside him at the realization that his own younger siblings very well could have been on one of those trains when he'd been without work last fall. What if they had been? The thought of his brothers or sisters being sent to live with just anyone wasn't right. What if they ended up with a woman like Mrs. Turner who belittled and beat them?

He started toward the door.

"Hold on there, sonny," Mr. Wilson called after him. "You don't want to leave without your letter, now, do you?"

Reinhold stopped. Lucinda bumped into him from behind and whispered a flurry of apologies.

He wanted to tell Mr. Wilson to hold the letter, that he'd get it next time he came to town, but his sense of responsibility to his family was too strong to ignore. He sighed and retraced his steps to the counter.

Mr. Wilson disappeared into his office and returned a moment later with an envelope. His aunt's handwriting was on the front this time. Lately she'd been the one writing to him, her complaints getting worse with every letter — mostly complaints about his mother's debilitating anxiety and how she wasn't doing enough to provide for or assist with the children.

Helplessness seeped through him every

time he read the letters. There was nothing he could do to make life better — at least until he had his own place and could afford to pay for his family to move west and live with him. All the more reason he needed to earn back what Higgins had stolen from him.

"Why don't you read it now," Mr. Wilson suggested, eyeing the letter, "then post your response right away like you usually do?"

It hadn't taken Reinhold long after moving to Mayfield to learn that Mr. Wilson was the best source of information in the community. He knew something about everything and everyone, mainly because he made it a point to stick his nose into everyone's business.

"I won't be able to send a letter home today," Reinhold said, folding his aunt's letter and stuffing it into his trouser pocket. He hefted Lucinda's packages and started back toward the door. The truth was, even if he'd wanted to reply, he couldn't afford a stamp.

"If you say so," Mr. Wilson said, his voice ringing with disappointment at not being able to hear the contents of Reinhold's letter. "Just make sure you tell Cal about the train of orphans coming in tomorrow. The meeting starts —"

Reinhold couldn't make himself answer and instead let the door close behind him, cutting off the proprietor's last instructions. Within moments he'd loaded Lucinda's parcels into the back and helped her up onto the wagon bench.

He took his place next to her, and the letter slid out of his pocket. Lucinda grabbed it before the gusting wind could carry it away. As she extended it back to him, he noticed the German word *Auchtung* written in all capital letters on the back of the envelope. *Attention.*

With a glance at the darkening sky, he realized he'd have to push the team hard to make it back to the Turners' before the storm unleashed its power. Still the word his aunt had penned on the envelope sent a shiver through him. What if something had happened to one of his brothers or sisters? His brothers at thirteen and ten were old enough by now that they could take care of themselves. When he'd left for the West, they both were selling newspapers and living at the Newsboys Lodging House to take some of the burden off Mother.

He was more worried about his sisters, Silke and Verina. They were only eight and six years old. What if his aunt had grown desperate enough that she'd taken them to the train station to join a group of orphans going west? Just like she had with Olivia and Nicholas, the two children the Neumann sisters had been caring for.

With a sick sensation in his stomach, Reinhold tore open the letter, unfolded it, and read.

"Dear Nephew, I regret to bear the news that your mother, my dear sister, is dead."

Drew stood at the back of Benton Presbyterian Church and bowed his head as Reverend Smith led the gathering in an opening prayer. The rumble of thunder above the church spire echoed the somberness of the moment. He was thankful the building was filled with eager families willing to consider taking orphans into their Christian homes to raise them with a godly influence. Still, he couldn't shake the lingering bitterness regarding all that had happened yesterday with the loss of George.

He'd slept for a few hours until dawn when he'd risen and gone out to the creek, once again to search for the missing boy. He scoured the surrounding area, but it had all been in vain. He'd seen no sign of George. The despair he felt last night threatened to overwhelm him again this morning. Images from the past, of a pale

lifeless face with blue lips and wide unsee-
ing eyes escaped from the dark recesses of
his mind to torment him. A body listless in
the tall grass, the bloody gash in his skull,
and the awful unnatural angle of his head.

No! Drew pushed the memory back into
the closet and tried to slam the door shut
before any more escaped. Yet the brief
glimpse of the vivid image sent his heartbeat
into a wild thumping against his rib cage.

He forced his attention to the front pew
where Marianne sat with the youngest
children, her head bowed in prayer. From
this angle he could see her peaceful profile,
the contours of her lovely face. The steadi-
ness of her presence calmed him in a way
he'd never been able to achieve on his own.
He stared, drinking her in until the racing
of his pulse began to even out again.

She'd come to him just in time last night.
With one gentle touch she'd rescued him
from the brink of the abyss, when the
memories from his past had come out like
demons to taunt him and call him a murderer. Again.

Even though he was to blame. Even
though he'd been at his worst. Even though
he'd deserved nothing more than her censure and disappointment. She'd tenderly
wrapped her arms around him and hugged

him. She cared about his pain. He'd felt it in every ounce of her being. She'd offered him the thing he needed the most — unconditional acceptance.

The thought of such a gift brought an ache to his throat. Charlotte hadn't been able to give him that after the accident. Neither had his family.

He hadn't had to ask Marianne for it. Instead she'd sought him out and given it of her own accord. It was almost as if she'd been waiting for him to return so she could come to him. Maybe she'd needed him as much as he'd needed her.

His attention drifted to the long neck now exposed, especially with her head bent. Had he really touched that beautiful neck last night or had he only dreamed it? He knew without a doubt he'd kissed her lips, and he had no remorse about doing so, except that he'd frightened her with his ardor. Even so, she'd kissed him back, however briefly, and she'd liked it. He'd sensed it in her response.

No matter that she'd liked it or that he couldn't stop thinking about it, he shouldn't have engaged with her in such a manner. Not only was such conduct strictly forbidden among agents, he didn't want to lead her on, didn't want her to think he was the kind of man she could ever admire. She may have praised him in his moment of despair, but she didn't know the truth about him or his past. If she had, she wouldn't have been so quick to comfort him and tell him he was a special man and that the children would be blessed for having known him. She wouldn't even want to be on the trip with him as an agent any longer.

As the prayer came to an end, her long lashes swept up, and her gaze flitted to him as though she'd sensed his staring at her. He didn't want to make her uncomfortable around him or cause her to be nervous whenever she came near. He wanted to continue their friendship, needed her support and encouragement. So he tried to mask the desire that seemed to grow stronger every day. And he winked at her.

The wink seemed to reassure her he was doing better. She smiled in return before tapping the shoulders of the two boys in front of her and pressing a finger to her lips, motioning for them to remain silent.

As much as he wanted to call off the meeting and continue with the search, he knew he had to move forward with their plan to place the children. He couldn't delay the happiness of all the others because of one.

Reverend Smith talked about the need to save the children of the slums, give them a change of environment, and replace the worst influences exerted on them with more Christian ones. "And that, my dear people," he said in a rich baritone, "is why we've gathered here today. Yes, these children shall be of help to you as well. But always remember to ask yourselves first what you can do to shape the lives of these little ones for the kingdom of God."

A pounding on the door of the church was followed by its swinging open, bringing with it the heavy splatter of rain outside along with another crash of thunder. An older man with a grayish-brown beard that hung halfway down his chest poked his head in. His hat and cloak were dripping with rain.

Drew pushed away from his spot against the wall and started toward the man, waving him inside. "Come on in, we haven't yet started. You're just in time."

The man broke into a grin that revealed tobacco-stained teeth. "Good to hear 'cuz I got a young'un with me says he belongs to a group of orphans goin' up for sale."

"The children aren't for sale," Drew started, but as the implications of the old man's words penetrated his sleep-deprived mind, he rushed forward and threw open the door all the way, not caring that it banged against the church with a reverberation that shook the walls.

He stepped into the downpour. Next to a wagon, a scrawny boy drenched to the bone huddled under a piece of canvas. His face was ashen and his eyes wide with fright. At the sight of Drew, he released a sob and took a hesitant step away from the wagon.

"George!" Drew ran to the boy, heedless of the rain and the mud. He threw his arms around George and pulled him tightly against his body. Relief coursed through Drew, leaving his limbs trembling. The boy's thin arms curled around Drew, and he clung to him with a fierceness that matched Drew's.

He didn't care where the boy had gone or why. Drew was overcome by the realization George was alive and standing here in front of him. He hadn't drowned in the river, hadn't disappeared downstream, hadn't been lost to them forever.

Drew lifted his face heavenward and let the rain pelt him. "Thank you, God. Thank you." He was grateful the boy was safe, but he was also grateful that God had saved him too — saved him from having another death on his conscience. He wasn't sure how he could have lived with himself.

He'd already run away from everything he'd ever known in order to forget his first mistakes. It already took all his energy to keep those memories from catching up to him. Where would he go if it happened again? He wasn't sure he'd be able to outrun any more demons.

"Thank you, God," he whispered again, but even as he voiced his thankfulness, fear settled deep in the core of his being. What had he been thinking to take this position as an agent? What had made him believe he could work with children again? Not when he'd failed as a teacher. What had Brace been thinking to let him supervise children? Brace knew his story. The man should have slammed the door in his face when he first set eyes on him.

"Mr. Brady!" Marianne's voice broke through his thoughts and the pounding of the rain. She'd grabbed someone's coat, spread it over her head like an umbrella, and began walking out of the church toward them.

"Stay inside," he called to her. "I'm bringing George in." He lifted the boy into his arms and trotted back to the church. Within moments the other children surrounded George, clamoring to touch him and slap him on the back. Peter shoved his way through the others until they parted for him.

Tears streaked the older boy's face. At the

sight of the lost boy now found, he flung himself at his brother. George buried his face against Peter, and together they stood holding each other and crying. At seeing them together, Drew's heart ached with the knowledge of the very real possibility the boys could be split up again soon.

As much as agents tried to keep siblings together or at least in the same vicinity, they couldn't always manage it. While he never liked the scenes where he'd had to physically pry crying siblings apart and send them home with different families, he'd always rationalized such moves. He consoled himself that he was doing the best for them, even if they didn't understand. After all, wasn't it better for siblings to have good homes away from each other than to have to return to the orphanages or streets of New York City together?

He pressed a hand against the burning in his chest. Maybe he'd been wrong in his opinion about sibling separations, too callous and uncaring. And if he'd been wrong about one thing, what if he'd been wrong about many things?

CHAPTER 11

Marianne took her place off to the side as the orphans filed to the front of the sanctuary and lined up before all those sitting in the pews. Dorothea had reluctantly let go of her hand and now stared at her with frightened eyes that pleaded with Marianne to save her from whatever was about to come.

Marianne clasped her hands behind her back to keep herself from running over to the girl and pulling her into a hug. She swallowed hard several times to dislodge the lump in her throat. Even then it rapidly returned at the sight of Peter and George standing side by side and holding hands.

The old man who'd brought George to the church claimed he'd found the boy six miles west of town wandering around his shanty. At first he thought the boy was trying to steal from him, but George kept talking about being on a train with his brother and other orphans. After some time, the old man remembered seeing an advertisement in town earlier in the week about the train of orphans that was to arrive.

He contemplated keeping the boy on to help him, since he was getting up in age. But George had continued talking about his brother and the need to get back to town before the train left without him. So at first light, the man hitched his wagon and came to town. Drew had been so appreciative he'd offered to buy the man a meal at the nearby tavern.

Marianne's sights shifted to Drew, who was speaking with Reverend Smith. He was still wet from running out in the rain to reach George, his blond hair flat against his head, and his shirt plastered to his body beneath his coat.

"Maybe we can have the children sing a hymn for us," the reverend suggested, "and that might help people in determining which child seems most suitable to them."

Sing? As in perform — like they were players in a traveling theater troupe? Protest rose swiftly inside Marianne. What would be next, having them dance and do magic tricks?

Drew nodded his assent, apparently accustomed to putting the children in the spotlight. For several moments he quizzed the children on the songs they knew. Of course, they didn't know many, as few had attended church during their short lifetimes. Finally he determined that the majority of them knew the words to "Amazing Grace."

Marianne glanced at the piano close by. She hadn't touched a piano since she'd left Seventh Street Mission. She hadn't the opportunity to do so, nor the desire. As a little girl growing up in Hamburg, she learned to play the organ from an older gentleman friend of her father. She'd relished the lessons in the old stone church, the music pulsing from the large pipes in the loft.

After her family moved to America, she no longer had access to an organ. It wasn't until later, while living at the Seventh Street Mission, that she was allowed access to their piano and received impromptu lessons from Miss Pendleton. Thankfully the keys and notes came back to her, and she played the instrument at every opportunity. And then she ran away from the mission, lied about being pregnant with Reinhold's baby, and lost everything — including her desire to make music.

Drew began the first stanza of "Amazing Grace," and his voice rose clear and strong above the children's. She watched him for a moment and couldn't keep from remembering the bold way she'd cupped his cheeks last night and how he'd leaned in and kissed her. And the kiss hadn't been a light one but powerful, deep, moving — much like the man behind it.

Her heart gave a rapid thump. As she watched the way his mouth moved and his lips formed the words of the hymn, that spark of heat for him flared in her belly. Even if he'd only kissed her in the heat of the moment, out of his sorrow and worry and frustration, and even if the kiss hadn't meant anything to him, she'd liked it and would never forget it.

He finished the first verse and started the second. By now, only a few of the older girls continued to sing with him. If anything, the children looked more frightened, the youngest especially. Dorothea's lower lip was sticking out and trembling, her eyes glossy with unshed tears.

Marianne knew she had to do something. Aside from running over to Dorothea and picking her up and spiriting her away from the eyes of all those watching her, she decided the next best thing was to distract Dorothea and the rest of the children.

Pushing aside her own discomfort, as she had so many other times already during the trip, Marianne approached the piano, scooted out the bench, and sat down. She listened carefully to Drew's place in the song and then pressed the appropriate keys, attempting to match his spot.

At the sound of the piano playing along with the song's melody, his voice wobbled and his expression radiated surprise. She nodded at him to continue.

He nodded in return, his lips turning up into a smile as he sang out the lines even louder. Marianne was delighted to hear the voices of more of the children joining Drew's until soon the entire congregation was singing. When she came to the closing notes, she glanced at Dorothea and noted that even though the girl wasn't singing, at least she wasn't crying.

"Thank you, Miss Neumann," Reverend Smith said as Marianne stood from the piano and pushed the bench back in. "That was quite lovely."

Behind the reverend, Drew mouthed the words *thank you.* She nodded once more, glad to have pleased him. She rather enjoyed playing for those few minutes, and at the realization, guilt wormed through her — telling her she didn't deserve the pleasure of music, not after all she'd done.

"Now that you've observed the children," the reverend said to the congregation, "we'd like to give you the chance to interact with them directly. Feel free to come up to the front, introduce yourself, and ask the children questions."

Some of the families stood and made their way out of the pews and down the aisle.

"If you decide upon a child, then please come speak to Mr. Brady, myself, or another member of the committee."

As more people came forward and milled about the children, Drew went to Marianne. For the first time since losing George yesterday, a genuine smile lit his face and brought out the dimple in his chin. "I didn't know you played the piano."

"So I surprised you?"

"Very much. It was beautiful." His face was unshaven, giving him a rugged appeal. She couldn't stop herself from glancing at his lips and thinking about how warm they'd felt against hers. As though reading her thoughts, his brows rose, revealing a glimmer of humor.

Stop fawning over him, Marianne. She mentally slapped herself and tried desperately to think of something else to say that wouldn't make her sound like a schoolgirl with her first crush. She was saved from further embarrassment by a young couple who approached Drew.

Before he turned to speak with them, he handed her the same black book he'd given her yesterday. The record book. The one that could contain the answers she needed for Sophie's whereabouts.

"The committee will take care of having the families sign contracts, but I need you to write down a few details for each of the children who are placed."

She nodded, trying not to appear overeager as she took the book. With all that had happened yesterday, she wasn't able to read through any of the older entries. Perhaps she finally would today.

She soon found herself much too busy to do anything but attempt to keep order among the children, as well as record as many details as she could about the first of the children being considered. When Dorothea left the platform and came to stand beside Marianne and cling to her skirt, Marianne didn't blame her. In fact, the more Marianne watched the proceedings, the tighter she held Dorothea. Some of the bolder townspeople who'd dealt with orphans before marched right up to the children and sized them up as if they were slaves on an auction block.

One burly farmer in particular was much too loud and pushy with the boys, requiring them to jog in place, stretch their arms above their heads, and roll up their sleeves so he could examine their arm muscles. Not only did he poke and prod them, but he barked out questions until Liverpool sassed him back with a defiant question of his own.

The farmer's face went red, and he drew back his hand into a fist. Liverpool and the other two older boys stiffened, bracing themselves for the first blow. But the farmer just gave a low, forced laugh before pushing Liverpool and Ned aside and instead grabbing Timmy, the tallest and quietest of the three boys.

"I'll take this one," he shouted over at the reverend as he gripped Timmy's arm and dragged him toward the committee finalizing the matches.

"I need your information, sir," Marianne called. "Your name and where you live." She was beginning to understand why the records of each child were so sparse. Even if she'd had more time to make notes, she wasn't sure what information was essential for the placement. Obviously she needed to record the name and address of each family. But what else was important? How much or how little would help?

"I'm n-n-not leaving w-without George" came a plaintive wail from the line of

children. The cry was filled with desperation and pained Marianne's heart even
before she realized what was happening.

A different man, this one with work-
roughened hands and brawny muscles, had
a hold on Peter and was pulling him away
from George, who'd been pinned to his side
since the moment of his return. "I can't
keep you both," the man said apologetically.
"I only got room for one in the loft above
the livery."

"We d-don't n-need much r-room," stuttered Peter, who clung to George's hand
even as the man was still attempting to
wrench him free.

"No, kid. I'm only taking one of you.
Besides, I don't want a boy who wanders
off whenever it fancies him. I need someone
responsible." The liveryman yanked Peter,
who refused to let go of George. Peter cried
out again, tears streaming down his face as
he fought to stay with his little brother.

"Wait!" Marianne called. She couldn't —
wouldn't — let anyone separate the brothers. It was clear they loved each other and
needed to be together. She untangled herself
from Dorothea and set the little girl off to
the side.

Before she could intervene, the commotion caught Drew's attention, and he rushed

over to the boys. She braced herself for his coaxing. He'd surely do what they'd been trained to do — place the children in interested homes, even if they had to split families. Mrs. Trott had warned her that although the arrangement would be difficult on the siblings at first, they would eventually adjust.

She was surprised when instead of prying George loose from Peter, Drew forced the man to break his hold of the boy. "These two stay together," Drew said in a low voice, his expression as hard as stone.

"I don't need two," the liveryman insisted.

"Then find a different boy." For a long moment, Drew held the man's gaze, and Marianne was afraid he'd protest again. Instead, he sighed and turned to another cluster of boys.

Peter and George were crying and embracing again. Over their heads, Drew's eyes found her. There was something haunted in his countenance, something that told Marianne his heartache went beyond this incident with Peter and George, that he was suffering much more deeply than he wanted to admit.

She gave a nod, hoping he could read her understanding as well as her appreciation for keeping George and Peter together, but then a piercing cry came from behind her. She spun around to see what was wrong.

Dorothea.

Marianne saw a couple kneeling before the girl, apparently attempting to converse with her. The smiles that had graced their faces were rapidly fading at the sound of Dorothea's high-pitched screams.

She returned to Dorothea, dropped to her knees, and dragged her into an embrace. She murmured reassurances and rocked her, attempting to quiet her sobs.

Marianne was rewarded when the orphan hugged her back. Dorothea breathed out a shuddering sigh that warmed Marianne's neck. The little girl's silky hair tickled Marianne's cheek, and the thin arms tightened into a hold Marianne didn't want to break.

She was needed. Again. And she liked that feeling.

Fingers touched her shoulder — Drew. She glanced up at him and smiled. "She'll be all right now."

"Good." He shot a sideways look at the young couple still watching Marianne and Dorothea. The husband had wrapped his arm around his wife's waist, and she had wound hers behind him.

She was wearing a stylish gown with large

hoops that made the skirt form into a bell shape. She had on gloves and a wide-brimmed hat that rested on her beautifully coiffed hair at a jaunty angle. Everything about her spoke of wealth and a life of ease. Her husband was attired in a gray suit that was very much like the expensive suits Thornton, her brother-in-law, wore most of the time.

"What's her name?" the young woman asked.

"Dorothea." Marianne said the name reluctantly. There was no sense in their knowing Dorothea's name when the girl clearly didn't want to have anything to do with them.

"That's very pretty," the woman replied.

"Yes, very," her husband echoed.

"I'm Elizabeth, and this is my husband, Harold. Harold Garner." She spoke the name as though it ought to mean something, but Marianne didn't care. She wished the couple would go away and bother another child, so Dorothea would be able to settle down again.

"Mr. Garner is president of the bank here in Benton," Drew offered. He lifted his brows and cocked his head at Dorothea. He was trying to communicate something. Was Marianne supposed to make more polite conversation?

"So," Marianne said, "you're here to give a home to one of the children?"

The couple glanced at each other and then down at Dorothea. Elizabeth leaned into her husband's shoulder briefly, as though gathering strength before replying. "Yes. I . . . we thought it might be nice to pick out a little boy or girl."

"Well, you're in luck because we have plenty of adorable children." Marianne made a point of turning toward the other orphans, particularly in the direction of the youngest at the end of the line. "I'm sure any one of them will make a good choice."

Again the couple exchanged a look, a look that made her hug Dorothea tighter.

Thankfully, Drew saw the silent communication between the couple. He'd know what to say and would come to Dorothea's aid just as he had with George and Peter. He'd help the couple find another child, one who wasn't quite as needy as Dorothea, one they could truly be happy with.

"Maybe you can introduce the Garners to some of the other children?" she asked him with a smile.

He didn't smile in return. Instead his expression turned almost sympathetic, as if he felt sorry for her.

Why would he feel sorry for her? Marianne buried her face into Dorothea's hair again and breathed in deeply.

"Why don't you let the Garners have another chance at speaking with Dorothea?" Drew suggested.

She shook her head. "Dorothea is already upset enough for one morning."

"She'll be fine." This time his words were not a suggestion.

Marianne pulled back a little and pleaded with him to understand. "No, she won't."

The blue-green in his eyes turned the color of steel. "I need to talk to you for a minute. In private." His tone gave her no room for arguing. Now she understood how one look or one word from him was enough to make the children comply.

She started to rise, but Dorothea clung to her. Marianne gently began the process of loosening Dorothea's hold, all while whispering to her that everything would work out for the best. When Dorothea was finally standing in front of her, Marianne brushed the girl's wispy hair from her tear-streaked cheeks. "I'll be right back. I promise."

Dorothea's bottom lip began to tremble. Marianne shot Drew an I-told-you-so glare.

He crossed his arms with a glare that said *I don't care.*

Marianne sighed and then placed a gentle hand upon Dorothea's head. "I won't be long."

Elizabeth Garner bent toward Dorothea so that she was at eye level. "While we're waiting, I can show you how to play the piano, if you'd like."

Much to Marianne's surprise, Dorothea didn't start screaming again. In fact, she studied Elizabeth's face as if trying to decide whether she was trustworthy or one more person who would end up breaking her heart.

Elizabeth held out a gloved hand in invitation. Dorothea's gaze dropped to the hand.

Marianne was about to issue a word of warning but grew motionless at the sight of Dorothea hesitantly placing her hand in Elizabeth's. The pretty lady smiled encouragingly at Dorothea before she stood and moved gracefully toward the piano, speaking quietly with Dorothea the entire way. When they reached the bench, Elizabeth slid it out. Dorothea offered no protest when the young lady picked her up and carefully situated her on the bench before sitting down next to her.

Marianne could only watch with a strange pain wrenching her heart. When Drew propelled her away, she didn't resist. He led her to an empty corner near the back of the sanctuary. She could still see Dorothea at the piano with Elizabeth. The young woman played a cheerful tune that was much more complex than anything Marianne could manage.

"Marianne," Drew said softly, his voice no longer steel.

Even so, she didn't want to talk to him. Her throat ached too much, and her eyes stung.

"They're perfect for her," he began.

"You don't know that," Marianne replied, blinking back tears before they could spill over. "She's going to cry again, and that woman won't know what to do to console her."

"You learned. What makes you think Elizabeth Garner won't be able to?"

"Because Dorothea is more sensitive than the rest of the children and having a harder time than the others."

"You've done well with her." Drew paused. "But you're not the only one who can love Dorothea."

The words hit her hard in her chest, knocking the breath out of her. Elizabeth had just finished playing a short song and was smiling at Dorothea in obvious delight. The amazing thing was that Dorothea was looking back. No, she wasn't smiling, but neither was she crying.

Elizabeth Garner seemed a gentle soul. The woman was handling Dorothea smoothly so far. But after only a few minutes of observation, how could they know for sure that Elizabeth would be a capable parent?

"The children need us for just a little while," Drew continued. "We're like a train conductor — there to help them during this part of their journey, this transition from one destination to the next. But we were never meant to have a permanent place in their lives."

His words made complete sense, yet she still didn't like them. She didn't like this process of not knowing these people, of not being able to screen the families more vigilantly, to see what they were really like when no one else was looking.

Shouldn't they exercise more caution? Shouldn't they conduct thorough investigations into the families' living situations, their motivations for taking the children, and their plans regarding the children's care? Surely they could sit down with each prospective parent and talk with them, ask them more questions and perhaps get character references from neighbors who knew them.

Although Elizabeth Garner seemed like a very nice lady, anyone could put forth her best image for a short while. Marianne would have felt much better if she'd been able to visit the Garners' home, learn more about them, and determine if they'd truly be the best match for Dorothea.

Instead, she'd been forced to hand the little girl over to a complete stranger. One minute Dorothea was safe with her, and the next she was gone to only God knew where, with people doing only God knew what.

"I just wish we could make sure this is right for Dorothea before giving her to them."

"We can never be completely sure of anything." Drew brushed back a stray strand of Marianne's hair from her eyes.

She stepped out of his reach. Deep inside, she knew he was right. But that didn't stop the frustration and sorrow that came pouring through her as the reality of the situation settled upon her. Whether she liked it or not, whether the Garners were capable or not, Dorothea was going home with them. Her little girl was leaving.

And that was exactly the problem. Dorothea wasn't *her* little girl. As much as Marianne had invested every ounce of energy and time into soothing and caring for Dorothea over the past week, the girl had never been hers and never would be.

"The first trip is always the hardest," Drew said, his brow lined with earnestness. "You'll eventually learn how to love them, but also be able to let go when the time is right."

Marianne shook her head and swiped at the tears that somehow managed to escape. "You're wrong. I'll never get used to this. I'll never be able to love with just part of my heart. And I'll never be able to make another one of these trips."

She was too weak to handle having her heart ripped out every time she had to say good-bye to the children. She cared too much to leave them with strangers. She cared too much to walk away before knowing if they'd be happy and safe. She cared too much to sever the ties without the reassurance that they truly were in a better place.

Once she was back in New York City, she'd resign from her job as an agent and live with the fact that she simply was never meant to be strong. She'd always be too tenderhearted, too emotional, and too tempted to fall in love with those she shouldn't.

CHAPTER 12

In spite of all her misgivings, Marianne somehow managed to do the right thing with Dorothea. She encouraged the little girl to go home with her pretty new mommy, who could play the piano for her whenever she wanted because she had one in her house.

She kissed Dorothea's head, and when the little girl attempted to cling to her, she placed Dorothea's hand in Elizabeth's, reminding the orphan of the piano that awaited her at her new home. Marianne held back the tears when Dorothea walked down the aisle toward the door. She even smiled and waved when the little girl looked back at her over her shoulder.

But when Dorothea disappeared out the door, she hadn't been able to stop the tears any longer. They slipped down her cheeks as silent sobs tore at her chest. She rapidly swiped them away and forced herself to go back to the other children who still needed her.

The train ride to Mayfield had been difficult without the little girl by her side. Her absence only stirred Marianne's worries, not only about Dorothea but about all the children. Through her turmoil she could only pray there hadn't been any mistakes in the placements and that each of the children would be better off, as Drew believed.

In the evening, they arrived at Mayfield, their next destination along the Illinois Central. They had dinner at the Mayfield Inn and went to bed early in rooms reserved for them. Marianne wasn't the only one who'd been quieter. Everyone seemed more subdued and contemplative, the thrill and newness of the trip stripped away and replaced by the cold, stark reality of what had happened in Benton and would happen again now in Mayfield.

The next morning, with half of the children remaining, she found them much easier to supervise as they played outside the church where the meeting was to be held at two o'clock that afternoon. Standing in the shade of the building, she was already sticky from the thick humidity that had moved in with yesterday's rainstorm.

Mayfield looked to be much like all the

other towns they'd been in, with its main street near the train depot, lined with the usual businesses and storage silos. The street was rutted and marked by mud puddles. She prayed the children would remain clean before the meeting but guessed many of the boys would be splattered and dirty in no time.

"Stay here in town," Drew said sternly to the boys as he prepared to go inside for a meeting. "Don't wander off this morning."

"What? Now you're my father?" Liverpool twirled a long stem of grass between his teeth.

"No," Drew said. "But after what happened in Benton with losing George, I want everyone to play close to Miss Neumann while I'm gone."

"Oh, so you think we're babies who need a nanny?"

"Just stay here."

"Mister, I'll do what I want, when I want."

In two long strides, Drew crossed to Liverpool and grabbed him by the front of his shirt. "Listen, so long as I'm in charge, you'll do what I want, when I want. Understood?"

Liverpool smirked and nodded behind him at passersby, who had stopped to witness their interaction.

Drew glanced over his shoulder at the townspeople, then released Liverpool with a shove. "If you hope to get a placement here in Mayfield, you'd better start behaving. I'd hate to have to take you back to New York."

"I'm not going back to the city nohow." Liverpool pulled himself up straight. "Me and Ned might just head out on our own. Ain't that right, Ned?"

Ned stared at Drew with hostile eyes. "All I know is that I didn't come out here to end up with a new family that's gonna take up where my pa left off. No way. I've had enough of that."

Marianne wondered if he was thinking of the farmers who'd poked and prodded them yesterday. She couldn't blame the boys for not wanting to go through that again.

Jethro and Sammy had stopped their game of chase to watch the big boys. Jethro's thick red hair was impossibly frizzy and unmanageable in the humidity, and it stood out from his head in all different directions. No amount of taming on Marianne's part had made the slightest difference today.

"I'm going in to talk with the committee right now." Drew's voice was threaded with frustration. "We'll do the best we can to place you both with families who will treat you fairly." The skepticism on Liverpool and

Ned's faces didn't waver. "In the meantime, stay out of trouble." His command was sharper than usual.

As he bounded up the wooden steps that led to the door of the church, Marianne caught a glimpse of the determination lining his face. Ever since losing George, Drew hadn't been quite the same. He'd been more on edge, the haunted glimmer always present in the depths of his eyes.

Even his admonishment for the children to play close to the church was a change from the carefree, relaxed attitude he'd had the rest of the trip. Maybe the temporary loss had frightened him and made him take his responsibility with the children more seriously.

He paused before the door, his hand on the handle, and glanced at her. "If the boys give you any trouble, don't hesitate to interrupt me." Then he turned and slipped inside the church building.

Marianne wondered if Drew was having second thoughts about bringing the older boys on the trip. As much as she tried to keep the children busy and contained within the vicinity of the churchyard, they wandered off anyway, especially as the long morning dragged by. By the time the committee exited the building, it was noon and the children's growling stomachs had brought them straggling back.

She wasn't surprised when Liverpool and Ned didn't return. Several of the other younger boys hadn't come back either, apparently having found a "swimming hole" somewhere. Drew was adamant with the children when they'd been in Chicago and playing along the canal that they were never to go swimming. At the news, Drew hurried off in the direction of the pond, his face tight with worry.

While Drew was rounding up the stray orphans, the children had lunch at the tavern. Afterward, Marianne helped the younger ones comb their hair and make themselves presentable before walking back to the church. Drew returned with some of the boys in time for the reception, which was nearly identical to the one yesterday in Benton, with the pastor giving a short sermon, followed by the children singing "Amazing Grace."

The difference today was that Marianne felt sick to her stomach because she knew exactly what was going to happen, and she dreaded it. She dreaded the fear on the children's faces, the worry about what their new lives would be like, and whether the families who took them in would love them.

And she dreaded the tears some of the children would shed as they were led away to strange places.

Her thoughts kept returning to Dorothea. Her heart ached at the image of the sweet girl possibly huddled in a corner of her new home, terrified, lonely, and confused. No doubt she'd sobbed inconsolably. Marianne prayed for Elizabeth Garner not to lose patience, that she'd be sensitive to all Dorothea had gone through in her short life.

"Have you seen Liverpool or Ned yet?" Drew asked under his breath as the families rose from the pews and moved to the front to meet the children.

She shook her head.

His shoulders sagged. He'd had such high hopes for helping the boys. He saw the good in them that so many people missed and was optimistic about their futures when so many others would have already given up hope.

He nodded and handed her the black record book. She let out a heavy sigh, knowing now what her job entailed. Even though she didn't like it any better today than she had yesterday, she'd do her best to record as much about the children and their new families as she could.

Perhaps today she'd find a way to hang on

to the book a little longer so she could search through it more thoroughly and look for information that might lead her to Sophie or Olivia or Nicholas.

Starting today, and every day hereafter, she had to remember why she'd joined on as an agent with the Children's Aid Society. Most certainly not to fall in love with the children and then have her heart broken. No. She was on a mission to find her sister. And so far she'd made no progress in discovering anything about Sophie. Since this was to be her first and last placing trip, she couldn't waste any more time. She had to focus on what really mattered.

When the door opened and Liverpool stepped into the sanctuary, Drew breathed a silent prayer of thankfulness. As rude and difficult as the boy could be, Drew knew it was only a front. He suspected Liverpool had erected many barriers over the years that masked all the hurts and disappointments he'd experienced.

Drew hoped to get past the barriers during this trip, or at the very least to begin tearing them down. But apparently that wasn't going to happen on his shift. He could only conclude God had someone else in mind for that job.

Drew lifted another prayer heavenward that God would bring the right family to Liverpool, if not here in Mayfield, then in the next town.

"Where's Ned?" Drew asked as Liverpool brushed past him.

"Gone."

"Gone where?"

"He decided he had enough of farm life and took off."

Drew felt his heart drop. "Do you know where he went?"

Liverpool shrugged. "Don't know and don't care."

For a moment, Drew considered running over to the train depot and checking for Ned there. Maybe he could stop the boy before he snuck aboard the train.

He let his shoulders sag. The truth was, if Ned wanted to leave, there wasn't much Drew could say or do to stop him. Like most street boys, he was an expert at hiding and avoiding authority. If he didn't want to be found, Drew wouldn't be able to track him down no matter how hard he tried.

Drew tried to be grateful that at least Liverpool had stayed. It was strange, though. He would have guessed that if either of the boys planned to strike out on his own, Liverpool would have been the one to do it, not Ned. Ned had always been more malleable, the one Drew thought would eventually come around, and maybe even begin to trust God.

He was under no illusion that boys like Ned and Liverpool would easily find their way to accepting the Heavenly Father who loved them, especially after having earthly fathers who were drunkards and had beaten and ill-treated them.

Only last week, Drew had spoken with Brace about the boys, and the man's response still lingered in his head: *"I suppose it is very hard for a poor boy to believe at all times that God loves him. Half-clothed, cold and hungry, sleeping in boxes, not knowing where he'll get his next meal, and utterly without friends, he can hardly imagine that there is someone close by who truly cares for him. And yet that is just the message we need to give — that God loves him."*

Drew prayed for each of the older boys every morning and night. He firmly believed no one was too far beyond the reach of God's love. Perhaps it would take more time and stretching to grab hold of these boys, but Drew had never been one to relinquish a challenge.

As Liverpool sauntered to the front, the young man shot Peter and George a narrowed look. The two brothers were standing at the end of the line, still alone, still unclaimed. At the sight of Liverpool, the two had turned pale and their eyes widened with fright. Peter reached for George's hand and pulled the boy closer.

Liverpool smirked at the younger boys and walked to the opposite side of the line where the rest of the older children stood.

"Please, God," Drew muttered. "Help that boy."

When a farmer about as tall as the church spire ambled up to Liverpool, Drew started to pray in earnest. Thankfully, the farmer seemed the quiet sort. He looked Liverpool up and down and wasn't daunted by the sullenness in the boy's expression.

"You wantin' to do farm work?" the man asked.

"Yep. I suppose so."

"You a hard worker?"

"Can be if I want."

"Good."

Drew exchanged introductions with the tall man, Mr. Turner, and shook his hand. "I think you'll appreciate having Liverpool's help. He's energetic and bright." Drew saw no reason to point out Liverpool's negative qualities — although there were more than a few. The boy would have a greater chance of success with the Turners if he started with his slate wiped clean.

"Got myself two grown men already," Mr. Turner said, "but I can always use another hand."

Liverpool scrutinized Mr. Turner as if picking him apart bone by bone. The farmer seemed harmless enough. He was likely a steady, hardworking fellow whose farm had prospered over the past few years, becoming too big to keep up with on his own.

"What do you think, Liverpool?" Drew asked.

Mr. Turner grunted but thankfully didn't make any comments about the boy's name as most people were apt to do when they first heard it. Apparently, Liverpool was waiting for the comment as well, and when it wasn't forthcoming, the boy nodded. "All right, mister. I'll come work for you."

Again the farmer snorted, perhaps humored by the irony that the boy thought he was picking his own home rather than the other way around. Drew wasn't so sure. Either way, he offered Mr. Turner another handshake. "Thank you, sir. And God bless you for your willingness to offer Liverpool a new start to his life."

Marianne crouched behind a shrub and

stifled her laughter as one of the children found Drew and began chasing him. She'd never played the game of hide-and-seek when she was younger. Her sewing for her uncle in the sweatshop had taken up most of her time, leaving her too exhausted to do much in her free time. However, over the past week of their trip, she'd learned and played more games than she had in her entire life.

Drew sprinted across the field toward the schoolhouse, the other children cheering him on. There were only six orphans left. After the meeting yesterday, eight of the children had remained. Then today following the church service, an older couple, a dairy farmer and his wife, had agreed to take Peter and George.

Marianne was happy the brothers could stay together, yet she hadn't been able to say good-bye since she had to stay back at the inn and miss church. One of the girls had complained of not feeling well enough to get out of bed.

The young girl in question seemed well enough now — running around with everyone else. Marianne couldn't keep from wondering if she'd come up with an excuse so she didn't have to return to the church and face the people who'd rejected her.

Tomorrow they were leaving for the last stop of their placing out, Dresden, which lay south of Mayfield along the Illinois Central Railroad. Drew seemed confident they would be able to find homes for the rest of the children there. And so for now, Marianne tried to put aside her concerns and sorrows and enjoy the beauty of the summer afternoon. She was taking a lesson from Drew. If he could so easily let go of his worries and enjoy life, then she ought to as well.

Drew made a show of tripping, allowing his opponent to catch up and tag him. As he congratulated the child, Marianne hopped out of her hiding spot.

"I won!" Marianne shouted, doing a little victory dance as she'd seen the children do and earning their laughter. "I guess I'm destined to beat Mr. Brady," she said, skipping across the schoolyard toward Drew. He'd begun working the pump handle up and down for one of the children to get a drink of water. "Last night I proved I was better at spitting watermelon seeds and playing checkers." She smiled at him in pretend innocence. "And now it looks like I'm also better at hiding than you."

"Oh, you think so," he said with a grin. "When I really put my mind to it, you wouldn't be able to find me."

"Prove it."

He let go of the pump handle and straightened. "Is that a challenge, Miss Neumann?" His eyes glittered with that irresistible sparkle that came whenever he was excited. She'd realized he wasn't the type who could back down from a challenge. He thrived on them, thrived on being impulsive, thrived on excitement.

And for a reason she couldn't explain, she loved to bait him. She supposed some might call it flirting. But she liked to think she was only having fun while keeping the children entertained.

True to his word, Drew hid himself so well that Marianne and the children called for him at the top of their voices as they scoured the school and church grounds. Some of the orphans raced around the train depot while two others checked behind the Mayfield Inn. The town was quiet on the Sunday afternoon, the businesses closed to observe the Lord's Day, so the children's laughter seemed even louder than normal.

At the sway of a shed door behind the church, Marianne veered toward the wooden shack. Even though one of the orphans had already checked inside, Marianne's pulse sped in anticipation. Without any wind, the door wouldn't have moved unless someone bumped it, someone big and bulky, someone who would get cramped in the tight space.

Slowly she opened the door. At first glance in the dark, the shed appeared to be full of crates and lawn supplies. But a closer look showed a pair of black leather men's oxfords at the edge of a piece of canvas.

Drew.

He had to be hot by now. Maybe she ought to make him wait just a little while longer. Inwardly grinning, she made a show of banging a rake and rattling a crate. "Nope. I guess he's not in here."

She was starting to back out when Drew's hand shot out, captured her arm, and dragged her all the way inside. She laughed but didn't fight him.

"Just for that, I'm trapping you in here with me," he said, pushing aside the canvas and stepping out from his hiding place. There was barely enough room for one person and certainly not for two, and she found herself almost pressed against him.

With the door still halfway open, the light revealed his handsome face flushed from the heat. His grin brought out the dimple in his chin and the playfulness in his eyes. As with the first time she'd seen him, she was aware of how his perfect smile could knock a girl from her feet, how he'd made a regular practice of knocking her from her feet this past week.

A strand of his sandy blond hair stuck to his forehead. Without thinking, she reached up, peeled it loose, and combed it back.

At her touch, he sucked in a breath and seemed to stop breathing altogether as though waiting for her to touch him again. The mirth in his eyes dissipated, replaced by something that made her stomach flip.

He didn't look at her lips, and she tried not to look at his. But suddenly she couldn't think of anything but kissing him.

"You ragamuffins settle down!" came a man's voice in the distance.

Drew's attention immediately shifted to the door and beyond. In an instant they both stumbled out of the shed. She hoped none of the children noticed that they'd been inside at the same time.

"Uh-oh," Drew said, peering across the street toward the train depot. "Looks like we've got trouble."

Marianne followed his gaze to a short, stout man with a long handlebar mustache and an even longer revolver. He caressed the ivory handle over and over like it was a pet puppy. He wore a shiny badge on his coat that announced his status as sheriff, although his scowl and sharp words seemed to announce it even more forcefully.

At the sight of Drew, the sheriff shifted his attention away from the children. "Mr. Brady?"

"That's right. I'm Andrew Brady."

"You get your orphans under control or I'm locking them up for the night."

"Now, Sheriff," Drew said in his usual unruffled tone, "we're just enjoying a few games on this beautiful summer day. You can't fault us for that, can you?"

"They're causing a ruckus and disturbing the peace."

Drew motioned for the children to gather near him. With fear on their faces, they rushed to comply. Marianne had no doubt that their experience with the New York City police was less than pleasant.

"There are plenty of us here in Mayfield who don't want you bringing this street scum to our peaceful town," the sheriff said, continuing to stroke his pistol. "We don't want them in our schools, tainting our kids, and running on our streets causing problems."

Marianne could see Drew's shoulders stiffen at the insult, but he nodded amiably at the sheriff. "I'm sure they won't be causing any problems, Sheriff. Give them a chance. They're all good kids in need of a loving and stable environment."

"If'n I wanted to give them a chance, I would have stayed in the big city. As it is, most folk here came west to get away from the garbage. And we don't like you bringing it here and stinking up our town."

The sheriff's statements were so shocking and offensive, they rendered Marianne speechless. How many people in Mayfield felt the same way the sheriff did? Marianne wasn't naïve enough to believe everyone supported Reverend Brace's Emigration Plan. But she'd never heard anyone speak so forcefully against it.

She reached for the hand of the nearest orphan, little redheaded Jethro, and wished he hadn't heard the sheriff's words. But as soon as she squeezed his hand, she realized he'd likely heard worse, and she wondered if there would ever come a day when he wouldn't have to face such discrimination.

CHAPTER 13

"Why doesn't anyone want me?" The child's voice at Marianne's side tugged her out of a sleepy daze brought on by the rocking of the train and the now-familiar clacking of the wheels against the rails. After nearly two weeks of traveling by train and staying in hotels along the Illinois Central, she was more exhausted than she'd realized.

"What did you say?" She blinked the sleep out of her eyes and stifled a yawn.

"I'm not good enough for anybody," Jethro said, his voice laden with anguish.

Marianne sat up and brushed a hand over the boy's freckled cheek, feeling the dampness of his tears. When he'd finally stopped talking an hour ago, she thought he'd fallen asleep. The silence had been a blessed relief after the boy's constant chatter.

On the bench across from them, Drew was sprawled out, his head on one end of the bench, resting on the suit coat he'd bunched up into a pillow. His legs dangled over the other side. He'd angled his hat over his face, shielding his slumbering face. The even rise and fall of his chest told Marianne he was still asleep, as he had been most of the day.

After several days in Dresden placing the last of the orphans, and Drew visiting the doctor to get the stitches in his arm removed, they'd departed on the first train that morning. Originally, Drew had made arrangements for them to stay in Dresden for another week before they started back along their route to do follow-up visits with the children they'd placed. But he'd easily agreed to her request to travel to Quincy for a few days instead.

They were less than a day's ride from the Illinois town her brother-in-law Thornton Quincy had developed last year. The town was still under construction and attracting settlers, but it was undoubtedly a very fine town. Marianne had visited a few months ago in February, and she was anxious to see Elise again, to hug her and know her sister still loved her — even if she'd failed once again regarding Sophie.

She'd scoured through Drew's record book on two different occasions, yet she hadn't seen any mentions of a child who resembled Sophie. There hadn't been any notice of two infants named Olivia and Nicholas either. In fact, the information was so vague for most children that she'd all but given up hope of using the records to help in her search.

Instead, she'd continued to make inquires wherever she went. But as with everywhere else, no one had seen a girl that fit Sophie's description or Olivia and Nicholas's.

Cuddled up next to her on the bench, Jethro seemed so small and vulnerable. Because of the stories he told about his survival, at times she forgot he was only seven years old. Unfortunately, he'd experienced too much of life already, too much that no one, not even an adult, should have to live through.

He sniffled and wiped the back of his hand across his runny nose. "Guess nobody likes my red hair."

"Oh, Jethro," she crooned and hugged him closer. "Your hair is a beautiful color. It reminds me of the sun when it's glowing on the horizon just before it sets, when it's a blazing fireball of oranges and reds."

"You might like it, Miss Neumann, but there ain't nobody else who does."

She didn't want to tell him he was close to the truth. Many people were prejudiced, and with his red hair they assumed he was

Irish — even though Jethro didn't know his family's ancestry and had lived in America his whole life. Still, he was the only orphan left. Even without his red hair, he was in the age group hardest to place. Families liked to adopt the youngest children whom they believed weren't corrupted by the degradation of poverty and city life. And families were willing to take in the older orphans, who had the capability of working hard and earning their keep.

But a seven-year-old like Jethro was often considered a burden. And one with red hair and possible Irish ancestry?

Drew hadn't been surprised that Jethro was still with them. "Don't worry, buddy," he said after they'd returned to the hotel last night. "We'll pray for God to provide you just the right new home." She was touched when Drew knelt down right then and there and prayed with Jethro.

Yet she couldn't keep from questioning the wisdom of the leaders who'd allowed Jethro to come on the trip. If they'd known he would be hard to place, why had they sent him? Didn't they know he'd face rejection? Didn't they realize how devastating such rejection would be for a young boy?

She hated to think about having to take him all the way back to New York City and place him in an orphanage there. He likely wouldn't stay in such a place and would end up back on the streets.

Drew had mentioned that during their follow-up visits, he'd attempt to find a family among those who'd already taken children. But Marianne worried that if a family took Jethro out of obligation and didn't really want him, he'd only suffer all the more. He deserved a family who wanted and loved him for who he was.

"You're going to make some mother and father a wonderful son," she reassured.

"My other ma and pa didn't want me." A tear escaped and rolled down his cheek. "You and Mr. Brady are the only ones who like me."

"That's not true. You're a loving boy and make friends wherever you go."

"Maybe you can be my new ma." He tilted his head up to gauge her reaction.

She attempted to hide her dismay and instead smiled. "As much as I'd adore having you for a son, I can't be your ma."

"Why not? I'd be a good boy."

"Oh, Jethro." She smoothed his hair back. "You'd be a very good boy. That wouldn't be the problem. The problem is me. I'm not in a position to have children since I'm not married."

"You could marry Mr. Brady." The words came quickly, as if he'd already planned everything out.

Marianne was tempted to laugh at Jethro's suggestion, but the sincerity of his expression stopped her. "Mr. Brady and I, well . . ." She slid a glance at the man in question.

"Mr. Brady's a real nice man," Jethro said. "And I can tell he likes you."

Against her will, her mind flashed back to the kiss he'd given her the night in the tavern after losing George. Since then, she'd thought of the kiss too many times to count. It was seared into her memory whether she wanted it to be or not. But she couldn't very well say that to Jethro.

"I agree. Mr. Brady is a fine man —"

"And intelligent, strong, and incredibly handsome." The voice came from beneath the hat covering Drew's face.

"But he's a tad too arrogant for me," she finished.

Drew pushed up his hat until he revealed his devastating grin. "Don't let her fool you, Jethro. She loves me, and she'd marry me in a minute if I asked her."

"I absolutely would not."

He pushed the brim of his hat higher until she could see his eyes. The sparkle there told her he was only teasing. Nevertheless, she felt flustered. The idea of marrying Andrew Brady didn't repel her in the least. In fact, it made her insides flutter in a strange but pleasurable way.

"Oh, that's right," he countered. "You wouldn't be at all interested in marrying me because you already have a dashing beau waiting for you somewhere here in Illinois."

Reinhold. She hadn't thought of him at all in recent days. She'd simply been too busy and too consumed with the orphans that her plans to search for him had all but vanished.

"As a matter of fact, I was planning to seek him out on the return trip."

Drew gave her a crooked smile, one that told her he knew she'd forgotten about Reinhold, and that he also knew who she'd been thinking about instead.

Jethro's gaze bounced back and forth between her and Drew. "Miss Neumann, you oughta marry Mr. Brady."

Drew's grin widened. "I am quite the catch."

Jethro nodded earnestly. "Mr. Brady's the nicest man I ever met."

She fanned a hand in front of her face, positive her cheeks were flaming with embarrassment. Even if Drew was only jesting, she couldn't deny her attraction. And she had the feeling he knew it all too well. "Mr. Brady is nice, Jethro," she replied, choosing her words carefully, "but he's not serious about asking me to marry him. He's teasing. That's all."

"You are?" Jethro said to Drew.

"He's not the marrying type," Marianne continued, this time challenging Drew with a narrowed gaze. She knew he'd been engaged once, that he'd been hurt, and ever since then he'd probably had a difficult time making a commitment to any woman. He was scared of a serious relationship and was more likely to flirt with pretty women, steal a kiss or two, but then cut the ties when things got too serious. He'd probably left a trail of broken hearts wherever he'd gone.

The truth was, he might be able to talk and tease about marrying, but when pushed, he certainly wouldn't follow through. She could play his game without any worries.

"As a matter of fact," she said, "I highly doubt Mr. Brady would get married, even if someone paid him to do so."

"Are you daring me, Miss Neumann?" He sat up in the bench, turning to face her squarely. After having slept most of the day, his shirt was wrinkled and his hair mussed. And yet nothing could take away from his incredibly good looks.

"I'm not daring you, Mr. Brady. I'm simply telling the truth. You can't do it. Some men are the marrying type. Some aren't." She smiled at him as if the matter were settled. "And you clearly fall into the second category."

"How about if we put your theory to the test, darlin'?"

She was enjoying sparring with him much more than she should. In fact, she loved challenging him. Their dares had become a highlight of the trip.

But for all his talk about daring to get married, he wouldn't. This was finally a dare he wouldn't be able to do. Marriage wasn't a part of Andrew Brady's immediate future. Perhaps that was one of the reasons he'd chosen the life of an agent, because then he didn't have to worry about settling down. He could constantly move around and so keep his relationships from ever becoming too serious.

"How would you like to put your theory to the test, *darlin'*?" she said, trying to imitate his Southern drawl.

"We'll get married just as soon as we get to Quincy."

She jutted her chin. "I'd like to see that. I know you won't."

"Try me." His eyes flashed with something that made her hesitate. Was he serious? Would he really go through with marrying her simply to win a challenge?

No. He wouldn't take it that far. He'd back out sooner or later. He was too afraid of marriage.

"All right," she said, her stomach quavering. "I'll try you."

Jethro was still glancing between them. "So you'll get married at the next stop and keep me as your child?"

"I'm planning on it. But Miss Neumann might be too afraid to commit." Drew's tone challenged her — no, dared — her to follow through, as though he didn't believe she was ready for marriage either. Did he think she was too frightened or too weak? The implication galled her, making her spine stiffen with the need to prove herself.

"For your information, I can commit just fine." She ignored the whisper at the back of her mind telling her she'd been using Reinhold as an excuse to hold other men at arm's length in her fear of getting too close and disappointing them.

As though reading her thoughts, Drew's grin slanted into dangerously irresistible territory. "Does that mean you'll marry me when we arrive in Quincy?"

How could she say no without making herself look like a frightened old spinster? Once more she hesitated. "Surely you don't expect to get married the minute we get off the train."

"I knew it!" With a smirk, he sat back, draping both arms across the bench. "You think I can't do it, but when it comes down to it, you're the one who's too afraid."

She bristled at his remark. "All I'm saying is that we would need a little time to make the arrangements. You aren't planning to walk directly to the church and ask the minister to marry us right away, are you?"

"Why not?" His eyes glinted, clearly relishing the challenge.

"Because . . . because . . ." She fumbled over her response. Because why, exactly? Elise had married Thornton without any preparation. What was to stop her from doing the same?

He tapped his fingers on the back of the bench. Jethro watched her expectantly, his eyes bright with hope. A part of her told her she needed to put an end to this whole discussion now before it got out of hand, if it hadn't already. She and Drew couldn't make plans and promises to each other only to break them at the altar once Drew's moment of impulsivity passed and the reality of what he'd done settled upon him. And they couldn't do this to Jethro — allow him to believe they would marry each other. He would be devastated when he realized they'd never really planned on it.

"I don't want anyone to get hurt," she finally said with a pointed sideways glance at Jethro.

"I'm not planning to hurt anyone," Drew replied. "In fact, I think Jethro's right. We're his best option. And since it's clear you like me —"

Her indignation rose swiftly. "I do not like you."

"You see the way she looks at me, don't you, Jethro?" Drew's expression took on an innocence that stirred her ire even further.

"I'm sure all Jethro sees is your infatuation with me."

Drew laughed, a deep belly laugh that soon had Jethro giggling. As she watched the play of sunshine and mirth between them, she couldn't contain a smile of her own.

When Drew's laughter faded, despite all the teasing and banter, something in his eyes beseeched her not to deny him. That something was powerful. It drew her in and made her breathless with anticipation.

"You better ask her to marry you proper-like, Mr. Brady." Filled with excitement, Jethro hopped up onto his seat. "Maybe then she'll say yes!"

Instantly, Drew slid from the bench and knelt in front of her. He reached for her hand and took it into his. The touch sent sparks into her blood. As he lifted her hand toward his mouth, she bit down on her lower lip in an exquisite moment of anticipation.

His kiss was soft and lingering and only stirred a longing for much more. It was the promise of more kisses and their exploring the secrets of married life together.

"Marianne," he whispered, "will you marry me?"

She should say no as quickly as she could. They were only asking for trouble by carrying on this charade. But somehow in that moment, with the undeniable attraction she felt toward him, she didn't want to say no. At least not yet. "We'll need at least a week to make the arrangements," she said in an embarrassingly winded voice.

"You'll marry me at the end of the week?" He gently maneuvered her hand so his lips were against her wrist, grazing her pulse, which she realized was throbbing. The contact was nearly hypnotizing, and she had to break it before he managed to get her to agree to anything else.

Besides, this open display in front of Jethro wasn't appropriate. The boy was hopping up and down on the bench, beaming with his toothless smile, watching her and waiting for her answer.

She couldn't say no now. She'd have to go along with the plan until she figured out a way to get them out of the hole they'd just dug and had now fallen into quite deeply. She nodded her answer.

Drew rewarded her with the most beautiful smile ever.

They arrived in Quincy at dusk. The soft blue of the sky was tinted with hints of purple and wisps of clouds. The tall grass of the endless prairie was still a fresh green that hadn't yet experienced the hot, dry days of summer, which would eventually turn it brown and brittle.

As Marianne stepped down from the train onto the platform, Drew held her arm to steady her. Her eyes snapped to his, revealing the stark desire there that had started to make him do crazy things — like get down on his knees and propose to her.

What had he been thinking?

For an instant, he lost himself in her bottomless brown eyes. The trouble was, he hadn't been thinking. With every passing day, he was finding it more and more difficult to make his brain work rationally around Marianne. And now somehow he'd ended up engaged to her with their wedding a mere week away.

"Marianne!" An elegantly dressed young woman with pale blond hair who'd been standing in the shade of the depot rushed toward Marianne.

Marianne squealed. "Elise!" The two women hugged and laughed and spoke all at once. When Elise pulled back, she held Marianne at arm's length and studied her like a mother would a child.

"I see you're getting good use of the dresses Fanny made for you," Elise said sarcastically in a German accent that was stronger than Marianne's.

Marianne glanced down at the skirt and flushed. "I'm sorry. I haven't had time to launder them since we started our journey. It's been incredibly busy and so much traveling and —"

"Then it's a good thing I had Fanny work on creating a few more dresses for you," Elise said. "Because this one is just begging for a day off."

"Marianne looks lovely all the time." The words came out before Drew could stop them and were much harder than he'd intended, a rebuke to Elise along with a warning not to hurt Marianne.

The young woman's attention shifted to him, revealing a face outlined by the same pretty features as Marianne's: long eyelashes, delicate eyebrows, and the same doe eyes. While Elise's coloring was fair, Marianne's was a shade darker, more exotic and enticing.

Elise's blue eyes were direct and almost intimidating. She was clearly a strong woman, a natural leader, and likely very determined when she set her mind on something. He understood more completely why Marianne had wanted to be on her own, to come out from under the protective wings of this capable woman and prove she had merit on her own.

"I suppose you're Marianne's supervisor from the Children's Aid Society?"

"No, I'm not technically her supervisor. Andrew Brady. Drew. We're working together as partners. Pleased to meet you, ma'am."

"They're going to get married in a week" came a small voice beside him. Drew felt Jethro's little hand slide into his. He glanced down to find the boy was peering up at him as though waiting for an introduction.

"Married?" Elise's tone rose several octaves.

Marianne looked away, embarrassment, fear, and insecurity rippling across her features. She obviously hadn't thought through how to tell her sister about their engagement. Maybe she hadn't been planning to; maybe she'd hoped to avoid any conversation about the subject so that all talk of marriage would simply die away.

It struck Drew then just how impulsive and irrational he'd been in proposing to Marianne. That was the way he usually operated — act first, think later. But at this moment, with Marianne bowing beneath the censure of her capable and intelligent sister, his heart welled with empathy and the strong, almost overpowering need to defend Marianne. With Jethro's hand still in his, he crossed to Marianne and wrapped his arm around her, drawing her to his side.

"She just agreed to marry me," he said, looking down at her and willing her to meet his gaze so he could reassure her that he would stand by her side. "I'm the luckiest man alive."

At his declaration, her lashes lifted, revealing startled, disbelieving eyes.

Before he could talk himself out of it, he bent and pressed his lips softly to hers. The touch was like a flicker of a candle flame, brief but searing.

When he pulled away, her eyes were focused on his lips, telling him the kiss had touched her with its heat too and she wanted more. Her look of desire had him dropping his attention to her lips again too. Just for an instant. Hopefully, though, it was enough for Elise to see that marriage by the week's end was probably in their best interests. At least that was the way he saw it just then.

"And exactly how long have you known each other?" Elise asked, her sharp gaze narrowing on him, suspicion and anger turning her blue eyes to ice.

"Less than a month," he replied before Marianne could.

"Well, that's hardly long enough to know you're ready to marry each other . . . unless of course you've been taking advantage of my sister."

Her words cut into Drew like a knife through his chest. At the same moment, Marianne gasped and started to pull away from him. He strengthened his hold before she could wiggle loose. "Marianne is not only innocent of all wiles, she's above them. Even though I'm incredibly hard to resist, she's done a fair job of rebuffing me." He winked at Marianne.

Elise's stern frown was frozen in place, and she apparently found no humor in his jest.

"Marianne is a much stronger woman than you realize," he continued, once again feeling the need to come to her defense. "But even if she were weak-kneed around me, I pride myself on being a man of high moral principles. I consider it my God-given duty to cherish a woman's virtue above my own selfish desires."

Jethro was taking in the whole interaction, and the enormous smile from earlier had all but disappeared. "They're going to become my ma and pa after they get married."

Elise's attention dropped to the boy, and her expression softened. She bent so she was at eye level. "And who are you?"

"I'm Jethro," he lisped, his freckles too numerous to count in his pale face. "Nobody else wanted me in any of the towns, so Miss Neumann and Mr. Brady said they'd become my ma and pa. Thataway I won't have to go back to New York City and sleep in a coal box."

Elise's eyes weren't as expressive as Marianne's, but the compassion they held was undeniable. "Of course you won't have to go back to New York City and sleep in a coal box. We'll find you a good home here in Quincy."

Jethro's fingers tightened around Drew's. "I don't need a good home here in Quincy. I'm gonna stay with Mr. Brady and Miss Neumann after they get married. They already told me so."

Something in the boy's tone warned of an escalating crisis if anyone tried to convince him otherwise. At least for the moment. As if sensing the same, Elise smiled at the boy and said, "I don't suppose you like strawberry pie, do you?"

His grasp stayed tight. Drew squeezed his hand to reassure him and at the same time hugged Marianne into the crook of his arm, unwilling to relinquish her just yet. He didn't know when he'd have another excuse to hold her and wanted to make this time last as long as he could.

"We had strawberries on the trip here, Jethro," Marianne reminded him gently. "Don't you remember? Mr. Brady gave them to me as my prize for winning the footrace?"

Elise's brows rose in question, yet she wisely chose to save the interrogation for another time. "I purchased strawberries just yesterday from a nearby farmer who brought transplants west with him. He has a small crop this year, but they're delicious."

Jethro nodded hesitantly. "I guess I won't get to be a farmer no more. But I won't mind riding the trains with Mr. Brady and Miss Neumann instead."

As the boy took hold of the hand Elise offered and dragged Marianne away from his side, Drew watched them, unable to move. Jethro's words ricocheted in his head. *I won't mind riding the trains.*

What kind of life could he give an orphan boy? Certainly not the stable life he would need. And he certainly couldn't offer Marianne a stable life either. How could he — not when he was running from a past that still haunted him?

Of course, he'd acted on a whim to go through with the challenge to marry Marianne. He probably should have resisted the urge to fall prey to her taunting him about not being the marrying type.

She'd been right. He wasn't that type anymore. Perhaps the reason he'd never gotten serious with another woman was because he hadn't wanted to drag anyone into his precarious situation, thinking he'd endure the heartache all on his own. He'd never envisioned himself settling down with a wife but pictured himself as single, as serving the Lord without the encumbrances of a family.

So what was he doing?

His heart began to pick up speed until it was thrumming with an uneven, nervous energy. What had he gotten himself into?

He watched Marianne reach for Jethro's other hand so that the boy was wedged between the two sisters. As Marianne entered the depot, she glanced at Drew over her shoulder as though sensing his eyes upon her. She gave him a shy but inviting smile, one that offered him the world and more if he had the courage to take it.

He hesitated only a moment before shoving all his worries to the back of his mind. Then he smiled at her in return and bounded forward, catching the door and following her inside.

CHAPTER 14

"Marrying to give an orphan a home is noble," Elise said from her spot in bed next to Marianne. "But it's also ridiculous."

"More ridiculous than your reason for marrying Thornton?" Marianne retorted.

In the darkness of the second-story bedroom, Marianne relished the time alone with Elise. Lying side by side on the big bed and staring up at the ceiling reminded her of when they were little girls living in Hamburg, sharing the dormer room above their father's bakery — when they giggled over silly stories, tickled each other with their cold toes, and listened to their stomachs growl from the yeasty aromas that wafted to the third story all the way from the basement oven.

"I married Thornton out of love."

"You also got married to help him win the contest against his brother."

"But I loved him and would have married

him either way."

Marianne couldn't find a response. How did she feel about Drew? She couldn't claim to love him, could she? Yes, she cared about him. And yes, she melted under his touch. But a noble cause and physical attraction weren't enough for marriage, were they?

A warm breeze blew in from the large bedroom window, lifting the lacy curtains and skittering across the bed, ruffling Marianne's thin nightgown and brushing her loose hair away from her shoulders.

She was selfishly relieved Thornton was on one of his trips east and that she had Elise to herself. After dinner in Elise's eating house connected with the depot, Marianne had tucked Jethro into bed in the extra room above the depot where he and Drew would stay for the week. It was more spacious and private than the hotel.

An older couple, the Grays, occupied the other room across the hallway from where Drew and Jethro were staying. Mr. Gray was the stationmaster and Mrs. Gray an assistant to Elise in her eating house.

Thornton had offered to build the Grays a house of their own, but the older couple hadn't wanted to move from the depot. Mrs. Gray was petite, thin, and weak from a bout of polio she'd suffered as a child. Since then, she'd had difficulty walking. The Grays decided to stay close to their place of employment and were loyal and kind to Elise and Thornton.

After kissing Jethro good-night, Marianne had walked back to Elise's new house, which hadn't yet been finished when she visited the last time. One street over from the depot on North First Avenue, Elise's house was by far the largest in town. "I told Thornton I wanted something simple," Elise had explained, unable to contain her smile, "and this is what he gave me." She waved a hand at the three-story home, painted white with ornate green trim.

Elise went on to describe the house as Italianate style, specially designed by architects whom Thornton had hired. It was elegant beyond anything Marianne had seen before — except perhaps Thornton's New York home.

The interior was as lovely as the outside. It was clear Thornton loved spoiling Elise and had granted her every wish and then some. He'd also hired New York City's best interior designer to come out to Quincy to help Elise decorate the home. As Elise gave Marianne a tour, the reality of Elise's new life and the vast difference in their status had finally struck Marianne. Marianne was the type of woman who would have considered it a privilege to live as a servant in Elise's attic. In fact, only a year ago, both of them would have been delighted to be hired as domestic help in such a beautiful home. Actually, they would have been happy with any job at all.

It wasn't until Elise crawled into bed with her that Marianne relaxed and was reminded they were still the same two girls they'd always been. Maybe life hadn't turned out the way they'd expected, but they still had each other.

"I'm sorry I haven't found Sophie yet," Marianne whispered into the warm night.

"I'm sorry I haven't found her too," Elise whispered back.

Marianne knew Thornton and Elise had done everything they could to locate Sophie. Thornton's private investigators had been searching for her for months.

"I've come to the conclusion we won't be able to find her until she wants us to," Elise said sadly. "Until then there's little we can do to help her."

"Then you're giving up looking for her?" Marianne asked.

"No," Elise reassured. "Of course not. Thornton has instructed his investigators to keep her case open indefinitely. But at the same time, I think we have to stop blaming ourselves. As hard as it is, we have to let Sophie grow up and make her own mistakes along the way."

Marianne knew Elise was right. Even so, she couldn't shake the guilt that she should have done more for Sophie and Olivia and Nicholas and that she still needed to keep searching. "Thornton has been a blessing. Next time you see him, tell him how much I appreciate all he's done for me — for us."

Elise nodded. "I miss him so much when he's gone." Her voice quavered as though she might cry. Marianne groped in the dark for Elise's hand and folded it in hers. "I didn't think it would be so difficult to be away from each other. I thought I could stay here and he could go to New York whenever he needed to."

The tremble in Elise's fingers was something new. She was never afraid or indecisive or weak; she was always strong, the one Marianne could count on. "What will you do?" Marianne asked.

"I don't know. I love my eating house here, but I love my husband more."

"Perhaps you can find a competent manager and then you'd be free to travel with Thornton more often."

Elise didn't say anything, and Marianne

knew Elise was thinking she'd never find anyone as competent as herself. Maybe she was right. Elise took after their father. Her hands worked magic with food and turned a simple fare into a feast fit for a king. The number of passengers dining at her eating house had doubled in just six months' time. Tonight over dinner, Elise had excitedly discussed her plans to expand and increase the number of tables.

"I just want you to find the kind of love I have," Elise said, sounding stronger and normal again. "I don't want you to marry this agent simply because you feel trapped into providing a home for an orphan."

Marianne was quiet for a moment, listening to the strange sounds of country life — the chirp of crickets, the squeak of bats, and the distant call of a barn owl. But most of all, it was the silence that had been the biggest adjustment from the constant clatter and rumbling of city life.

Did she feel trapped into providing a home for Jethro? Did she feel forced into marrying Drew? She didn't think so. Nevertheless, she could admit their decision to get married had been rash and based on a silly challenge rather than sound reasoning.

"I used to think I was in love with Reinhold," Marianne said. "I even told myself I would find him on this trip and tell him I wanted to marry him."

Elise didn't react with the least amount of surprise to her revelation. "You could visit him if you wanted to. He finally contacted me this week. He's north of here, working on a farm in Mayfield."

Mayfield had been the second stop of their placing-out trip. She'd been so close to him. Maybe they'd even passed each other without realizing it. She expected her stomach to flutter at the news, but nothing happened. No blood rushing faster. No heart thumping harder. Not even a single regret that she hadn't seen him.

"His mother died recently," Elise added. "He's worried about what will become of his sisters."

"Will Tante Brunhilde keep the girls as her own?" Marianne's thoughts returned to the months she'd lived with Mrs. Weiss and Tante Brunhilde in the cellar tenement, the dark, damp one-room hovel that had only a single window at ground level. Reinhold's sisters deserved better than that.

"Reinhold is afraid Tante Brunhilde will put the girls on a train like she did Olivia and Nicholas. And that then he may never see them again."

Marianne knew it was possible. If Tante

Brunhilde had done it once, she could do it again.

"But if he continues to send money to support her, then Tante Brunhilde will keep the girls, won't she?"

"Let's pray so. In the meantime, he hoped I'd get a message to you. He wanted you to check on the girls. Of course, he didn't realize you'd left the city."

He would have if he'd stayed in touch with her, if he'd ever written back to her. As quickly as the thought came, it flitted away. If Reinhold was in trouble, she'd help him in whatever way she could. "I'll check on them when I get back," Marianne said. "But what if it's too late? Our follow-up visits to the children might take us several more weeks."

"Perhaps you can arrange to see Reinhold before you return east?" Elise suggested.

Marianne hesitated. Wasn't that what she'd wanted?

"At the very least," Elise said, squeezing her hand, "don't you think you should see Reinhold before you go through with your crazy plans to marry Mr. Brady? What if you meet with Reinhold and discover you still have feelings for him?"

"Maybe you're right." She'd tell Drew she needed more than a week. She'd postpone, stall, and keep him at arm's length until she figured out the best course of action.

CHAPTER 15

"You've been avoiding me." Drew stepped in front of Marianne as she exited the seamstress shop. In a new yellow silk gown, she was breathtakingly beautiful, her creamy skin and brunette hair standing out even more in contrast to the pale gown. She wore a new hat as well, and her hair was pulled back into dangling curls that hung down her back.

"I've just been very busy." She sidestepped him, but he snagged her hand before she could get away.

"No. You're most definitely avoiding me. Even Jethro noticed." He nodded toward the depot down the street, where the little boy was standing outside watching them.

Marianne smiled and waved at Jethro.

They'd been in Quincy for three days. At first, Drew had taken her at her word that she was busy spending time with her sister and having dress fittings. But that morning, after breakfast when Marianne had scurried away, Jethro was the one to say what they'd both concluded. "She's mad at you, Mr. Brady. You better do something real quick to make her like you again."

Faced with another challenge, Drew spent the morning with Jethro plotting ways he could win Marianne's favor. Drew wasn't exactly sure why he'd lost her goodwill or why he felt the need to woo her, except he was driven by the desire to prove to himself that he could win her if he really wanted to.

Marianne tugged against his hold, but with Jethro watching, Drew knew he was at an advantage. She'd do anything so she didn't have to hurt the boy's feelings, even play along with whatever plans Drew had concocted.

"I have a special afternoon planned," he said.

"I'm helping Elise in the kitchen a little later."

"She told me she would be able to get by without you."

"You spoke to her without consulting me?"

Drew slipped Marianne's hand into the crook of his arm and started to stroll toward the wagon and team he'd hitched in front of the depot. "As a matter of fact, Elise is the one who gave me the idea for the afternoon."

Marianne almost stumbled. "Elise wouldn't have."

Drew smiled. Elise hadn't been overly friendly toward him. It was clear she didn't approve of the hasty marriage plans and was likely doing whatever she could to talk Marianne out of it. He wasn't sure why that fueled his desire to marry Marianne all the more, but it did.

"Elise didn't anticipate I'd take you along," he admitted. "But you can't disappoint Jethro, can you? He's looking forward to spending the afternoon with us."

The boy had climbed into the back of the wagon and was watching their approach with unbridled excitement.

Marianne forced another smile for Jethro's sake. "What exactly are we doing?"

"It's a surprise."

"I don't want a surprise."

"I thought you liked them."

"You have me confused with you."

He laughed, and this time her responding smile was genuine.

When they reached the team and wagon he'd borrowed from Mr. Gray, he helped her up onto the bench.

"Are you in on the surprise too, Jethro?"

she asked the boy as the wagon rumbled out of town.

He nodded from his spot in the bumping wagon. "Me and Mr. Brady were trying to figure out a way to make you like us again."

Guilt flashed across her face. She glanced at her gloved hands folded in her lap before lifting her eyes and meeting Drew's gaze. "Don't worry," she said to Jethro even as she looked at Drew. "I still like you both. Very much."

Her words sent both warmth and wonder to Drew's heart.

"I'll sure be mighty glad when you're married," Jethro said. "Mr. Brady said he ain't so sure you'll do it. But I keep tellin' him you won't go back on your word."

Marianne's expression betrayed her once again, but only long enough for Drew to glimpse the doubt and confusion. Truthfully, it mirrored his own. He'd been plagued with such conflicting feelings over the past few days. He knew he should find a way to release them both from their impulsive engagement. He'd allowed himself to get caught up in the moment, and he shouldn't have rushed either of them into something so serious.

But every time he was with Marianne, he could think only of all the reasons why he wanted to be with her. Besides, they still had a few days until the so-called wedding was to take place. Surely he'd figure out something before then — a way to break things off without hurting Marianne or Jethro.

"Once you're my ma and pa, you can move in with us above the depot," Jethro said. "You can take my spot in the bed, Miss Neumann. I don't mind sleeping on the floor."

"Oh my." Marianne gasped at his words.

Drew grinned. "You're too kind, Jeth. I'm sure Miss Neumann would be more than delighted to have your place in the bed."

"Only if you agree to sleep on the floor too," she said while looking away.

The thought of sleeping beside her stirred his blood, and he had to fight hard to keep the image from his mind. "I don't snore too loudly, do I, Jeth?"

"I don't think so. Leastways, Mr. Brady don't kick in his sleep," Jethro responded cheerfully, completely unaware of the undercurrent between Drew and Marianne.

Marianne began fanning herself with one of her gloved hands.

Drew chuckled. "Hopefully, Miss Neumann doesn't snore."

"I do nothing of the sort," she said, flashing indignant eyes at him. "I'm quite docile when I sleep. Or so I've been told."

"Then we'll make a boring pair." As he spoke, his attention strayed to her mouth, and he knew they'd be anything but boring together.

As though sensing his thoughts, she clamped her pretty lips together. Kissing her again was all Drew could think about for the rest of the ride, so he was grateful for Jethro's steady stream of chatter that filled the heated silence between him and Marianne.

The road north of town eventually turned into a rutted wagon path through tall grass. All around them, startled grasshoppers and butterflies rose up and flitted away. With but a few scattered clouds the June afternoon was promising to be a hot one, though the prairie breeze kept them from scorching in the sun.

When finally the path descended into a valley and a copse of trees, Drew halted the team. Ahead was the creek, the clear water glistening in the sunlight.

"We're here." Jethro jumped from the wagon and raced eagerly toward the bank.

Drew was watching Marianne's reaction to the shaded spot, relishing the delight that rippled across her features as she took in the surroundings — the oaks lining the creek, the wildflowers growing in abundance.

"It's lovely." She rewarded him with a smile that made his heart expand with something he couldn't explain, something he'd never felt before.

"Your sister said there are wild raspberries around here." He hopped down and retrieved several baskets from the wagon bed. "And she promised to make me fresh raspberry tarts if I picked her all the raspberries I could find."

With the childlike abandon he loved about her, Marianne joined in the raspberry picking, laughing and singing with him and Jethro as they attempted to fill their baskets, eating more than they picked.

He realized again, as he had other times during their journey together, that even though she was much more organized than he was and took life more seriously, she adjusted quickly to his whims. She didn't get exasperated or frustrated but rather accepted him for who he was, quirks and all. No one had ever done that before. Certainly not his family who'd tried to mold him into the proper Southern gentleman. Certainly not Charlotte who'd liked his flirting and fun ways but had ultimately expected him to fit a certain image as well.

"Is it time to go swimming, Mr. Brady?" Jethro asked, looking longingly at the cool water of the creek.

"I didn't know you could swim," Marianne said to the boy.

"Oh, I can't," he responded. "But Mr. Brady told me he'd teach me today. And you too, Miss Neumann. He's gonna teach us both to swim, so we never have to be afeared of drowning."

Marianne pushed up the brim of her hat, and her pretty but shocked brown eyes met Drew's. "It would be unseemly for me to swim —"

"Not in the least," Drew said. "It'll be fun." Elise had told him the creek was shallow and slow moving, the perfect place to teach a young boy to swim.

"I'll sit in the shade of that lovely oak tree and watch you." She picked up both hers and Jethro's baskets and started toward the tree.

Drew stepped in front of her to block her way. "Now, Miss Neumann," he said in a low voice, "it'll be no fun without you. Please, you have to join us."

She glanced again at the creek. He could tell she wanted to go in. And now it was his job to convince her that she could in fact do so. She shook her head. "I absolutely can't. It would be entirely inappropriate."

"No one else will ever have to know."

She stared again at the water. "No. I really can't. I have nothing to wear."

"I asked the maid at Elise's house to pack a bag with an old dress." He nodded to the back of the wagon where a small valise sat.

Her eyes widened.

Jethro was grinning. "See, Miss Neumann? You can go swimming with me after all."

A smile tugged at the corners of her lips. "Maybe I'll get my feet wet."

Drew wasn't about to tell her he was planning to make sure she was thoroughly soaked by the time they were done. He merely handed her the bag and nodded to an area of thick brush. "You can change over there. I promise Jeth and I will keep our backs to you and eyes on the creek."

In no time, she'd changed and was tiptoeing gingerly in the creek behind Jethro, who'd stripped down to his linen drawers. Drew had shed his coat and hat and socks and shoes, rolled up his pants and shirtsleeves, but had decided against baring himself any further in the presence of a lady.

Their clothing would weigh them down a little, yet the creek wasn't deep, only up to their waists. Jethro plunged into the creek while Drew hung on to him, swirling the boy around and letting him get accustomed to the feel of the water. Marianne stood close to the bank, ankle-deep in the creek.

As he was working with Jethro, he tried not to stare at her bare calves. But his gaze kept returning there nonetheless. When at last Jethro started making progress, he crooked a finger at Marianne, grinned, and beckoned her to step deeper.

"I'm perfectly fine where I am," she said, stirring the water with one of her feet.

"Don't make me come and get you."

Next to him, Jethro was doggy-paddling, and he stopped to watch the interaction with a wide grin. With his feet touching the bottom, he had to hold his chin high to keep it out of the water.

"Mr. Brady," she said, "You wouldn't dare drag me out there."

He started toward her, the water and his wet trousers slowing his steps.

At his advance, her eyes widened, and she took a wobbly step backward.

"Miss Neumann, you should know by now not to dare me to do anything."

"Ah yes, I should have remembered that. Even so, I don't believe you're so callous to my wishes that you'd force me deeper into the water against my will."

"Don't worry. I'm not callous to your wishes." Then he sent a spray of water her way so that it splashed against her dress.

Surprise registered on her face momentarily, but then she reached down and sent a wave of water back at him.

He grinned and continued toward her.

She splashed him again. And then again, as if the water would slow his progress. When he was almost upon her, she spun away and started to run toward shore — or at least made a brave attempt at it. He was much more nimble in the water than she was, and within a few seconds he had hold of her waist and scooped her up into his arms so that he was holding her like an infant.

As he turned and headed back toward the creek, she squirmed and squealed with laughter. "Jethro!" she called. "Save me!"

The boy's laughter mingled with Marianne's, and Drew couldn't imagine a sweeter sound than the two of them together.

By the time he reached the middle of the creek, she was clinging to him as the water came up and bathed her, soaking her back and legs. For a long moment he just held her, content to feel her arms around his neck and the press of her body against his.

"This isn't so bad, now, is it?" he asked.

"I guess not," she said, dropping one of her hands into the water and swishing it back and forth.

"Then I think you're ready to go under."

"Go under?"

"Yes. Plug your nose." Before she could protest, he sank down, dragging her with him.

She barely had time to pinch her nose before he plunged them both underwater. The creek was clean and clear enough that he didn't close his eyes but instead watched her reaction. With the sunlight streaking through the water and the bubbles, he took in the delight and fascination on her face. Her long hair swirled around her, and his heart ached at her beauty.

He kept them submerged for only a few seconds before pushing back up and breaking through the surface. She spluttered and laughed and gasped, all the while clinging to him as if her life depended upon it.

"Do it again!" Jethro cried happily. "Do it again!"

Drew was all too happy to oblige and sank back under the water again. Before long, Marianne had wiggled free of his embrace and was splashing around on her own, dipping below the surface. They attempted to swim and floated on their backs and played tag until finally Jethro called out that he was hungry.

Drew spread a blanket in the sun and unpacked the basket of sandwiches, sweet pickles, oatmeal cookies, and lemonade Mrs. Gray had provided for their outing. Dripping wet, they settled themselves on the blanket and devoured every bit of the food. Satisfied and full and drying out, they moved into the shade of an oak on the side of the gently sloping bank.

Drew lay back and pulled Jethro into the crook of one arm and Marianne into the other. He was glad when Marianne snuggled against him, settling in as though it was the most natural thing in the world for her to lie next to him. He didn't bring any attention to the fact that her damp clothes clung to her body and outlined her curves. He was unwilling to disturb the peace of the moment. Instead, he kept his eyes on the leaves overhead and entertained them with escapades of his own childhood swimming adventures.

Eventually the deep rise and fall of Jethro's chest told him the boy had fallen asleep. He glanced down to see that Marianne's eyes were closed and that she seemed to be on the verge of sleep as well.

He allowed himself to stare at her delicate features, the graceful lines of her eyes and nose, the smoothness of her cheeks and chin, and the dip in her upper lip. She released a soft sigh, and he tightened his hold. She responded by burrowing further into his side, laying her hand across his chest and turning her head so that her lips were only inches from his.

The desire to lean in and kiss her was so powerful, his body tensed with the need. *God, help me, but I want to marry this woman.* His silent prayer rose in a plea for help. He needed God to keep him from hurting her in any way. He truly wanted to cherish her. And surely a soft kiss on her brow wouldn't hurt anything.

He bent in and pressed his lips against her forehead in the spot between her eyebrows.

Marianne smiled at the tenderness of his touch. The day had been wonderful in just about every way. And now in the shade, with a soothing breeze lulling them to sleep, she couldn't imagine a more perfect way to end the outing.

His touch moved to one of her eyelids, and only then did she realize the feathery brush was from his lips. Her heart jumped in her chest, and she held her breath as he sweetly and gently moved to her other eye and left a whisper of a kiss there too.

She didn't stir, didn't want the moment to end, especially as he moved his mouth to her cheek. She expected the trail of kisses to continue until he made it to her jaw. So when he began to pull back, as though wrenching himself away from her, she decided not to let him. She chased after his lips, finding them with her own. Lifting her hand to his hair, she whispered against his partly open mouth, "Drew . . ."

He needed no other invitation. His lips came against hers with a hunger the other, softer kisses had apparently awakened. The hard, devouring pressure consumed her all at once. She would have moaned with the pleasure of the kiss, but it was so deep that she could only dig her fingers into his hair to communicate her need for more.

"Mr. Brady?" came a small voice. "Why are you eating Miss Neumann?"

Drew jerked back at the same time she scrambled away from him. She crawled off the blanket and stood in the sunshine out from under the shade of the tree at an appropriate distance from Drew.

Drew hadn't moved except to grin down at Jethro. "I wasn't eating her, buddy."

"Then what were you doing?" Jethro didn't move from the crook of Drew's arm but was wide awake now.

Marianne twisted at the tangled loose strands of her damp hair, mortified the boy had witnessed such an impassioned outburst between her and Drew.

"That's the kind of kiss you give the woman you're about to marry," Drew said in his Southern twang. When he looked up at her, the passion simmering in his eyes made her breath catch. For a moment, she could almost believe he really did want to marry her, that his proposal was more than just an answer to a challenge.

"I ain't never seen a kiss like that," Jethro said with disgust in his voice. "Believe me, I ain't gonna kiss a girl thataway."

Drew ruffled Jethro's red curls. "See that you don't. At least until you find the right woman." Was she the right woman? As if he'd heard her unasked question, he added unabashedly, "Like I have."

It was then she realized she wanted to marry him too, that she didn't just want to do so for Jethro or because she had to prove something. She wanted him.

She offered him a shy smile and was relieved when he gave her a big, happy grin that told her he felt the same way.

Jethro seemed to forget about witnessing their kiss and ran off to swim in the creek again. Drew joined him for a while, and Marianne changed out of her damp clothes into the new yellow gown Fanny had made for her.

It still amazed her that Fanny had her own shop. The young Irish woman had been among the poor women at Miss Pendleton's Seventh Street Mission when she and Elise worked there last year. Fanny acted as their tormenter, inciting the other women against them.

The Irishwoman had been part of Elise's group of women sent to Illinois by the Children's Aid Society during the financial crisis, which hit the major cities in the East last fall. Somehow, during all the hardships of those early months in Quincy, Fanny and Elise became friends. And now Fanny was operating a flourishing business as Quincy's main seamstress. Every time Marianne had gone for a fitting, it was clear that the young woman was quite satisfied with her new life.

Marianne returned to the blanket with a hairbrush and watched Drew and Jethro play together. She was too distracted by the sight of Drew to make much of an effort at brushing the tangles out of her hair. His shirt clung to his body, outlining his muscular chest and arms and making her think about being wrapped against that chest within those arms.

When he climbed out of the creek and shook himself like a wet dog, she had to look away lest he read her thoughts. He came and sat down next to her, and for a little while they watched Jethro, applauded his efforts as he yelled "Watch me!" over and over.

"He's quite the fish," she said once Jethro was distracted by collecting rocks from the creek bed. "He learned to swim quickly."

"All children should learn how to swim," Drew said somberly. "For their own safety."

Was he thinking of George again, of how he believed the boy had drowned?

Before she could ask him, he reached for the brush in her hand. He took it from her and held it up. "May I?"

"Of course."

He scooted behind her and placed the brush against her hair. She leaned out of his reach. "I thought you were planning to brush your own hair," she said with a laugh. "You most certainly cannot brush mine."

"Why not? You're not making any progress, and I only want to offer my expert services."

"Expert services? Exactly how many

women have given you the privilege of brushing their hair that you're such the expert?"

Even though she teased, she couldn't keep a tiny prick of jealousy at bay or the realization that she didn't know much about Drew's past. Sure, he'd shared funny stories, like he had earlier about swimming with his brother, but he never divulged the more serious memories such as how he felt about his family, his parents, or his life.

"To be honest," he said, "I've never actually brushed any woman's hair. But I've watched you and other agents comb the girls' hair. Doesn't that qualify me as an expert?"

She pretended to weigh the decision as if she were a judge handing out a sentence. "Very well. I'll allow you to put to the test your expertise. But under one condition."

He quirked a brow.

"You'll tell me more about your family and your past."

His expression fell, and clouds blew through his blue-green eyes as swiftly as a summer storm forming on the horizon. He twirled the brush in his hand and didn't answer her.

"Would it help if I promised to tell you my dark secrets too?" she asked, not entirely sure she wanted to reveal everything to him either. But if they were planning to go through with marriage by the end of the week, didn't they owe it to each other to be completely honest?

He studied the brush and then met her gaze. "You drive a hard bargain."

She smiled with what she hoped was sympathy and encouragement and then settled back into the spot she'd occupied before. He tentatively touched her hair, which made her body tense in anticipation.

His fingers moved higher and then skimmed down. When he lifted them and dug into her thick hair again, she closed her eyes in pleasure. "So you've decided to comb my hair with your fingers instead of the brush?"

"I can't help it." His voice was low.

"Then I may have to relieve you from the job." She tried to keep her voice light and playful, knowing it would be all too easy to fall back into his arms again.

"Your hair is so beautiful." This time he brought the brush up and began to stroke gently, almost reverently.

She savored the tenderness and the delicious feelings he was eliciting in her. The ripple of the wind in the leaves overhead and Jethro's splashing nearby were the only sounds until Drew finally spoke again.

"My father didn't want me to be a teacher." There was a hint of bitterness in his tone.

She wanted to ask him why. But she held her questions, deciding it was best to let him share what he wanted to in his own way.

"He told me he wouldn't support me or pay for any more of my education if I became a teacher, said there wasn't any prestige in teaching children. He had his heart set on my becoming a minister, had connections at one of the largest churches in Savannah. And he had hopes I'd eventually move into politics. Later, when I dropped out of seminary and returned home, he threatened to disown me."

"He sounds like a hard man to please."

"Very hard. He's well educated, a lawyer, and thought teaching was beneath me."

"But you became a teacher anyway?" she asked.

"I guess he expected me to tire of it and see the error of my ways."

"I have no doubt you proved him wrong and became the best teacher Georgia has ever known."

She expected him to agree or at least to make a jest, but he was silent.

"What about your fiancée?" Marianne

couldn't stop herself from asking about the other woman in Drew's life. She wanted to ask what had happened and if he still cared for her, but she forced herself not to pry too deeply. "Did she support your teaching?"

"She tolerated it, but in the end she persuaded me to return to the seminary and continue my theological studies. After being wed, we planned to move back to Virginia so I could finish."

Marianne suddenly didn't like his former fiancée at all. "Then she didn't see you with the children to realize how wonderful you are with them."

He didn't respond, but instead brushed her hair in long strokes. She'd almost begun to believe he'd shared all he could, that he'd reached the limit, when he spoke again in a choked voice. "There was an accident a week before the wedding. One of my students died. I left and haven't been back since."

Marianne twisted around to face him. His expression was etched with the same anguish she'd seen there the night he'd thought George was dead. Now she understood.

He hung his head as though expecting her condemnation. Instead, she pressed a hand to his cheek as she had that night and swiveled his face so he was looking in her eyes. His turmoil tore into her. Had his fiancée rejected him because of the accident? Maybe his father had as well.

"I'm sorry," she whispered, her eyes filling with tears at the thought of the incredible pain he must have gone through.

"Don't be sorry," he whispered back. "I'm the only one to blame for all that happened."

She wanted to ask him exactly what had happened. How had his student died? But she had the feeling she'd already pushed him to share more than he had in a long time with anyone else. She prayed that in time he'd heal enough to share the rest with her.

"I lost my sister." She blurted the truth, and once the words were out, she started to tremble.

He didn't seem the least surprised by her declaration. "Is she who you've been looking for in the record book and asking about everywhere we go?"

She nodded, and it was her turn to drop her head as the shame of all that had happened fell upon her. "I was hoping to find a lead of some kind on this trip. But I haven't found a single clue."

"I'll help you," he offered.

When she chanced a peek at his face, there wasn't a hint of condemnation there, only understanding. Surely, he wouldn't be so kind if he understood how much she was to blame. "When Elise left for her new job in Quincy, she put me in charge of Sophie and Olivia and Nicholas. I was supposed to keep them safe, supposed to keep us together, supposed to be strong enough to handle it all. But I failed." The words poured out about living at the Seventh Street Mission, the lie about being pregnant, moving in with Reinhold's family, and then losing Olivia and Nicholas, as well as Sophie.

He watched her with serious eyes, his brows slanted.

She waited for him to pull away, for disappointment or disgust to flitter into his eyes.

"You were with Reinhold?" he asked.

Of all the things she'd just bared to him, that was his only question? Did he think she was a loose woman now? Embarrassment slashed through her. "Of course not," she murmured. "I've never even kissed anyone, until you . . ."

Nice job, Marianne. Way to make yourself look like a bumbling idiot.

"Good. Because if he dared to use you, I'd have to find him and beat him to a pulp." This time Drew's voice contained a distinct note of possessiveness.

"Reinhold would never do anything to dishonor me. He's a good man. In fact, he's wonderful —"

"You could have stopped at 'good man.' "

"Are you jealous?" She managed a smile.

"Absolutely." He smiled back, but it wasn't lighthearted. It smoldered. "The merest thought of any other man touching you makes me crazy."

Before she could study him further, he turned her around so she was facing forward again. He ran his fingers through her hair, and she expected him to resume the brushing. Instead, he slid his arms around her middle and pulled her back against his chest. He folded her against him, and she relaxed in his embrace, wrapping her arms over his. Her chest ached with the sweetness of the moment. He hadn't rejected her or thought any less of her for losing Sophie and Olivia and Nicholas. He still wanted her.

She snuggled against him, and when his lips pressed against her hair above her ear, she released a breath and for the first time in a very long time felt as though she was finally home.

"Are you eating Miss Neumann again?"

Jethro called from the bank.

Drew's laughter rumbled against her. As if to defy Jethro, Drew angled his head and pressed his lips against her neck, this time below her ear.

She gasped and wiggled to free herself from him before she totally embarrassed herself in her reactions to his touch.

He laughed and moved after her.

She climbed across the blanket out of his reach. "Andrew Brady," she chided, "we have an audience."

"Marianne Neumann." His eyes twinkled with merriment and desire. "We may have an audience now, but in four days we won't."

"Then you must wait." As much as she longed to be back in his arms, they needed to be careful not to give in to any more intimacies, not until they were married.

As if realizing how easy it would be to let their passion spiral out of control, Drew nodded. "It might be the longest four days of my life, but I'll wait. You're worth it."

CHAPTER 16

Reinhold finished hitching the mare and rubbed a hand along her muscled flank.

"Your girl Lucinda wants you," Liverpool said from the wagon bench where he was waiting.

Reinhold didn't bother to look up or respond to the youth's snide comment. The orphan came home with Mr. Turner last week and had been trouble ever since. The only good thing about the situation was that the boy seemed to take to him more than Higgins. Perhaps Higgins and Liverpool were too much alike to stand each other. Higgins would have only soured the boy's attitude all the more. Whatever the case, he'd become Reinhold's shadow.

Reinhold was used to boys like Liverpool, had lived and worked with young men even more hardened than this one. He always put up with them and hoped they could see in him a better way of life. Maybe Liverpool would eventually too. Even so, there were times, like now, when he longed for peace and quiet.

"Looks like she's got food for you," Liverpool continued. "Think there's enough for me too?"

After a full day's work, Reinhold didn't particularly want to ride into town and miss supper. But Mr. Turner had paid him today, and he was desperate to send word to his aunt that money was on the way. He just prayed it wasn't too late, that she hadn't decided to give up his sisters yet.

He couldn't chance waiting another day, even though he was exhausted and hot and hungry. If he waited, tomorrow would be just as busy as today with hoeing the cornfields. And tomorrow evening he'd feel exactly the same as tonight.

Reinhold straightened as Lucinda neared the wagon. She held a dish that was heaped with pieces of fried chicken, golden-brown biscuits slathered in butter, string green beans, and beets. His stomach growled at the sight of it.

"I thought you might be hungry," she said shyly. Her thin face turned as red as the beets. She bowed her head, giving him full view of her dark hair, parted down the middle as usual and pulled into a severe knot at the back.

"Thank you, Lucinda." He took the plate gratefully, hoping Mrs. Turner wouldn't discover her daughter had fed him in spite of her strict rules about mealtime. He didn't want Lucinda getting into trouble on account of him.

Lucinda nodded, watching him a moment as if waiting for him to take a bite.

He obliged her by picking up a chicken leg and tearing off a hunk of meat with his teeth. The warm, flavorful juices ran into his mouth and made his stomach rumble all the more. "It's delicious," he said.

Her face beamed, making her long pointy features come to life. "I'll leave a piece of cake for you on your bed."

Liverpool snorted in a way that made Reinhold keenly aware of the fact that Lucinda was perhaps growing too attached to him. He hadn't meant to lead her on in any way. He'd only tried to be kind and appreciative, the same way he'd treated his mother and sisters.

Had she been reading more into his actions? He started to shake his head. "You don't need to leave me any cake —"

"But it's your favorite." The pleasure in her eyes faded, and her shoulders slumped.

How would she know his favorite kind of

cake? He didn't even know himself what he liked best.

"You can leave me his piece," Liverpool said, still sitting on the wagon bench.

"Never mind," Reinhold interjected. "I'm sure I'll be hungry again when I get home and would appreciate the cake."

Her smile returned, albeit more hesitantly.

"That girl's got it bad for you," Liverpool said as the wagon rattled down the rutted path toward town. He stuffed a biscuit into his mouth, devouring it in only a few bites. While the Turners kept the boy well fed, Reinhold knew it was difficult for street children to shed the habits formed after years of starving and scrounging. Liverpool had likely learned to eat fast or lose his meal to someone stronger and quicker than him.

"Mister, all you need to do is show her a little more interest," Liverpool said through another mouthful, "and you'll get more than just the cake on your bed."

Crass talk was nothing new to Reinhold. He'd heard it all and then some. But that didn't mean he liked it. "Listen, Miss Turner is a fine woman. Not the woman for me, but still, she deserves my respect. And I won't use her to sate my own pleasure."

Liverpool stopped chewing and stared at him as though he'd gone crazy. "She's practically throwing herself at you."

Was she? Reinhold shifted uncomfortably on the hard bench. He needed to be more careful not to give her the wrong impression. "I'm not planning to be intimate with any woman until I get married — *if* I get married."

Liverpool's mouth dropped open even more. "What's wrong with you? You planning to be a priest or something?"

"Do I look like one?"

Liverpool shook his head.

"I'm just an ordinary man, but I'm not rushing ahead and doing my own selfish thing by having any woman I want. Too many problems come from that kind of living." Reinhold didn't have to spell out for Liverpool the problems that resulted from infidelity. They'd been surrounded by it in the city: prostitutes with unwanted, abandoned children, wives cast aside by unfaithful husbands who had no means to support themselves, drunken and abusive men who beat their women and children.

"No, when the right woman comes along," he continued, "I'm planning to get married first before sharing my bed. In the long run, waiting until marriage is the safest and most satisfying way. That's the way God designed it. Unfortunately, a lot of people ignore the guidelines He set in place, do it their way instead, and get hurt."

Liverpool was silent, and Reinhold prayed he was taking his words to heart. Actually, the words belonged to Reverend Bedell from the Seventh Street Mission. Reinhold had sat in on some of his church services and seen the way the reverend treated his fiancée, Miss Pendleton, with restraint and respect.

Of course, Reinhold had never gotten any words of wisdom while growing up, especially not from his father. No, all he'd gotten from his father was the sting of his belt and the bruising force of his fists. Reinhold tried to be different with his own siblings, giving his brothers the encouragement he'd never received. And now maybe he could encourage this young man too.

Reinhold surveyed the neighbor's cornfields on either side of the road and gauged the growth of the corn. It was knee-high, perhaps a little taller than the corn belonging to the Turners. But the tender shoots were growing fast in the hot and humid weather they'd had recently and promised to be a bountiful harvest. Reinhold prayed his potato crop would be just as plentiful.

He still hadn't figured out how he'd be able to earn enough by autumn to put a down payment on a place of his own. But he wasn't giving up just yet.

"So you got someone else then?" Liverpool finally asked.

Reinhold shook his head and debated whether to say anything more or not. His past was still too painful to dwell on. And yet perhaps he needed to face his pain and talk about it if he was ever going to heal. "The woman I love and thought I would marry ended up falling in love with someone else."

"Serves you right," Liverpool said. "If you'd claimed her while you could, maybe she wouldn't have walked away from you."

"I'm glad she got someone better than me," Reinhold said. "She's happy now, and that's what matters most."

Liverpool snickered. "You're pathetic."

Maybe, but the truth was, Elise was much better off with a wealthy man like Thornton Quincy. Thornton could give her everything she wanted or needed much more than he ever could. As hard as it had been to leave her behind in Quincy, he'd done the right thing by heading out on his own.

He just hoped she'd received his telegram from earlier in the week and sent word to Marianne to check on his sisters. Marianne would do it. She was a sweet and caring girl.

Although she'd tricked his mother and aunt last fall with a false pregnancy and claimed he was the father, he knew she'd done so out of desperation because she needed a place to live. She'd cared so deeply about her family that she was willing to lie for them. If there was even a hint of trouble now with his sisters, she'd do everything she could to help them. He had no doubt about it.

Even so, he wanted to make sure Tante Brunhilde received the money as speedily as possible. He gave the reins a shake to urge the horses into a faster trot.

The miles passed quickly, and as they rounded a bend in the dirt road on the final stretch before town, he saw several boys jumping in Percy's pond. The small body of water belonged to Mr. Percy as part of his farmland, but he allowed the kids to swim in it whenever they wanted.

As Reinhold drew nearer, the boys waved in greeting. Reinhold tipped the brim of his hat in response and noticed Liverpool was looking the opposite way, almost as if he didn't want to watch the boys having fun.

"I can drop you off here if you want to go swimming while I'm in town," Reinhold offered.

Liverpool shook his head. "No. I don't swim."

"It's not hard to learn," Reinhold said.

"I ain't going and that's the end of it." Liverpool's voice rose in anger.

Reinhold shrugged. "Suit yourself."

At a sudden chorus of shouts from near the pond, the skin at the back of Reinhold's neck prickled. Was someone hurt? He scanned the boys, counting the three from before. They were all accounted for. But had one of them hurt himself?

Reinhold tugged on the reins and slowed the wagon. "Everything all right over there?" he yelled.

One of the boys shook his head. Even from a distance, Reinhold could see he was terrified. Before the frightened boy could speak, one of his friends called out, "Ernie said he saw something at the bottom of the pond."

Reinhold steered the team off the road toward the pond.

"What are you doing?" Liverpool asked. "Don't go over there."

"I need to make sure the boys are all right." Reinhold guided the team into the tall grass, slowing them down.

Liverpool shook his head. "Do you have to be a do-gooder wherever you go?"

"If you were one of those boys in trouble, you'd be happy to see me."

Liverpool cursed under his breath. And when they arrived at the edge of the pond, he sat stiffly on the bench while Reinhold jumped down and headed to where the boys were clustered.

The three of them were younger than Reinhold first thought, likely around the ages of ten, eleven, or twelve. "What's going on, boys?"

"Ernie here saw a dead body lying in the muck at the bottom," said one of the boys, his eyes the size of the mare's when she was spooked.

Ernie hugged his arms across his chest. In spite of the sun beating down on him, his teeth were chattering. Boys his age were apt to tell tales just to frighten their pals. "You sure you saw something down there?" Reinhold pressed.

The boy nodded. And when he peered into the water, he shuddered too visibly to be making up his story. Either that, or he was a very good actor.

"One of you want to dive down there and see for sure?" Reinhold asked. "It might just be a deer or calf that wandered off —"

"Ernie said it's a boy," explained the friend.

"I ain't goin' down there," the other said at the same time.

Reinhold took off his hat and scratched his sweaty head. Then he rubbed a hand across the back of his sunburned neck. It too was sticky and hot. The pond was as still as a looking glass and seemed to beckon him to jump in and cool off.

He shed his clothing and shoes until he was down to his drawers, then plunged in. Ducking his head underwater, he took pleasure in being submerged. The water was tepid, but it still felt good against his mostly bare body. He swam out to the middle before resurfacing. "Where did you see the body?" he called to the boys.

After the three boys directed him to a spot not far from the shore, he dove down again. The water was so murky that he doubted the boy had been able to see anything at all. Regardless, he swam down until he touched the bottom, which was no more than twelve feet deep. He felt around with his hands, stirring up leaves and rocks and mud.

With the pressure building in his lungs, he flipped around and surged to the surface. "Nothing," he called.

Liverpool was still up on the wagon bench. "Come on then!" he shouted. "Let's go."

"Try again," Ernie said. "A little to the

left this time."

One more try wouldn't hurt. Reinhold drew in a breath and dove back down. Once at the bottom, he swept his hand around in a wide arc back and forth. He shifted positions and tried again and was about to give up when his hand grazed something soft. He patted the fleshy object. It took his mind several seconds to register his discovery.

He jerked his hand away and almost gagged.

It was a human face — or at least what remained of it.

Reinhold had to make several more dives before he was able to remove the large stone that had been tied to the corpse. It took even more time to drag the slimy, bloated body to shore. The boys were all too scared and sick to their stomachs to be of any help as he worked to get the body out of the pond.

Once the person was laid out on the grass, Reinhold could see why the boys were retching. The flesh had begun to decompose, and the sight and smell was nauseating. However, the face was still mostly intact. Hopefully the body would be identifiable. Going by the slight size and build, Reinhold guessed the dead boy to have been twelve or thirteen.

Reinhold stood dripping in the grass next to the corpse. There hadn't been any news recently about a missing boy. Not that he'd heard about anyway. One thing was clear, though. Whoever this boy was, he'd been thrown into the pond on purpose. What other reason could there be for having a stone tied to him, if not to weigh him down and make his body sink to the bottom?

Had the boy been murdered? Had someone drowned him? Or was he killed first and then tossed into the pond?

Reinhold shook his head as he stared down at the poor dead boy. "Any idea who this might be?"

With their hands covering their noses and mouths, the three boys mumbled something about not knowing who it was.

Liverpool hopped down from the wagon and walked over to where the body lay. He looked down at the dead boy's white, almost translucent face. The eyes and mouth were wide open. "I know who this is," he said matter-of-factly.

"You do?" Reinhold asked in surprise. Liverpool had been in Mayfield only a week, and most of that time was spent in the Turners' cornfields.

Liverpool nodded and looked away. "It's

Ned. He's one of the other kids like me who came to Mayfield looking for farming work."

"Then you knew him?" Reinhold reached for his trousers and jerked them up over his wet legs.

"Yeah, I knew him. I thought he jumped the rail and left town."

"Do you have any idea how he ended up here?"

Liverpool peered into the distance, his eyes as black and deadened as the pond scum that stuck to Ned's body. "I think I know what happened."

CHAPTER 17

An urgent knocking on the front door of Elise's home woke Marianne. She sat up in her bed with a start, her heart pattering hard in her chest. Her feet were tangled in her covers, and her hair spilled in disarray over her shoulders.

Through her open window that faced the front of the house, she heard the knocking again, more insistent than before. Had something happened to Drew?

She wasn't sure why that was her first thought, except he'd been a part of her restless dreams. She'd had a difficult time falling asleep, unable to put him and their marriage out of her mind. The ceremony was scheduled for tomorrow at noon.

All week she'd kept the thought of the marriage at a distance by telling herself they still had time to change their minds. But the week had passed all too quickly. She and Drew had fun helping Elise in her kitchen. They shucked peas, plucked feathers off chickens, peeled carrots, and a dozen other tasks Elise had given them. They'd spent all their time together either helping in the eating house, taking walks, or playing games with Jethro, their constant companion.

Marianne decided that spending time with Drew in public places was for the best, as even then the heat between them flared all too often. Elise had wryly mentioned she could start a fire in a cold coal stove with the sparks that flew between Marianne and Drew. She hadn't exactly given her blessing on the marriage, but she seemed to be accepting the fact that Drew genuinely cared about her.

Marianne let her feet slide from the bed to the thick rug covering the floor. She reached for the summer robe Elise had given her to go with the frilly nightdress, slipped it on, and tied it closed while she moved to the window.

She had no doubt Drew cared about her and that she did for him. But should they get married so hastily? The question had plagued her until she'd finally dozed off, only to be awakened by the knocking on the door.

Yes, they'd spent almost every waking moment together over the past month of traveling. She'd gotten to know Drew better than she had almost anyone else. He'd finally opened up and shared about his past. Maybe not everything, but it had been enough for now.

Besides, if they were going to be traveling together for at least the next month, wouldn't they be better off married? Then they wouldn't have to worry about falling prey to temptation or about any further improper conduct, especially in front of Jethro.

But was their physical attraction enough to justify getting married?

She pulled back the curtain and peered out at the dark street and then down to the door. In the moonlight she caught a glimpse of Drew's blond hair.

Her breath caught with renewed worry. She'd been right to have the premonition. Something *was* wrong. "Drew," she called, sticking her head out the window.

At the sound of her voice, he stepped away from the door. She didn't have to see his face to sense he was tense with anxiety.

"What's wrong?" she asked in a loud whisper.

"Jethro's sick," Drew answered. "He's burning up with a fever."

"I don't understand. He was fine when I tucked him in earlier. He had a runny nose, but that was all."

"He woke up crying and complaining of a sore throat."

"Did you send for the doctor?"

"Yes, he's with Jeth now and so is Mrs. Gray."

"I'll be down as soon as I can," Marianne said.

Drew nodded. He'd come to care deeply for Jethro as much as she had. He was a special little boy who'd taken up residence in both of their hearts.

Marianne hurried to get dressed, not bothering to fix her hair. Instead, she rushed downstairs and reassured the young maid who'd responded to the knocking that she could go back to bed and that she didn't need to awaken Elise, who would only reprimand Marianne for leaving with Drew in the middle of the night.

With Drew's hand in hers, they ran back to the depot and clattered breathlessly up the stairs. The doctor was closing up his leather case as they tiptoed into the room. The lantern on the bedside table was lit and illuminated petite Mrs. Gray, who had pulled a chair up to the double bed and was holding a cloth against Jethro's forehead.

"How is he?" Marianne asked, releasing Drew and stepping to the bedside.

"Sleeping again," Mrs. Gray whispered.

The lantern's glow turned Jethro's face a sickly yellow. His red hair was curly from his perspiration and stuck to his face. His breathing was quick and shallow. Otherwise, Marianne couldn't see anything else wrong with him.

"I believe he has the measles," the doctor said. "He's showing the early signs of it — inflamed eyes, a few white spots in his mouth. But we won't know for certain for a day or two more, when or if he develops a rash."

Everyone knew that measles was highly contagious. But Jethro hadn't been around anyone who had the illness. "Where could he have caught it?" Marianne asked. "Are there any reports of the measles in Quincy?"

The doctor shook his head. "Not at the moment. Even so, we'll need to keep him quarantined. We can't take any chances."

"Of course." She reached for the boy's hand and held it. Children — especially younger children — died every year from the measles. A new worry seized her heart. What if Jethro didn't make it? Because of his years of malnutrition, he was weaker and smaller in stature than other seven-year-olds.

As if sensing her anxiety, Drew slipped an arm around her waist. "He's stronger than he looks, Marianne," he reassured her. "If he does have the measles, he'll make it through just fine. You'll see."

She nodded and took strength from Drew's embrace and also his confidence.

The doctor picked up his bag and moved toward the door. "If any of you haven't had the measles yet, I suggest you leave now and quarantine yourselves."

Nothing would make Marianne stay away.

Drew pulled back to meet her gaze, but she avoided it. She wasn't leaving. Before she could say anything in her own defense, Drew muttered angrily under his breath and at the same time swept her off her feet into his arms. Cradling her against his chest, in three long strides he was out the door and already starting down the stairs.

"Put me down this instant!" she insisted.

"You're going back to Elise's house and staying there."

She wiggled in his arms, trying to free herself from his hold. "Jethro needs me."

"Mrs. Gray is with him."

"But he doesn't know her. When he wakes up he'll be worried, and he'll want me."

"I'll be with him too."

She tried to free herself again, but Drew was strong and his hold unbreakable. He didn't stop until he barged through the front door of Elise's home, this time making enough noise to wake the entire household. He barked orders to the maid and followed her up the stairs as she directed him to Marianne's room. Once inside, he stopped in front of the enormous canopy bed.

"If I put you down, do you promise you'll stay here?" His voice was firm.

She hesitated. She didn't know if she could follow through on such a promise.

"Please, Marianne," he said more gently, "if not for your sake, then for the sake of others. Think about the people you'll expose. You don't want that, do you?"

"No," she whispered. She didn't realize there were tears on her cheeks until Drew bent and kissed a spot below her eye where a tear was escaping. She wrapped her arms around his neck and buried her face against his chest as more tears trickled down.

"It'll be all right, darlin'," he whispered against her hair.

"What's going on?" Elise asked. She was standing in the doorway, holding a lantern high. The light fell over the rumpled bed and the two of them in their intimate hold.

Marianne pulled back from Drew. As if realizing how compromising their situation appeared, Drew lowered her to her feet but kept his arm around her to steady her.

She wished she could come up with a witty remark as easily as Elise would have. But she wasn't a quick talker and neither could she mask her heartache. "The doctor thinks Jethro has the measles, and now it's possible I could catch the illness too."

"How about you, Elise?" Drew asked. "Have you ever had the measles?"

She shook her head. The lantern light cast a pallor over her face and caught the glint of fear in her eyes.

"Then the two of you will keep each other in good company over the next few days while you're in isolation."

Elise's face registered a resignation that Marianne wished she could muster.

"What about the wedding?" Marianne asked. Once the words were out, she felt silly for bringing it up, like a petulant child who'd been denied her dessert. She wasn't that eager to be married to Drew, was she?

His grin was slow and knowing. "Don't worry. I'll check with the reverend tomorrow and see if he's willing to come here and perform the ceremony."

"Or perhaps this is God's way of intervening," Elise suggested, "giving the two of you more time to think about what you're doing."

Maybe Elise was right. Now that Jethro was sick, what was the rush? Should they take more time to think about it?

"I've had more than enough time," Drew said in answer to Elise's question as well as Marianne's silent one. "I want to marry Marianne, and nothing will stop me."

His declaration went straight to her heart, filling it with a warmth that chased away all the doubts she'd had earlier in the night. He reached for her hand and lifted it to his lips. Then he kissed the tip of each finger softly, one after the other. But it was the shining look in his eyes that caused her pulse to patter to a halt.

She knew he was crazy about her, and she couldn't deny she felt the same way. But was it love or infatuation?

"If the reverend is willing and able," he whispered, "promise you'll marry me tomorrow."

Marianne shifted so she couldn't see her sister but instead focused on Drew. She brushed the dampness from her cheeks and tucked a strand of hair behind her ear. Jethro would want them to get married tomorrow. In fact, he'd be disappointed if he learned they'd postponed their wedding on account of his illness. Besides, if Drew was so eager, how could she deny him?

She smiled and nodded.

"Good." He kissed her hand again before releasing it. "Until tomorrow, then."

Marianne slept fitfully and woke up tired. Her eyelids were heavy, and with every swallow of her coffee at breakfast she felt something like an ache in her throat. She knew she was only imagining symptoms and that if she caught the measles, she'd know it.

Nevertheless, the morning passed with agonizing slowness. She kept worrying over Jethro and watching out the window for Drew coming down the street, listening for his confident steps or his friendly voice.

Had he really meant what he said last night, that nothing would stop him from marrying her?

Mr. Gray finally came by to let her know that Drew was relieving Mrs. Gray at Jethro's bedside. The stationmaster's wife had spent the rest of the night keeping the boy's fever from spiking higher. Now that Jethro was resting more peacefully, Mrs. Gray had decided to get a few hours of sleep for herself.

Marianne dressed in another new gown Elise had given her, this one a deep amethyst that made her eyes and hair appear darker and her skin creamier. She'd also taken extra care with her hair, even accepting the maid's help to style it with cascading ringlets.

"You look lovely," Elise said when Marianne came down to the parlor where they'd decided to hold the wedding. The room had a tall ceiling with elaborate cornices like all the other rooms. A large marble fireplace took up nearly one entire wall and had a gilded mantel mirror above it. The furniture was simple but tasteful, brightened with colorful cushions that matched the Venetian rug covering the polished black oak floor.

Marianne pressed a hand to her stomach to settle the butterflies that kept fluttering every few minutes. "I only wish Sophie were here."

"Remember, Sophie wasn't at my wedding either," Elise said as she adjusted the bow in Marianne's hair.

Elise was silent as she walked around Marianne and inspected her, like a mother of the bride. Marianne waited for Elise to say something more, to object, to try to talk her out of the wedding. But she hadn't said anything of the kind all morning.

"I thought you'd be trying harder today to persuade me against getting married," Marianne said.

Elise stood back. "Since you've apparently made up your mind to go through with this impulsive wedding, I decided I need to be supportive and do my best to help you make it work."

Marianne had been prepared to defend herself again but instead faltered for a reply. "Then . . . you like Drew?"

"Oh, I like him well enough. In fact, as I've gotten to know him better, I like him more every day."

"But . . . ?" Marianne could hear the hesitation in Elise's words.

"But I'm still not sure if he's in love with you or simply having fun trying to woo you. Once the conquest is over, I hope he doesn't have regrets about getting married." As usual, Elise's observations were astute.

Marianne lowered herself into one of the wing chairs and sighed. "Once we're back in New York City, what if he decides he made a mistake?"

Elise took the elegant chair next to hers. "Has he told you he loves you?"

"No," Marianne admitted slowly, wondering if the shine in his eyes last night counted.

"But I haven't told him that yet either."

"Well? Do you love him?"

Marianne picked at a loose thread that dangled from her sleeve. "I think I do."

"Then tell him so."

"Don't you think he should be the one to tell me first? What if he says it in return only because he feels pressured to?"

A knock on the front door halted their conversation. The knock was followed by men's voices, one of them distinctly Drew's, another Mr. Gray's, and the third was the reverend's. The butterflies in Marianne's stomach took flight again.

As Drew entered the room, she rose from her chair. She smoothed a hand over her silk skirt and waited for him to see her. When his gaze found her, his conversation came to an abrupt halt and his eyes widened. "You're absolutely stunning," he said in a winded voice.

A laugh of delight bubbled over before she could contain it. "You look quite handsome yourself." Wearing a dark suit coat with matching vest and tie, he was indeed dashing, especially because he'd taken the time to get a haircut and shave.

He introduced her to the reverend, and then they all talked about how Jethro was doing and if there were any other cases of

316

measles in the area. Finally the reverend pulled out his pocket watch. "I'm sorry to say I'm in a bit of a rush today. I have a baptism in an hour for a baby born last night out at one of the farms."

"Then let's get started," Drew said cheerfully.

Marianne tried to tell herself that Drew's smile wasn't forced and his cheerfulness wasn't strained, but she sensed something tight around the edges of him, like a drawstring pulled too tight right before it breaks.

"Jethro's disappointed he can't come to the wedding," Drew said, taking his place next to Marianne. "But when I suggested we postpone it until he's feeling better, he grew so agitated I thought his fever would spike again."

She nodded, pushing at her stomach and wishing she could calm her nerves. So Drew had been attempting to find a way to postpone the wedding? "Drew, we can wait," she whispered to him. Should she tell him she loved him right now to see what his response would be?

"No, Marianne," he whispered back. "There's no reason to wait. Let's proceed as planned."

Mr. Gray stood next to Drew to serve as a witness. He looked official in his stationmaster suit and hat, his beard and long mustache threaded with hints of silver. Elise had positioned herself next to Marianne and was beautiful in her emerald gown with its wide hoop skirt and velvet trim.

As the reverend opened his book of prayers and paged through it, Drew shifted his weight from one foot to the other. Was he getting ready to bolt from the house?

She cast him a glance at the same time that he looked at her. Once again he gave her a smile, yet it did nothing to soothe her mounting anxiety.

The reverend cleared his throat, but before he could begin, another knock sounded on the door, this one loud and determined.

"More wedding guests?" Elise asked, lifting her brow.

Marianne shook her head. She and Drew had decided to keep the occasion simple with only a few people attending. Elise had originally planned to prepare a special dinner in the couple's honor at her eating house, but now that they were quarantined, the wedding meal would be a quiet affair.

The maid answered the door, and a man's deep voice carried into the parlor. "I'm the sheriff from Mayfield, and I've come to arrest Andrew Brady for the murder of the orphan boy, Ned Colson."

CHAPTER 18

Drew couldn't move, couldn't breathe, couldn't think.

Murder? The word paralyzed him.

The Mayfield sheriff had one hand on his pistol and the other on his handlebar mustache.

"You must be wrong, Sheriff," Marianne was saying. "Ned ran away on the day of the placing out. He got tired of all the people inspecting him like he was a farm animal and decided to strike out on his own."

The sheriff hadn't taken his eyes off Drew from the moment he'd stepped foot in the parlor. "We had several of the orphans who were recently placed in Mayfield come into town and identify the body. Every single one said the same thing — that the boy was Ned Colson."

Drew's stomach churned with the need to vomit. He swallowed hard, forcing down the bile. Ned was murdered. He hadn't run off, hadn't decided to hop the next train out of Mayfield. He'd been killed.

"Even if that's true," Marianne protested, "Ned wasn't murdered, and certainly not by Drew."

"He was murdered, all right. Found his body at the bottom of Percy's Pond." The sheriff's eyes were like marbles, hard and glassy, and they were unrelenting in their appraisal of him, as if through sight alone he could discover Drew's part in the murder.

"What if he drowned?" Elise suggested. Drew was surprised Marianne's sister decided to come to his defense. She'd been slow to accept him this past week, had almost seemed suspicious of him.

Mr. Gray and the reverend remained silent observers. He didn't blame them for not speaking up. They'd only just met him.

"Appears the boy was hit over the head," the sheriff continued. "Can't be one hundred percent certain of the blow since . . . well, the body isn't in the best shape, if you catch my meaning."

It had been well over a week — going on close to two weeks — since the placing-out meeting in Mayfield, the day Ned disappeared. With the warmer temperatures, the body would have begun decomposing, and the fish would have taken a toll on it. Nevertheless, if the bottom of the pond was cooler, the body might still be identifiable, along with any trauma to it.

"And the other thing is certain," the sheriff said without taking his eyes off Drew, "someone wanted to hide the evidence of the murder by tying a big stone to the boy. Then he wouldn't float to the surface. I got the rope and stone retrieved as evidence."

"But that still doesn't prove Drew was behind the murder," Marianne said in a desperate tone.

Drew wanted to comfort her and assure her everything would be all right. But one word drummed through his head over and over: *murder, murder, murder . . .*

"Got some of the townspeople who've come forward and said they saw Mr. Brady roughing up some of the older orphan boys the morning of the reception. Say he was arguing with the boys and shoved them around a bit. That he was angry with them."

"He was telling them to stay out of trouble." Marianne had sidled next to Drew. "You just wanted everyone to stay close to the church so we didn't have anyone else wandering off and getting lost like we did with George. Right, Drew?"

He could feel her eyes upon him, pleading with him to rise to his own defense, to say something to refute the sheriff. But Drew couldn't look at Marianne, and he couldn't find his voice.

"Even if I didn't have the townsfolk coming forward to testify to Mr. Brady's rough treatment of the boys, I have an eyewitness to the murder."

Eyewitness? Drew sucked in a sharp breath.

The sheriff nodded, watching every one of Drew's reactions, his eyes seeming to catalog them for future reference.

"Boy by the name of Liverpool said he saw the whole thing."

"Liverpool's the witness?" Marianne gave a shaky laugh as though relieved. "I can tell you right now — Liverpool isn't reliable. Not in the least. He's an angry, disrespectful young man who hasn't liked me or Mr. Brady since the moment he joined our group. If he was trustworthy, he would have come forward with his story earlier, right after the incident happened."

The sheriff shrugged. "His testimony matches what some of the townspeople are saying. And it's enough for me." Of course, it would be enough for the sheriff. The law officer had made it mighty clear when he'd confronted them during their game of hide-and-seek that he didn't want the orphans in his town.

The sheriff probably speculated that if he could stir up trouble with an agent from the Children's Aid Society and cause the organization's good name to have a blemish, then he'd be able to get more people to join him in opposing the orphans.

Drew inwardly shuddered, but outwardly he remained calm. Maybe this was his due punishment. He hadn't deserved to walk away free after the accident five years ago. He'd deserved to pay for his irresponsibility, for his lack of attention, and for his failure to protect those who'd been in his care.

Now he'd failed again. He'd failed to protect another one of the children in his charge. If only he hadn't persuaded Ned to leave the Newsboys Lodging House, if only he'd left the older boys back in the city instead of being so determined to bring them along. Ned might have been in danger from his abusive father, but at least he'd still be alive.

Marianne's hand slid into his. Her fingers were warm against his cold flesh. "Say something, Drew," she whispered.

He heard the fear in her voice, felt the

tremble in her hand and knew she was scared for him. He wanted to look down into her big brown eyes and reassure her he was innocent and that this was all a misunderstanding. But if he did that, he'd be a liar.

He hadn't been the one to tie the stone around Ned and drop him into Percy's Pond, but he was just as guilty. By bringing him west, he'd led him to his death. Maybe if he'd been a better man, stricter and more serious like most of the other agents, he would have seen the trouble brewing, noticed signs of problems, and stepped in and done something to avoid such tragedy.

"Mr. Brady, if you come with me peacefully," the sheriff was saying, "then I won't have to use this thing." He tapped his revolver as though wanting an excuse to pull it.

"He's not going with you," Marianne said. "We're supposed to get married."

"My train's leaving for Mayfield in thirty minutes, and I aim to be on it with Mr. Brady one way or another."

"You can't take him," she insisted. "He's innocent."

" 'Course you're gonna feel that way, young lady," the sheriff said tersely. "As his intended bride, you've got quite the bias, don't you?"

She protested again, and this time Elise joined her. Drew was afraid the sheriff might decide to implicate Marianne as well. He wouldn't be able to live with himself if he let anything happen to her.

"Marianne," he said, breaking into the stream of protests, "I'll be fine. I'll go with the sheriff, straighten everything out, and be back in a few days."

Her hand in his began to relax. "Are you sure?"

He nodded and tugged her to the side of the room where they could have a semblance of privacy while he worked at convincing her to stay. "I'd go anyway to find out what happened, even if the sheriff hadn't come for me."

She nodded reluctantly, her face pale and forlorn. "I want to come with you."

That was the last thing he wanted. He needed to keep her far away from the situation and from any chance of threat. "You can't go anywhere right now until you know if you're free from the measles."

"Please, Drew," she whispered, clinging to him. "I'll be so worried about you."

Even though he was playing unfairly, he threw out his last attempt, the only thing left that would make her stay. "You don't want to leave Jethro, do you?"

She was silent a moment before shaking her head and releasing a resigned breath. "Promise you'll telegram me every day to let me know how things are going?"

"I'll do my best."

"And you'll come back just as soon as you can make arrangements?"

"Yes."

"Please be careful."

"I will."

She stood close enough that he could smell the lavender scent on her skin. Her breath was warm, her body willowy and supple. This beautiful, delicate woman who felt things so deeply and allowed herself to love so freely. She'd almost been his. He'd been minutes away from claiming her as his wife.

He'd never forget her. The past month, especially the past few days . . . they were engraved on his heart forever. She was indeed a priceless treasure. But he had to let her go. Though he wanted her so desperately, he supposed a part of him had always known he wasn't worthy, that he didn't deserve her or the happiness they could have together. Perhaps that was why he'd been so anxious to marry her. Deep down he'd suspected that what they had together wouldn't last, that in the end she'd be ripped away from him somehow.

She peered up at him from behind her long lashes. Her upturned lips were an invitation.

"Good-bye, Marianne." He took a step away before his resolve broke and he swept her into his arms. If he did so, he wouldn't be able to let go.

Confusion and disappointment rippled across her face.

His throat burned with the words he wanted to say to her. He cared about her and would until the day he died. But he couldn't say those words now. He couldn't offer her marriage and commitment when he had no way to offer her anything else.

"Mr. Brady, are you coming nice-like or am I gonna have to prod you along?" At the sheriff's words, Drew put several more steps between himself and Marianne.

Her eyes welled with tears, and he could see she was fighting bravely to hold them back.

He spun away before he embarrassed himself with tears of his own. He stalked past the sheriff toward the door. Only when he passed through did he glance over his shoulder for one last look at Marianne.

She offered him a wavering smile. He

captured her in an instant portrait, her beauty, her sweetness, and her strength. He tucked it into a pocket of his mind where he could easily pull it out. He had the feeling he'd need that picture of her often during the trying days and weeks to come.

Then he pushed forward, walked out the door, and didn't look back again.

Three days passed without a single word from Drew. On the fourth morning, Marianne was inconsolable.

"I'm going to Mayfield on the first train out of town today," she said, tossing garments into her trunk and swiping tears from her cheeks. "And don't try to stop me."

"I'll telegram Reinhold and see what he can find out for us," Elise suggested from where she stood across the bed watching Marianne, dismay creasing her forehead. Elise had already sent a telegram to the sheriff and several to Drew, yet no reply had been forthcoming.

"How would Reinhold know anything?" Marianne said. "He's probably out working in the fields and has no idea anything has happened. Why would he? This doesn't involve him."

Marianne's insides had turned sour like curdled milk, growing more unsettled by the day. She'd been heartbroken watching Drew walk away with the sheriff, and she'd cried in Elise's arms for hours after he left.

She'd told herself he would be back soon enough. He was an intelligent and persuasive man. She had no doubt that once he arrived in Mayfield, he'd clear his name and discover what really happened to Ned.

But now, after three days, she couldn't shake the premonition that perhaps there had been more to their parting than a simple good-bye.

She stuffed the last dress into her trunk and then began filling her valise. "The doctor said if we haven't shown any signs of the measles by today, then we're free to go about our normal activities."

"Yes, but that doesn't mean you should race off to Mayfield the first chance you have. What if Drew is already on his way back?"

Marianne paused and glanced out the window in the direction of the train depot. The steady tapping of rain against the windowpane and the streaks running down the glass prevented her from seeing far. The rain had moved in after Drew left, as if sensing her gloom, and hadn't departed since. That was just fine with her. She wasn't in the mood for sunshine and rainbows and reminders of swimming and picnics and raspberries.

"With Thornton arriving today," Marianne said, "you'll be glad to have me gone. I'm sure you'll have more important things to do tonight than try to console me." Elise had been sleeping with her, always the strong one, the one Marianne could lean on no matter what.

When Elise didn't offer any protest, Marianne glanced up in time to see Elise squirm. If her sister had been a blushing woman, her cheeks would have been bright red. "You know I'll be here for you if you need me," Elise said and then cleared her throat. "And I'm sure Thornton will want to see you too."

Marianne lifted the music box from on top the dresser where she'd placed it. She hadn't turned it on again since the train ride when she used it to distract Dorothea. How wrong Mutti had been to think God could give music and joy during the difficult situations, at least not for her.

Maybe some people were born more naturally optimistic, like Drew. He could laugh effortlessly and worry so little. But for her, every heartache she'd experienced clung to her like a burr in her skirt. No amount of singing and smiling could take away the deep pain that came whenever she thought of losing Vater and Mutti. Or of how lonely, lost, and hurting Sophie and Nicholas and Olivia were.

No amount of reassurances from Mr. Gray could chase away her worry over Jethro and her longing to be the one smoothing back his hair and kissing his hot cheek while he suffered this week.

No amount of singing and sunshine could take away the sharp pain in her heart whenever she thought of Dorothea and wondered whether the little girl was happy or miserable in her new home.

And of course nothing could ease the ache whenever she thought about Drew's farewell, how sad he'd been, almost as if he'd been saying good-bye to her forever.

"I need to go, Elise." Marianne looked her sister in the eye. "Don't you understand? I need to see him. I can't function if I don't know he's okay."

Elise nodded. "Very well. I'll buy you a ticket for the first train heading north."

CHAPTER 19

Marianne stepped off the train in Mayfield and dashed through the steady rainfall into the depot. All she could think about was being here the last time with Drew and the children and that now she was alone.

After she retrieved her luggage, she made arrangements for its transportation to the Mayfield Inn where they'd stayed before. She figured that was where Drew had taken a room and it would be the best place to find information of his whereabouts. But when she arrived, the hotel proprietor shook his head and pursed his lips. He recognized her from her last visit and wasn't pleased to see her again.

"Mr. Brady's not staying here. He's locked up in jail where he should be."

The proprietor's words smashed into her with the power of a cannonball. "Jail?" Her lungs didn't work, and she could hardly squeeze the word out.

"He's a murderer. Where else would he be?"

"But he didn't commit the crime," she sputtered.

"The sheriff said Mr. Brady is taking full responsibility for the drowned boy. If that isn't a statement of guilt, I don't know what is."

"He's not guilty."

"We all think so. And the sheriff is holding him in the jail until the circuit judge comes through here for a trial in a few weeks. We haven't ever had a hanging, but that's what folks are saying he deserves."

Panic rushed through Marianne, leaving her weak and stumbling and dizzy. She reached for the nearest chair and fell into it.

Thankfully at midafternoon the dining room was nearly deserted. Several long trestle tables contained empty tin plates, cups, and bowls from the midday meal, showing the dried remains of a creamy chowder. A few crusts and crumbs littered the table and floor. From previous experience, Marianne knew the disorder would remain there until the end of the day.

The Mayfield Inn hadn't been the cleanest establishment they'd stayed in during their journey. Marianne had tried not to care about the bedbugs and the sheets that smelled of sweat and someone else's body odor. But now, after having spent the past week in Elise's grand home and wearing clean, luxurious garments, she experienced a twinge of disdain for the hotel and immediately felt guilty for it.

She buried her face in her hands and wanted to weep with despair at the news of Drew. What had Drew done? She'd assumed he was coming to Mayfield to identify Ned's body and investigate the crime. But had he left with the sole intention of handing himself over? And if so, why? He hadn't been the one to drown Ned. Why would he take the blame for it?

Feeling helpless and with mounting despair, she pushed away from the table and stood. Her legs wobbled, and she grasped the sticky table edge to keep from buckling back into the chair.

"Where can I find the sheriff?" she asked the proprietor, who'd moved to the far wall and was lifting down an empty barrel that dribbled leftover beer onto the floor.

With his directions ringing in her head, she stumbled back outside.

Mayfield was a small community built along the railroad. The land closest to the railroads was the most coveted due to the ease of transporting goods to market. Her brother-in-law, Thornton, had attempted several times to explain the nature of developing a town along the railroad, that most of the land belonged to the investors in the Central Illinois Railroad, given by the government in the form of land grants. In order to pay for the railroad coming through, the investors parceled off land and sold the parcels to farmers. But to attract the farmers, they first needed to develop towns along the railroad.

Whatever the case, most of the Illinois towns were new and still in the process of expanding. While Mayfield was small, it was larger than most others, which was why Drew had made it one of the stops for the placing out.

Dodging puddles and attempting to avoid splashing wagon wheels, Marianne stopped by the train depot and placed a telegram to the only person she could think of who might be able to help Drew. She conveyed the urgency of Drew's predicament and need for legal counsel. In fact, if Drew didn't get help, he was liable to end up swinging from the end of a noose.

After sending the telegram, she hurried down Main Street and was muddy and soaked by the time she arrived at an office with a sign over its door that read *Sheriff* in bright red letters. She entered and tossed off the hood of her cloak. She'd hoped to see Drew somewhere in the room, but was disappointed to see that, besides the sheriff's desk, the tiny room contained nothing more than a stove with an empty coal box in one corner and a brass spittoon in the other.

The sheriff, who'd been dozing in his chair with his mouth wide open, stood and tipped his hat at her politely. "Miss."

"Good afternoon, Sheriff." She paused and waited for recognition to dawn in his eyes.

Instead, he attempted to smooth his long curling mustache with one hand and his vest with the other.

She took a deep breath and forced herself to be brave and say the words she'd rehearsed on the walk over. "I heard you're unlawfully holding Andrew Brady in your jail. I've come to secure his release."

The sheriff stiffened and regarded her again, this time more closely.

"I'm Mr. Brady's intended," she offered.

"That's right," the sheriff said, hefting up his belt so that his revolver was well displayed. "You're the other agent." He spoke the word *agent* as if it were a curse.

"I'm here to see Mr. Brady." She hoped her voice didn't wobble. She wasn't used to being so impudent. "Please take me to him."

He shook his head. "Can't do that, miss."

"I insist."

"He told me he don't want no visitors."

"I'm sure he'll want to see me."

"He said no one — and he was mighty firm about it."

"But he didn't know I'd be coming."

The sheriff tugged on his mustache, staring at her with his keen eyes. "Fine," he said with an exasperated sigh. "I'll go ask him. Wait here."

He disappeared through a door behind his desk. If she'd been braver, she might have gathered the courage to follow him. Rather, she fidgeted with her cloak. She was uncomfortably warm under its damp weight, and she couldn't quell the sense of doom that had enveloped her since the hotel proprietor's statement about Drew taking responsibility for the crime.

She peered out the dusty front window, envisioning the children outside the church the morning of the placing-out meeting. Drew had gone inside to confer with the committee. When he emerged later, many of the children had already dispersed throughout town, the youngest ones staying close to her side.

Ned and Liverpool hadn't come back for

lunch at the hotel. But neither had a few of the other boys who'd apparently skipped the noon meal so they could go swimming. Were they swimming in the same pond in which Ned had drowned? If so, they could give more information on what had happened that day.

She tried to recollect which of the boys had gone swimming. Maybe she could give the sheriff their names, so he could go speak to each one privately.

When the door clicked open behind her, she spun in anticipation, hoping to see Drew. Her heart lurched at the sight of the sheriff standing there alone.

"I'm ready to see him, Sheriff." She started toward the back door.

He closed it firmly. "Like I said, he don't want to see no one. Not even you."

The sheriff's words froze her feet to the floor. "That can't be true."

"He said to tell you to forget about him."

For a moment, her heart was too chilled to utter a word in response. Drew didn't want to see her? He wanted to cut himself off from her? How could that be?

Her mind replayed his farewell, and now she understood why she'd been so anxious the past few days. His good-bye had been filled with a finality she'd tried to ignore but no longer could.

"He told me to tell you to make follow-up visits to the orphans you placed," the sheriff continued. "And I say, while you're at them visits, you just pack those young'uns up and take them all back east with you."

So Drew didn't want to marry her anymore? Maybe he never really had to begin with. Maybe she'd just imagined his eagerness and desire. The chill inside spread to her limbs until she was frigid with hurt and anger. He'd led her on. He'd made her believe he cared about her. He'd even made her like him in return.

She closed her eyes momentarily to ward off the sting of tears. Elise had been right. He'd never said he loved her. He'd only been enamored with the conquest.

Marianne had known from the start of their engagement that Drew wasn't the type of man to commit. Hadn't she predicted his fickleness that day on the train when he proposed to her? He'd had fun with the challenge. But when it came down to actually marrying her, no matter how attracted he'd been or how earnest he'd seemed, he was looking for a way out. And now that he'd found one, he was taking it, even if he had to sit in jail to avoid her.

"Very well," she said, finding her voice. It

came out as coldly as she felt. "You may tell Mr. Brady I'll visit the children, that at least one of us is grown up enough to see the job through to completion."

She yanked up the hood of her cloak, swung open the door, and stepped out into the rain. If Andrew Brady didn't want to see her, then she'd make sure his wish came true.

At the slamming of the door, Drew buried his face in his grimy hands and allowed himself to shudder.

"She's gone!" the sheriff called through the thin wall.

"I heard."

"She weren't too happy neither."

"I could tell." Drew had clung to every word she'd said from the moment she stepped into the building. The wall between the sheriff's desk and his cell was as thin as newsprint. He'd held his breath each time she'd uttered a word, drinking in her voice and imagining her beauty like a desperate and dying man.

He leaned forward on the wooden bench built into the wall, which had served as his bed for the past week. The cell was no more than four-by-eight feet, the size of a horse stall. With only one high window set outside the bars of the cell, the place was dark and dank — only magnifying the rancidness of the chamber pot.

The sheriff brought him two meals a day, as well as a basin of water for washing. The only thing he'd wanted was a Bible, something the sheriff had also supplied.

The truth was, he didn't want to make things worse for Marianne. He'd already made it hard enough on her by letting a relationship develop between them. He should have been more careful. But how was he to know he'd be responsible for the death of another child?

He loathed himself for giving her hope of a future with him, only to toss it all aside. And he loathed himself for hurting her now. He hadn't wanted to ignore her. He wanted her to come back to his cell so he could pull her into his arms and hold her tight.

As much as he needed her, he'd forced himself to remain quiet and distant. Maybe he hadn't kept his distance all along like he should have, but he was doing it now. He didn't want her linked to a twice-murderer. Any association with him would ruin her reputation. Already her job with the Children's Aid Society was in jeopardy because of him and this murder case. If she lost it, how would she be able to continue her search for her sister?

Drew pressed his fingers against his temple to ward off a headache. What good would it do to see Marianne now? Even if he was exonerated, people would always speculate about him. Brace would have to fire him, and he'd have nothing to offer Marianne.

He needed to let her go. She was better off without him, and she'd realize that soon enough. Before long she'd find someone else and be happy again.

Reinhold. Last week, shortly after arriving in Quincy, Marianne had discovered Reinhold's whereabouts from Elise. Marianne confided the news to him that Reinhold lived near Mayfield and had asked for her help caring for his sisters once she returned to New York City. And although he'd teased her at the time, he was slightly jealous of the man she'd once wanted to marry.

Drew sat up on the hard bench. "Sheriff, do you know a German immigrant who goes by the name Reinhold Weiss? Works as a hired farmhand?"

"Sure enough do," the sheriff replied from the other side of the wall, likely back in his chair now that Marianne was gone. "He was the man who pulled the orphan boy's body from the pond."

Reinhold had found the body? Marianne's Reinhold? Drew's muscles flexed in protest for what he knew he had to do. He couldn't bear the thought of Marianne finding solace in anyone else's arms. It was the same reaction he'd had that day they'd gone swimming when she told him more about Reinhold.

He shook his head and tried to loosen his hold on Marianne. He had no right to her. If he couldn't be there to help her, then he wanted her to have someone.

"Could you get word to Reinhold that I'd like to meet with him?" He forced himself to say the words.

The sheriff hesitated before answering. "You ain't planning to question Reinhold and try to talk your way out of the murder, now, are you?"

"No, sir. Just hoping to find a good man to take care of the woman I love."

Love? The word slipped out before he could think about what he was saying. Was it true? Did he love Marianne?

He cared about her more than any other woman he'd known, even more than Charlotte. Of course, at the time he'd believed that he loved Charlotte and was devastated when she'd canceled their wedding.

Charlotte had been a bright flare in the

344

sky who had lit up his world for a little while. But the intensity of all he felt for Marianne was like an explosion of the sun that would never diminish but would continue to burn within him forever.

He held back an agonized groan. Yes, he loved Marianne. And because of how deeply he loved her, he wanted to provide her with someone who could comfort and care for her in his place.

Marianne had once loved Reinhold. Even if she'd transferred her feelings to Drew temporarily, perhaps she would switch them back to Reinhold — especially once Drew talked with the young man and convinced him what a treasure Marianne was.

CHAPTER 20

The telegram weighted Reinhold's trouser pocket more than a handful of heavy coins. It didn't jangle as he plodded down Main Street, but he was conscious of it with every step he took nonetheless.

His boots were heavy in the muck that remained after the past week of rain. Almost as heavy as his heart.

Tante Brunhilde had finally responded, had likely had one of his brothers post the telegram. He was relieved to hear she still had his two sisters living with her. But she'd only agreed to keep them if he sent her more money every month. And only until autumn. In October, she'd made arrangements to marry a distant cousin who would be arriving in America. This cousin was in need of a wife for his children and had agreed to marry Brunhilde when he arrived.

His aunt explained that if Reinhold didn't make other provisions for the care of his sisters by the time her new husband arrived, she'd have no choice but to put the girls into an orphanage. Between her own children and those of her new husband, they would have enough mouths to feed and didn't need two more.

Reinhold was glad his sisters were safe for the time being. But that meant he had four months to figure out something else for them. Of course, he'd hoped to be able to put a down payment on the land for his own farm by autumn. But after Higgins had stolen his savings, Reinhold had to start saving all over. And now that Higgins had the extra cash, he'd be able to purchase the land first.

Holding in a sigh, Reinhold stopped, kicked his boot against the wooden step, and dislodged some of the mud before banging his other boot. Even if by some miracle he managed to earn enough to beat Higgins to the land, it would take time to build a house. In his wildest dreams, he didn't know how he'd ever have the means or ability to take care of his youngest sisters by October. Besides, how would he be able to work *and* take care of two little girls?

It was an impossible situation. Yet he couldn't abandon his family, couldn't let his sisters be split up and possibly shipped off on a train to go live with strangers. Didn't his brothers also deserve a chance to live free of the dangers of the city?

Reinhold pushed open the door and stepped inside the building.

"Ah, there you are." The sheriff uncrossed his legs from where they were resting on his desk and dropped them to the floor with a *thud.* "Took your sweet time coming into town, didn't you?"

"I'm sorry, Sheriff." Reinhold stuffed his hands in his pockets and once again felt the weight of the telegram against his fingers. "Just haven't had the chance this week."

He wouldn't speak ill of Mrs. Turner in front of anyone, but privately he was irritated that she'd complained to her husband regarding Reinhold's trips into town. She'd convinced Mr. Turner to give him more work, saying that if Reinhold had enough time to ride to town every other day, then he had too much free time.

The sheriff stood and stretched. "Well, come on then. My prisoner has been asking to see you all week, and I'm tired of hearing his yapping."

Reinhold didn't need the sheriff to explain further. The whole community was talking about the murdered orphan and the suspect, Andrew Brady. Of course, after Liverpool's description of what happened that day, it was difficult to refute his claim that Mr. Brady was the one responsible for Ned's death.

Mr. Brady had gone out to the pond to call the boys back for the meeting. He'd been mad at them for disobeying his instructions to stay in town. He'd had strict instructions not to swim, and when he found the boys in the pond, he became agitated. The sheriff had visited several other orphans who'd been swimming that day and confirmed Mr. Brady's anger toward them for swimming after he expressly told them not to.

Not only had Mr. Brady been upset about their disobedience with the swimming, but he'd also supposedly gotten angry with Ned, who refused to go through with the placing out. The two started arguing after the younger boys headed back to town. Liverpool claimed Mr. Brady shoved Ned, who'd slipped and fallen, hit his head on a stone, and died upon impact. Liverpool said he'd been scared Mr. Brady would hurt him too and so ran off. And now everyone speculated that once Ned was dead, Mr. Brady dumped the body in the pond to hide the evidence.

Accident or not, Reinhold agreed with the

sheriff and others in town that Mr. Brady didn't deserve to be working with orphans, especially because the sheriff also learned Mr. Brady had lost one of the orphans earlier in the trip during their stop in Benton. One of the younger boys had wandered off and was later rescued by a squatter.

Whatever the case, Reinhold tried to keep himself out of the whole messy business. Sure, he'd been the one to bring the murdered body into town. But other than uncovering the corpse, Reinhold didn't want any other part in the situation. He was too busy trying to figure out his own future and save his family to worry about what a murderer may or may not want from him.

The sheriff led Reinhold behind his desk and into the back room of the building. Bars ran from floor to ceiling through half the room and formed a cell that was much too small for a grown man. Even so, a man sat on the wooden bench, a blanket bunched against his back serving as a cushion against the wall. He had a thick book spread open on his lap. At the sight of Reinhold, he closed the book, which Reinhold could now see was a Bible.

"Got you the visitor you wanted," the sheriff said.

Even with the window open, the air in the back room was sour from body odor and urine. Flies buzzed around the chamber pot and an empty dish that sat on the floor outside the cell.

Mr. Brady moved slowly and stiffly, like a much older man with arthritic joints.

"You should let Mr. Brady out to walk around now and then," Reinhold suggested.

"I ain't taking any chances on this one running off."

Reinhold stared at the young man. His face was unshaven, his hair unkempt, and his clothes were dirty. Aside from that, he appeared to be a nice-looking man, perhaps one the ladies would consider handsome. He didn't look like a child-killer.

Mr. Brady remained on the edge of his bench and seemed to study Reinhold with the same measure of scrutiny, as if Reinhold was the one about to undergo a trial and not the other way around.

"So you're Reinhold," Mr. Brady finally said in a voice rusty from disuse.

"Yes." The man seemed to know him. Should he know something in return? Reinhold studied Mr. Brady more closely. He'd only seen him briefly at the church service the Sunday the orphans had been in town.

"I'm glad you found Ned's body," Mr. Brady said softly. "Thanks for pulling him out of the pond so he could have a proper burial."

Reinhold crossed his arms, not sure how to respond. He didn't make a practice of fraternizing with murderers, so he wasn't an expert in the matter of innocence or guilt. But the man's statement didn't sound like something a murderer would say.

"Ned was a good boy," Mr. Brady continued. "I thought he could escape the city and find a better life here. I never imagined it would end this way for him."

Again, Reinhold didn't know how to respond. So he said nothing. For a long moment the only sound was the whistle of a train and the whirring *chug chug* as the engine picked up speed.

"What can I do for you, Mr. Brady?" Reinhold asked.

Mr. Brady glanced at the sheriff, who leaned against the doorframe, clearly not intending to allow them any privacy. "I'd like for you to consider marrying Marianne Neumann."

The statement was so unexpected that Reinhold started to choke. "What?" he managed to say.

"Marianne Neumann," Mr. Brady repeated. "You do know her, don't you?"

"Yes, I've been friends with her family for a while now."

"Good. Then you need to marry her." Mr. Brady closed his eyes as though it had cost him all his strength and will to speak the words.

Reinhold had never been witty or eloquent. He was more deliberate and liked to think things through before answering or making decisions. He supposed that was one of the reasons why he'd lost Elise. He hadn't been quick enough to claim her. He'd been too deliberate and had wanted to plan his life before asking her to marry him.

But marry Marianne? He didn't have to think about that for even a second to know he didn't love Marianne Neumann the same way he'd loved Elise. He wasn't sure that he'd ever love anyone else the way he loved Elise.

Even now, he pictured her sitting on the train the day they'd parted ways in Quincy. She'd been so regal and strong. His heart beat painfully just thinking about how beautiful she looked then. Even when he'd first met her in Kleindeutschland, when she was scrawny and pale, he still loved her.

"Mr. Brady," he started. How did Mr.

Brady know Marianne? And why was he making this strange request? Was Marianne in some kind of trouble? "You'll need to explain yourself better."

"Miss Neumann — Marianne — is my partner, the other placing agent who came with to help the orphans find homes."

The news didn't surprise Reinhold. After Sophie had run away, he expected Marianne to take the responsibility upon herself to locate the missing girl, and she wouldn't stop until she found her along with Nicholas and Olivia. That's just the way Marianne was. She had a tender heart. Not that Elise didn't, but Marianne's was more fragile.

"Marianne told me she was looking for you," Mr. Brady continued. "She confided in me that the two of you had talked about getting married."

Surprised, Reinhold was rendered speechless. Why had Marianne mentioned such a thing when they'd never spoken of it, not even once? His thoughts returned to Marianne's claim last year that she'd been pregnant with his child. At the time he'd received the news from his aunt, he was baffled since he'd never touched Marianne, except to hug her as he would one of his sisters. He'd never imagined her feelings for him went deeper.

"I'm sorry to say," Mr. Brady said, dropping his head into his hands, "she thinks she's enamored with me." The thick tension in his voice gave away his feelings for Marianne. He'd apparently become enamored with her too. "I have nothing to offer her anymore. She'd be better off with someone else who can give her happiness and security."

"And you think I can give her that?"

"Yes. She talked about how much she admired you. I know you can make her happy so she forgets about me."

Reinhold shook his head.

"You can help her find Sophie," Mr. Brady cut off his protest. "And she can help you. She told me about the situation with your sisters in New York City. Surely she can be a mother to them now that they have none. As your wife, she could become their guardian and watch over them in New York until you can send for them."

Reinhold wasn't sure he'd be able to find a rebuttal even if he'd wanted to. Mr. Brady was handing him the perfect solution to his difficult predicament. If Marianne admired him and had already talked about marrying him, then why not make her his wife and secure a caretaker for his sisters?

Maybe he didn't love Marianne the same way he loved Elise, but over time he'd grow in his love and desire for her. There were plenty of marriages that started from convenience but turned into something rich and deep as time passed. That would be the case for Marianne and him.

Reinhold hesitated. "Mr. Brady —"

"Call me Drew." His voice had gained strength during their conversation. "You'll bring me great peace if I know Marianne will be taken care of. I'll be able to go forward and accept my fate if I know she'll find happiness."

Reinhold's mind spun with the possibilities. Marianne could find a small apartment in New York City for herself and the girls. He'd send her money, and his brothers would help as much as they could too. Maybe Marianne would even be able to secure work as a seamstress again. He'd heard some of the businesses were recovering from their financial problems and were hiring workers once more.

Then after he bought the farmland and built a house, he would send for them. Marianne would be here to mother the girls and help him with all the work that needed doing. Even if she didn't know anything about farming, she'd learn quickly. She was cheerful and made the best of situations. He'd always liked that about her.

"What do you think?" Drew gripped the bench with both hands so tightly his knuckles turned white. His sad eyes pleaded with Reinhold to say yes.

Reinhold decided he liked Drew. Drew had enough worries of his own, and yet he was more concerned about Marianne's well-being. He was putting her interests first, trying to secure her future. He was a strong man, a good man.

So how could such a good man commit murder? The longer Reinhold stood talking with Drew, the more out of character it seemed that Drew would even consider such a thing.

"I like your plan," Reinhold said, "but I need to discuss this with her first —"

"Don't discuss it," Drew interrupted. "You shouldn't have any trouble finding her. She's in the area doing follow-up visits on the children we placed. When you see her, pull her in your arms and tell her you love her and want to marry her. She'll melt like butter."

Reinhold suspected Drew knew this information from firsthand experience, and he was surprised by the twinge of jealousy that slashed him. "You seem to know her well."

"We became close," Drew replied more vaguely. "And maybe there was a time when we both thought it could work out between us, but I'm not the man she needs. You are."

Reinhold watched as emotion played across Drew's face, and then he realized something. Drew was in love with Marianne. "What if she doesn't think I'm the man she needs?"

"Then convince her." Drew's expression turned desperate. "Please."

Reinhold didn't look away. He studied this man before him intently with growing unease. He didn't seem guilty of murder. Not in the least.

If it meant so much to Drew to take care of Marianne, how could he say no? Especially now? Reinhold swallowed his objection and nodded. "I'll do my best."

"Will you keep our conversation private? I don't want Marianne to think I was meddling."

"I won't say a word."

Drew nodded, then dropped his face into his hands again. His shoulders sagged in defeat. Reinhold had the feeling Drew was done with the conversation, that he wanted to be alone to grieve in private over all he'd lost.

Reinhold could relate to the depth of

Drew's loss. His chest tightened with a burning he hadn't felt since walking away from Elise. With a nod at the sheriff, Reinhold spun on his heels. If for no other reason, he'd take Marianne as his wife because he didn't want to let Drew down.

CHAPTER 21

As the wagon came to a halt in front of the white clapboard farmhouse, Marianne expelled a full breath, the first since leaving the last farm. They'd gotten stuck in the muddy roads only once. Her hired driver had gotten out and pushed while she directed the team.

"I'll try not to stay as long this time," she said, climbing off the wagon and trying to remain graceful but tangling in her wide hoop skirt anyway.

"No matter to me, miss," the old driver said, "so long as you pay me what you said."

Even though she tried to find firmer ground, one of her feet sank into a puddle. Overhead, the skies were still gray, but thankfully the rain had taken a day off. The wet days of late slowed her follow-up visits by turning the roads into rivers of mud. She was bruised and sore from the constant jostling and jerking. However, after almost two weeks in Mayfield, she'd finally managed to visit all but two of the orphans they'd placed in the area.

She hadn't been able to find one of the orphans, since the child had been relocated to a different family, and no one was able to give her any information on the new situation. This visit was one she'd been dreading, and so she put it off until last. After it was finished, she'd move on to the next town. Maybe she'd leave tomorrow or the next day.

She never imagined the follow-up visits would be so time-consuming and difficult. Not only had the weather and roads played a factor, but she'd had to travel quite a distance to reach some of the families. In fact, she'd been obliged to stay the night at one of the homes because of how late she'd arrived.

"If you'd be so kind as to hand me my valise." Marianne nodded at her bag, which contained the record book. She'd taken the book to each visit and had attempted to put down as much information as possible about each of the children's homes, new families, and how they were adjusting.

The driver nudged the bag toward her with his muddy boot.

She would have preferred to talk with the

children alone, so they could honestly respond to her questions. After all, the orphans would feel they must answer positively or face repercussions from their family after she left. As it was, only one of the boys mentioned that he was hungry. Upon further inquiry, the father stated that he'd disciplined the boy once or twice for his laziness by depriving him of meals. "He who does not work, neither shall he eat" was the father's motto.

In another home, the child was found to be exceptionally dirty, the outfits provided for him by the Children's Aid Society already stained beyond recognition. The other four or five children in the family were equally filthy and their clothing more ragged. Marianne had taken note of the state of the home, the unwashed dishes, filthy linens, and dilapidated furniture. She'd come to the conclusion that any child would have a difficult time remaining clean in such an environment. However, the parents had been kind enough, and the children seemed not to be suffering from any ill treatment.

Marianne left that home and others with great uncertainty. Were the children really better off in such places? Or had they merely traded one kind of oppression in the city for a different kind in the country?

Of course, the poor living conditions of some of the children had only brought back nightmares about Dorothea. The little girl's cries would jolt Marianne out of a deep sleep at night, and she'd tremble at the thought of Dorothea lying alone in the night with no one to hug her or comfort her.

She wished she could discuss her questions and fears with Drew. He would have known whether to remove the children and try to find new and better homes for them, or to leave them where they were.

But she hadn't attempted to see Drew again since the day last week when she walked out of the sheriff's office. She'd wanted to go visit him again. At times, the need to be with him had almost pained her. She'd passed by the sheriff's office and had to physically force herself to keep walking, reminding herself he hadn't wanted to see her. If she went in and he refused to see her again, she'd be utterly humiliated and devastated. She couldn't risk it.

She squared her shoulders and faced the two-story farmhouse, trying to squelch the unrest within her, especially the thought of facing Liverpool. Even though she'd considered skipping his visit, she knew she couldn't. She simply had to put aside her fears and do her job.

Remember the good, she told herself. Amidst the questionable situations, some of the children seemed genuinely happy in their new homes. She'd visited George and Peter two days ago, and she was delighted to find them both still together and seemingly content in their home with a dairy farmer south of town. The couple who'd taken them in was older. They had two grown sons, who helped with the business. One was already married and lived in a small home next to the farm, and the other was engaged to be married. Even though the couple hadn't needed the extra help with the milking, they'd decided to do their Christian duty by taking in an orphan boy. Somehow Drew had persuaded them to take both.

When Marianne arrived, she'd hardly been able to believe the two were the same timid and scrawny brothers who'd survived the trip. They were well fed and properly clothed in shirts and trousers their new ma had made for them. They'd been proud to show her the clothes and their bedroom on the second floor across the hall from their ma and pa. And they'd wanted to demonstrate how they'd learned to milk the cows.

The couple seemed just as proud of the boys as the boys were of themselves. They praised the boys and encouraged them and hugged them. But they also weren't afraid to reprimand or correct the boys when necessary. After only a few hours with the family, Marianne sensed theirs was a special home and that the couple would change George and Peter forever.

If only the Children's Aid Society could find more families like that for all the children.

Marianne made her way up a stone path that led to the front door of the farmhouse. The marigolds on either side were planted in neat rows and had been recently weeded. A big fenced-in vegetable garden behind the house also appeared to be well tended. The bleating of sheep in the barnyard and the clucking of the chickens in their coop were welcoming sounds, better than the dog barking that usually greeted her arrival.

Late in the afternoon like this, she figured any womenfolk would be inside preparing supper and that the men were in the barn feeding the animals. She knew it was an inconvenient time to be paying a call, but she'd learned she had little control over the roads and weather and that she was lucky to arrive to any of the houses at all, much less at any particular time.

Even so, she expected someone to step outside to greet her and was surprised by the quiet of the place. She raised her fist to knock when the clatter of another team and wagon caught her attention. It was approaching on the road that came from Mayfield, and it turned onto the lane that led to the farmhouse. A stocky man and a thin boy sat on the bench.

Marianne stepped away from the door and waited patiently for the wagon to approach. As it drew nearer, she realized that the thin boy was Liverpool. The cocky, almost defiant, way he held himself was easy to spot.

From first glance, he seemed to be faring well. Maybe she would greet him quickly, ask him the standard questions, and then be on her way. She could check him off her list. Surely if there were any problems, Liverpool would have run away by now.

A gust of wind blew against her, bringing with it the scent of manure and wet soil. She grabbed her hat to keep it from blowing off, and as she did, her sights landed upon the driver.

She found herself looking at the handsome ruddy face of the man she'd loved for so many years. He was hunched over the reins, but his familiar brawny build and broad shoulders were difficult to miss.

"Reinhold Weiss?" she exclaimed, unable to contain her smile.

He smiled in return, not the dimpled, self-assured smile that only belonged to Drew. But the calm, steady smile Reinhold always had — one that never failed to make her heart sing. He brought the wagon to a jerking halt, jumped from the bench, and went to her at the same time she ran to him.

She launched herself against him and threw her arms around his neck. When his stocky arms came around her, she gave a squeal. "It is you!"

He hugged her for a long moment. She waited for the usual feeling of heavenly bliss she'd always felt whenever he'd hugged her in the past. But the heart singing and the heavenly bliss were absent. She held him tightly, trying to conjure the depths of her feelings, knowing it would just take a moment. After all, she hadn't seen him since last autumn, and a lot had happened since then.

She pressed her face into his neck, hoping the contact would elicit her long-buried feelings. She expected him to peel himself away. But he didn't seem in a hurry to break the connection either.

"Looks like you and Miss Neumann have

a thing going," Liverpool cajoled from the wagon bench.

At the boy's crude words, Reinhold released her and took a rapid step back. He was still smiling, but his expression turned strangely shy. "I didn't know you were in the area until today," he said, his voice thickening with his German accent, "or I would have come to visit you."

She ignored a thorn of guilt that pricked her. She'd been in Mayfield close to two weeks and hadn't made an effort to seek him out even though she'd known he was living here. She'd been busy, she told herself. Without Drew's assistance, she'd had too much to do.

"Do you live on this farm?" she asked, hoping he wouldn't ask her why she hadn't sought him out.

"Yes. I work for the Turners." He regarded her, starting at her hat and working his way down to the muddy tips of her boots showing beneath the soiled hem of her skirt. An appreciation lit the green of his eyes, turning them the color of dark moss.

For years, she'd longed to see that kind of look in his eyes — the one that said he saw her as a woman and not just a sister. But now that it was there, she squirmed with a sudden bashfulness she hadn't expected.

"How are you?" she asked. "Are you enjoying your work as a farmer?"

Instead of answering, he nodded at Liverpool. "Why don't you drive the team over to the barn and start unhitching the mares? I'll be over to help you soon."

Liverpool scooted over on the bench eagerly and grabbed the reins. Once the wagon started rolling, Reinhold stared after it almost as if he regretted sending the boy away.

"Aren't you glad to see me, Reinhold?" she asked.

"Yes, very." He glanced at her again but then just as rapidly returned his attention to Liverpool. "You look so grown up and pretty in your fancy dress."

"Thank you." Marianne swished her skirt back and forth, appreciating the gentle sway of the hoop and the loveliness of the silky material. She adored the new clothes. While she still missed many things about her old life with her family in New York City, she didn't miss the coarse peasant-like garments that most of the German immigrants wore.

"Farming life seems to agree with you," she said. He was sun-bronzed and muscular and more handsome than she remembered.

"I'm hoping to buy my own place." He stuck his hands in his trousers and shifted.

"Looks like it will take more time than I wanted, but I hope to have enough saved by the end of the year."

"That's wonderful, Reinhold. I'm so happy for you." And she meant it.

He cleared his throat. "I want to bring Silke and Verina to live with me as soon as I have a place. And maybe Peter and Jakob, if they'll come."

"I'm sorry about your mother," she replied softly. Mrs. Weiss had been too delicate for the toils of the new life in America. The problems and worries had drained the life from her until all that remained was a shell of the beautiful woman she'd once been.

"Praise Gott my Tante Brunhilde will take care of the girls until October."

Marianne couldn't think of Tante Brunhilde without bitterness forming in the pit of her stomach. She realized she'd deceived the woman with the fake pregnancy and claimed to be Reinhold's fiancée. Even so, Reinhold's aunt was heartless and hadn't shown an ounce of compassion when Marianne had most needed it. Thankfully, Tante Brunhilde was being kinder to Reinhold.

"October will be here soon," Marianne said.

Reinhold toed a rock sticking up in the mud. "Marianne," he started, then stopped.

She didn't understand this awkwardness between them. They'd always been able to relate freely. What had changed?

"Marianne," he said again, embarrassment turning his voice deeper.

"What is it, Reinhold?" She touched his arm, wanting to reassure him that he had nothing to fear from her. If he had something to tell her, he could do so. Surely he knew that.

He laid his hand over hers and looked into her eyes. "Will you marry me?"

The question pummeled into her with the force of a steam whistle blast. She tried to formulate a response but only grasped at the air.

From behind her, inside the house at one of the open windows, she thought she heard a cry of protest. But when she glanced over her shoulder, the only thing she saw was the fluttering of a curtain.

"I promise I'll give you a good life and that I'll be a good husband," he said more earnestly. "And I'm sure over time we'll grow to love each other deeply."

She was speechless and could only stare at him in wonder. She'd always imagined him asking her to marry him, had longed for it so intensely. "I sent you a letter last year . . ." She was now embarrassed to admit that the letter had contained her declaration of love. She'd waited for the chance to ask him why he'd never written back, but realized it didn't matter anymore. Perhaps she was finally able to accept what she'd always known — that he liked Elise more than he had her.

Nevertheless, now that he was actually proposing, she wasn't reacting quite the way she'd envisioned with the scream, the jumping up and down, and the tears of joy. Instead, she was filled with uncertainty.

What about Drew? Even if Drew had told her to forget about him, even if her heart still ached with his rejection, she couldn't so easily put aside all that had happened between them and the feelings she still harbored, although she wished she didn't.

Reinhold's fingers against hers were strong and secure. "I never received your letter, Marianne." His expression was open and honest. "If I had, I would have written back."

She believed him. He was too honorable and too kind to ignore her. And she had no doubt he'd be a good husband and that he would continue to be honorable, kind, and loving in every way. But was that enough for her?

"I don't know," she started. Before she

could finish her sentence, he pulled her against his chest, wrapped his arms around her, and lowered his mouth to hers. His touch was surprisingly tender and poignant. And it was over in an instant.

He held her close, and she laid her head against his shoulder, tasting the lingering warmth of his kiss on her lips. She'd always dreamed of what it would be like to kiss Reinhold. She'd expected it to change her, to make her feel like she'd been turned inside out and upside down — like Drew's kisses had. But strangely, Reinhold's kiss felt anticlimactic, almost brotherly.

If she allowed more time, would passion develop between them? She was clearly thinking of Drew too much to have room in her heart for another. Maybe eventually she'd stop caring for Drew. And maybe once she forgot about Drew, she'd regain her feelings for Reinhold.

But what if she couldn't stop thinking about Drew? That wouldn't be fair to Reinhold.

As if sensing her inner turmoil, Reinhold extended her to arm's length and met her gaze without pretense. "I need a mother for Silke and Verina." There was a quiet desperation in his eyes that told her the truth about his proposal, that the real reason he was asking her to marry him was because he needed someone to care for his sisters.

How could she say no to that? And yet how could she say yes?

"I don't want you to think that's the only reason I'm asking for your hand in marriage," he rushed to add. "But it is there, and I want to be honest with you."

Reinhold was offering her marriage. It was what she'd always wanted. Until she met Drew. She closed her eyes for just a second, but it was long enough to picture Drew's handsome face, his devastating grin, and the bottomless excitement in his eyes.

But no. He'd led her on and then rejected her. In the end, he'd failed the challenge. He hadn't wanted her enough to fight for her. Swallowing the helpless frustration that taunted her too often of late, she pushed the picture of him from her mind and tried to focus on Reinhold.

Maybe if she accepted Reinhold's offer, Drew would hear of it. And maybe, just maybe, he'd regret giving her up.

"Yes," she said impulsively, almost defiantly. "I'll marry you."

Reinhold lowered his gaze, but not before she saw the guilt there. She knew he felt remorse for proposing marriage because he needed her more than he loved her, but she appreciated his honesty.

"I promise I'll work hard to be the best husband you could ask for."

"I know you will." She pressed a hand against his cheek.

Perhaps her time with Drew this summer had been an infatuation, a distraction from her real destiny with Reinhold. And now that she was finally here with Reinhold, she simply needed a little more time to get back on the right track and allow her feelings to catch up.

When she started to drop her hand, Reinhold reached for it and held it in place against his cheek. "I'll help you find Sophie and Olivia and Nicholas. They can come to live with us too."

She smiled. "I'd like that."

He smiled back, his eyes crinkling at the corners with relief. As he moved her hand to his mouth and gently pressed a kiss to her palm, she waited for her heart to give an extra thud or her pulse to jump in her chest. She waited to feel something — anything — for this sweet, tenderhearted man standing before her.

But all she could think about was another man sitting in a jail cell and how desperately she wanted to see him. One last time.

CHAPTER 22

Marianne had been waiting so long next to the granary that her feet ached and her stomach rumbled from hunger. She'd expected the sheriff to leave long ago for lunch, relieved by his deputy. But he hadn't come out of the office yet.

After her visit with Reinhold yesterday — and his proposal of marriage — she'd thought of little else but seeing Drew. She knew it wasn't right to be engaged to one man and obsessed with another, which was why she needed to see Drew. She had to put him out of her mind once and for all. If she could see him one last time, then she'd be able to move on and marry Reinhold.

He'd said he wanted to marry her as soon as possible. But she wanted to wait until after she'd finished her follow-up with the orphans. She was planning to leave tomorrow for Benton to visit the first children they'd placed in homes, including Dorothea.

Then she'd finish in Dresden with the handful who had been placed there.

She'd collect Jethro from Quincy and stop in Mayfield again on her way back. She'd marry Reinhold and spend a few days with him before she returned to New York City to find Silke and Verina. She'd have to begin the job search all over again and would likely have to rely upon Thornton's connections rather than her own merits. But she was not so proud that she wouldn't accept his help, especially because she'd have to take care of Reinhold's sisters along with Jethro until Reinhold was able to send for them. She'd told Reinhold about Jethro, and he was as willing to take the boy as she knew he would be.

Even though she'd already determined to make this her last trip with the Children's Aid Society, she had to admit that the thought of not working with the orphans saddened her. The placing out had been wrought with difficulties and disappointments, but she realized that she loved working with the children more than anything else she'd ever done. Perhaps she'd eventually be able to find work helping orphans in another capacity.

In the meantime, the need to see Drew had overtaken her to the point that she hadn't been able to focus on anything else. Although he'd said he didn't want to see her again and sent her away, she needed to say good-bye for her peace of mind. But she couldn't do that with the sheriff in the building. He'd likely end up sending her away again.

She fanned her face with one of her gloves she'd removed. She'd taken great care with her appearance, had wanted to look her best when she visited Drew. But now in the hot morning sunshine of early July, she was wilting.

Maybe she would have to go over and demand to see Drew whether the sheriff allowed it or not.

She took a step away from her hiding spot, and at that moment the door of the sheriff's office opened. She darted out of sight, pressed herself against the metal of the storage container, and counted to five before peeking across the street.

At the sight of the sheriff and a distinguished-looking gentleman leading Drew between them down the street, Marianne gasped in surprise. Drew's head hung so that she couldn't see his face, yet she could see the haggardness of his appearance, his uncombed hair, unshaven jaw, and rumpled filthy garments. He limped along slowly and could hardly walk, even with the aid of the two men on either side.

Marianne moved onto the street. She wanted to call out to him, but she didn't want to make a public spectacle. Already she guessed everyone in town was watching and gossiping about the accused murderer walking through town. All she could do was follow his every faltering step with the ache in her chest growing, until the men ushered him inside the private vacant residence at the end of the block.

Once he disappeared from her sight, she slumped against the granary. Was that the judge? Had they taken Drew away for questioning? Did that mean his trial would take place soon? Although she dreaded the thought of the trial, she didn't want to miss it.

Maybe she would have to postpone her trip to Benton. She stared at the front door of the large new home. She'd heard that a banker had planned to move to Mayfield to live in it. But after the recession in the fall, the banker had fallen on hard times. He was no longer moving to Mayfield and was attempting to sell the massive home he'd built, except none of the simple townspeople could afford such an extravagant residence.

Did she dare walk down to the house,

knock on the front door, and ask to see Drew?

Before she could make up her mind, the sheriff came out and started back toward his office. She hadn't expected him to re-appear so soon, had thought he'd stand guard and eventually bring Drew back to the jail.

But now he was just the person she needed to speak with. He'd have information about Drew's predicament, the trial dates, and what would happen next.

"Sheriff!" she called, picking up her skirts and hustling in his direction.

He cast her a cursory glance but continued with his purposeful stride.

She fell into step next to him. "I'd like to know what is happening to Andrew Brady."

"I'm not at liberty to say."

"Sheriff," she said, unable to contain her exasperation, "I have every right to know what's going on. He's my erstwhile fellow employee." And erstwhile fiancé.

The sheriff lengthened his short stride, and she struggled to keep up. "He's in capable hands now, and that's all you need to know."

"Whose hands? The judge's?"

"No, his father's."

Marianne stopped. The sheriff walked

ahead without her.

Drew's father was here? Her body sagged with relief. She spun and examined the house at the end of the street again. So Mr. Brady had received her telegram? He must have left immediately. She could only imagine how long of a train trip it was from Georgia to Illinois.

Now that he was here, he'd be able to find a way to help Drew. As a lawyer, he'd know what to do. He'd be able to prove that Drew was innocent and save him from needless pain.

Should she go and introduce herself? She took several steps toward the fancy house, but then halted. Uncertainty swirled around her as thick as the hot prairie breeze. She'd wait a little while, give Drew and his father time to talk before she imposed on their reunion.

Disappointment choked Drew. He stared unseeingly out the second-story window, his hands stuffed into his trousers.

Behind him, his father's slaves were working silently to carry away the dirty bathwater. In addition to the long and hot bath his father had ordered, his father also paid a barber to come and give him a haircut and shave.

The bay rum scent of the aftershave lotion lingered on his skin, eradicating the stench of his filth and the prison cell.

Once again, his father had come to bail him out of his troubles. At the first sight of his father walking into the back room of the sheriff's office so clean-cut and confident, Drew had sucked in a bitter breath and the bitterness had only grown with each passing hour.

Somehow his father had found out about his predicament. Drew had told him to leave him and go back home. "You're acting like a child," his father had said in his no-nonsense tone. "Stop the wallowing, pick yourself up, and start behaving like a man."

"I'm a murderer," Drew had said in reply. "You can pay everyone off like you did last time, but it won't change who I am."

"I'm not paying anyone off." His father's face looked older, more lined, and harder than five years ago when Drew had last seen him. "These people have no compelling evidence to hold you in jail. Without solid proof beyond the hearsay of an unreliable and highly volatile orphan boy, who is a convicted criminal himself, they have no legal recourse for imprisoning you."

"I turned myself in."

"For what? Because once again you feel

responsible for the loss of a life?"

"Yes."

"There's a difference between *feeling* responsible for a death and actually *being* responsible for causing it."

Drew had known there was no sense in arguing with his father. He'd learned long ago his father would win every time. Even if his father was wrong, he'd still win. There was a reason he was one of the best lawyers in the South.

The sheriff hadn't contradicted his father when he told him to release Drew and assist him to the house his father had rented for the duration of his time in Mayfield. The sheriff had apparently sensed Mr. Brady's power and hadn't been able to resist any more than Drew.

Even now as Drew stared out the window, he felt the need to escape from his father's clutches. But his joints were too stiff from his days of inactivity to move more than a few shuffling steps without pain shooting through his limbs. He turned away from the window and limped out of the room toward the winding stairway. One of the slaves followed a short distance behind, having been instructed by his father not to let Drew out of his sight.

His father didn't have to worry, at least

not today. Drew wasn't about to leave until after the trial. Of course, his father would win Drew's freedom just like he had before. And if for some strange reason he didn't win, then he'd pay the judge and any other official to reverse the decision and secure Drew's release. Money wasn't an issue for his father. The family plantation was thriving, and his father was making money faster than he could spend it.

No, his father wasn't worried about finances. The real issue was the Brady reputation. And his father didn't want a convicted murderer for a son. It would blemish the family's name. Since Drew had already done that once, he had no doubt this most recent incident caused his father to squirm with quite a bit of embarrassment. His wayward son, the irresponsible one, the black sheep of the family — once again in trouble.

His father had likely hastened to Illinois just as fast as he could in order to fix the damage that had already been done as well as cover up the rest.

Drew held on to the curved banister of the wide stairway, determined to rebuild his strength. But at the sound of voices coming from the front parlor, Drew stopped. A woman's voice.

Marianne was here.

His heartbeat leapt in his chest involuntarily, and he continued down the stairs more quickly, causing the slave behind him to cluck her tongue. "Whoa now. Careful."

A warning sounded in his mind telling him to go back upstairs instead of down, telling him to rush away from Marianne instead of toward her, to let her go instead of wanting to hold on. But the hum of anticipation coursing through his blood drowned the warning.

He'd been wrong to think he could let her go so easily. His time apart from her had been torture. When he wasn't reading his Bible, his thoughts had turned to her. Even his sleep had been filled with images of her. And yesterday the agony had grown unbearable after Reinhold had walked out of the sheriff's office. All Drew could think about was Reinhold wrapping his arms around Marianne and kissing her.

The thought had driven him wild with jealousy. Even if he'd been the one to suggest Reinhold pull her into his arms, he couldn't bear the idea of Reinhold actually carrying through with it. He'd wanted to punch the wall and pretend it was Reinhold's face on more than one occasion throughout the long night.

But now that Marianne was here, he had to see her. Maybe Reinhold hadn't gone to her yet and asked her to marry him. Maybe he still had time . . .

He halted outside the parlor door. Time for what? To tell her he loved her? What good would that do, except to shackle her to a man who had nothing to offer except a blemished reputation and a future as an outcast? No, he had to let her go.

Once the trial was done, his father would expect him to return home like an obedient chastised son, then pick up his life where he'd left off five years ago. His father had already mentioned Drew finishing seminary.

But Drew couldn't return to Georgia any more than he could return to being an agent with the Children's Aid Society. The only option left for him was to run away again. And this time he'd go west, maybe to California. Yes, he knew God had forgiven him for his mistakes. And he had no doubt God still loved him and would be there for him, no matter his failings.

The trouble was, he couldn't forgive himself for allowing another child under his responsibility to die.

"So you didn't know each other very long before my son proposed to you," his father was saying to Marianne.

"I'm sure you know your son is rather spontaneous and unconventional," Marianne responded.

"Yes, I'm quite aware." His father didn't sound pleased. "Which is why it's a good thing you both came to your senses."

"I don't think we came to our senses. Rather, Drew never intended to carry through with the plans. The murder charge allowed him an escape from his obligation to me."

Drew almost called out a word of protest. He most certainly had planned to marry her. He'd gone to Elise's house the morning of the wedding, hadn't he? He'd been nervous, but he *had* wanted to marry her. There was no questioning that fact or that he loved her.

His father was quiet for a moment, and Drew pictured him, broad-shouldered and well built in his finely tailored garments. His sandy brown hair was untouched by age, his expression of displeasure unchanged as well.

Drew leaned his head against the wall. He couldn't remember too many times while he was growing up when he'd ever pleased his father. Maybe the time when he won first prize in the youth oratory contest. But otherwise he'd garnered more raised brows, frowns, and scoldings than praise. Granted, as a boy he was full of energy and enthusiasm, perhaps too much so. He could admit he'd gotten into his fair share of trouble. Drew always seemed to fall short of pleasing his father. And in recent years he'd been nothing but a headache for the man.

"I can see why Andrew was taken with you," his father said. "You're very lovely and forthright."

"Thank you. I —"

"But you have to realize a union between the two of you would never have worked."

Drew pushed away from the wall. Of course, his father would make that kind of conclusion without knowing Marianne.

"I know all about your history and background, Miss Neumann," his father went on. "Although you may think you can imitate your sister and marry into wealth and prestige, you wouldn't fit into Andrew's world."

Drew shook his head in frustration and moved forward, holding on to the wall for support. He wasn't surprised his father had investigated Marianne. The man had a network of friends all over the East Coast, and information could be bought — especially for the right price.

"Father," Drew said, stepping into the

room, "my relationship with Marianne isn't any of your concern."

At the sight of her, all coherent thought vanished from his mind. She was as fresh and beautiful as the daisies someone had arranged in a vase on the side table. She wore her yellow silk dress that showed off her rich brown hair, which had been styled into a fashionable loop with a few dangling curls by her cheeks. The light contrast of the dress also set apart her eyes that were now fixed upon him.

Although he could mask his hunger and need for her, hers was written in every line of her face. Not only could he see it, but his father was gauging her reaction as well.

"Drew." His name on her lips was an invitation, a plea and so much more. The longing in her eyes was his undoing. This was why he'd sent her away when he was in jail, why he didn't ask for her even though he'd gone nearly mad with needing to see her. He couldn't resist her; he was too weak. And even though he hated himself for his weakness, he wanted to hold her one last time, to feel the softness of her skin and breathe in her womanly fragrance.

He shuffled forward a step, hating that he wasn't physically strong enough to sweep her into his embrace the way he wanted.

She took a tentative step toward him.

He loved her. How could he ever give her up?

"It was so good of Marianne to send me the telegram regarding your imprisonment," his father said. "Don't you agree, Andrew?"

His father's words froze him into place, just as the man had known they would. While he wanted to be angry at Marianne for involving his father, he knew it wasn't her fault. In fact, he wouldn't doubt that was exactly what his father was attempting to do — cause a rift between him and Marianne. But he wasn't falling for it.

His father studied him shrewdly. "Perhaps we can credit Marianne for bringing us back together after so many years apart." Before giving Drew a chance to reply, he said to Marianne, "Thank you, my dear, from the bottom of my heart. After not hearing from Andrew for five years, I'm delighted to be reunited with him."

"Drew told me he hadn't gone back home," she said, glancing between him and his father as though afraid of saying the wrong thing.

"I don't suppose he told you why he left —"

"I told her enough."

"He mentioned an accident." She answered at the same time he did.

"Yes, it was a tragic accident," Father continued. His tone was nonchalant, but from the calculated gleam in his eyes, Drew knew he was scheming and there was nothing he could do to stop him.

"During the last week of school, Andrew took his students out of class for a picnic and to swim."

Drew's stomach churned as his father dug up the buried memories. "There's no need to talk about it —"

"Of course there is," his father said smoothly. "I'm sure Marianne would like to hear why you ran away from home."

Marianne's eyes widened, and she started to shake her head. "If Drew doesn't want to speak of the matter . . ."

"His students were swimming. Instead of supervising, Andrew had decided to join them."

Drew swallowed hard and gripped the edge of the nearest chair to keep from sinking to his knees. It wouldn't do any good to try to stop his father from telling Marianne what had happened. No one could stop his father from saying what he wanted, not the toughest judge or the most seasoned politician. Certainly not his lowly, irresponsible son.

"Andrew was busy playing with the youngest boys and had his back turned on the older students. One of the boys decided to dive into the gorge. He hit a rock, snapped his neck, and died instantly." His father paused for effect, and of course his voice was laced with tragedy. He was a good actor when he needed to be.

Drew didn't look at Marianne. He wouldn't be able to bear her pity. And he didn't want her censure either, although he deserved it. He'd been irresponsible with his students and that hadn't changed in five years, even though he'd hoped it had.

The parents of the boy who'd died were wealthy neighbors, the boy their only son. Heartbroken, their grief spilled over into the entire community. Just thinking about the sadness of the other students and families made Drew's chest ache all over again.

It hadn't taken long before the grief turned to anger and then to blaming. All fingers pointed at him. At first he'd been defensive. After all, he'd warned the boys not to dive. And even if he hadn't warned them, they knew it well enough for themselves. It was common knowledge the gorge was filled with boulders.

Even so, the boy's parents had gone after

Drew with a vengeance, accusing him of being inattentive to his duties as a teacher. With their grief staring him in the face, he'd been too consumed with guilt and brokenness to resist.

His father had stepped in and defended him, had used every oratory skill he possessed to push the blame onto the young boy who'd died, showing him to be a willful child, one who commonly questioned authority and who'd blatantly ignored Drew on that fateful day.

In the end, his father had won Drew's innocence with his smooth talking — or had paid the judge for it. Drew had never been certain. Whatever the case, after the trial, Drew left without a good-bye. He hadn't spoken to his family or friends since.

"You can imagine my gladness to see Drew again," his father was saying, "but also my deep disappointment to learn my son was involved in another tragic accident and that I would have to save him from self-destruction once more."

"I already told you I didn't ask you to come." The vehement words escaped from Drew before he could stop them. "And I don't need you to save me."

His father lifted his brows. "Really?"

"I know I've never been anything to you

but a disappointment," Drew went on, the words spilling out now. "I know I've caused you untold grief, and I've been a miserable failure in just about everything I set out to do."

"No, Drew!" Marianne interjected, rushing to his defense. "That's not true."

He shook his head. Even if she accepted him for all his faults, he was a man who bore the responsibility for two deaths, who would be forever running from his guilt and grief. She needed a much better man, someone who wasn't so broken.

"Go away, Marianne," he said in a cold tone. He avoided looking at her. If he saw the pain he was causing her, he'd break down and go to her. "I told you I didn't want to see you again and I meant it."

He heard her sharp intake of breath and loathed himself for stabbing her tender heart. He turned and stumbled toward the door. He had to get out of the room before he admitted to her how much he loved her. The words rose and threatened to strangle him.

"Drew, please . . ." Her footsteps padded across the rug toward him.

If she touched him, he wouldn't be able to pull away. He braced himself against the doorframe and held out a hand toward her to stop her.

Her steps faltered.

"Go marry Reinhold," he rasped out. "He promised to take care of you. He'll be able to give you a better life than I ever could."

She didn't respond.

His father didn't say anything more either. Drew guessed his father felt he'd said enough. He'd accomplished what he set out to do — push Marianne out of Drew's life.

Drew straightened as best he could and forced himself to walk away. This time for good.

CHAPTER 23

Marianne sat on the edge of the claw-foot sofa and admired the pineapples carved into the mahogany armrests. She ran her fingers over the gold velvety material. A pedestal table next to the sofa was etched with a matching pattern and held a lantern with gold leaves painted into an intricate pattern around the globe.

An enormous piano graced the opposite side of the sitting room and was polished to a glossy sheen. The wall sconces behind the piano dripped with crystals that glittered in the sunlight streaming through the open front windows.

Marianne had arrived in Benton late last night and wanted to rush over to see Dorothea. But she'd forced herself to go to the inn and attempt to get a few hours of sleep. She'd arisen early and made herself wait for as long as possible before walking the short distance to the banker's large home.

From the outside, the Garners' house rivaled the size of Elise's new home in Quincy. On the inside, however, the Garners' tastes far exceeded Elise's. Elizabeth Garner had a flair for the extravagant. Everything was opulent, as if imported from a royal English palace.

How could a little girl be happy in such a fancy place? Although Marianne was awed, her unease had grown with each passing minute. A servant had ushered her into the front parlor, informing her that Mrs. Garner was still eating her breakfast.

If Marianne had her way, she would have preferred to visit the family unannounced. Then she'd have the chance to see firsthand the living conditions without Mrs. Garner having the chance to cover up any problems.

"Miss Neumann." Elizabeth glided into the sitting room, already immaculately attired. She was as pretty this time as she'd been the day Marianne met her in the church. "What a pleasant surprise."

Marianne rose and returned the woman's gracious smile, noting how she seemed happy to see her. Immediately Marianne's thoughts raced in a hundred different directions. Why would Elizabeth be happy to see her unless something was wrong with Dorothea? What if something had happened to

Dorothea, and Elizabeth was trying to smooth things over first before telling her the bad news?

"How's Dorothea?" The words fell out before Marianne could offer a return greeting.

Elizabeth's smile only widened, revealing the pleasure in her eyes. "I hope all agents are like you, Miss Neumann. Your love for the children is so commendable I've already written once to your superiors in New York City to praise your efforts, and now I really must write to them again."

The compliment brought an abrupt halt to Marianne's careening thoughts. A peace settled in her spirit that she didn't quite understand. "Why, thank you, Mrs. Garner."

"I am relieved every time I think about Dorothea having you to hold her and comfort her during those difficult days of her trip here." Tears sparkled in Elizabeth's eyes.

Suddenly Marianne felt a pricking in her own eyes and a tightness in her chest.

Elizabeth took a lacy handkerchief out of her pocket and dabbed at the corner of one eye. "I don't know how you do your job with so much love and compassion and kindness."

Marianne swallowed the lump in her

throat. "I honestly don't know how I do it either."

"You're a strong woman, Miss Neumann."

Marianne gave a wobbly laugh. "I'm afraid you have me mixed up with my sister. I've always been the weak one compared to her."

Elizabeth dabbed at the corner of her other eye. "I've always considered myself a weak woman too," she admitted. "I've been particularly frail in health, and as you can likely deduce, I've never been able to conceive any children of my own."

Elizabeth lowered herself to the edge of the golden sofa. Marianne sat down next to her. "For the past several years, as I've accepted my barrenness, my dear husband said something I've never forgotten." The pretty young woman turned toward the window that overlooked a spacious front yard full of blooming flower beds. "He told me he was proud of the way I'd adjusted to the news I couldn't have children. He said it takes great courage to accept what I can't change, and even more courage to move forward and live my life to the fullest in spite of how achingly hard it is to face each new day."

Elizabeth reached for Marianne's clammy hands and held them in her soft unblemished ones. "What I've learned is that courage takes many forms. And it takes a very special kind of strength to love these orphans and then to let them go."

Marianne's eyes welled with tears in earnest, and her throat was too thick to speak.

"You have that special strength and don't let anyone convince you otherwise, especially yourself. Sometimes we're our own worst enemies."

A soft rap at the door of the sitting room was followed by a maid entering, holding the hand of a talkative child who was dressed in so many layers of pink ruffles and white lace she looked like a dainty porcelain doll. Her blond hair was styled in perfect dangling ringlets and tied in place by a big matching pink bow.

At the sight of Elizabeth on the sofa, the child broke free of the maid and ran to Elizabeth. "Mommy!" she called, her smile wide with delight.

For a moment, Marianne could only watch the little girl in stunned disbelief. Was this Dorothea? The skinny frightened child with red puffy eyes and splotchy cheeks who'd cried through most of the trip?

Her beautiful brown eyes filled with adoration as she flung herself into Elizabeth's open arms. Elizabeth hugged the girl so tightly that Dorothea giggled.

"We have a guest, darling," Elizabeth said, pulling back and helping to smooth all the ruffles back into place on Dorothea's dress.

Only then did Dorothea seem to notice Marianne's presence. Marianne smiled at the child. But instead of the cheerful welcome that Marianne expected, Dorothea shrank against Elizabeth, and fear transformed her face into the one Marianne remembered.

"Good morning, Dorothea," Marianne said, suddenly filled with uncertainty. Maybe she shouldn't have come.

"It's fine, darling," Elizabeth said, holding Dorothea's hand but maneuvering the young girl so she was standing up straight and no longer clinging. "Miss Neumann is only here for a visit. She's come to make sure you are happy and like your new home."

At the words of reassurance, some of the fear in Dorothea's face fell away and she looked at Marianne shyly. "Your mommy is right, Dorothea," Marianne said. "I've been worried about you and have been praying you like your new home."

Dorothea glanced down at her shoes, which were shiny white patent leather with tiny pink bows on top.

Elizabeth exchanged a glance with Marianne, one that told her everything would be all right and to be patient. Marianne nodded in understanding.

"Why don't you tell Miss Neumann all about your new home?" Elizabeth suggested.

Dorothea glanced up, but only halfway, and whispered, "Please don't take me away."

The trembling statement was like a dagger plunging into Marianne's heart. Though she felt like weeping for the girl, Marianne smiled bravely. "You don't need to worry about going away again, Dorothea. This is your new home now, and you'll never, ever have to leave it."

Dorothea's head lifted a little higher and she met Marianne's gaze, this time with a glimmer of hope shining in her eyes. "I won't?"

"Never." Marianne pushed the word past her tight airway and blinked back more tears. "Your new mommy loves you, and you get to stay with her forever."

Dorothea smiled and turned to Elizabeth. "I love my new mommy too."

Elizabeth wrapped Dorothea into another embrace.

The day with Dorothea and the Garners

was one Marianne would treasure forever. It was a joy to see Dorothea blossom before her eyes into a talkative child full of laughter and smiles and inquisitiveness. Elizabeth doted on her, and it was clear the two were meant for each other.

It wasn't until Marianne was back at the hotel and in bed that she realized she hadn't thought of Drew all day. Lying in her bed and staring out the open window into the starry summer night, her chest ached with a pain that felt as deep and dark as the universe.

She pictured him as he'd first appeared when stepping into the parlor. He was thinner and with dark circles under his eyes. But he was as devastatingly handsome as always with his sandy hair combed into submission, his cheeks and jaw smooth from a recent shave, and his lips hard and determined.

When she gazed into his blue-green eyes, she'd seen that look again, the one that made her believe he loved her. If it wasn't love, then it was definitely something close to it. The desire for her had been so palpable, it was a living force that swirled between them and would have drawn them together, except it had become increasingly clear Drew's father intended to do all he could to keep them apart.

A fine Southern gentleman like him might have once intimidated her. Yet based on what Drew had told her about his father, she'd already disliked him before she'd made his acquaintance. She supposed he loved Drew in his own way. After all, he'd traveled to Illinois with all haste and had managed to free Drew from jail.

Even so, Mr. Brady didn't understand his son, didn't see what a good man he was, nor realize how talented he was with children. If only the man would open his eyes and see Drew for who he really was and not what he wanted him to become.

Marianne kicked off her sheet, slipped out of bed, and padded to the window. Elizabeth Garner's words had been echoing through the corridors of her mind. *"It takes a very special kind of strength to be able to love these orphans and then to let them go."*

She hadn't thought of that before. But Elizabeth was right. It took more courage to love in the face of loss than to close oneself off out of fear of getting hurt. The children had needed her unconditional love. She'd given freely of herself, poured everything into them. And in the end she'd had to let them go, which tore at her heart.

It had taken courage to be an agent. And

it would take even more strength to do it again. Could she handle another trip? She peered up into the starry sky. There were as many orphans in New York City roaming the streets and languishing in the orphanages as there were stars that she could see.

Maybe she wouldn't be able to find them all homes and parents like Dorothea's or like George and Peter's, but if she helped even a few of the children to find happiness, wasn't the pain and heartache worth it?

Was that the lesson her mother had been trying to teach her?

Marianne turned and crossed to the bedside table. She touched the girl figurine on the music box and reverently fingered each of the geese. She cranked the handle until it was wound tightly, then watched as the music box spun, listening to the sweet melody that filled the quiet of the bedroom.

She didn't have to let the difficult situations take away her joy. God could help her walk through the hardships so she could find new strength and joy on the other side. If God could do that for her, could He do the same for Drew?

Something else Elizabeth Garner said had stayed with Marianne throughout the day. *"Sometimes we're our own worst enemies."*

For too long she'd let her insecurities dictate her life — long before Sophie had run away. But once Sophie had gone, she'd let the insecurities clamp down on her like chains, holding her prisoner.

She wanted to break free, to live the way Elizabeth did. Even if the day was challenging and hard, she wanted to get up and live life to the fullest. Could she help Drew come to the same realization, that he too could break free of the chains he kept locked around his heart?

The melody of the music box drifted into silence, leaving the room with a stillness and peace that made Marianne sense the presence of God in a way she hadn't in a long time.

"I want to help him, God," she whispered as she fell back onto her bed, the rusty frame squeaking beneath her. His trial had been set for a week from today. Her mind began to spin, and a plan slowly took shape until she smiled up at the ceiling.

"I promise that after I help him, I'll let him go." She knew that would be the hardest test of her courage she'd faced yet. Could she pour out herself for Drew, let herself love him, and in the end be willing to let him go?

She had to be honest with herself, that

yes, she loved him. She probably had all along. But she was bound to let him go the same way she was bound to let the orphan children go. Drew didn't want her. And even if he did, she'd promised Reinhold she would marry him and couldn't go back on that now. She was a woman of her word. Besides, Reinhold and his family needed her. She couldn't let them down, even if it cost her the man she loved.

CHAPTER 24

Reinhold sat stiffly on a pew near the front of the church. The building was already packed full of people, and still more were entering and standing along the sides and in the back.

At least half of the faces were unfamiliar. He hadn't lived in Mayfield all that long, but he thought he'd gotten to know most of the farmers and townsfolk. So where had these families come from? Had news of Andrew Brady's trial spread, attracting the attention of people outside their community?

At the front, Drew sat next to an important-looking man dressed in a crisp black suit and matching vest. His white shirt had a high collar set off by a black bow tie. Drew was similarly attired, and it was easy to tell from their build and mannerisms they were father and son.

"When is this thing gonna start?" Liverpool muttered next to Reinhold. The boy had been resistant to coming, but when the judge had specifically requested his presence, Mr. Turner gave Reinhold the morning off in order to bring Liverpool to town.

"It's supposed to start at nine o'clock," Reinhold said, glancing around again for Marianne. He'd been looking for her since he pulled up in the wagon. She'd been gone all week visiting orphans in Benton to the north. But she said she'd be back for the trial.

Strangely, all week he'd been worried about her. Now that she was his wife-to-be, he felt a new sense of responsibility for her and didn't like that she was traveling alone and unchaperoned. He'd thought often of her going back to New York City and having to fend for herself and his sisters there, and he didn't like that either.

Mr. Turner had just paid him. Slowly and steadily, he was beginning to save again, and this time he'd buried his savings in a crock out in his potato field in a spot only he knew about. He only added to his savings when no one else was with him. He wasn't taking any chances this time. He'd also been asking around for additional work, hoping he might find ways to earn extra cash.

He'd thought the idea of having Marianne

as a wife to take care of his siblings would ease his mind and give him more time to get settled. Yet he realized now his sense of urgency had only increased. He wanted to care for and protect Marianne every bit as much as he did his sisters. The sooner he could settle into a place of his own, the better.

"I don't want to go up there and talk," Liverpool said, glaring at the judge, who sat at a table positioned at the front of the sanctuary. He was a short older man who was chatting in a friendly manner with the reverend.

For Drew's sake, Reinhold was glad the judge didn't seem too severe. After having met Drew and talked with him, Reinhold couldn't shake the feeling that Drew was innocent. The man was defeated and hurting. That much was clear. Still, he was no murderer.

Liverpool had remained consistent in his version of what had happened the day of the murder. Although Liverpool hadn't come right out and blamed Drew for Ned's death, there was no other way to interpret the boy's story. According to Liverpool, Drew had pushed Ned. And if Drew didn't deny it, which he hadn't yet, then what else could the judge do but conclude that Drew had killed Ned out of frustration?

"You've got to tell the truth." Reinhold shifted in the packed pew so he was looking at Liverpool.

Liverpool's eyes were hard and unflinching. "I already told you the truth."

"I think you know more about what happened than you're saying."

"You think I'm lying?" Liverpool's tone turned defensive.

Reinhold stared at the boy and attempted to see past the hard exterior. As much as he'd tried over the past few weeks to set a good example for Liverpool in what it meant to live with integrity, kindness, and fairness, he hadn't seen much change in the boy — if any at all.

He was still just as sullen and antagonistic as he'd been the day he arrived at the Turner farm. In fact, Higgins seemed to take special delight in riling up the boy with snide comments so now Liverpool seemed more defensive and sullen than ever.

The only time Liverpool let down his guard was when they were alone together in the potato field. Every few evenings, Liverpool would follow Reinhold out to the field and help him hoe weeds. And on those nights, the boy would talk about his life in New York City, which filled Reinhold with sorrow because he realized the boy had never had a home — a real home, with a mother and father who cared about him.

Instead, Liverpool's earliest memories had been of scrounging on the streets of Liverpool, England. He'd never known who his father was, and his mother had died in a brothel. At the age of six, he'd stowed away on a steamship with a friend and had arrived homeless and penniless in New York City, where he'd lived on the streets ever since and taken the name of the city of his birth.

Reinhold hadn't asked about his real name. And he'd tried not to show any pity, which he guessed would only frustrate the boy. Reinhold had tried to be more patient and purposeful, taking extra care to show Liverpool how to tend the livestock, sharpen the tools, and work the fields. "Then you'll be ready, just like I am, to have your own place someday."

Although Liverpool complained often about the hard work and missing his life in the city, Reinhold suspected the boy was more satisfied with living on the farm than he let on. Reinhold hadn't given up hope yet that God could transform Liverpool.

But at times like this, when Liverpool was sour and testy, Reinhold couldn't keep from feeling discouraged.

"It'd be a shame for a good man like Mr. Brady to take the blame for something he didn't do," Reinhold said.

"He's not a good man."

"He did a good thing by bringing you out here, didn't he?"

Liverpool glared at the back of Drew's head. "He's bossy and always thinks he knows best."

Reinhold shifted his attention to Drew, who sat with his head bowed in his hands and his shoulders slumped. Drew probably did know what was best for Liverpool. But the boy had never had any discipline and had always been his own authority. How could he appreciate the sacrifices Drew and Marianne were making for orphans like him?

At a commotion at the back of the sanctuary, Reinhold craned his neck, along with everyone else, to see what was going on. To his surprise, Marianne breezed into the church with a wide smile on her face, as though she were arriving at a baptismal ceremony rather than a murder trial.

Not only was she exuding confidence and poise, but he couldn't help but notice just how pretty she looked in the silk gown — likely one Elise had given to her. And she appeared so mature, so grown up and womanly.

She really was beautiful, especially her vivacious brown eyes that sometimes danced with merriment and other times with deep sadness. He was marrying her next week. After that, he'd get to take her in his arms and hold her. And he'd take her to his bed. The thought came to him unbidden and burned a slow trail through his gut. He hadn't talked to Marianne about the finer details of their arrangement, but he had no intention of marrying a woman without making their marriage real in every sense. He didn't anticipate Marianne would protest, but maybe he needed to clarify the nature of their marriage first.

The thought of speaking to her about such intimacies heated his face, making him watch her more closely and anticipate pulling her into his arms and burying his fingers into her thick hair.

Maybe God had ordained this marriage with Marianne. After all, if not for Drew calling him to his cell and revealing Marianne's desire for him, the thought of marrying her never would have occurred to him.

He couldn't stop from watching her march forward, realizing at the same time as everybody else that she hadn't come alone but had a trail of children following her. The children were in order from shortest to tallest. Some were smiling shyly while others looked terrified.

Marianne searched the front as though looking for someone in particular. Reinhold waited for her to notice him, almost raised his hand to draw her attention. But her gaze came to rest on someone else, and her smile widened.

Reinhold noticed she was looking directly at Drew and that he'd snapped out of his broken stupor — at least momentarily — and was staring back at her. He wasn't smiling, but his attention was riveted to her like a thirsty man to a cold, fresh creek. As before, when he'd seen Drew in jail, Reinhold could tell that the man loved Marianne.

Reinhold returned his attention to Marianne. She was close enough that he could have whispered her name, snapped his fingers, or done something to remind her he was here. But something shining in her eyes stopped him. Love.

Everything within Reinhold ceased functioning as the realization seeped into him. Not only was Drew in love with Marianne, she obviously loved him too. She had eyes and thoughts for no one else in the room.

Not even him — her fiancé.

After several long seconds, Reinhold's pulse and breathing resumed but at twice the speed. What should he do? Why had Marianne agreed to marry him if she was in love with another man? She shouldn't have given him such a promise. She shouldn't have led him to believe she'd eventually care about him.

Even as he silently chastised her, self-reproach pointed a finger at him. He should have known the day he'd proposed to her. She was hesitant then and likely would have said no. Except he'd played his last card, and it had been trump. His sisters. He'd known Marianne would marry him to help him and his sisters. She was too tender-hearted to turn away from someone in need.

Drew watched Marianne, the longing in his eyes palpable and the yearning in his expression almost desperate. He nodded at Marianne and then slowly turned, resignation tightening his features.

Marianne's smile faltered for only a second, and the sparkle in her eyes dimmed. But she strode forward nonetheless until she reached the front of the church. There she directed the children to sit on the floor in front of the pews, then took her place standing off to the side.

Only after the judge began to address the gathering did Reinhold finally catch her attention. He nodded and gave a slight wave of his hand. Her smile in return was forced, almost sad. The truth was there for all who wanted to see it. Marianne loved Drew, but he'd given her up. After all that had happened, he was doing the honorable thing and setting Marianne free to find a better life rather than being tied to a man charged with murder. He'd tasked Reinhold with helping him. And now Reinhold couldn't let him down, could he?

Drew sat stiffly in the front pew. The room was stuffy, even with the windows open, and his shirt clung to his back. He wanted to tear off the bow tie his father had made him wear and throw aside the suit coat that confined him. Deep inside, though, he realized that even if he tossed off the shackles, he still wouldn't be free.

His father had been talking for some time and making a case for his innocence. But Drew had heard it all before. A general in a battle couldn't be held responsible for the deaths of the men under him. He was only the leader, and as carefully as he attempted to protect his regiment, he wasn't God. He couldn't prevent accidents either from within or outside their camp. Although a general might feel sorrowful when he lost good men, it was inevitable at times because life was a battle. Their enemy, the devil, was sneaking around seeking whom he may devour.

His father had used the same line of defense the day of the last trial. Drew understood the rationale behind it. Nevertheless, it didn't ease his guilt. And likely never would. But that wasn't his father's concern. His father had one goal in mind. He wanted a declaration of innocence for Drew, and he'd stop at nothing to get it.

Drew stared at his shoes, which had been polished to a perfect shine. Only a dozen steps away, Marianne stood against the wall. He didn't dare look up from his shoes or he'd lock eyes with her again. And it was torture to see her and know he was leaving her behind. As soon as the trial was over today, he was catching the first train out of Illinois.

"Your Honor," his father was saying to the judge, "although the sheriff has gathered testimonies from townspeople as well as from other orphans, none of them were at the pond when Ned Colson was killed and tossed into the water. All the sheriff's so-called evidence is pure conjecture."

The sheriff sat several seats back. The stout man had done nothing but scowl since Drew and his father had entered the church.

"In fact," his father continued, "I'd even go so far as to say the sheriff has a bias against my client. He's made his dislike and opposition of the orphans and the Children's Aid Society very clear in this town. As a result it would appear he has ulterior motives for smearing my client's good name."

The sheriff started to grumble, but a sharp look from the judge silenced him.

"We have only one true witness of the murder, a young lad by the name of Liverpool."

"Your Honor," Marianne interrupted, "I hate to contradict Mr. Brady, but I've brought a couple dozen witnesses."

At her declaration, Drew's head snapped up, and he couldn't keep himself from looking at her. Again she smiled at him in such a way that told him everything would be all right. It was the same confident smile he'd always given her to assuage her worries. It was strange to be on the receiving end this time.

"A couple dozen witnesses?" The judge was a friend of his father; his father had made sure of that. Thus Drew didn't need a couple dozen witnesses to rise to his defense. He really didn't need any. His father would bring Liverpool to the front, tear him apart in front of everyone, and then the judge would rule in Drew's favor. The proceedings would be over in less than a quarter of an hour. There was no sense dragging this out.

"Your Honor," Marianne said, waving her hand toward the children sitting on the floor in front of him, "surely you can't deny these eager young children the chance to speak on behalf of Mr. Brady?"

Drew sat up straight and took stock of the children. He hadn't paid them any attention when they'd come in with Marianne, but now he saw that they were the orphans. Familiar faces peered back at him, smiling tentatively. They were the children he'd grown to love during the long days and nights of travel.

He smiled back, touching each dear face with his gaze before landing upon the last one, a little girl with blond curls and big brown eyes. She wasn't with the others. Instead, she was dressed in the most exquisite white dress, almost as if she were a princess. She was standing next to an elegant woman, clinging tightly to her hand.

Dorothea?

His sights snapped to Marianne. As if sensing his unasked question, she nodded. And this time he saw the peace in her eyes and knew she'd finally accepted the hardest part about loving the children — letting them go.

"Please, Your Honor," Marianne said more earnestly. "Many of these children have traveled for miles to support Mr. Brady. Won't you let them each say a sentence or two? I promise it won't take long."

His father perked up at the word *support.* He exchanged a glance with the judge, clearly giving the judge permission to allow the unusual proceedings.

As one by one the children rose and stood facing the crowded room, they began to list off all the things he'd done on the trip.

"Mr. Brady stayed up all night to empty the buckets in our leaky room at the hotel the night it rained."

"When I was sick, he gave up his seat on the train so I could lay down."

"I left my shoes behind at one of our stops and he bought me new ones the very next day."

"I liked his stories and games. They kept me from cryin' and missing my grandma."

"He listened to me and prayed with me every day."

"I had a big sliver in my finger and Mr. Brady got it out."

"He always had a cheerful attitude and made me smile or laugh."

The children looked straight at him when they spoke, and each word filled his heart until it felt like it would burst.

"You cared about each one of us like we were real people, and no one's ever done that before," the last little boy said with a toothless smile that made Drew's eyes sting with unshed tears. "We love you, Mr. Brady."

Around him, sniffles filled the air. Marianne walked to the front, wiping tears from her cheeks. She hugged the boy, who then scampered back to his spot on the floor amidst the others.

"As you can see, Your Honor," Marianne said, "Mr. Brady has done an exemplary job with the children. I too bear witness to the love Mr. Brady showed. I watched him day in and day out tirelessly sacrifice for these children. Time after time he put their needs ahead of his own."

Her gaze radiated a pride for him that rushed through him, running into the cracks and crevices of his past hurts — the hurts of a young boy who'd never received praise, who'd always lived in the shadow of his older brother, who'd somehow never been able to live up to his family name.

"Mr. Brady is a rare kind of man who deserves to be lauded for all the many things he's done right and not singled out for something over which he had no control. His great concern and sense of responsibility for the loss of Ned Colson proves just how deeply he loves the orphans. Even though he wasn't involved in the boy's death in any way, he still holds himself accountable for it."

Neither his father nor the judge made any effort to stop Marianne. Drew had to admit, she was making a good case for him. Maybe his father wouldn't have to say anything more.

"If you must hold anyone accountable for Ned's death, then it should be me, not Drew," she continued.

He sat up straighter and shook his head.

She didn't look at him but instead spoke in a rush. "I was the one watching the children when the boys wandered off. I should have tried harder to make them obey. At the very least, I should have gone after them. I should have sensed there were problems. If I'd been a better leader, I would have been able to stop them —"

"That's ludicrous." Drew stood to his feet.

His pulse was thumping erratically, and he was suddenly overcome with fear for Marianne. He wouldn't be able to live with himself if his father or the judge or the townspeople decided to blame her for the crime. "You know you weren't involved."

"I'm just as much involved as you, if not more," she replied.

He turned around and looked out over the sanctuary. People stood in every inch of space available. The doors were open, and there were people standing outside too.

He had to make them understand that Marianne wasn't to blame. "You cannot accuse Miss Neumann. She wasn't the one who killed Ned Colson and tied the stone to his body."

"Neither were you."

"I know that, but as the leader of the trip, I should have done more to protect him."

"And as the co-leader of the trip, I should have done more too."

With each of her rebuttals, his frustration mounted. "You're being irrational. There's nothing more you could have done!"

"And there's nothing more you could have done either."

Her words rang out over the deathly silence of the sanctuary and echoed down to the deepest part of his soul. *There's noth-*

ing more you could have done. There's noth-ing more you could have done.

Every pair of eyes in the room was fixed on him waiting for his answer. But what could he say? She'd backed him into a corner. If he demanded she free herself of responsibility for the crime, then how could he do any less for himself?

He'd clung to his guilt for so long he didn't know that he could let go. And yet, if he held on, would she do the same? He didn't want her to be strangled by the same chains that bound him.

"You're a good man, Andrew Brady. Everyone in this room knows it, and it's time you accepted it too."

Someone in the back of the room began to clap, and soon the entire room joined in. People surged to their feet clapping. The children jumped up and cheered. Even his father was clapping, slowly, almost begrudgingly.

Marianne smiled at Drew, her eyes daring him to defy her. In doing so he'd have to defy a hundred or more other people. And she knew it.

A whisper of release blew gently through him. It was soft, but it was there, almost as if someone had turned the lock that had held him prisoner for so long. He was free.

All he had to do was let go of the chains. Could he do it?

"Now that we've heard from all the children," the judge said after the clapping had faded and everyone sat back down, "I do need to call forth our witness —"

A commotion at the back of the sanctuary halted the judge. Two young boys had burst into the room and were followed by an older couple. Immediately Drew recognized George and Peter and the dairy farmer he'd placed them with.

"Sorry we're late, Mr. Brady," George said, dragging his older brother behind him. Peter stumbled along after his brother. He stopped every few feet, causing George to stop and jerk him forward.

Drew was satisfied to see the two boys still together. From a quick survey of their new parents, who'd stopped at the back of the aisle, Drew could once again tell from their demeanor they were good people and the boys would be well taken care of.

"When Miss Neumann rode out to the farm yesterday and told us you were being put on trial today for murder, we knew we had to come to town even if we had to walk the whole way to git here." George had been the more talkative of the two boys, and that apparently hadn't changed.

426

So Marianne had ridden all over the countryside to gather the orphans? He studied her, noting the dark circles under her eyes. She must have spent hours during the past week spreading the news of his trial and imploring the families to come.

"Young man," the judge said, frowning at George and Peter, "we're ready to move on to our next witness. If you'd like to say something nice about Mr. Brady, you'll need to wait until we've finished the trial."

George proceeded to the front, regardless of the judge's dismissal. Peter had no choice but to follow his brother. When the pair stood side by side near the desk the judge occupied, George stared out over the crowd with a solemn expression.

"Me and Peter didn't want Mr. Brady to get hanged on account of Ned's death," George said. "Mr. Brady don't deserve to swing from the end of a rope any more than you do, Judge. We can swear on it."

The judge started to dismiss the boys again, but Drew's father held up a hand. "Boys, are you telling us you can prove Mr. Brady's innocence beyond a shadow of a doubt?"

"Yes, sir," George replied. "I'm a-sayin' that Mr. Brady didn't kill no one nohow."

"And how do you know this?" His father's

voice remained calm and kind, the same tone he used when trying to win someone's favor.

"Me and Pete," George said, "well, we saw what really happened the day Ned drowned."

"You did?" Mr. Brady stepped forward. "Then why are you only now coming forward to tell us the truth about what happened?"

George glanced at Peter, who hung his head. "We wanted to, mister, but . . . well, we were afeared."

"Frightened?" Mr. Brady said gently. "And why's that?"

George turned to face the crowd, his gaze fixed on Liverpool, who was sitting next to Reinhold. "Because Liverpool told Peter not to say anything or he'd drown me."

Liverpool glared back a warning.

But George quickly turned back to Mr. Brady. "We decided Liverpool never said he would drown Peter if I said anything, so I'm doin' the telling. Besides, my new ma and pa told me God would want us to come clean with the truth. Thataway we can be forgiven and grow up to be good men."

The dairy farmer at the back clutched his hat in large work-roughened hands. His face was plain but kind. He nodded at George, the earnestness in his eyes imploring him to tell the rest of his tale.

George nodded back and then faced the judge. "I'm here to tell you that Liverpool got spittin' mad at Ned and hit him over the head with a rock. When he realized Ned weren't alive, he rigged up Ned's body to the rock, dragged him out into the pond and let him go. He sank clear away."

At the new revelation, murmurs and whispers filled the air around Drew.

Liverpool shot to his feet. His face had gone pale, making his pocked scars stand out. "He's lying through his teeth! That ain't the way it happened. Mr. Brady tied him up and dropped him in."

"Were you there to see this happen?" Drew's father asked sharply.

Liverpool hesitated and then jutted out his chin, his expression taut with defiance. "No, I already ran off by then. But —"

"So you're asking us to believe your account of what happened that day when supposedly you ran off and didn't see everything. But we're to ignore two witnesses who claim they saw the murder firsthand?"

"They're lying, I tell you!"

"They have no reason to lie. In fact, with the threat leveled against them, it's quite a feat of courage for them to come forward and say anything at all."

Liverpool's retort died in the air.

"Your Honor," Drew's father said, his lips curling in disgust, "we have an unreliable witness, one who quite clearly has the ulterior motive of shifting the blame away from himself. And now we have two witnesses who have come forward with the truth."

"I'd like to hear from the other witness." The judge nodded at Peter.

Peter visibly swallowed and turned his attention to his boots. Drew was tempted to jump up, cross to him, and squeeze his shoulders. But he held himself back. Such a move could be taken as collaboration and arouse suspicion.

"I know you're worried about keeping your brother out of trouble," the judge said to Peter. "But if I'm going to count you as a witness to the crime, I need to hear directly from you too."

Peter glanced up, and for a moment Drew thought he was going to look at Liverpool. Instead, Peter looked at the dairy farmer standing at the back just inside the door in his scuffed boots, faded trousers, and patched shirt. The man nodded to Peter the same way he had to George. His kind eyes, crinkled at the corners from age and the elements, encouraged Peter to go on.

"What did you see, young man?" the judge asked.

Peter again swallowed hard. "I s-saw Liverp-pool h-hit Ned." Peter's voice constricted, and for a long while he couldn't seem to get another word out. Seeing Peter's predicament, George slipped his smaller hand into his brother's and squeezed.

Peter took a deep breath and spoke again, this time as smoothly as if he'd never stuttered in his life. "Liverpool killed Ned and then tried to cover up the murder by sinking him to the bottom of Percy's Pond."

When he finished his statement, he looked at the dairy farmer again. The man smiled at Peter, pleasure shining in his weathered face. At the sight of the man's approval, Peter's eyes rounded, revealing pride in himself for his courage, for facing his fear and coming out stronger as a result.

Once again, whispers and chatter rose around the church. The judge silenced the gathering with a bang of his gavel. "I think I have more than enough information to make a decision regarding the murder of Ned Colson."

"If you ain't gonna believe me, I'm leaving." Liverpool started to rise, but Reinhold laid a hand on the boy's arm. Reinhold's expression contained everything Drew felt — sadness but determination to help the boy. Sullenly, Liverpool sank back down on the pew next to Reinhold.

Drew's father's closing statement and the judge's pronouncement of his innocence passed in a blur. When the trial was adjourned, the children swarmed around him. He spoke to each one by name, thanked them for coming, and made a point of going to each of their new parents and thanking them as well.

Out of the corner of his eye, he saw the sheriff and Reinhold lead Liverpool away at his father's instructions. He wanted to go to the young man and try to talk to him, but even if he'd been able to break away from the crowds of people around him, he knew the boy wouldn't want to see him today — maybe never. But that didn't mean Drew planned to give up on him.

The thought took him by surprise. Could he give up on any of these children?

Families loaded into their wagons and began to roll away. Eventually only a few lingered. Drew finally went to George and Peter, hugged them tight, then handed them over into the capable hands of their new parents. It took only a moment of watching the boys interact with the couple for satisfaction to settle into his soul.

"They've found a good home, haven't they?" Marianne asked.

He nodded in reply and stared after their wagon bumping over ruts, the two boys in the back bouncing up and down with it.

From where Drew stood outside in the shade of the church building, he'd known she'd been nearby. All throughout the greetings after the trial, he was conscious of her presence, heard her laughter and felt himself drawn to her, though he'd tried not to stare. Now that most of the people were gone, part of him was dying to talk to her, but the other part was afraid.

"I thought the trial went well," she said. "Your father is brilliant."

"You are too." He meant it.

She smiled shyly and shook her head. "No, it was nothing —"

"It was everything." His chest swelled with the realization of what she'd accomplished by bringing in the children. Their testimonies about all he'd done for them might not have granted him freedom from the murder conviction, but it had given him freedom in a different way — a way he couldn't quite explain. Maybe in hearing all the many things he'd done right and done well, he could shift his focus off the one thing he'd done wrong.

"It must have been a lot of work to get everyone here the way you did," he said.

She shrugged. "You would have done the same for me if I'd needed it."

Even in the heat of the July afternoon, she was beautiful. Her long lashes rose off her cheeks, and he found himself falling into her eyes, falling and tumbling and falling until he was nearly breathless with his need for her.

"Thank you," he whispered and lifted a hand to brush a wisp of hair back behind her ear. He stopped himself at the same time she stepped back. Again she ducked her head almost apologetically.

He didn't blame her. After all, the last words he'd spoken to her were to go away and marry Reinhold. He'd been rude and cold, and yet she'd worked tirelessly to help him. He'd been right before. He wasn't worthy of her. But that didn't stop him from wanting her anyway.

"What will you do now?" she asked. "Or is it too soon to know?"

Before he could formulate an answer, his father clapped him on the shoulder and held out a hand toward Marianne. "Good work in there, Miss Neumann."

She shook his father's hand. "Thank you. Same to you."

"Your ploy to gain sympathy for Andrew was perfect —"

"It wasn't a ploy," she interrupted. "It was an intentional effort not only to help Drew see how much of a difference he's making, but also to help you understand your son, to hopefully give you a glimpse of what a loving, dedicated, and godly man you've raised."

His father smiled but with a hint of condescension. "Yes, I see that —"

"And I hope you also see how hardworking and tireless he is in his efforts to better the lives of these homeless children. He's touched many lives, and they're better because of it."

His father fumbled for a response, and inwardly Drew smiled. He rarely saw his father speechless, and he wanted to savor the moment. But his satisfaction was cut short when Reinhold called Marianne's name from across the street.

She waved a hand at him, and he began jogging toward them, his strength evident in every rippling muscle. When he stepped next to Marianne, close enough for his arm to brush against hers, Drew couldn't keep from tensing.

He wanted to tell Reinhold to move away from her, but when he lifted his gaze to meet Reinhold's direct one, Reinhold pierced him with both accusation and anger. The burly German man slipped an arm behind Marianne's shoulders as though to claim his possession — the treasure Drew had handed over to him on a silver platter and practically begged him to take.

Marianne didn't move into Reinhold's embrace, but neither did she resist it. Drew had to look away or he feared he'd put his shoulder down and plow into Reinhold to force him away.

The truth was, Drew didn't have any claim on Marianne. She was Reinhold's now. The sheriff had made a point of letting him know Reinhold had proposed and that Marianne had accepted. And now Drew had no right to step between them — perhaps he never had.

The other truth was, even if Marianne had been free, Drew still didn't deserve her. Maybe he'd felt some peace today, maybe the children's affirmation had brought about the start of healing, but he still had a long way to go. And he didn't want to drag Marianne into his confusion and guilt.

He had to stick with his earlier conviction to walk away from her. He couldn't go back on that now. No matter how hard it would be. When a few minutes later she left with Reinhold, he had to physically hold himself back from going after her.

"You did the right thing in letting her go," his father said next to him.

"I know you don't think she's good enough for me." Each word came out low and clipped, and Drew's fingers tightened into fists. "But you have it wrong. I'm not good enough for her. And that's why I'm letting her go."

His father squeezed his shoulder again as though they were the best of companions. "I know you care about her, but she wouldn't fit into life in the South. You'd only make her miserable by bringing her into a way of living that's foreign to her."

Drew shook off his father's hand with a shrug. "I want you to know I appreciate you coming here and helping me to make sense of this situation. You've forced me to begin putting it into perspective. I see that now."

"Good —"

"But I'm not going back home."

"Sure you are. I've already purchased your train ticket. We're leaving tomorrow."

"If I ever come home, it will be to visit, not to stay." Drew couldn't bear to see the disappointment creasing his father's forehead. He didn't want to be the cause of his father's frustration once again, but perhaps that was his father's issue to deal with now and not his.

He peered down the street in the direction Reinhold and Marianne had gone. Reinhold was opening the hotel door for Marianne, and she stepped inside. His chest tensed, yet he took a deep breath and tried to think of anything but her. "I'm not sure what my plans are. But this time I promise I won't run away without telling you where I am. I'll let you know once I decide what I'm going to do."

His father was silent for a long moment. Too long. And when Drew dared to meet his gaze again, he saw sadness but also something else he'd always craved yet had never gained. Acceptance. Was his father finally accepting him for who he was and not the man he wanted him to be?

"You're good with the kids," his father said slowly.

The words brought a lump to Drew's throat, and he could only manage a tight "Thank you."

His father nodded, reached out to shake his hand, and then at the last minute, when Drew had stuck out his hand in return, his father hooked him into an embrace.

It was a quick hug, but it was a start. When they stood back from each other, Drew felt a new respect for his father, and he sensed his father's new respect for him too. Whatever the future would bring, he needed to trust that God was in control and that He would continue to loosen the chains that had bound him for far too long.

CHAPTER 25

Marianne stared out the open window at the night sky as she'd begun to do whenever she couldn't fall asleep, which had been quite often lately. The cooler breeze soothed her hot skin, and the quietness of the sleeping town eased the tension from her body.

She breathed in deeply of the humid air that contained the now-familiar scents of farmland — the earthiness of plowed soil and the sweetness of clover. She would miss it when she returned to New York City. But one day, soon enough, she'd be back and begin her life as a farmer's wife.

She folded her arms across her chest and sighed. She wasn't frightened, she told herself. She would adjust to being a farmer's wife, including all the responsibilities that came with it. After visiting the orphans who'd been placed at farms, she'd witnessed a variety of tasks women were expected to do, such as preserve berries, churn butter, and much more. She didn't know much about any of it, but somehow she'd learn. She had no choice.

"Marianne, is that you?"

She glanced down to find Drew standing beneath her window, still wearing the fancy suit from the trial, except the bow tie was gone, the collar was open, and the buttons loosened.

Against her will, her heart thrilled to see him. "What are you doing out at this time of night?"

"I couldn't sleep so I decided to take a walk and clear my head."

He wasn't wearing a hat, and the moonlight hit his face revealing strong lines and the tautness in his jaw. He was the most handsome man she'd ever met.

"Come down and join me," he whispered loudly.

"I can't."

"Why not?"

For a million reasons. "I'm in my nightgown."

"Then change. I'll wait."

"It's too late." In more than one way it was too late.

"Actually it's the perfect time to stargaze." He smiled up at her, the dimple in his chin making an appearance.

Why did he have to be so irresistible?

"Come on," he pleaded. "You won't regret it, I promise."

"Fine." She couldn't hold out against him. Not when he looked up at her with so much expectation shining in his eyes. "But only for a few minutes."

She tugged a gown over her nightdress and didn't bother with her shoes or stockings. Instead, she tiptoed out of the hotel to where he was waiting for her.

As she approached, his grin widened, and he reached for her hand. "Come."

When his fingers closed about hers, heat enveloped her and raced to her chest, filling her with delight and confusion and frustration all at once. She couldn't allow an attraction to grow again. She'd been working hard all week to stop thinking about him and to put an end to any feelings she was harboring. How was it that one touch could bring everything back in a tidal wave of emotion?

Being outside with him in the dark was a bad idea. A very bad idea. She grabbed the front porch post. "Wait."

He stopped. The moon and starlight reflected so much hope in his eyes that she didn't know how to formulate the words to express her fear and hesitancy.

"I don't think this is a good idea," she began.

"Why not?" His tone was playful and free-spirited.

Would she crush him if she said she didn't want to spend time with him? And if she told him that, would he sense she was lying? She hesitated and tugged at her skirt. "Because . . . because I'm not wearing any shoes."

With a soft laugh, he tugged her forward, giving her no choice but to step away from the porch railing and follow him. "We won't go far. I promise."

"Where are we going?" she asked, stepping gingerly after him as he wound around the hotel.

"It's a surprise."

She should have known he wouldn't tell her. "You said it wasn't far."

"It's not." His voice was light and cheerful, and after the past weeks of seeing him so melancholy, she couldn't begrudge him a moment of happiness, now, could she?

He led her through the thick cool grass behind several businesses until they rounded the train depot. The tracks were as silent as the rest of the town but reminded her that tomorrow she was leaving to do the follow-up visits in Dresden and then afterward going to Quincy to collect Jethro. She'd sent a telegram to Elise earlier in the day to give her the good news about the results of the trial.

Elise had wired back to inform her that Jethro had recovered from the measles and was still talking about Marianne and Drew getting married. Marianne didn't know what she'd tell the boy when she saw him. But she had at least another week to think of some way to share the news with him that she was marrying Reinhold instead of Drew. She dreaded breaking his heart. She knew how much he'd been looking forward to being a family with her and Drew.

Drew stopped at the foot of the large water tower that was used to service the trains' steam engines. The steel cylinder stood on a pedestal that was at least twelve feet off the ground for the ease of pumping water into its tank.

A ladder ran up the length of the tower from the ground to the sloped metal roof. As Drew directed her to the ladder, she laughed her protest. "You can't be serious."

"I'm always serious," he said.

She laughed again and tried to step away, only to find him lifting her onto the first rung.

"Climb up," he said. "It'll be fun."

She peered up the ladder that gleamed in the moonlight. It rose to a frightening height. She shook her head and started to lower her foot to the ground again.

"You're not afraid, are you?" His voice hinted at a challenge.

She had to lean her head back to see all the way to the top. The ladder seemed to climb to the stars. Yes, honestly, she was afraid. But she pursed her lips and started up. She certainly wasn't going to let Drew win this challenge.

The metal rungs were cold against her bare soles but surprisingly easy to climb. She soon found herself at the top and heard Drew right behind her.

"Crawl onto the roof," he instructed, his hand brushing against her toes.

"Roof?" she squeaked, studying the slanted metal. "You never said anything about going on the roof."

"You won't regret it. I've been up here almost every night this week watching the stars, and it's amazing."

She hesitated only a moment longer before forcing herself to climb over the top bar and onto the slanted roof. Within seconds, Drew was beside her, his hand on her arm steadying her. With his help, she tentatively turned and sat down, tucking her legs under her skirt. He lowered himself next to her.

For a minute they didn't speak. She was too nervous to look down, afraid she'd fall over the edge if she moved even a fraction. Beneath her, the roof was still warm from the heat it attracted during the hot summer day. She relished the smoothness and warmth against the bottoms of her bare feet and at the same time lifted her face into a gentle night breeze that carried a hint of coolness.

Drew looked up to take in the night sky. She did the same and gasped at the sight. Millions upon millions of stars spread out in every direction as far as her eyes could see.

"It *is* amazing," she whispered.

He nodded his agreement, and they sat in awed silence for a while, gazing at the constellations of stars and breathing in the night air.

"That one is Corona Borealis, the Northern Crown," he said, pointing to a ring of stars that looked like half of a crown. He went on to regale her with one of his stories, this one of Theseus and the Minotaur and the beautiful princess Ariadne. "And after Theseus defeated the Minotaur with her ball of thread," he finished, "the young warrior gave her the crown when they were married."

During his story, Marianne felt herself relaxing so that by the time he ended, she peeked over the edge of the water tower. She grabbed on to Drew and sucked in a sharp hiss at how high up they were.

"Don't worry. I've got you," he said, slipping his arm behind her.

At his touch, she stiffened. Part of her warned that sitting on this roof with her ex-fiancé wouldn't make her current fiancé very happy, especially now that her ex-fiancé had his arm around her.

But Drew didn't make any move to pull her closer or hold her tighter. Since he was apparently only trying to ease her fears, she decided she wouldn't say anything or make a bigger deal out of his hold than he likely intended.

"There's Hercules." He outlined another grouping of stars. "He's the son of Zeus and known for his strength and courage. Would you like me to tell you how he defeated Leo the Lion or the many-headed beast called Hydra?"

"Are you attempting to distract me from my fear with your stories like you do the orphans?" she asked, smiling at him.

"Maybe." He smiled back, his dimple much too attractive.

"Well, it's working." She focused her attention on the sky, away from him, away from his allure. "Tell me about Hydra."

She loved listening to him just as much as the children did. And by the time he finished with the story of Hercules not only defeating Hydra but also killing Cancer, a vicious crab, all her fears had dissipated.

"Lay back like this," he said and lowered himself against the roof so that both his back and head rested against its surface.

She imitated his action until she was lying next to him, the starry sky a canopy above them. "Thanks for challenging me to come up here," she whispered. "Look what I would have missed if you hadn't pushed me."

"You're a stronger woman than you know," he replied.

"And you're a stronger man than you know." She wasn't sure if he was ready to discuss his past with her yet or everything that had happened recently with Ned. But they were parting ways tomorrow, and she didn't know if she'd have another chance to speak with him.

She took a deep breath and plunged forward before she could talk herself out of responding. "Too often when we think of courage, we think of Hercules and having extraordinary strength to face a mighty foe like Hydra or battle nature."

Drew lay silently without moving. He didn't refute her or change the subject, so she took that as her cue to keep talking and share the lesson she'd been learning lately for herself. "But don't you think sometimes it takes even greater courage to accept our losses? And not just accept them, but move on and continue to live?"

He didn't answer her.

When she glanced sideways at him, he was staring straight up at the sky, and in the dark his expression was unreadable.

She swallowed the fear that rose and threatened to constrict her voice. After all, what did she have to lose by encouraging him to make peace with his past? "I lost Sophie and Olivia and Nicholas. I can hate and blame myself forever. That's actually the easy thing to do. What takes strength is to finally forgive myself and make peace with what happened. No, I won't ever forget about them, but I can't continue to live in the shadow of my mistakes." She held her breath, praying she hadn't offended him.

"So you're saying that sometimes it takes courage to stop living in the shadows and move into the sunshine?" His question was genuine and warm.

She exhaled her relief. "Yes."

A distant bleat of a sheep and the continuous song of crickets settled around them. When his fingers brushed against hers, she didn't move them away. And a moment later when he laced his fingers through hers, she smiled and didn't fight against his hold or the deep joyous ache that sprang to life inside her.

She simply gazed into the night sky and let herself savor the moment thoroughly. She wanted to imprint every second of it on her mind so she could treasure it long after it was over. It wouldn't last forever, even though she wished it could.

"So," he said quietly after a long while, "maybe the first thing I need to do to move out of the shadows is honor my commitment and finish the work on this trip."

"I'd like that."

"Are you sure you can put up with me?"

"You are rather difficult to endure," she teased, "but I'll do my best."

"What do we have left to do?"

With his hand still intertwined with hers, she told him about the children and families she'd already visited over the past weeks. He listened attentively to her concerns about some of the children whose new homes had appeared questionable.

"We'll revisit them together," he suggested. "And if we don't like the situation, then we can work on finding new homes or take the children back with us."

She nodded. She didn't want to remind him that Jethro was still in Quincy and waiting for their return.

"I'm sure Jethro is worried about us by now," Drew said, reading her mind. "I hope he doesn't think we've abandoned him."

She prayed so too. He was a good boy, but curious and talkative and sometimes very tiring. She could only imagine the hassle he'd been to Mrs. Gray when he'd started to feel better and had gotten out of bed. Marianne would have to think of some special way to thank the dear woman for taking Jethro under her wing.

"How do you think he'll react when he discovers . . ." She was about to mention her upcoming marriage to Reinhold but suddenly felt embarrassed about bringing it up.

"Discovers what?" Drew tightened his hold on her hand. "That we're not getting married anymore?"

"Do you think he'll accept Reinhold as a father instead?" she asked in a rush. "Reinhold said he was willing to keep Jethro . . ." Again the awkwardness of the conversation stopped her.

At the mention of Reinhold, Drew sat up and frowned. She rose more slowly and at the same time extricated her hand from his. Guilt pushed at her, urging her toward the ladder to put an end to her time with Drew.

She wasn't being fair to Reinhold. She shouldn't be spending intimate time with Drew, holding his hand and talking so deeply with him. If anything, it was something she should be doing with Reinhold, although she couldn't imagine practical, level-headed Reinhold coming to her hotel window and asking her to come out and see him. He would have considered such a thing scandalous. And she couldn't imagine him climbing a water tower to stargaze, much less goading her into it.

She reached for the ladder, but Drew beat her to it. "Let me go first so I can assist your descent if you need it."

She nodded mutely and waited for his head to disappear before beginning to climb down after him. When he reached the ground, he waited with his arms stretched toward her. As she touched the last few rungs, his hands encircled her waist, and he lifted her effortlessly the rest of the way down.

With her bare feet just inches from the

tickly grass, she expected him to release her, but he didn't. His hands fit perfectly on her hips, spanning her waist around to her back. All he had to do was put the slightest pressure at the small of her back and she'd stumble against him.

She wanted to lean into his touches, feel the strength of his presence, to rest her head against his chest and hear the ever-quickening thud of his heartbeat.

Though he didn't tug her closer, he didn't move away either. He drew in a ragged breath, one that made her pulse increase with sudden need.

"Marianne?" His whisper was hoarse and laden with longing.

She closed her eyes for a second to block him out, to stay rational, to keep herself from doing anything she would later regret. She forced out the words she knew she must. "I'm engaged to Reinhold."

Her statement had the wake-up effect she'd hoped for. Drew released her and took a step back. "I'm sorry . . . I shouldn't have brought you here."

"No, Drew." She crossed her arms over her chest to ward off a sudden chill. "I'm glad we could talk. I'd hoped for the chance."

"But . . ."

"But we have to remain friends now."

"I understand." He tugged at his collar, sliding another button open as though his shirt was strangling him.

"Can we go back to being partners, like we were at the beginning of the trip?"

He blew out a long breath. "I don't know if I can ever go back, Marianne. But I'd rather be your friend and partner than nothing at all."

She wanted to throw away caution and tell him she couldn't go back either and that she wasn't sure how they could be only friends and partners. Not when the attraction between them was still very much alive.

But she'd made a commitment to Reinhold that she'd marry him, and she couldn't go back on her word. He needed her now more than Drew did. And she wouldn't let him down. Besides, everything that had happened between her and Drew had been impulsive and reactionary. They could both recognize that they'd acted hastily, couldn't they?

"Yes, I'd like to remain friends," she said, hoping that would be enough for them both.

"Then friends it shall be," he said with forced cheer.

"Drew, I'm sorry —"

"Don't be. It's my fault. I was a weak

man. I pushed you away when I should have cherished you most."

"Our relationship happened so fast. We hardly knew each other when we made our decision. And it was all because of Jethro —"

"It was long enough for me to know," he added, cutting her off.

"We let things get out of hand and became infatuated. That's all." She tried to keep the longing out of her voice. "And now we need to set boundaries and keep them there."

He didn't answer. Instead he blew out a tense, exasperated breath.

"Reinhold is a good man, Drew, and I don't want to hurt him. He needs me to take care of his sisters. And I can't go back on my word to him. I just can't." If she rejected Reinhold, she'd not only hurt him, but she'd hurt his sisters too. And she wouldn't do that to either Reinhold or the girls. Not even for Drew.

Drew stood rigidly for a long moment, staring at the sky again.

She reached out to touch his arm but then caught herself. If they were going to remain friends and nothing more, then she'd have to do her part and not lead him on. She clasped her hands together and put another foot of distance between them.

"You and I . . . we can't be anything more than friends. We have to agree to that or it won't work for us to travel together."

He radiated frustration and seemed to be waging a private battle within himself. Finally he cleared his throat. "If that's what you want, I'll respect your decision."

"Thank you." She knew she was doing the honorable thing, but the pain in her heart kept deepening. "Now promise me."

"Promise what?"

"That you and I will be friends and nothing else."

He nodded. "Friends and nothing else, I promise."

She wasn't sure why his words didn't reassure her. And as he started to walk her back to the hotel, she couldn't keep from wondering if this time she'd made her worst decision yet.

CHAPTER 26

Drew sprawled out on the train bench, his hat low over his eyes. It was low enough he could stare at Marianne on the seat across from him without her realizing it. It was a trick he'd perfected with the orphans, and now it came in handy.

Marianne was reading through the notes she'd made in the record book and now and then jotted something new down. He loved the way she chewed at her bottom lip when she was trying to make a decision. Or how she tapped her pencil against her chin when deep in thought. Or how she scrunched her nose at something that bothered her.

As if sensing his staring at her, she glanced at him. He feigned sleep for a few seconds before looking again. She'd shifted her attention to the landscape, prairie mostly, passing by outside the train car. The light coming in from the open window high-lighted her elegant chin and cheek. Her thick wavy hair was pulled back, revealing her long and smooth neck, where he imagined burying his face and getting lost in the sweetness of her skin.

He'd done his best over the past ten days to remain strictly friends with her. The self-restraint had nearly killed him. He wanted to keep his promise but didn't know how much longer he could hold out.

They'd finished visiting the orphans placed in Dresden and had also gone back to some of the placements Marianne had found questionable during her first round of visits. Drew had found one excuse after another to extend their time together. But finally he'd run out of reasons to prolong their trip. This morning they'd boarded the train bound for Quincy where they'd pick up Jethro. In a few days they'd return to Mayfield, where she was planning to get married to Reinhold.

Panic seized him, as it had done every time he thought about how the clock was ticking and he still hadn't figured out a way to win Marianne's affection. Even after hours of contemplating the problem, he couldn't think of a way to convince her to marry him instead of Reinhold.

The problem was, she couldn't let Reinhold down. He needed Marianne. And she'd made a commitment to him. Drew was hesitant about stepping between the couple. Besides, she'd eventually feel guilty for not honoring her commitment to Reinhold. And he'd feel guilty for breaking his promise to her. Hence they'd always have a wedge between them.

No, if he was going to win her heart, he had to do it right, honorably. He just hadn't figured out what that right way was yet. And now he was running out of time.

"Drew?" she said softly.

He pretended he was sleeping and hadn't heard her. If she knew he'd been staring at her, she'd only be self-conscious and sit in a different seat. As uncertain as he was about the future and what to do after this trip, he'd never wavered in how much he loved Marianne. His time in jail and especially the trial had made him want her even more. After she'd heard the details of his past, he expected her to be disgusted with him. Charlotte certainly had been. He didn't blame her for calling off the wedding. Who wanted to be married to a man who'd stood trial for murder?

Even worse, who would want to be associated with a man who'd stood trial for murder twice? And yet Marianne hadn't bolted. Instead, she'd stood beside him,

459

never wavering in her belief in him, and had even gone to a great deal of trouble to help him. He loved her for her unswerving and unconditional acceptance and wished he could tell her.

More than that, he wished he could go on loving her for the rest of his life. She'd been strong when he was weak. And now he wanted to do the same for her. Over the past week of thinking and praying, Marianne's example had helped him begin to understand the verse from the Second Epistle to the Corinthians: *"And he said unto me, My grace is sufficient for thee: for my strength is made perfect in weakness. Most gladly therefore will I rather glory in my infirmities, that the power of Christ may rest upon me."*

He'd likely experience times where the guilt of all that had happened would overwhelm him again. But perhaps God was trying to show him that during those times, He wouldn't leave and would in fact be strong in the midst of Drew's weakness — just as Marianne had been.

"Drew, wake up," she said louder.

He pretended to stir.

"Before we arrive in Quincy, we have to talk."

He pushed up the brim of his hat and

460

made a point of yawning noisily. "Talk?"

They'd spent hours over the past week discussing all the things that were right and wrong with the Children's Aid Society placing-out program. He appreciated seeing things from Marianne's perspective as a new agent. But he also knew from experience that she was a bit idealistic. In Drew's opinion, even though there were problems with the system Brace had developed, overall the resettlement was working well.

Nevertheless, he'd taken her concerns to heart and was pondering them. Especially because in Dresden the stationmaster had handed him a week-old copy of the *Chicago Tribune,* which had an editorial comparing the Emigration Plan to slavery. The editor said, "If an agent had taken that many little Negroes from the plantations of Louisiana to Springfield and should have prepared to do the very thing with them that everybody knows will be done directly or indirectly with these poor children from New York, our good abolitionist friends would all have fainted at the horrid thought."

While the article had irritated Drew, he simply attributed it to ignorance. The editor clearly didn't understand the stipulations of the placing out. There was some truth raised in that Brace's plan did contain similarities to the indenture system that had been prominent for decades during the early days of the country's founding, but it also contained significant differences.

For example, the children were not bound to the families they went to live with. The relationship could be dissolved at any time if either the child or family was dissatisfied with the arrangement. Marianne had argued that such an open-ended policy contributed to turnover for certain children rather than stability, that it allowed for parents to give up a child at the smallest hardship rather than stay committed.

Drew, however, saw the flexible nature of the agreement as beneficial to the children who could then be placed in better living situations or brought back to New York City instead of being relegated to a family who didn't want them.

Drew could admit that Marianne had raised many good points, and he'd thoroughly enjoyed discussing them with her. She'd challenged him to move beyond the complacency he'd fallen into during his years of working for the Children's Aid Society and to realize that even if they were doing well on behalf of many children, they needed to evaluate ways to improve the program.

He sat up and stretched his arms above his head before settling back into his seat. "What would you like to discuss this time? Better methods for interviewing prospective parents? Or establishing regulations for children's work?"

They'd already discussed both, but he loved listening to her talk and watching the emotions that played across her face, the way her eyes lit up, and the sincerity that made lines in her forehead. She was smart and logical and full of interesting ideas.

"We passed through Wellington," she said. "Quincy is the next stop."

Actually, he was well aware of exactly where they were and how little time they had left together.

"So we need to discuss something that won't take all day?" he asked.

"I'm afraid this one will take all day and longer."

Something in her tone and expression set him on edge. "Which one?"

"Jethro."

"I'm sure he's much better by now and able to travel."

"That's not what I'm worried about."

"Then what's worrying you?"

"Elise said he's excited to see us again. And I'm sure he's still expecting us to get married and adopt him as our child."

Drew was tempted to tell her in that case they would simply have to go through with marriage plans so they didn't disappoint Jethro. But he knew such an answer would frustrate Marianne, so he made an effort to weigh their options. "I think we have to be honest with him, don't you?"

She nodded. "Then should we tell him I'm marrying Reinhold?"

"If we don't, he'll find out soon enough." Unless Drew could find a way to get Marianne to cancel her plans. But how?

She was contemplative for a moment. "I don't want to hurt him."

"I don't either, but unfortunately he'll be disappointed."

"He'll be absolutely crushed." Marianne sniffled, fighting back tears. "I hate to do this to him, especially since he's so excited about it."

Drew considered playing on Marianne's sympathy for Jethro and in that way making her change her mind about marrying Reinhold. But he had to be completely honest with her, even if doing so cost him his last chance at having her.

"Marianne," he said gently, "Jethro's a resilient young boy. With the kind of life he's lived, he's had to be. In the short term, the news that we're not getting married and adopting him will make him sad. But he'll get over it soon enough and will be fine."

"Do you really think so?"

"I'm positive." If only he could say the same thing about himself.

Marianne stepped hesitantly off the metal step onto the train platform. The slant of the late afternoon sun blinded her. Before both her feet hit the ground, a small figure shot against her. Little arms wrapped around her waist. The force pummeled her backward so that she lost her balance and would have fallen, except Drew caught her from behind.

He stepped down behind her, his hands moving from her shoulders to her upper arms, steadying her and at the same time making her conscious of his chest brushing against her back. For an instant, she was tempted to recline against him and relish this closeness even if for a moment. But she hadn't given in to temptation during the time she was with him over the past week and a half, and she couldn't start now. She wanted to return to Reinhold with a clean conscience and with the knowledge she'd maintained integrity in their relationship.

"Miss Neumann!" A freckled face topped

with rooster-red hair peered up at her. With his wide eyes and impish gap-toothed grin, Jethro melted her heart. He released her and stood back to take in Drew behind her.

"Hi, Mr. Brady," he chimed. "I can see you still like holding Miss Neumann every chance you get."

"That I do, buddy." His voice was tinged with humor and rumbled near her ear, making her neck tingle in response.

"Oh, dear," Marianne murmured, breaking away from Drew. Her cheeks felt suddenly hot, and as Mrs. Gray limped toward them from the depot, Marianne prayed the woman hadn't heard Jethro's bold statement.

Marianne attempted to cover her embarrassment by busying herself, greeting Mrs. Gray and getting an update from her about how Jethro was doing in the aftermath of his measles.

"I can't thank you enough for taking care of him," Marianne said.

"It was my pleasure," the kindly woman said with a smile aimed at the boy. "He was a good patient."

"Aunt Elise and Mrs. Gray have been letting me help in the kitchen," Jethro said.

Aunt Elise? Marianne's heart sank even further. If he was already calling Elise his aunt, then he would be more devastated by the news than they realized.

Jethro slipped his hand into Marianne's and walked next to her as they made their way inside to the waiting room. His chatter was nonstop with all the things he'd gotten to do in the kitchen — washing vegetables, peeling potatoes, snapping beans, and more. "I get to eat the carrots that still have their green tails. And I bit into a tomato thinkin' it were an apple."

"You were a saint for taking him under your wing," Marianne said to Mrs. Gray as Jethro scurried to open the door for Drew, who was carrying her trunk. "I know he's busy and talkative and full of energy."

"Oh, no worries, dear." Mrs. Gray watched Jethro with shining eyes. "He's been a bigger help than I imagined he would be."

"I'm stronger now," Jethro was saying to Drew as he made a show of helping Drew place the trunk on a bench. "Can't you tell?"

Drew praised the boy liberally and then bent down and pretended to be impressed with Jethro's muscles. Jethro strutted in response, his smile as wide as a prairie mile.

Drew chuckled at the same time that Marianne did. But then just as quickly her heart panged with the realization they would have to hurt this precious boy all too soon.

"Aunt Elise let me help her make a wedding cake for you," he said with a proud smile.

"A wedding cake?" Marianne's voice squeaked a little too high, and she exchanged a glance with Drew. Of course, when she'd telegrammed Elise yesterday to confirm their arrival, she hadn't told her sister she was marrying Reinhold instead of Drew. That wasn't exactly the kind of information one could explain in a telegram. She'd planned to inform Elise in private later.

Mrs. Gray smoothed a hand over Jethro's frizzy hair. "The minute he heard the two of you were returning, he's been busy planning your wedding."

"Mrs. Gray helped me make a gift," Jethro said, this time jumping up and down with exuberance. "And we picked flowers for the tables."

She caught Drew's gaze again. His brows cocked, revealing his concern. How would they be able to break the news to him now?

"Maybe we should wait until tomorrow to tell him," she whispered under her breath to Drew while following Jethro into the dining room.

"It won't be any easier then," Drew replied.

"Please," she whispered, even as she pasted on a happy smile at the sight of the flowers beautifully arranged on all the tables. A few passengers from the train had come into the eating house, and Elise was busy serving them.

Drew didn't protest. Instead, he oohed and aahed appropriately over everything Jethro had done to prepare for their wedding.

"And exactly when is this momentous occasion to take place?" Drew asked once they'd admired the cake in the kitchen.

"Aunt Elise said the wedding will be tomorrow morning," Jethro replied, reaching for both of their hands so that he was standing between them and beaming brighter than a full moon.

Elise returned from the dining room with the coffeepot in hand. "I see Jethro's been showing you all our wedding preparations."

"Yes, he's quite excited." Marianne tried to keep the dismay from her voice and was glad Elise was distracted making more coffee and couldn't read her face. "I wasn't expecting so much trouble for the wedding."

"It's been no trouble at all," Elise replied

469

with a wave of her hand. "Jethro was so excited yesterday and today about your return that it actually gave Mrs. Gray and me a way to keep him busy."

Mrs. Gray added her agreement from the range where she was dishing up two plates with crispy fried chicken, mashed potatoes, and green beans. The scents would have tantalized Marianne if she hadn't been so worried about the enormous hole she was sliding into with every tiny lie she told.

"We would have been perfectly happy with a simple wedding," she said weakly.

"It'll be simple enough." Elise opened the stove door and shoveled in more coal.

Marianne was at a loss for words, and she silently implored Drew to say something. He only lifted his shoulders in bewilderment. Since just a few minutes ago she'd asked him not to say anything tonight.

"Besides," Elise continued, "we wanted to celebrate the good news regarding Drew's trial. Jethro was worried sick about the whole thing. So when we received Marianne's telegram letting us know the real murderer had been discovered, we wanted to do something for Drew when he returned."

How could she protest, especially with

Jethro smiling up at them with such radiance?

Elise closed the stove door with a clang and then stopped to eye her with a look of confusion. "I thought you'd be happy that I'm supporting you."

Considering Elise's hesitation regarding her marriage to Drew the last time she was in Quincy, Marianne should have been thrilled to have Elise's support. If only she'd had the chance to explain all the events that had happened over the past month while she'd been gone. As it was, Elise had no clue that everything had changed. And now Marianne would have to find a way to tell Elise and attempt to get herself out of the awful mess she'd created.

At present, though, she had no other option but to continue the charade. She took a deep breath and smiled at her sister with what she hoped was reassurance. "I'm happy. We're happy." She turned to Drew. "Aren't we, sweetheart?"

Drew nodded, and this time humor lit his eyes. She didn't blame him for finding their dilemma silly. Part of her warned that she needed to simply state the truth. Even if it would hurt everyone for a few minutes, they'd adjust — at least Drew seemed to think Jethro would get over it quickly.

471

But another part of her couldn't disappoint anyone. At least not tonight. She needed more time to figure out how to gently deliver the truth to Jethro. Surely once she told Elise later about the predicament, Elise would help her figure out something.

Drew released Jethro's hand and tugged Marianne into the crook of his arm. His expression had turned decidedly mischievous. "I agree, darlin'. We're extremely happy." He pulled her close. "Tomorrow can't come soon enough."

She wrapped her arm around Drew's back and attempted to look like the happily engaged couple they were supposed to be. "Thank you for going to all this work on our behalf."

"I'm just relieved for your sake everything worked out." Elise paused with her dinner preparations and smiled at her. "After your last visit, and seeing how much you loved Drew, I admit I was worried."

Drew pulled her closer. "And exactly how much does Marianne love me?" he asked, his tone mirthful.

Marianne bit the inside of her cheek and prayed Elise wouldn't say too much.

"She said she couldn't function without you," Elise said wryly. "And it was absolutely true. Marianne was a wreck. I thought I was going to have to pick her up off the floor and stitch her back together."

"Is that right?" Drew's voice dropped, and his hand at her side splayed out possessively.

Marianne didn't dare meet his gaze. "Elise has a tendency to exaggerate."

"I'm not exaggerating," Elise said.

"Your sister said she's not exaggerating," Drew said innocently.

"I heard," Marianne replied just as innocently.

Drew chuckled, and the sound wrapped warmly around Marianne's heart. Even though she was embarrassed by their conversation, she couldn't keep from smiling. When Drew hugged her tighter and pressed a kiss against her temple, the gesture seemed the most natural in the world. She was exactly where she wanted to be, in the shelter of his arms, by his side. And for that moment she could pretend it would last, that she truly did belong with him.

With a grin, Elise returned to the coffeepot on the stove. "It was as clear then as it is now that the two of you are in love. So I decided that rather than stand in love's way, I might as well do all I can to make sure you end up married this time."

"That's very kind of you," Drew remarked. "Don't you think so, darlin'?"

This time she made the mistake of glancing up into his face. His blue-green eyes were the color where the sky met the prairie. And they were filled with such tenderness she couldn't resist when he bent down. With his attention fixed upon her mouth, she realized he wanted to kiss her. She needed to move away and break free of him. But when he hesitated, then dipped in a little further, she was already breathless with her desire for him.

She lifted her lips just a fraction, and it was apparently the invitation he'd been waiting for. He closed the distance between them, sweeping his mouth against hers. The pressure was hard and urgent and full of longing, letting her know quite clearly that although he'd kept his promise to be her friend over the past week, he hadn't liked it and wanted to be so much more.

She wanted him to be more too. But how could she ignore her commitment to Reinhold?

"Mr. Brady, I see you still like eatin' Miss Neumann," Jethro called.

Elise burst into laughter, and Drew broke his kiss enough that Marianne felt his lips curve into a smile against hers.

She started to smile in return, but his lips

closed against hers again, softer this time, almost teasing, dropping a kiss and then pulling back out of reach and doing it over, not giving her enough time to respond except to leave her breathless and melted beneath his touch.

"Save it for the honeymoon, you two," Elise called.

Somehow during the kisses, Drew's arms had come around her, fully and completely. At Elise's teasing, he refrained from his soft shower of kisses, but his hands pressed at the small of Marianne's back, giving her no room to move away. "When did you say we were having the wedding ceremony?" he said over his shoulder to Elise. "Come to think of it, I'd like to have it tonight. Maybe right now."

Elise chuckled, clearly enjoying Drew's banter. Marianne was too overcome with Drew's nearness and the headiness of his kisses to think. His labored breath brushed her cheek and tantalized her already sizzling nerves.

"The reverend is coming to my parlor tomorrow morning at ten o'clock. I realize that's an eternity to wait," Elise replied, her voice laced with sarcasm, "but I know how you can keep your hands busy someplace else besides my sister."

"Elise!" Marianne said, tugging free of Drew, having no doubt she was showing just as much mortification on the outside as she felt on the inside.

Drew was grinning as he reluctantly released her.

"Go over to North Second Street and pitch in with the home being built for Quincy's new doctor."

"And leave my bride-to-be? I don't think so." Drew reached for Marianne, but she dodged out of his way.

"Help me, Jeth," Drew called, darting after her. "You go one way and I'll go the other."

Jethro laughed with excitement and started toward Marianne until the two had her cornered near the pantry. As Jethro and Drew tickled her, Marianne squealed with laughter until finally Elise pulled her free.

"Go!" Elise pointed to the back door of the kitchen and then at Drew. She was working hard to contain her smile. "You need to cool off."

Drew ran a hand through his tousled hair. Did he know how dashing he looked when he did that? When he winked at her, she realized he was enjoying her ogling.

"Besides," Elise said, "my husband would like the chance to meet you before he

476

welcomes you into the family."

Drew's grin dropped away. What would Thornton think of Drew? She was sure Drew was wondering the same thing. Thornton was a compassionate man, but he was also tough and business-minded. He was a large contributor to the Children's Aid Society. What if he discovered Drew had been kissing and handling her even though they weren't engaged? What if he got angry at Drew and decided to withdraw funding from the Children's Aid Society?

"He's helping out over on the doctor's home." This time Elise propelled Drew toward the door. "Go see if you can impress him."

Within seconds she'd pushed Drew out the door. He seemed to take the sunshine with him. And as the door closed, a dark cloud settled over Marianne. What were they doing pretending they were still engaged? This whole charade was no good. One little lie had led to another and another until she was so tangled in the lies she didn't know how she'd find a way out.

She pressed a hand to her chest to calm her erratic pulse. But all she could think about was how her lying had been the source of her problems before — when Sophie had run away. She'd lied because she hadn't wanted anyone to get hurt. And she was doing it again. If it hadn't worked before, what made her think it would work now?

She took a deep breath hoping to ease the pressure building in her chest, for she had the terrible foreboding that, one way or another, she would have to hurt someone and no matter how hard she tried not to.

CHAPTER 27

Reinhold's back and shoulders ached from stooping all day, but he'd managed to finish hoeing his potato field. The bushy rows almost touched now, their white blossoms reminding him of snowdrops.

Everything was growing well in the hot sunshine and humidity. The oats swelled a gray-green, and the wheat's thin heads had shot up with husks where the kernels would grow. The corn was nigh to his shoulder with tassels forming.

Mr. Turner had indicated they'd start an early harvest on the hay, and he'd spent the day with Higgins sharpening the scythes. Higgins was needed to turn the grindstone and pour a constant stream of water on it while Mr. Turner braced the steel edges against the whirring stone until the scythes were razor-sharp and ready for cutting hay.

Reinhold kneaded his neck before stooping to dig in the spot where he kept his crock of money. He didn't need to add more. Mr. Turner wouldn't be able to pay him any more cash until after the haying. Even so, Reinhold liked to count his earnings to make sure it was all still there.

He dug with his fingers into the thick damp soil. He liked the way the dirt got into his fingernails and stuck there. He liked the stain that it made in the grooves of his hand. He even liked the soil's strong aroma.

As he pulled the crock out and began to brush away the dirt, he stopped abruptly at the angle of the lid. It hadn't been screwed on correctly. It was crooked, as if someone had attempted to put it back on hastily.

Reinhold dropped to his knees, ignoring the dirt that would now be engrained into the fibers of his trousers and the extra work that would cause Lucinda who washed the clothing. He was too panicked to think of anything but getting the lid off and assuring himself the past two months of income were still stashed safely inside.

But even as the lid popped off and tumbled to the ground, Reinhold's body sagged with defeat. He didn't have to look inside to know it was all gone. Every last note and coin. But he looked anyway, tipped the crock over and shook it, pounded the sides, and blew into it.

Finally he let it fall with a thud to the dark, upturned earth. Who could have known his crock was here? He'd been so careful to cover the spot. He'd tried only to check it whenever he was alone. But apparently he hadn't been careful enough. Or perhaps someone had followed him out at a discreet distance and watched him without his knowing it?

Reinhold scanned the area, stopping to peer in the direction of the house and barn. Higgins had said he was going out to fish yesterday. Maybe he'd backtracked to the potato field first. With a growl, Reinhold pushed himself up from the ground. He snatched up the empty crock in one hand and his hoe in the other and stormed across the fields. By the time he reached the barnyard, he was hot and sweaty and more than ready to confront Higgins.

Luckily for him, Higgins was at the well, washing his hands and face in the bucket Lucinda kept filled.

"Where is it?" Reinhold shouted without breaking his stride. Higgins was splashing water on his face and didn't look up. But Mrs. Turner and Lucinda, who were both weeding in the vegetable garden nearby, stopped and watched him.

Reinhold reached Higgins, grabbed him

by the back of his neck, and jerked him to his feet.

Higgins let loose a slew of curses, but Reinhold cut them off by shoving the empty crock into Higgins's chest.

"What?" Higgins said, glancing at the crock. "I didn't drink your stash of whiskey, if that's what you're thinking."

"You stole my money!" Reinhold roared. "Again!"

Water dripped from Higgins's face. Slowly, understanding dawned in the man's dark eyes. He started to laugh, a chortling sound that was clearly intended to goad Reinhold.

Reinhold could only think of the months of hard work he'd endured. The hours of sweating and hurting and saving. In a single moment it was all gone, and he was back to being a penniless pauper, always dependent on someone else for his survival.

That thought more than any other stirred rage deep within him, a rage that had swirled in his gut from time to time but that he'd hoped would never surface. He expelled a breath and tried to clear his mind. He released Higgins with a shove that sent the man falling back into the wash bucket, causing it to topple over.

"Tell me where you put it," Reinhold demanded, trying to keep his voice level.

"Or what?" Higgins sneered. "You gonna beat me up since you're so mean and tough?"

Reinhold's hands closed into fists, and he fought back the anger that was rising in a powerful surge.

"You're too nice to do anything," Higgins taunted, standing. "If you were half the man you think you are, you could have kept Liverpool under control."

Reinhold could feel his blood pumping faster. His thoughts raced to the last time he'd seen Liverpool the day of the trial, when he'd gone to say good-bye before the sheriff escorted the boy to prison in New York City. He'd wanted to encourage him to take responsibility for his part in the murder, but Liverpool had blamed everything on Ned.

Reinhold stared at Higgins, who'd always relished riling him. Of course, Higgins was trying to irk him again, but maybe Higgins was right. Maybe Reinhold was a weak man. Maybe he'd tried so hard not to be like his father that he'd ended up being too soft.

He took a deep breath and tossed aside those kinds of thoughts. "All I want is my money. Just give it back and I won't hold it against you."

Higgins wiped his hands on his trousers,

which were covered with a fine gray metal dust. He beckoned Reinhold with his fingers. "Come on. Come get me. I dare you."

Reinhold's biceps contracted into bricks, but he held himself back. "Give. Me. My. Money." He ground out each word in a low growl.

Higgins laughed. "If you fight me, then I'll give you the money back."

Reinhold's fingers closed around the crock — the *empty* crock. He glared at Higgins for a long minute, wanting to rush at him and pummel him the way he deserved. "Tell me where you put it."

"You might talk tough," Higgins spat, "but you're nothing but a weakling." With that, he began to saunter toward the barn.

As Reinhold watched him walk away, heat rushed to his chest, arms, and legs. He tossed down the crock and hoe and lunged after the skinny farmhand, reaching him in several long strides. With a roar that came from deep within, from all the anger and frustration he'd been holding in, Reinhold spun Higgins around. Before he could stop himself, he slammed a fist into the man's gut.

Higgins's eyes rounded in surprise. "Well, well, well —"

Reinhold swung again, this time punching

Higgins in the mouth, cutting off his words. Blood oozed from his split lower lip, and the sight of it seemed to heat Reinhold's blood all the more.

Higgins stumbled backward, but Reinhold followed after him, hitting him in the nose and then stomach. Each punch brought a strange surge of satisfaction that only fueled his thirst for more.

"Okay!" Higgins cried out. He crossed his arms in front of his head in self-defense. "You made your point. You can fight."

"Where's my money?" Reinhold's voice was strangely raspy. He could hear Mrs. Turner scolding him, but it was hollow as though from a great distance away.

"I don't have your money!" Higgins shouted.

Reinhold grabbed the man's arm and twisted it. Higgins squealed like a baby pig. "Tell me where it is."

"I swear!" Higgins fell to his knees, his face contorted with pain. "I don't have it!"

Reinhold kept hold on Higgins with one hand and swung at him with the other. He slammed and slammed, over and over, ignoring Higgins's cries of protest. Reinhold's thoughts blurred, and all he could think was that he was tired of being bullied, tired of holding back, tired of being weak.

A gunshot broke through his haze. His fist froze in midair.

Silence descended. I was so heavy, so terrible that Reinhold blinked his eyes as if waking up from a nightmare. The first thing he noticed was the blood. He lifted his hand and stared at it. Blood covered his knuckles and ran down his fingers. It was splattered on his sleeves and across his chest.

"Step away from Higgins nice and slow" came a hard voice nearby.

Reinhold took a step back and realized his chest was heaving as if he'd been running. He took a deep shuddering breath, and his head began to clear.

Why was Mr. Turner standing a dozen feet away and pointing his hunting rifle at him?

"That's right," the farmer said as he stared down the barrel at Reinhold. "Step away."

Mrs. Turner was cowering behind her husband, clutching her wooden spoon. Lucinda stood on the front porch step, wringing her hands, tears running down her thin face.

Reinhold lowered his hands to his sides. What had he done? Lying on the ground in front of him was a body covered in blood, motionless.

His heartbeat slowed to a deathly crawl.

It was Higgins, facedown in the grass, his

arm twisted at an odd angle behind him. Had he killed the man? Reinhold took several more steps away from the body and sagged to his knees, hitting the ground with a jarring force.

He couldn't breathe, could only stare at Higgins. *Oh no . . . what have I done?* In one moment of insanity, had he become his father? "I'm sorry," he said, his voice hoarse.

As if he'd been waiting for the apology, Higgins grunted and lifted his face out of the grass. At the movement, he cursed profusely and cradled his arm.

Higgins was alive. Tears burned at the back of Reinhold's eyes, and he buried his face into his bloody hands, wanting to weep with relief.

"I don't know what's going on between the two of you," Mr. Turner said, "but I won't have any more trouble like this."

"You need to fire Reinhold," Mrs. Turner declared in her no-nonsense tone. "I don't want a dangerous man like him living here. He would have killed Higgins if you hadn't come along."

Reinhold held his hands out in front of him. His knuckles were raw and bleeding. The truth of Mrs. Turner's words stabbed him to the core of his being. He was dangerous. He hadn't killed Higgins, but he'd come close. And he probably would have if Mr. Turner hadn't intervened.

"I want you to send Reinhold on his way, tonight, right now," Mrs. Turner continued. "I don't want him around here another minute."

"No!" came a shrill scream.

The sound was so loud and startling, Reinhold turned toward the source of it to find Lucinda wide-eyed and red-faced on the front step, covering her mouth, as though she too was surprised by her outburst.

"Young lady," started Mrs. Turner angrily, "how dare you —"

"You can't send him away," Lucinda said forcefully. From a woman who rarely spoke above a whisper, and even then only briefly, the protest was startling and left Reinhold as speechless as Mr. and Mrs. Turner.

At the sight of their gaping, Lucinda ducked her head. She was twisting her hands together again, this time so tightly Reinhold thought she might twist them right off.

"Higgins didn't take Reinhold's money," she said more quietly.

Higgins had rolled to his side. His eyes were swollen and turning a shade of purplish-black. His nose was bent and still bleeding. His lips were busted and bleeding too, but still he managed a sneer at Reinhold. "Told you I didn't take it."

Reinhold shook his head, and the rage inside surged easily this time. "You're a liar." He had the overwhelming urge to kick the man until he couldn't move.

"I took it." Lucinda raised her voice, her declaration ringing out and echoing in the silence that followed.

Reinhold sat back on his heels. He stared at Lucinda, unable to formulate a response. She looked at the ground, the lines in her face taut, her lips pursed and almost white. She refused to meet anyone's gaze.

Lucinda had been the one to steal from him? How? When? And more important, why?

"I took it all," she said again, digging her hand into her apron pocket. When she lifted it out, she held a bulging leather pouch.

Mrs. Turner gasped. "You wretched, wretched child! What came over you to do something so evil?"

"I thought if Reinhold didn't have any money to buy his farm, then he'd want to stay here." Lucinda's confession dropped to a whisper.

"I should have known you'd do something like this," Mrs. Turner said. She lifted the wooden spoon and smacked it against her hand. "You're a worthless and wicked girl. All you do is embarrass us."

Lucinda's chin dropped against her chest.

Reinhold could only stare at the bag of money in the young woman's hand. She'd taken his earnings because she wanted him to stay here? But why?

Liverpool's teasing rose up in answer. *"She's practically throwing herself at you."* His mind flashed to all the times she'd slipped him an extra piece of cake or packed him a special lunch pail or offered to patch a hole in his trousers. She'd even sewn him new shirts.

Had Lucinda been attempting to win his affection? Maybe Liverpool had been right.

Mrs. Turner huffed and started toward Lucinda. "You're not only going to repay Reinhold every penny you took from him, but I'm going to give you a thrashing you won't ever forget."

Mr. Turner stopped his wife with a touch to her arm. The motion was unexpected, because she stumbled to a halt and turned to look at her husband with an open mouth.

"Give him the money, girl," Mr. Turner said to Lucinda.

She nodded mutely and rushed to obey. As she approached Reinhold, he couldn't make himself rise to meet her as he knew he should. Tentatively she held the pouch out to him.

He took it. The familiar weight of the bundle should have made him happy or at least relieved. Instead his stomach churned, and his head ached. He felt like he might throw up.

"I'm sorry," she whispered. She didn't immediately back away from him. When she lifted her head, her eyes held a tiny flicker of hope. "I wasn't planning to take any more, but once you asked Miss Neumann to marry you, I just wanted to try to find a way to keep you here."

Keep him? Did Lucinda think if he stayed long enough working for her father, that eventually he'd want to marry her? That was ludicrous. And he wanted to tell her so. She had to know he'd never consider marrying a woman he didn't love.

But even as the words rolled through his mind, he realized that was exactly what he was doing with Marianne. He was marrying her even though he didn't love her. Even though she was in love with another man. He'd seen how she looked at Drew during the trial and afterward. He'd wanted to ignore it, wanted to believe she'd eventually love him instead, wanted to hold on to her because he needed her.

Essentially he was using her. Perhaps it was for a worthy cause, but he was using her nevertheless.

Suddenly he was disgusted with himself for how low he'd sunk. Not only had he nearly beaten an innocent man to death with his bare hands, but he'd also intended to marry a woman for what she could do for him.

He shoved the heavy bag into his pocket and stood to his feet unsteadily. He'd turned into a monster, the kind he vowed he'd never become, the kind his father had been. No matter how hard he'd tried to be different, somehow he'd ended up there anyway.

"I'm sorry too," he said to Lucinda before lurching past her toward the barn. He'd barely turned the corner before he doubled over and vomited.

As he straightened and wiped the bitterness from his mouth, he knew it wouldn't be so easy to get rid of the bitterness that filled his soul. But there was one thing he could do to make things right. And tomorrow he'd ride into town and do it.

CHAPTER 28

Marianne stiffened as the front door of Elise's house opened and ushered in excited voices. The clock above the mantel signaled ten minutes until the top of the hour. Ten minutes until the wedding started. Ten minutes for her to figure out some way to get herself out of the current mess.

Coming from the hallway, she heard Jethro's excited nonstop chatter, followed by Drew's laughter.

"You seem more nervous this time," Elise said, straightening the lace on another new gown she'd had made for Marianne. This one was especially beautiful. It was white with a full skirt and had silk roses of varying colors of pink sewn into the waist and at the sleeves.

Earlier that morning, a local farmer had delivered an enormous bouquet of fresh-cut roses that matched the roses on the dress. And now Marianne buried her face into the soft petals to soothe the heat that climbed into her cheeks whenever she thought about the charade.

"I didn't sleep well last night," Marianne said. She'd waited for Elise to join her in the big bed, kept telling herself she'd confess the truth about Reinhold and Drew when Elise came in. But as the hours ticked away with no sign of Elise, Marianne had finally fallen into a restless sleep.

"We don't need to worry about any interruptions to your wedding today," Elise said with a laugh. "I've instructed the servants to send away anyone who knocks on the door."

Marianne tried to muster a smile. This time she desperately needed an interruption, a way to extricate herself from marrying Drew. She couldn't go forward with the plans. But with each passing minute, it was becoming more impossible for her to back out.

She hadn't had the opportunity to talk with Drew privately again since they'd departed from the train. He'd been gone most of the evening, helping with the construction of the new doctor's home. When he'd returned to the depot with Thornton, the two had been inseparable, laughing and talking like they were long-lost brothers.

She'd thought when they tucked Jethro into bed, she'd have a private moment with him in the hallway, but Mrs. Gray had insisted on laying Jethro down so she and Drew could have more time together with Elise and Thornton. It would have been a lovely evening of talking if she hadn't had the constant thought at the back of her mind that everything was a sham and Elise would be angry with her when she discovered she'd been lying again.

"Miss Neumann!" Jethro exclaimed, running into the parlor. His hair had somehow been combed into submission and lay in neat waves. He was wearing one of the new suits the Children's Aid Society had given him, and it was washed and ironed. "You look mighty purty. Don't she, Mr. Brady?"

Drew stepped into the room behind Jethro. At the sight of her, he came to an abrupt halt. His smile faded, his eyes widened, and his Adam's apple dropped like a bundle of dry hay into a trough.

"Why she's prettier than a princess," Mrs. Gray said, slipping past Drew and grabbing on to Jethro's hand in time to keep him from touching a small porcelain plate with gold trim that decorated the pedestal side table.

"I couldn't have said it better myself," Drew managed, swallowing hard again. "You take my breath away."

Thornton appeared behind Drew and with a laugh clamped a hand on his shoulder. "Spoken like a man in love." Thornton was attired in a finely tailored gray suit that contrasted his dark wavy hair and suave good looks. He was sleeker and slimmer than Drew and more refined-looking, but standing side by side, they made a handsome pair.

As the reverend entered the room along with Mr. Gray, Marianne's chest squeezed with anxiety. She needed a moment with Drew alone, but the men surrounded him, patting his back and teasing him mercilessly for his reaction to seeing his bride.

As Jethro and Mrs. Gray and Elise gathered around her, the quiet panic inside began to swell. When a few short minutes later the mantel clock chimed ten o'clock, she found herself stationed next to Drew and standing before the reverend.

"Dearly beloved," the reverend began, "we are gathered together here in the sight of God, and in the face of these witnesses, to join together this man and this woman in holy matrimony, which is an honorable estate, instituted of God."

How had this charade gone so far? She glanced up at Drew and tried to catch his eye. But he was looking at the reverend and not paying her any heed.

She shifted so that she brushed against him and attempted to elbow him. Only then did he glance down at her, but only for an instant before closing his eyes as the reverend led them in prayer.

"Drew," she whispered. They had to stop the wedding now.

He pried open one eye and peeked at her.

She raised her brows and cocked her head toward the hallway. She needed to speak with him alone. Now.

He smiled and closed his eyes again, apparently not understanding her silent message.

She slipped her hand into his and squeezed. He squeezed back. She jerked on his arm, but he only tugged back playfully. She frowned, but he continued to smile throughout the entire prayer as though everything was perfectly okay.

But it wasn't. And he clearly wasn't planning to cooperate with her.

When the reverend said "Amen," Marianne took a deep breath and opened her mouth to speak. Before she could get a word out, the reverend had already launched into his reading of Genesis, chapter three, and the uniting of the first man and woman as their example for matrimony.

I'm sorry for lying, Lord, she silently prayed. *I knew it was wrong. And I've done it again. I've allowed myself to believe a small deception won't matter. But it does. And now it's become a big mess. Forgive me and help me to tell the truth, even though it will be hard and will hurt the people I care about.*

The reverend smiled at them. "I require and charge you both, as you will answer at the dreadful day of judgment when the secrets of all hearts shall be disclosed, that if either of you know any impediment why you may not be lawfully joined together in matrimony, that you do now confess it."

"I confess that I'm engaged to another man," Marianne said quickly before she could find one more reason to refrain.

The room grew so silent Marianne was sure everyone could hear the rapid whirring of her pulse. The reverend's mouth stalled around the next words of the ceremony. And Drew's head sank as though he'd been defeated once and for all. She didn't dare look at Jethro and see the shock and disappointment on his face.

"I don't understand," Elise said. "I thought Drew was your fiancé."

"Drew and I aren't getting married." Marianne forced the words, even though they stuck in her throat.

"Why not?" Thornton asked from where he stood by Drew's side. "You both love each other, don't you?"

"Yes." The word fell off Drew's lips as if he needed to say it or burst. "I love Marianne. I love her more than my own life."

Her lungs constricted at his words. And she lost her breath completely when he gazed down at her with love radiating from his eyes — a love so sweet and strong she wanted to weep that she would never get to experience it.

"Don't you love me too, Marianne?" he whispered hoarsely.

She did. But telling him would only make the parting that much more painful.

"If you can honestly tell me you don't love me, then I'll walk away from you today and I won't pressure you again."

Her heart ripped apart, and the pain in her chest brought tears to her eyes.

"Just say it," he pleaded, reaching for her hand. "Please, Marianne."

"Yes, I love you." She couldn't hold back the words any more than she could hold back the tears that had begun to spill over. "But you know I have to marry Reinhold.

He needs me."

"We'll talk to him," Drew said. "We'll explain the situation. We'll work with him to find someone else to take care of his sisters."

"Stop right there," Elise said, spinning Marianne. "You mean to tell me you agreed to marry Reinhold even though you were in love with Drew?"

Marianne dropped her head and nodded miserably.

Mr. Gray cleared his throat loudly. "Speaking of Reinhold." The stationmaster reached inside his suit coat pocket and pulled out a telegram. "This came earlier in the morning. I didn't realize there was any question — I just assumed with the dewy-eyed way Drew and Marianne acted that everything was as it should be. If I'd known differently, I would have given the telegram to you right away."

Marianne took the telegram. Her fingers were shaking too much to open it, so she handed it to her sister. Elise unfolded the short note, read it silently, and then expelled a relieved breath. "Reinhold says he'll do just fine looking after Silke and Verina by himself. He says he hopes you and Drew will be happy together in your new life."

"What?" Marianne and Drew asked at the

same time.

"Here." Elise shoved the telegram into Drew's outstretched hand. "Read it for yourself and then maybe we can get back to the business of having a wedding."

Drew held the telegram, and Marianne noticed his hand was trembling. Reinhold's telegram was brief, but it was enough for Marianne to realize he understood she loved Drew and was releasing her from their engagement.

Elise began explaining to the others Reinhold's situation with his aunt and his sisters, and Drew used that opportunity to pull Marianne off to the side.

"What a relief," Drew said, sucking in a shaky breath. "It's a good thing he sent that telegram or I was planning to ride up to Mayfield today and tell him he couldn't have the woman I loved."

Marianne was grateful to Reinhold for his understanding of her situation, but she still planned to do all she could to help him with Silke and Verina. She'd let him know she would be there, only this time as a friend, not a wife.

The only man she wanted was standing next to her. And now they were free. *She* was free. Once she'd finally admitted to her deception, the truth had set her free.

He lifted a hand to her face. With exquisite tenderness, he grazed her cheek down to her chin. "I should have just told you I was marrying you regardless of Reinhold."

"So you were planning to go through with this wedding today even if I'd never said anything?"

He nodded sheepishly. "I wasn't about to let you marry a man who could never love you the way I do." His fingers trailed around her chin and then to her lips.

"What way do you love me?" she asked, not caring that her voice came out low and sultry.

Sparks flickered to life in his eyes, and she glimpsed his desire before his hands slid around her waist and pulled her against him.

She had the feeling they would face many more trials and hardships, especially if they continued working with the orphans. But they would face them together, just as they had this trip. And they would be stronger because of it.

"I love you, Andrew Brady," she said into his neck.

"And I love you, Marianne Neumann," he whispered into her ear before pressing a kiss there. The kiss echoed throughout her body and made her shiver with anticipation at the promise of many more to come. "Please, will you marry me now? Right this instant, before anything more happens to stop us?"

"Nothing can stop us or separate us ever again," she whispered.

"Promise?"

"I promise you. We'll be together forever."

"I pronounce that they be man and wife together, in the name of the Father, and of the Son, and of the Holy Ghost. Amen." The reverend made the sign of the cross above their heads and then closed his prayer book.

"Are they finally married?" came Jethro's voice behind Drew.

Drew had expected more protest from Jethro when Marianne had spoken up about being engaged to Reinhold. But he'd handled the news well. The boy was resilient, just as Drew had predicted.

"Yes, buddy, we're finally married," Drew said with a grin over his shoulder at the boy. "Isn't that great? After I kiss my bride, then we can be a family just like we all talked about."

Jethro didn't grin. Instead he looked down at his polished black shoes.

Drew exchanged a glance with Marianne, but she shook her head firmly with a look that told him he wasn't getting a kiss until they made sure Jethro was all right first. He gave an exasperated sigh, but inwardly smiled because he felt the same way. He and Marianne made a great team, and he prayed God would give them many more opportunities to make a difference in the lives of children together.

He released Marianne's hand and knelt in front of Jethro. A second later, he felt her hand upon his shoulder and loved her all the more for her constant support in whatever he did.

"What's wrong, Jeth?" he asked. "I thought you wanted me and Marianne to get married so you could be our child."

"I did want that," he said in a small voice, still staring at his shoes. "But maybe you can find another little boy with red hair and freckles that nobody wants."

Drew glanced up at Marianne in confusion. But her eyes widened with the same questions he had. What was Jethro saying?

Drew focused his attention on the boy again. "Why's that, Jeth? Why do you want us to find someone else?"

Jethro looked up at him finally. "You'd make real good parents," he said solemnly. "You and Miss Neumann both."

"But . . . ?"

"But I was wondering if Mr. and Mrs.

Gray could be my new pa and ma instead."

At Jethro's words, Mrs. Gray released a soft sob before cupping a hand over her mouth. Her eyes brimmed with tears, and Mr. Gray wrapped an arm around his wife to keep her from crumpling.

At the sight of Mrs. Gray's tears, Jethro's face fell. "It's okay if you don't want me," he said. "No one else ever has except Mr. Brady and Miss Neumann —"

Mrs. Gray broke away from her husband, fell to her knees before the boy, and grabbed him into a fierce hug. "I want you, honey," she said through another sob. "Oh, I want you very much."

Jethro circled his arms around Mrs. Gray's neck and hugged her back tightly.

"I've always wanted a little boy just like you," Mrs. Gray said. "And you'd make me very happy if you'd be my son."

"Even though I got red hair and freckles?" His voice wobbled.

"Not *even though* you have them, but *because* you have them." Mrs. Gray kissed his forehead. "I can't imagine a more handsome boy than you."

Jethro gave her a gap-toothed grin, and his eyes shone with an adoration that had apparently developed during the time he'd spent with her when he had the measles.

Mr. Gray bent down and placed a hand on Jethro's head. "We never thought we could have any children, but you've proved us wrong."

"Thank you, Jesus," Mrs. Gray whispered.

Tears streaked Marianne's cheeks. Drew stood and pulled her into the crook of his arm, placing a kiss onto her cheek and tasting the saltiness. She smiled and snuggled against him. Nearby, Thornton had wrapped his arms around Elise.

"Then you won't be mad at me, Mr. Brady?" Jethro asked as he pulled free from Mrs. Gray.

"No, buddy. I won't be mad. In fact, I'm mighty happy God brought you to the perfect family in His perfect timing just like we prayed for."

Jethro smiled and nodded. He reached for one of Mr. Gray's hands and one of Mrs. Gray's and stood between the couple. "God's pretty good about working things out, ain't He?"

"He sure is." Drew turned his attention upon his new bride and whispered a silent prayer of thanksgiving for how God had worked things out for him and Marianne too.

"Do you think I can finally kiss my bride?" he asked.

Marianne lifted her head in response, her tender smile beckoning him, her lovely brown eyes inviting him to come home, where he belonged.

AUTHOR'S NOTE

Thank you for reading this second book in my ORPHAN TRAIN series, for joining in the ride as Marianne, the middle Neumann sister, takes a journey both literally and figuratively, discovering more about who she really is, as well as finding true love along the way. She learns many things during her journey, including how to come out from the shadow of her sister and embrace a new kind of courage she never believed she had.

In casting Marianne Neumann in the role of a placing agent, it was my hope to give readers a glimpse into the orphan train movement from the perspective of those men and women who rode the trains with the orphans. The Children's Aid Society (CAS), started by Charles Loring Brace, was the major organization in New York working to place orphans from its inception in 1853 and well into the twentieth century. CAS hired numerous ministers, single men and women, as well as married couples, to escort orphans from the East to their new homes in the West.

One of the most well-known placing agents was Clara B. Comstock, who traveled west with children from 1911 to 1928. During these years, she made seventy-four trips and wrote about her experiences. I drew from her notes about what it was like before the trip, the clothes the orphans were given, and the detailed lists of supplies and food she packed. She also recorded what it was like during the journey west and what happened once they arrived at their destinations, including an incident where she was quarantined with a five-year-old boy who'd contracted diphtheria.

Toward the end of her life, Clara Comstock said this about her experiences: "The work was a great adventure in faith. We were always helped and grew to expect kindness, deep interest and assistance everywhere. A sense of responsibility was keenly felt by all the workers. My life has been greatly enriched by the varied experiences found in everything the Children's Aid Society and the contacts made. It is an honor to have followed from afar, the founder of this work."

In *Together Forever,* I hoped to portray

the struggles that placing agents felt right along with the struggles of the orphans. I have no doubt what the orphans experienced was far more emotional and painful; nevertheless, the job of the placing agent was not an easy one. It consisted of weeks of demanding travel, difficulty in placing children, plus the logistical challenges in revisiting each child before returning to New York.

I also hoped to reveal the dichotomy of the placing-out movement, the positive aspects as well as the heartbreak. Even in the best of situations (like Dorothea's), fear and confusion were constant companions. Amidst the adventures, mishaps and accidents happened. The incident with George getting lost and separated from his brother, Peter, is based on a true story that occurred during one of these trips. Of course, there were the "unwanted" children like Jethro, who were neither young nor old enough to be of much appeal to families.

The agents not only faced the ups and downs of handling such a wide variety of children, but they also faced the challenges of the job itself. Since nothing had ever before been done like the placing out, agents had to learn on the job and make up the rules as they went. In the early years, record-keeping was inconsistent, placements irregular, and the screening process nonexistent. While many of the agents like Drew and Marianne meant well and truly cared about providing better lives for the children in their care, unfortunately the lack of consistent practices provided further hardships to many orphans.

I pray that in reading this story, not only have you gained greater insights and a different perspective of the orphan train movement, but that you've also been encouraged to know God is present in our weakest moments. He doesn't necessarily promise to give us the courage of a lion or to make everything perfect. But He does promise that His strength is available and that His power will rest upon us. Perhaps that strength will be just enough to get out of bed for another difficult day. Or perhaps it will be just enough to face the illness or hurt or heartache we bear.

We can rest assured it will always be just enough. His strength is made perfect in our weakness. May His power rest on you today and always as you move forward each tiny step with His courage.

ABOUT THE AUTHOR

Jody Hedlund is the award-winning author of multiple novels, including the BEACONS OF HOPE series as well as *Captured by Love, Rebellious Heart,* and *A Noble Groom.* She holds a bachelor's degree from Taylor University and a master's degree from the University of Wisconsin, both in social work. Jody lives in Michigan with her husband and five children. Learn more at JodyHedlund.com.

Check Out Receipt

Hayner PLD - Alton Square Branch (HYAP-ZED
)
618-462-0677
www.haynerlibrary.org

Saturday, August 31, 2019 2:50:56 PM
ROSE, MERRY L

Item: 0003006060994
Title: Together forever [text (large print
)]
Call no.: S F HED
Due: 09/14/2019

Total items: 1

You just saved $30.99 by using your librar
y. You have saved $290.87 this past year a
nd $5,305.55 since you began using the lib
rary!

Thank You!